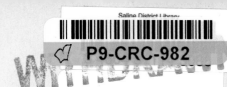

WRONGFUL DEATH

ALSO BY LYNDA LA PLANTE

WRONGFUL
DEATH

An Anna Travis Novel

LYNDA LA PLANTE

**BOURBON
STREET
BOOKS**

An Imprint of HarperCollins*Publishers*
www.harpercollins.com

First published in slightly different form in the UK in 2013 by Simon and Schuster UK.

HarperCollins books may be purchased for educational, business, or sales promotional use. For information, please e-mail the Special Markets Department at SPsales@harpercollins.com.

FIRST U.S. EDITION

Library of Congress Cataloging-in-Publication Data is available upon request.

ISBN 978-0-06-235593-5

15 16 17 18 19 RRD 10 9 8 7 6 5 4 3 2 1

To my dear friends Richard and Jonny,
at whose wedding I was honoured to be an invited guest.

Acknowledgements

Special thanks and gratitude for the outstanding research and work on this novel by Callum Sutherland, whose in-depth knowledge of police procedure and dedication to working alongside me has proved to be very productive and gratifying. Sincere thanks also to Detective Superintendent Simon Morgan, for his expertise with FBI research and policy. Having two such capable professionals working to produce the necessary research was a big bonus. I would also like to thank Karol Griffiths for her support; she was and is always a pleasure to work with. As always, my sincere thanks go to the rest of the team at La Plante productions, Liz Thorburn and Richard Dobbs-Grove.

Many thanks also go to Stephen Ross, his son Daniel Ross and Andrew Bennet-Smith at Ross, Bennet-Smith, my financial advisors and dear friends.

The publication of this book would not have been possible without the constant support from my literary agent Gill Coleridge and the team at Rogers, Coleridge & White Literary Agents.

It is always a pleasure working with my ever-supportive book editor Susan Opie, whose care and attention to every detail is impressive and always encouraging.

I also wish to thank Simon and Schuster, my publishers, for their constant support of my work – their encouragement and long-lasting friendship makes me very fortunate to be one of their authors. Ian Chapman, Suzanne Baboneau, Kerr

MacRae are a great influence and their kindness is deeply appreciated. They are a very strong creative group. I would also like to thank Dawn Burnett and especially Nigel Stoneman. Nigel is one of the dearest and most professional publicists I have ever worked alongside. He is always encouraging and I can think of no better travelling companion to promote my novels around the world with. My appreciation of his friendship is increased by his ability to create the best titles; *Wrongful Death* was his suggestion.

Spending so many hours over the computer, I am thankful to have a very trusted and dear woman who takes great care of me and makes sure I eat healthy and good dinners. Rose Mary Skidmore is very much a part of my family. In reality, most of these people have become close and beloved friends and with their support, working is always a joyful experience.

Chapter One

'Good morning, nice to see you all hard at work,' Detective Chief Inspector Anna Travis said cheerfully as she made her way across the newly refurbished major incident room in Belgravia Police Station. Both Joan Falkland and Barbara Maddox, busy setting up computer equipment, turned sharply on hearing her voice. Taken aback by her tanned glowing appearance, their jaws dropped.

'Oh, ma'am, it's so good to see you and you look so well. I told my mum last night that I felt it in my waters you'd be heading up our next case,' gasped Joan.

'Well, your waters were right,' Anna said, smiling at the detective constable's choice of words.

'You look stunning,' Barbara Maddox conceded enviously as she looked Anna up and down.

'I finally took some leave and had the voyage of a lifetime sailing around the Aegean. I only got back last night.'

'Bit young for a cruise, aren't you?' Barbara remarked.

'It was a large clipper yacht not the QE2, Barbara. So who's the DI on the team?' Anna asked.

'I am. Believe it or not, they finally promoted me,' a voice from behind her replied.

Anna, recognizing the voice, turned to see Paul Barolli with a proud grin across his face coming out of the DI's office. She immediately noticed how neat and tidy he looked in a new pinstripe woollen suit, white shirt, red tie and well-polished brogues. She was surprised that Paul had recovered so quickly since the serial killer Henry Oates had shot him the previous October.

'It's well deserved and I'm glad to see you're fully fit again.'

'Doctor advised me to stay off a bit longer but I was bored to tears sitting at home doing nothing,' Paul told her.

'So who's replaced you as the team DS?' Anna enquired.

'Now you really are in for a surprise,' Joan said.

'I can answer for myself, Joan, and my promotion was also well deserved,' Barbara said tersely.

'I'm sure it was, Barbara, and well done. I've no doubt Paul will give you the benefit of his experiences as a former DS,' Anna said.

'My office door is always open for advice, Barbara,' Paul added.

'It will never be closed now,' Joan muttered under her breath.

Anna asked if anyone knew anything about the case they were to investigate but everyone shrugged their shoulders. All she herself knew was that she'd got back late last night to find an answerphone message left by Detective Chief Superintendent James Langton, requesting her to be at the Belgravia station for a 10 a.m. case briefing. Joan remarked that all the office equipment was new and state-of-the-art. Barolli wondered if the case was a sensitive one, only to be discussed within the four walls of the incident room.

'Has Langton appointed a superintendent on this team?' Anna asked Paul.

'Not that I know of; be great if it was Mike Lewis.'

Although Anna had enjoyed working alongside Mike Lewis on a number of cases, she doubted it would be him, as he was now overseeing all the murder teams in North London following his recent promotion. She wondered if Langton himself, seeing as he was being so secretive, would head up the inquiry.

Anna could not help but be impressed by the new high-tech incident room and the abundance of computer screens on every officer's desk. Instead of the traditional incident-room board, on which all details of the case were pinned, there was a huge plasma touch-screen monitor, which would be used to load information and photographs direct from any one of their office computers. Paul said that one of the local officers had told him the whole office had been gutted, rebuilt, decorated and furnished in just over three months.

Intrigued, Anna couldn't wait to see her office and was instantly struck by how plush it was, with a modern computer desk and chair, a two-seater sofa and two armchairs placed around a small coffee table. It all made her wonder not only why everything was brand-new but also who, in times of major police budget cuts, had authorized this kind of spending. Sitting down at her desk she began to check through her work e-mails that had piled up during her holiday leave, but before long she was interrupted by the beep of her mobile. It was a text message from Langton saying he was running an hour late. Exasperated but not surprised, she went into the main office to tell everyone.

Shrugging at her news, Paul Barolli headed into his office and Anna followed. 'Do you have time for a catch-up?' she asked.

'Come on in,' he said proudly. Anna smiled, knowing that this was the first time in his career that he had had an office of his own.

'It's not as glamorous as yours, but I'm well pleased,' he said, pulling out a chair for her, then walking behind his desk to sit opposite.

Anna looked around and noticed there were pictures on the walls of classic sports cars.

'It's nice, but why all the photographs of cars?'

'Classic cars are my hobby,' he said proudly. 'So, have you seen Langton recently?'

Anna nodded, somewhat amazed that you could work with someone for so many years without knowing about a personal interest such as this.

'After the Oates case, I went back to cold casework at the Yard and bumped into him a few times in the canteen. You?' she asked.

'It's been a while, but he came to see me in hospital after Oates shot me and then at home when I was on sick leave. Last time, he brought me a big bottle of malt whisky. Said it was the best medicine money could buy.' Barolli chuckled.

An hour later found Anna and Paul deep in discussion with the rest of the team when Langton finally made his appearance. He looked as if he had taken a well-earned rest; he was tanned and had lost weight, his hair longer. Everyone welcomed him, Barbara remarking to Joan that the new hairstyle suited him – he had always worn it in a crew cut, but now it was combed back, making him look younger. He stood in front of everyone, beaming, and apologized for keeping them waiting, then loaded a USB stick onto a computer and asked them all to gather round.

'How do you like the new office?' he demanded as he quickly removed his suit jacket and hung it over a chair. Everyone nodded in approval and commented how modern it was.

'Well, I'm glad that's the case as this is the first of its kind under a new modernization scheme for the Met Homicide Command,' Langton informed them.

'So every murder team across London is going to get equipment like this?' Barbara asked.

'Eventually. This however is your new working home and you will be permanently based here.'

'I live in Harlow. It will be a three-hour round trip every day and if they stop our free rail travel the cost will be astronomical,' Barbara blurted angrily but Langton ignored her.

'You're probably all wondering what your new case is,' he said as he opened his briefcase, removed a file and placed it on the table.

Anna was slightly irritated that he hadn't discussed the details with her before informing the team, but she let it go for now.

Langton touched the large plasma screen and a picture came up of a handsome light-skinned, mixed-race man. Langton informed the team that their victim Joshua Reynolds had been age thirty-one, and married to Donna Reynolds, now twenty-seven, and he had died just over six months ago from a single gunshot wound to the head. At the time of his death, Reynolds was co-owner of a club called the Trojan.

As Langton spoke, Anna whispered to Joan to run Reynolds' name on the major investigation database. Quietly, Joan typed in the victim's details but could find no sign of anyone by that name having been the subject of a murder investigation.

'Excuse me, sir, but there doesn't appear to be a computer record concerning the murder of Reynolds,' Anna said.

If Langton was annoyed by the interruption he didn't show it. 'That, DCI Travis, is because he was believed to have committed suicide and the inquiry was dealt with on Borough by the local detective inspector. It has since been alleged that he may have been murdered and I have decided that the allegation will be properly investigated. Treat it like you would a cold case.' He held up the thin case file.

'There is not much contained here other than scene photographs, copy of a suicide note found on his laptop, a statement from his wife who discovered the body, pathology and closing report by DI Paul Simms.'

Anna knew Paul Simms well; he was an openly gay officer whom she had previously worked with on the Alan Rawlins murder. She had found him to be a dedicated and competent officer and doubted he would have made mistakes or come to the wrong conclusions in this case.

'Has the Coroner's inquest hearing been held?' Anna asked.

'Yes, just over a month ago ...'

'And the verdict was?' Anna enquired.

'Suicide,' Langton replied.

'And the new evidence that has come to light is ...?'

'I was about to inform you all so if you would kindly let me finish, DCI Travis.'

Langton then brought up a mug shot of a black male that bore the caption: Delon Taylor, age twenty-eight years.

'Taylor is currently in custody at Belmarsh Prison awaiting trial for armed robbery and serious assault on a police officer. He has told one of his guards that he has information that Joshua Reynolds was murdered. And before you ask, Travis, Taylor's allegation was only made last week and he refuses to say any more until he speaks to a murder squad detective. It may well be a totally unfounded allegation.'

'Is Taylor going to be pleading guilty?' Barolli asked.

'It would appear so, yes,' Langton replied, becoming irritated with the obvious lack of enthusiasm from the team.

'So he could be making it up. Looking for a way to get a reduced sentence?' Anna remarked, to nods of agreement from around the room.

'There's no deal on the table. If it's lies then he gets nothing and will be prosecuted for wasting police time,' Langton snapped.

'Will you be overseeing the inquiry personally, sir?' Joan asked.

'No, and as yet I haven't decided who will be.'

Anna was somewhat confused, as the case didn't really seem to merit Langton's involvement, but now he was in effect stating that he had no interest in it himself. Then he gave his reason. Smiling, he gestured to everyone and said that he would not be overseeing the inquiry because he had been given a rare opportunity to be seconded to the Federal Bureau of Investigation in the United States for a year. He was to work at the Quantico Academy, specializing in the study of serial killers, alongside some of the most highly regarded and experienced agents who had made their careers creating offender profiles. His enthusiasm was obvious as he revealed he would also be working on unsolved cases at Quantico.

Anna couldn't help but smile — sometimes he was so child-like, beaming from ear to ear, unable to disguise his pleasure at what this invaluable opportunity meant to him. Everyone was congratulating him, but Anna was also slightly disappointed. It was almost as if he was retiring from the Met and although he expressed his eagerness to go, it didn't feel right.

Langton had always been an old-school detective, often politically incorrect, abrupt and averse to new policies or procedures.
Obstinate he could be, yet he had a suppleness about him, not
only in the way he bent the rules, but also in how he treated his
colleagues. There was one thing no one could or would ever
deny and that was that James Langton got results.

Anna knew that he had ruffled a few high-ranking feathers
along the way. Most notably, since his promotion to chief
superintendent, those of Deputy Commissioner Walters over
the case of Anthony Fitzpatrick, a notorious drug dealer and
murderer, or 'the one that got away', as Langton referred to him.
More recently, there was the shooting of Paul Barolli during
the escape from custody of the serial killer Henry Oates. Walters
had been appointed to investigate Langton's alleged breaches of
discipline in both cases.

Walters had really given Anna a grilling to establish exactly
what had occurred in the Fitzpatrick case. Langton had warned
her to keep her mouth shut about the mishandling of evidence
that would have led to the capture of the highly elusive drug
dealer. Anna knew she had been at fault and Langton had
warned her at the time that it was a possible career-ending
fiasco, but assured her that he would resolve the entire screw-up.
Initially, it had appeared that he was as good as his word as
Walters accepted Langton's version of events. However, a year
later the Deputy Commissioner called in Anna just as she was
being fast-tracked for promotion, for what he misleadingly
called an 'off the record' meeting, in which he duped her into
believing he already had all the details regarding the Fitzpatrick
mess. The truth was that the notorious drug dealer had had the
audacity to walk into the team's incident room posing as an FBI
agent, thereby gaining information about where his stolen drugs
were hidden. He committed three murders and then to top it all
evaded arrest by flying off in his own plane with his haul of
drugs, worth millions, and his young son on board.

For Anna, Fitzpatrick's escape had been an unforgettable
moment. She had witnessed at first hand Langton's fury, which

escalated further when she admitted that she had actually seen a photograph of the plane at a country cottage owned by the dealer's brother and had failed to connect it to their suspect.

Although Anna had inadvertently let it slip to Walters that mistakes were made during the Fitzpatrick investigation, she never confessed her own concerning the plane, or revealed that Langton was present in the murder squad office when Fitzpatrick had posed as an FBI agent. She had always felt somewhat relieved that the Deputy Commissioner never reopened the case against Langton. She could only surmise that Walters still felt there was not enough evidence for disciplinary action.

Similarly in the Oates case, Langton had ensured that everyone on the team was 'singing off the same hymn sheet'. When interviewed by Walters, they all stuck to the story that the sudden atrocious turn in the weather could not have been foreseen and had led directly to Oates's opportunity to escape. Langton actually told Walters he saw it as 'an indiscriminate act of God' and played on the fact that the suspect was quickly rearrested and had confessed to a number of murders. Anna knew deep down that Walters was Langton's nemesis and the real reason behind his failure to make Commander. However, Langton's promotion was a subject she had decided to never again raise in his presence for fear he would discover she'd unwittingly betrayed him to the Deputy Commissioner. That would be something he could never forgive.

Many cherished moments had passed between Anna and Langton and they had both known their own tragedies; Langton with the sudden death of his first wife, and Anna herself when a prison inmate murdered her beloved fiancé, Ken. She had fought to salvage her career, and had even worked alongside Langton since the Fitzpatrick case, but he had never been as friendly or as close to her – in fact the reverse. He appeared to be watching her progress as she rose quickly through the ranks, as if loath to ever again become emotionally involved.

Anna had not worked with Langton since the Oates inquiry.

She had no current personal relationship or could even contemplate one. Work had become her priority and her whole life, and she had managed to earn the respect of all her colleagues. However, this new case Langton had given them just didn't sit right with her. To reopen a suicide as a cold case, because of a spurious allegation from an untrustworthy source like Delon Taylor, was highly irregular. Anna knew Langton better than anyone and was suspicious that there was a hidden agenda to his allocating an apparently simple case of suicide to a highly experienced murder team. She wondered if Langton had some personal connection. If that was the case, as the DCI she needed to know before he left the office.

'Could have a quick word with you?' she asked him.

'As it happens there a couple of matters that I need to speak to you about,' Langton said as he removed his jacket from the chair.

'We can use my office then,' Anna said, starting to head that way.

'I've got to go to the US Embassy in Grosvenor Square for a meeting at their FBI office. I will be back about four p.m. and we can talk then. In the meantime, you can get cracking uploading the Reynolds case onto the computers, he threw at her as he turned away.

'Well that should take up about ten minutes of our time,' Anna retorted, irritated.

'That's a nice glowing tan you've got, hides the red face when you're annoyed with me.'

Langton was quickly out the door, leaving Anna even more convinced he was hiding something from her.

Chapter Two

Deciding that she might as well make good use of her time until Langton returned, Anna picked up the file Paul Simms had prepared on Joshua Reynolds' death. Although the contents were sparse, it seemed to her the verdict of suicide was correct. She knew that if the Coroner had any doubts he would have given an open verdict or requested a more in-depth police inquiry.

Anna spread out the scene photographs across her desk. Reynolds was lying beside the sofa on his right side with his right arm outstretched in front of him, the revolver still in his hand. His knees were in an almost foetal position and on the left temple there was a bullet exit wound. There was a very large pool of blood around Reynolds' head and upper torso, which his white shirt had soaked up like blotting paper. Blood spatter, along with brain and skull tissue, was distributed on the seat and upright cushions of the sofa. Amongst the post-mortem photographs, one showed a bullet entry wound to the right temple. The wound had many pinprick-sized black burns around it, indicating a close-range shot. The exit wound, the pathologist's report remarked, indicated the gun being held by the victim at a slight upward angle. The forensic swabs taken from Reynolds' right hand revealed heavy traces of firearms residue and were consistent with him pulling the trigger. The wall safe in the bedroom fitted wardrobe was open and contained four loose bullets, which were the same kind as the single empty cartridge case in the gun. Firearms residue matching that on the gun and Reynolds' body was found in the safe, indicating it had been kept there. His blood alcohol level was high, indicating he was drunk at the time he shot himself. The pathologist's report concluded death by injuries to the head from a gunshot wound. From the state of rigor mortis the pathologist estimated the body had been dead between eight to twenty hours prior to its discovery at midday on the sixth of November.

Anna didn't have the enthusiasm to read through what little else there was in the case file, as the pathology and forensic reports spoke for themselves. Like the rest of the team she was finding it hard to work up any interest and she was deeply annoyed that Langton, for reasons she was unable to fathom, had lumbered her with such an open-and-shut case of suicide. There was a knock at her door and Paul Barolli entered.

'We've finally got all the computers set up and linked, so if I can take a copy of the file we can get the contents uploaded.'

'By all means take a copy for yourself and a couple for the office but hold off on the upload for now,' Anna told him.

'I thought DCS Langton wanted it treated as a cold case investigation and put on the computer system.'

'I know what he said, Paul, but honestly, read the file and tell me if there's something I'm missing. Reynolds even left a suicide note on his laptop.'

'Why has Langton given us this case then?'

'I haven't a bloody clue. The sooner we interview Delon Taylor the quicker we can be freed up for a proper murder investigation. You and I will pay him a visit in Belmarsh.'

'You want me to go with you?'

'Well you are my number two now.'

'You think Taylor is lying?'

'We won't know until we speak to him.'

Anna handed Paul the file and followed him back into the main office.

'Right, listen up,' she said, attempting to hide her own frustration. 'I know you are all feeling a bit down-hearted, what with all this wonderful new technical equipment and no case to play with. DI Barolli and I will see Delon Taylor tomorrow and hopefully by the next day we will be free to take a live case. I know you all kindly came in at seven a.m. this morning to set up the office, and it's nearly three p.m. and—'

'Don't tell us there's no overtime, ma'am!' the voice of Detective Dan Ross shouted jovially from the back of the room, resulting in a chorus of laughter from the team.

'Ten out of ten,' Anna said with a wry smile to the detective, a dapper dresser in his early thirties who was renowned as the office joker.

'For you, ma'am, we'd work for nothing,' he said.

'Go on, bugger off, the lot of you,' Anna said, knowing that whatever the outcome of the interview with Taylor, this team had already gelled and, she felt, accepted her as their leader.

It was just before four p.m. when Langton finally walked into Anna's office with a cup of coffee in each hand, sitting himself down in one of the comfortable armchairs and putting the cups on the small coffee table.

'White no sugar for you, as I recall.'

'Thanks.' Anna went over to join him, sitting opposite on the sofa.

'Any Scotch?'

'No. But I'll put it on the shopping list.'

'Where is everyone?'

'They'd all done their eight hours so I told them to call it a day.'

'Good. They'll have to get used to it as there's no overtime allocated to this case.'

'So this new state-of-the-art office is budget money well spent, is it?' Anna enquired.

'I knew this was going to be the first of the new high-tech murder investigation offices and I pulled a few strings to make sure your team was permanently based here.'

'Is it a fixed post for a DCI as well?'

'Yes, and before you get on your high horse, you've worked with nearly everyone out there. They respect you and above all you know how to motivate them. The best team for the best SIO.'

Anna leaned forward with a sharp grin and looked Langton directly in the eye.

'Please don't flatter me, James. I know you too well. The best team with the best office and SIO, I'll give you, but why lumber us with a crap job?'

'If I gave the team a case before this office opened I couldn't guarantee to get you based here. The Reynolds thing is just something to tide you over and shouldn't take long to put to bed. Anyway, there were no live murder cases to allocate you.'

'I know you're hiding something. Joshua Reynolds isn't some long lost relation or friend of an auntie's uncle twice removed, is he?'

Langton now mimicked Anna, leaning forward with a grin and staring her in the eye.

'How would you feel about joining me . . .?'

'You can't fob me off with dinner.'

'I meant at Quantico.'

Her jaw dropped in surprise. 'Joining you! At the FBI Academy?'

'There's a place that's just become available on their Senior Command course. But if you have too much on your plate at the moment then . . .'

'Not at all, I'd love to do it!' Anna exclaimed.

Langton stared at her and nodded.

'Good. Sorry it's short notice but we leave in eleven days on the Thursday-morning flight from Heathrow. It'll mean being away for nearly three months. Well, for you. As you know, I will be staying on longer.'

'Thank you, but why me?'

'Well, Mike Lewis was supposed to be going but he pulled out after his daughter was in a car accident last week . . .'

'Elisa? She's only twelve, please tell me it isn't serious,' Anna said, shocked at the news.

'No. A drunken cyclist hit her on a zebra crossing. Broken leg, a few cuts and bruises, but she'll be fine.'

'That's a relief. I hope Mike doesn't mind me taking his place.'

'Of course he won't. Anyway, he's pencilled in for the next course and I knew that you had no current commitments. I told Deputy Commissioner Walters you'd be the best replacement for Mike and he agreed.'

'Thank you, it'll be an amazing experience.'

'For both of us, and good for your future promotion prospects.'

'And yours, I hope.'

'Maybe – it's hard to say where Walters is concerned, but I live in hope,' Langton said optimistically.

'What about arranging my flight?'

'It's just a case of changing your name and details from Mike's, so e-mail me your passport details.'

'Great. I can't wait – and again, thank you for putting my name forward.'

She was suspicious about Walters' involvement, especially knowing that he did not like Langton, and she wondered why he was allowing them both to go. Perhaps this might be Walters creating a façade, a way of ridding himself of Langton and in his absence ensuring that he would never make Commander.

'About the Joshua Reynolds investigation . . . If it isn't done with before we leave, who is going to take over from me?' Anna enquired.

'Paul Barolli's perfectly capable of dealing with it. Also I've arranged for an FBI agent called Jessie Dewar to do some work experience with your team.'

'Why?'

'All part of her research for a doctorate in Forensic Psychology. She's in France at the moment.'

'Have you met her?'

'Yes, at a European homicide conference in Paris. She's pleasant and seems very capable.'

'Well, if you're happy and you think she will fit in with the
team . . .'

'She starts tomorrow morning. Show her the ropes before we
leave for the States. She'll no doubt give you a heads-up about
what to expect on the FBI course.'

'Any more surprises for me?'

'Yeah, I forgot that she lands at eight p.m. this evening,
Terminal Five Heathrow. I've got a prior engagement and I
wondered if you could . . .'

'I'm sorry, I can't, but I can arrange for a local detective to
meet her.'

Langton never ceased to amaze her, even after all these years,
still trying to offload what he saw as the mundane things in life.
She was annoyed that he hadn't given her more notice.

They were interrupted by a knock at the door and Paul Barolli
walked in, to tell them he had finished reading the Reynolds file
and was now off home. Langton was quick to seize the moment
and ask Paul if he was doing anything that evening.

'No, sir. You fancy a pint then?' Barolli asked, thinking his
new rank had knocked him up the social pecking order.

'Maybe another time, but I need a favour.'

'Then I'm just your man,' Barolli smiled.

'DCI Travis will be joining me at Quantico and FBI Agent
Jessie Dewar will be working with the team in her absence.'

'Right. I see,' Barolli said with a forlorn look.

'However, you will be running the show as SIO in DCI
Travis's absence.'

Paul was chuffed with Langton's faith in him and remarked
that he wouldn't let Langton or Anna down. He turned to leave
the room but Langton continued.

'Running the team's not the favour. I was wondering if you
could pick up Agent Dewar from the airport this evening.'

'Sure, it'll be a good opportunity to brief her on the
Reynolds case.'

'I've arranged the use of a Met-owned flat in Vauxhall for her,' Langton said, handing Barolli a set of keys.

'What does she look like?' Paul asked.

'Five seven, medium build, blonde hair.'

Barolli felt none the wiser about Agent Dewar as he put the keys in his pocket and said good night.

It was only after Langton had left the building that Anna had a chance to think about what it would mean for him to spend a whole year in the States working with the FBI. Like Mike Lewis, he too had a family. There was Laura his second wife and her daughter Kitty from a previous marriage, whom he had adopted. There was also their young son Tommy. She contemplated how Laura and the children would be feeling about his long-term absence. Although Anna did not know Laura, she could not believe that she would be happy about the situation. Anna's past relationship with Langton had made her more than aware that he was never a man who put his family obligations above his career. Anna knew from experience that Langton could be difficult to live with and envisaged that he and Laura also had many ups and downs. It crossed her mind that maybe Laura didn't care any more and was perfectly content to let him go to America. His family life was something he never discussed and a subject she knew was absolutely taboo.

The automatic doors of the Terminal Five Arrivals area slid slowly open revealing a number of people pushing luggage trolleys, pulling suitcases, mothers with stroppy children. Barolli, holding a small sign with MS J DEWAR written on it in black marker, noticed a lone middle-aged, plain-looking blonde woman pushing a luggage-laden trolley. She matched the brief description Langton had given him of their new team member. Paul raised his sign and waved it at her.

'I believe it's me you should be waving at,' an American voice said.

The Jessie Dewar standing beside him was not what he was expecting. Stunningly attractive, she had soft, shoulder-length shiny-blonde hair and wide hazel-grey eyes. She wore little makeup; she didn't need to with her flawless, lightly tanned skin. She was wearing a pink Solaro blouse and smart grey tailored suit, while the cut of her clothing and her high heels accentuated her curvaceous figure. She gave off an air of knowing she was a sexually attractive woman but also one who would take no nonsense.

'I was expecting Jimmy Langton,' Dewar said, causing Paul to rouse from his transfixed stupor.

'He's blind . . . I mean he got stuck behind . . . at work with a meeting. I'm Paul Barolli, the Detective Inspector on the murder squad you'll be working with. It's a pleasure to meet you, Agent Dewar.'

She gave him a small cool nod and shook his hand firmly.

'I'm a supervisory special agent, Detective Barolli,' Dewar replied in a matter-of-fact tone as he took hold of her suitcase.

'That's a mouthful. We use rank initials as abbreviations. Like DI for my rank, DCI for Chief Inspector . . .'

'I hardly think SS Dewar would be appropriate.'

Although Paul Barolli felt that Agent Dewar was somewhat abrupt, he put it down to her having had a long tiring day. As he drove to Vauxhall he sensed that she was not in the mood for conversation so he pointed out various sights of interest and suggested that when she felt like it he would be only too pleased to give her a proper tour round London. Dewar thanked him for his offer but doubted that her work commitments would allow time for sightseeing. Paul told her that there was a copy of the Reynolds file for her on the back seat and started to give her a run-down on the case, to which Dewar said nothing but leaned over to retrieve the file and began reading. Paul knew she wasn't listening to a word he said.

It was just after ten p.m. when they reached Nine Elms Lane in Vauxhall. The sat-nav voice informed them that their destination was two hundred yards on the left and Paul could see that meant St George's Wharf, an award-winning development of luxury flats and penthouses with riverside views of the Thames. He was somewhat surprised that Dewar was being provided with such upmarket accommodation and suspected that it must be one of the flats used by the top brass at Scotland Yard.

As Dewar looked round the apartment, Barolli followed her and explained how to use the kitchen equipment, under-floor heating and air-conditioning.

'There's a garage with a Tesco Express down the road. Do you want me to get you some groceries while you unpack?' he offered, but she said that she'd prefer to do her own shopping the following day. Paul told her that he would pick her up at nine a.m. to take her to Belgravia to meet the team. Dewar thanked him but said she would make her own way into the station, and then turned and walked off into the bedroom, leaving Barolli with little option but to bid her good night. He had just placed his hand on the door latch, about to open it, when there was a loud repeated knock, which made him jump. Opening the door he was surprised to see DCS Langton standing there with a bouquet of roses, bottle of champagne and bulging bag of groceries.

'And there I was thinking you didn't care about me any more,' Paul quipped.

'It's past your bedtime, Barolli,' Langton replied.

Jessie Dewar walked out of the bedroom and suddenly came to life, greeting Langton with a howl of pleasure as she leaped into his arms and gave him a big hug.

'How come you weren't at the airport to meet me, Jimmy?'

Paul watched Langton disentangle himself and explain he had been caught up at work.

'Well, I'll be off then, shall I?' Paul asked.

'Yeah, yeah, you take off,' Langton said, wafting his hand and following Jessie into the living room.

Paul let himself out, still not knowing exactly what to make of Agent Dewar. It was more than obvious Langton and Jessie knew each other well but he wondered how the rest of the team would take to her, especially DCI Travis, who thanks to Langton's description would be expecting to meet a plain Jane

Chapter Three

Anna was in good spirits the next morning, thrilled about her trip to the FBI Academy at Quantico. She knew that she should be drawing up things about the cold case to go over with Dewar but a list of what to pack and take with her seemed more important. She had decided to wait and tell the rest of the team about her US trip when Agent Dewar arrived at the office and introductions were made. In her excitement it hadn't crossed her mind to tell Paul Barolli to let her be the bearer of the news to the rest of the team.

Barolli entered the main office with a spring in his step.

'Morning, ladies, have I got a bit of news for you two,' he said to Joan and Barbara, who were sitting drinking coffee.

'You've got a girlfriend,' Barbara said, sarcastically.

'Ha-ha.' Barolli looked around the room to make sure no one else was in earshot. He moved closer to the two women.

'Just between us, Travis is off to the States on the FBI course with Langton, and Special Agent Jessie Dewar is attached to the team as from today.'

'You serious?' asked Barbara.

'Yes. Langton told me last night. I had to pick Dewar up from the airport. Langton got her a Met flat in St George's Wharf. He even turned up there after ten o'clock with champagne and roses.'

'How romantic,' Joan said.

'Did he stay the night?' Barbara asked, always wanting to know the gritty details when it came to gossip.

'Don't be stupid!' Barolli said in Langton's defence.

'Who's taking over as SIO while Travis is away?' Joan asked.

'Me. Langton said I will be team leader in her absence,' Paul said proudly.

'You must be joking. You've only been a DI two minutes,' Barbara exclaimed loudly.

Anna, distracted by Barbara's booming voice, looked up through her office window and instinctively knew that gossip had to be on the menu.

'What's Agent Dewar like?' Joan asked.

'Drop-dead gorgeous, thirty-ish, great figure, amazing complexion and sensuous lips,' Barolli said, wanting to irritate Barbara.

Joan and Barbara suddenly pretended to be busy on their computers, but the Detective Inspector failed to recognize the significance of this.

'And to whom are you referring, DI Barolli?' Anna asked, coming up behind him.

Paul cringed, looking as if he wished the ground would open up and swallow him. He turned to face her.

'Sorry, ma'am, I wasn't talking about anyone in particular.'

Anna took Paul into her office and reminded him that throwaway sexist remarks could lead to an official complaint and discipline.

'While I am away you're the one who will have to lead by example and make the important decisions. It's all about earning their respect, and believe me that doesn't come easily.'

'I'm sorry, ma'am, it won't happen again.'

'Right, that's the bollocking over. So drop-dead gorgeous and sensuous lips aside, what's this Dewar like?

'A bit abrupt, but I put it down to her being tired after a long day,' Paul said, deciding it was best not to mention Langton turning up at the flat.

'Our interview with Taylor at Belmarsh has been arranged

for tomorrow morning at half-eleven.' Anna showed Paul the signed document the prison had faxed her.

Paul again apologized and went back into the main office as Langton and Jessie Dewar entered the incident room. Barbara, never one to miss a trick, was straight out of her seat, introducing herself to Dewar and informing her that Barolli had told them all about her. Langton glared at Barolli, wondering what else he had told the team, and ushered Dewar away into DCI Travis's office.

Anna looked up from her desk as Langton entered with Dewar. The agent was wearing a neat navy-blue jacket, matching knee-length tight skirt, sensible shoes and a pristine white shirt with starched collar and cuffs. She was also carrying a laptop bag and two zip-up clothes carriers, which she hung on the coat stand. Anna stood up and Langton made the introductions as they shook hands. Anna asked her if she would like tea or coffee but Dewar declined her offer of refreshments, adding that in any case she only drank bottled water.

'DCI Travis is a fount of knowledge when it comes to murder inquiries. I hope you don't mind sharing an office until she goes to Quantico,' Langton remarked.

'No, if it's all that is available.'

'Good, you'll get to know each other in no time.'

Dewar got her copy of the Reynolds file out of her laptop bag and placed it down on Anna's desk.

'From what I've read so far the original investigation is poor and raises quite a few questions.'

'And they would be?' Anna asked, unimpressed with Dewar's blunt attitude.

'I'd rather finish reading it first and then I can compile a full list of all my observations, DCI Travis.'

Anna took a breath, determined not to react. 'Let me introduce you to the team then.'

Anna had everyone gather round as she introduced Agent Jessie Dewar who would be working with them while she was on the FBI course. The team gave Anna a round of applause and shouted out their congratulations. Dewar said she looked forward to working with them all but was quick to point out that her full title was Supervisory Special Agent and she worked at the FBI Behavioural Science Unit. Dewar went on to inform them that she advised police forces across the United States and the world about how criminals think and behave and had helped to solve many serious crimes.

If first impressions were anything to go by, Dewar had not done very well in the eyes of the team, Anna thought as she headed for the canteen to get herself a coffee. She consoled herself that having just met the agent it was too early to make any firm judgement on her character or working practices.

Returning with her drink, Anna was surprised to be told by Joan that Langton had left. She had wanted to have a word with him in private about Agent Dewar's role on the case. Anna also felt that Langton, having met Dewar before, might have given her more of an insight into what she was really like.

Dewar was sitting at Anna's desk, typing away on the laptop she had brought, and Anna immediately noticed that her own filing trays and paperwork were heaped in a loose pile on the floor. Her usually tidy desk was in disarray with the Reynolds papers and photographs strewn around, covering every part of the large work surface. Post-it notes of various colours were stuck onto different pages of DI Simms' reports and photographs.

'Hard at it, I see. Anything I can help you with?' Anna asked Dewar.

'Jimmy said I was to go with you to interview Delon Taylor,' Dewar said without even making eye contact.

Anna was caught off guard by Dewar's information. 'Oh, right, well I had told DI Barolli that he would be going with me.'

'I'm sure you can find him something else to do.'

'Yes, well I'd better have a word with him then. He's in the canteen having a sandwich, so would you like to join us?'

'No, I'm too busy at the moment. Could you bring me a pastrami on rye sub?' Dewar asked, again without looking up at Anna, who couldn't believe the cheek of the woman.

'The canteen's pretty basic, will ham on brown do?'

'No,' Dewar said, and sighed.

Abandoning her coffee, Anna made her way back to the canteen to speak with Barolli. She still didn't know what to make of Dewar. Was she actually just nervous or, as Anna feared, rather full of her own perceived self-importance?

Having got herself a chicken sandwich and fruit juice, Anna went and sat with Barolli.

'There's been a change of plan, Paul. Agent Dewar will be going with me to see Delon Taylor.'

'Is it because of my earlier indiscretion?' Paul asked anxiously.

'No. Dewar must have seen the prison-visit document on my desk and asked Langton if she could go with me.'

'Looks like she used Langton to force your hand.'

'Possibly, but look on the bright side – if she's with me, I can keep an eye on her.'

No sooner had Anna placated Barolli than Barbara came into the canteen looking furious, followed by a very flustered Joan.

'Joan and I had just started preparing a house-to-house enquiries file for where Joshua Reynolds lived when Dewar demanded to see it,' Barbara said.

'She didn't demand, Barbara, she asked,' Joan pointed out.

'Dewar grabbed it out of my hand, took a brief look, and tossed it back, saying that it wasn't good enough and needed to be extended to the surrounding streets and not just Reynolds' block of flats.'

'She didn't grab it, but she did throw it back down on the desk and say she expected better,' Joan admitted.

'I'm beginning to wonder if FBI stands for Fast But Ignorant,' Barbara said.

'Better not say that in front of Langton as he's clearly supportive of her,' Barolli remarked.

'She even wanted Joan to go out and get her a pastrami on rye sub!' Barbara said crossly.

Joan nodded that it was true but said that Barbara told Dewar there were no delis near the station and Dewar had stormed off in a huff.

Anna realized that things were going from bad to worse where Dewar's attitude was concerned.

'Okay, points made and noted. Sometimes first impressions can be misleading, but I will have a word with her,' she said but it fell on deaf ears.

'That's all well and good but what if she's like this while you're in Quantico?' Barbara said, and Joan nodded.

Barolli was quick to interject, taking some of the heat off Anna.

'In DCI Travis's absence, I will be in charge of the team, so if there are any problems, then come to me and I will deal with them.'

Barbara was about to make a remark but Travis cut her off. 'Paul is right. I back him one hundred per cent and expect you to do the same.'

Having finished placating everyone, Anna decided that she would speak with Dewar privately to advise her on how the team worked and hopefully make her realize that she was not endearing herself to them.

'Looks like Jessie is the only one doing any work round here while everyone else is having extended lunch breaks!' Langton said with a frown as Anna entered her office.

'Actually, Barolli and I were discussing the case over lunch. I did invite Agent Dewar but she said she was busy.'

'Well, she's made some interesting and impressive observations,' Langton remarked, whilst Dewar placed her laptop in its carrying case.

'Really. I'd be interested to hear them.'

'Sorry, I'm done for today, be ready to start talking to the team tomorrow morning,' Dewar said, and Langton stood up.

'You got everything you need?' Langton asked her.

Dewar grabbed her jacket then picked up her handbag and laptop.

'Sure thing, but I am starving. Did you track down a good grocery store? I'd like to stock up with provisions. I need gluten-free biscuits, bread and pasta, and fresh vegetables.'

As Langton ushered her out of the office, Dewar turned at the door.

'Don't tidy anything up, it's laid out in a specific order,' she said, pointing to Anna's desk that was still strewn with the Reynolds file, paperwork and photographs.

'I'll use the coffee table as a desk,' Anna remarked curtly, but Dewar ignored her and walked out the door with Langton.

Anna drew up a list of do's and don'ts to discuss with the agent and then looked over the documents Dewar had left on her desk. Anna was unable to decipher the notes, which had been written in a personal form of shorthand. However, the scene and post-mortem photographs were marked in red felt-tip pen, highlighting around the wound, the position of the body, the gun, the sofa, and, strangely to Anna, the washing machine in the kitchen. There were crosses marked on the victim's knees, head and hands in the post-mortem photographs. Written in the same red ink on an attached Post-it note was, GDR, DTT, STIP, BD. Anna was not sure exactly what the abbreviations meant and decided any guesswork would be pointless. Turning to the copy of Donna Reynolds' statement, she noticed that it too had been annotated with a marker pen. Anna had just begun to read through the highlighted areas when Barolli knocked and walked in, making her jump.

'Did you get a chance to speak with her?'

'No. Langton was here and she was off like a shot. I think she's avoiding discussing the case with me.'

'And no doubt filling Langton with crap and trying to find fault.'

'No comment,' Anna said, and Paul laughed as he sat down.

'I've gone over the file myself. It's not an in-depth investiga-tion but I don't think what Paul Simms has or hasn't done would have made any difference to the Coroner's verdict,' Paul said.

'I agree with you but I think Dewar will take delight in pointing out areas where she feels DI Simms should have been more professional. That'll embarrass Langton, who will want answers as to why more wasn't done at the time.'

'We've all been guilty of cutting corners on suicide cases,' Paul remarked.

'I suspect Dewar will try and find fault wherever she can. I think I might touch base with Paul Simms, give him a heads-up about her.'

'I've got to go out and restore some property on an old case then I'll head home from there if that's okay with you?'

'See you tomorrow then. And thanks for the backup in the canteen with Joan and Barbara.' Anna smiled in gratitude.

'No problem, good practice for me when you're in the States. See you in the morning.'

Barolli hesitated at the door as he watched Anna collecting up Dewar's paperwork and photographs, placing them on the floor next to the desk and putting her own filing trays and papers back where they had been before Dewar had moved them. She looked up at Paul.

'Childish, I know, but it's still my bloody office!'

Chapter Four

The next morning, Anna went into the office early, conscious that she had left a list of things to discuss with Jessie Dewar on her desk and worried the agent might see them. It was 7.30 a.m. and Anna was surprised to find Dewar already planted at her desk working away, Anna's filing trays and papers tucked neatly to one side. Dewar was dressed in a figure-hugging running suit, her long blonde hair held back with a headband, and there were drops of perspiration on her brow.

'Good morning, DCI Travis,' Dewar said with a smile.

'Morning. Been out for a run?'

'Yes, four point three miles,' Dewar said, checking her iPhone running app. 'Daily routine for everyone on a course at the FBI Academy.'

'Is it compulsory?' Anna enquired.

'Yes. Initiated by our founder, J. Edgar Hoover.'

'Really,' Anna remarked with a distinct lack of interest.

'Physical fitness is a big part of the Senior Command course.'

'I'm looking forward to it,' Anna said.

'I can give you a run-down on what to expect at Quantico on the way to Belmarsh,' Dewar offered.

'Thanks. I'd appreciate that.'

'Just going to shower and change. Would you mind if I gave a team briefing this morning? I sensed an air of hostility yesterday and I'd like to start again. Put them at ease with me.'

Anna looked directly at her and smiled. 'That would be good, they should all be in by nine.'

Dewar nodded as she went off for her shower.

Anna couldn't get over Dewar's sudden change of personality, and wondered if she had seen the do's and don'ts list on her desk. The other possibility was Langton had spoken with Dewar, and advised her about her interaction with the team. Yet Anna doubted that was the case, as she knew Langton would have been straight on the phone to her to see what the problem was. It seemed that Dewar must have realized the tension she had created and wanted to rectify the situation. Anna was pleased and felt it was a step in the right direction.

Paul Barolli arrived just before nine and Anna told him to make sure the team were all gathered for a briefing by nine-fifteen. Paul asked what it was about and Anna explained that it seemed Dewar had 'seen the light' and wanted to apologize to the team.

'You spoke with her?' Paul asked, trying to keep the disbelief out of his voice.

'Actually, she approached me. Said she felt there was an air of hostility towards her and wanted to start again.'

'Langton's influence?'

'I don't think so. Her own decision by the looks of it and one we should respect her for.'

'I'll hold on that until I hear what she has to say,' Paul said and went to his office.

Jessie Dewar returned from her shower and once again she looked immaculate, wearing a black two-piece suit and white silk shirt. Anna thought she looked very professional and eager to make a good impression. As members of the team arrived, Barolli told them to grab a tea or coffee from the canteen and bring it to the incident room for an urgent briefing. Barbara moaned that she wanted to have a cooked breakfast but Paul told her it was not an option and she should grab a sandwich if she was hungry.

Everyone was sitting at their desks as Dewar linked her laptop to the projector and, using a remote control, opened up a PowerPoint display.

'What's all this about?' Paul whispered to Anna.

'No idea,' she muttered back. 'I thought we were getting an apology, not a show.'

Dewar pressed the remote and a picture of the blue-and-gold FBI seal came up on the screen. In its centre was a set of scales, five alternating red and white horizontal bands and the words FIDELITY, BRAVERY, INTEGRITY. Members of the team looked at each other, wondering what was going on.

'Good morning and thank you for your time. Don't worry, this is not a history lesson,' Dewar said.

'We know ... because America hasn't got any,' Dan Ross joked, causing the others to laugh.

'Tell me about it ... In more than thirty seconds,' Dewar smiled and everyone laughed again.

Anna had expected Dewar to react badly to the gibe, but the humorous reply had got their attention.

'I realize that I did not get off to a good start yesterday and may have upset some of you, but that was not my intention. As a supervisory special agent at the FBI, I know that not everyone is going to like me or what I may have to say during an investigation but it goes with the territory, or job, as you say in the Met.'

Dewar then brought up a slide with the Met Police Statement of Common Purpose written on it.

'Although I work on the other side of the pond under different laws, we as investigators all do the same job, that being ...' Dewar pressed the remote to highlight the words: 'to pursue and bring to justice those who break the law'.

'It is a great privilege for me to be here and work alongside you and I believe that along the way we can learn from each other.'

Anna was impressed. Dewar was clearly a good speaker who knew how to use PowerPoint to not only get an audience's attention but also get her point across. Anna could see members of the team nodding in agreement as the agent, it seemed, was winning them over. Anna, thinking that Dewar had finished, stepped forward to say a few supportive words, but Dewar suddenly brought up another slide showing a wide-angled photograph of Reynolds lying dead in his living room.

'I have had the opportunity to read through the Joshua Reynolds file and record my observations regarding his death,' Dewar said, and glared at Travis, who took a step back.

Anna would rather have discussed Dewar's 'observations' in private, but since the agent had their attention and Anna did not want to appear rude she gestured with a nod for Dewar to continue.

Dewar pressed the remote and the word SUICIDE? came up on the screen.

'I believe that the original investigation by DI Simms is flawed and the scene of Reynolds' death may have been staged to look like a suicide,' she said bluntly.

As Anna looked around the room she could see that members of the team were instantly agitated at what they perceived to be an attack on 'one of their own', even though many of them had never worked with DI Simms. Upset by the remarks, many of the officers looked at each other in amazement and began to fidget in their seats.

Barolli, standing next to Anna, leaned closer and whispered, 'Might be best to stop her before the gloves are off and one of them says something.'

'No. She wanted the floor so she can have it,' Anna replied.

'Reynolds' death was assumed to be a suicide from the outset and because of this DI Simms sought, or conveyed, information that confirmed his belief.'

'But the pathology and forensic reports both confirmed that Reynolds committed suicide,' Barolli said.

'As did the Coroner's verdict. Are you seriously saying he was wrong as well?' Barbara added in support of Barolli.

'Confirmation bias is not necessarily intentional but it does affect us all and we don't even realize it. We look for evidence to support our theory about what happened at a scene. This in turn causes us to ignore or miss evidence that opposes it,' Dewar calmly replied and brought up a copy of Joshua Reynolds' suicide note on the screen.

'I'd ask you all to bear with me on this and read Reynolds' *alleged* suicide note.'

My Dear Wife, please forgive me for having left you all with the troubles that my death has caused you. I loved all of you very much and more than you can ever know. Everything had become too much for me and I have felt very depressed since mothers death and the money problems with the club.

I know I have let you all down but your mother and sister will help you through this. Bye for the last time, and never forget that you were the best thing that ever happened to me.

Love Joshua

Dewar paused while everyone read the note.

Anna, who was already aware of the dangers of confirmation bias in an investigation, wondered how and why Dewar was implying that someone else had written the suicide note.

'The problem here is the design of the note is wrong. It's set up for an audience rather than just the addressee and even that's wrong. Can anyone tell me why?' Dewar asked, but no one answered her.

'My Dear Wife? Surely, Reynolds would write his own wife's name. "Mothers" should be apostrophe "s" and there are other grammatical errors – this man was university-educated!' Dewar said with conviction.

'He was just about to kill himself. His state of mind must have been all over the place so that would affect the way he wrote the note,' Barbara suggested, but Dewar ignored her and continued.

'He refers to Donna's sister and their mother yet he never once writes their actual names. Some of the note is written in the past tense. It's as if he was already dead when he wrote it and that's impossible.'

'The toxicology results showed he was pissed. So that coupled with his state of mind would explain—' Barbara argued, but was cut off by Dewar, who replied calmly but firmly.

'I am not talking about his state of mind or how drunk he may have been. What I am saying is I don't believe he wrote this note.'

'Well, only Reynolds can tell us that and he's dead,' Barbara replied.

'I understand what you're saying. But there's no direct evidence that the note's a fake. It is what it is,' Barolli said, trying to be diplomatic.

'This note was taken on face value for what it was perceived to be. It supported a suicide theory. The validity of the note was never challenged. Was a forensic linguist asked to examine it? Why leave it on a computer screen and not hand-write it? Did they check his computer for other notes? The answer to every question and many others I haven't yet raised is, NO.'

'So you're saying if the note is a fake, the scene was staged and Reynolds was murdered,' Barolli said.

'Yes,' Dewar replied, emphatically.

Anna thought Dewar was conducting herself reasonably well and that she had remained calm and collected, even when challenged. She had raised valid points about the authenticity of the note, indicating that the contents should have been further investigated at the time. Anna knew this was something Dewar would tell Langton, meaning that she needed to discuss it as soon as possible with DI Simms.

Anna looked at her watch. 'Sorry to interrupt you, Jessie, but we're running late for the Taylor interview.'

'There are other observations concerning the crime scene that I'd like to bring to everyone's attention.'

'You and I can discuss them on the way to Belmarsh.'

'It will only take a few minutes—'

'Time is pressing and we really need to leave now,' Anna said.

'If you insist, DCI Travis.' Dewar was clearly annoyed as she then picked up her laptop and walked off into Anna's office.

Anna asked Barolli for a quick word in private.

'You give her the floor. She spouts a load of psycho-babble and because we don't agree, she storms off,' Barolli remarked.

'At least you were tactful, Paul, unlike Barbara who wanted to go head to head with her,' Anna replied.

'Agreed, but Barbara's comments were justified and as valid as Dewar's.'

'I'd like you to check over the house to house file, extend it beyond Reynolds' block of flats and draw up a list of everyone who was close to him.'

'Do you want full background and intelligence enquiries as well?' he asked.

'Keep it close to home to start with – the wife, his family, business associates . . .'

'His wife already made a statement.'

'It's not very detailed and gives little insight into Joshua Reynolds' lifestyle. To be honest, I only skimmed over it myself.'

'Do you think Reynolds was murdered?'

'As yet, no, but I can see Dewar stirring things up with Langton so we need to be one step ahead of the game.'

Dewar hurriedly put down the desk phone as Anna entered her office, leading Anna to suspect that she had been speaking to Langton.

'Everything all right, Jessie?' Anna asked, knowing full well it wasn't.

'First names is fine between us in private but in front of the office, I'd appreciate it if you referred to me as Special Agent Dewar.'

'I thought you gave an excellent presentation about the suicide note,' Anna said, trying to soothe Dewar's mood.

'Really? Then why didn't you back me up out there when I was being challenged by Maddox and Barolli?'

'What you said has given me food for thought but as the SIO on this case I need to keep an open mind,' Anna reminded her.

'Well, if your DI Simms had kept an open mind last November, you'd have started a murder investigation then and there.'

'Paul Simms is a good detective and, as you said, confirmation bias is not necessarily intentional.'

'What's with you guys? It's all shock, horror because I show someone fucked up and then you get defensive!' Dewar barked, waving her hands as if frightened.

Anna shook her head in disbelief at Dewar's theatrics.

'It's how you said it. The team took it as an attack on a colleague and thereby on the Met as a whole. You instigated the barrier, not them.'

Dewar paused, looking at Anna, and sighed before continuing.

'That wasn't my intention. Sometimes my passion for a case leads to frustration, which makes me angry and then people misunderstand what I say.'

'It would have helped if you had discussed your thoughts with me before the briefing.'

'You only had to ask and I would have. If the suicide note is fake then the most likely person to have killed Reynolds is his wife.'

'She was at the Savoy Hotel all night at a big charity do. DI Simms confirmed it,' Anna observed.

'She could have hired someone to do her dirty work.'

'There were no signs of a struggle or forced entry.'

'If I knocked on your door then stuck a gun in your face, you would do exactly what I told you. I shoot you in the side of the head, stick the gun in your hand and type up a fake suicide note.'

'There was firearms residue and bullets for the gun in the wardrobe safe. Only Reynolds knew the code, so how did your

killer get the gun out?' Anna demanded, beginning to get bored
with the conversation.

'How do you know he was the only person who knew the
code?'

'Donna said so in her statement.'

'Of course she would if she took the gun out and gave it to
the killer or told him the code.'

'This is all very interesting, but a lot of what you're saying is
conjecture.'

'I like to think of it as an alternative proposition. It helps to
work out the balance of probabilities.'

'Any other alternative propositions?'

'Not for the moment.'

Anna couldn't help but think that Dewar was rather self-opinionated, with an answer for everything, and in many ways
wanted the pieces of the puzzle to fit together her way. The
manner in which she presented her theory made it seem possible but Anna knew a story could be twisted. She felt that Dewar
was biased towards Donna Reynolds being responsible for the
murder, although there was not a shred of evidence to show that
she was involved, and Dewar's inflexible attitude worried her.

Anna looked at her watch.

'We're running late. Grab your stuff, we need to get a move
on,' she said, picking up her briefcase and bag while Dewar did
the same.

'One other thing, if it was a suicide and the neighbours were
in, how come no one heard a loud bang that night? The killer
must have used a silencer of some sort.'

'It was November fifth. No one would have noticed.'

'What?'

'Guy Fawkes Night.'

'What's he got to do with it?'

'I'm so glad you didn't raise this in front of the rest of the
office or they would still be laughing now.'

'Why?'

'English tradition. Bonfires and fireworks. Guy Fawkes tried to blow up the Houses of Parliament with gunpowder.'

'Shit, I know nothing about your history,' Dewar said, and laughed loudly as they both left the office.

Chapter Five

Dewar had insisted on driving and Anna was beginning to regret letting her as it was very nerve-wracking. She was constantly over the speed limit, and on a few occasions verging onto the wrong side of the road. Dewar was very tense, her lips pursed as she muttered about the ridiculous road signs being outdated and dangerous. When Dewar ignored a red light and turned right into the path of oncoming traffic Anna had no alternative but to remind her that it was illegal to do that in the UK. Dewar grimly replied it was force of habit as it was allowed in the States.

However, she seemed to relax as the journey continued and Anna gradually felt more at ease with her driving.

'Have you known DCS Langton long?' she asked.

'Yeah, a while, he was over in Los Angeles on a case about an actor, be a few years back now, and we met up again recently at a homicide conference in Paris.'

'LA, yes, I remember he went there once.'

Anna had accompanied Langton to Los Angeles on that inquiry but she was certain that she had not met Dewar before, and that he had never mentioned her name until two days ago when he referred to them meeting at the homicide conference.

'In case you are fishin' for information, my relationship with him is purely business. I know he has quite a reputation. Is he married?'

'Yes, to Laura. His first wife died of a brain tumour, so it's his second marriage. He adopted Laura's daughter Kitty from a previous relationship, and they have a young son Tommy. He likes to keep his private life close to his chest.'

'Well that was very concise. What about you, married or single?'

Anna hesitated. She didn't want to talk with someone she didn't really know about the tragic death of her fiancé Ken or her past relationship with Langton.

'Me? Footloose and fancy-free, apart from work, that is.'

Dewar nodded and laughed. 'Same with me. It's hard in this job being surrounded by men, but I've never mixed work with sex. There are so many divorces and separations due to the pressures, not to mention the shagging around, but I live in hope.'

'I'm really looking forward to the FBI course,' Anna said, deliberately changing the subject.

'Good. You'll really enjoy it. No walk in the park though. It's rare but some people do fail it and there's no going back for a second chance.' Dewar's tone made Anna feel she was implying that was what she expected to happen to her.

'I was on the Met's accelerated promotion course so I know what hard graft is,' Anna countered.

'Jimmy said you were a degree entrant like me. I joined the FBI at twenty-three after completing my master's degree in Forensic Psychology. After three years' fieldwork I became the youngest agent ever to be asked to join the Behavioural Science Unit.'

'You have done well.'

'Within seven years I was promoted to supervising level. As well as profiling on live cases I now head up the behavioural profiling input on all the courses at Quantico. So you will be studying some of my cases,' Dewar said in a rather pompous manner.

'What else is on the course syllabus?' Anna asked, tired of hearing about Dewar's achievements. She thought that three years in the field was not a lot of ground experience and wondered if, as a profiler, Dewar actually visited crime scenes or based her opinions on photographs and statements like the UK profilers did.

'I'll give you some advice: keep your mouth shut unless you have something of value to add. They jump on anyone who likes to think they know it all.'

Anna thought this was rich coming from her.

'There's a wealth of knowledge and experience at Quantico. Especially on the behavioural module I designed. Don Blane is standing in for me while I'm away so I'll give him a ring and tell him you're on the course. See if you can accompany him on a live case over a free weekend. Watching Don working is a masterclass in itself. His interview technique is so good he can make a virgin open up.'

'Thank you,' Anna said, not appreciating the analogy and hoping that Dewar would forget her offer to ring Don. If he was anything like Dewar, she didn't fancy getting stuck with him, especially not over a free weekend.

'Jesus, these frickin' traffic circles, you got cars comin' at you from all directions.'

They drove on in silence before arriving at the vast modern-looking prison, which held some of the UK's most dangerous and violent criminals. As they walked over to the visitors' centre, Dewar said she would like to conduct the interview with Taylor, but Anna tactfully suggested that as he was expecting someone from the Met, it would be best for her to handle it and she would introduce Dewar as a US detective over on work experience.

Once inside, Anna produced her warrant card while Dewar showed her FBI badge, after which they had their fingerprints scanned and a photograph taken before being issued prison passes. The receptionist pointed to the lockers behind them as he explained that mobile phones, handbags and other personal belongings had to be locked away during the visit. They were allowed to take in writing paper, pens and a Dictaphone if they had one, which Anna did and showed it to the guard, who checked it over. They were asked to sign a form agreeing to abide by the rules and then told to wait for a prison officer to escort them to the main building.

'I thought it was bad in the States trying to visit a prisoner but this is ridiculous,' Dewar moaned.

'Well this is a maximum-security prison housing terrorists and—'

'It's hardly Guantanamo Bay, is it!'

Anna was surprised by Dewar's disparaging remark and now realized how impatient the woman could be.

She herself was feeling very uneasy and her stomach was churning. It wasn't so much the interview with Taylor that worried her, more that she had not been inside a prison since the death of Ken. They had actually met when he was a senior officer on a segregated high-security wing at a different prison. She had been interviewing an inmate, the same one who later murdered Ken just after their engagement. Anna was dreading stepping inside the prison gates and the sad memories it would reignite, her greatest fear being how she would react when she saw prison officers all dressed in the standard-issue uniform that Ken had worn with pride. She was so absorbed in her thoughts that she hadn't noticed the male prison officer approach.

'Detective Travis, Agent Dewar, if you would like to follow me, please.'

On hearing his voice, Anna was afraid to look at him, fearing that she would see an image of Ken in front of her. She felt her heart pounding and her breathing increase as she stood up too quickly. Suddenly she felt faint and the room began to spin. 'Pull yourself together,' she thought and, in fear of falling over, sat back down.

'You all right?' Dewar asked.

'Yeah, I just stood up too quickly. It made me feel dizzy.'

'Would you like some water?' the prison officer asked.

'Yes, please,' Anna said and looked up to see that the officer was not only Asian but much younger than Ken. She smiled, somehow feeling as if Ken was with her and telling her not to be stupid and get on with the interview.

After Anna drank her cold water they were escorted through

the main entry gates and into a holding room with a set of air-lock doors. Anna entered the first then proceeded into the second one before Dewar was allowed to follow. Once through the air-locks, they had to go through an X-ray machine and metal detector and were then patted down by a female officer with a sniffer dog. Anna wondered how on earth visitors still managed to smuggle anything in. For her the real irony was that prisoners were still able to make weapons from almost anything they could get their hands on. Ken, her fiancé, was stabbed in his neck artery with a homemade knife and had bled to death.

The interview room was small, with only a table and four chairs. To the left of the table there was a panic alarm that could be pressed if assistance was needed. The escorting officer told them that Delon Taylor would be brought from his cell shortly and Anna sat down and placed her Dictaphone, notebook and pen on the table. Dewar sat next to her.

'I can't believe all the rigmarole for a police officer and senior FBI agent to come and see some lowlife prisoner,' Dewar complained.

'The officers are just doing their job.'

'I wonder if the pain-in-the-ass bureaucrats will put us through the same irritating process on the way out?'

'Do me a favour and cut the cynical remarks about the prison officers, please!' Anna said bluntly.

'Well, excuse me if I offend you.'

'You didn't offend me. You offended someone I knew.'

Before Dewar could say anything else the interview-room door opened and Taylor was brought in and sat opposite them. Delon Taylor was black, in his mid-twenties, very muscular and six feet tall. Anna had looked at his criminal file and noted that he was a professional cage fighter, which accounted for his mis-shapen nose and numerous facial scars, but nevertheless he had a very handsome face.

Anna introduced herself as the DCI investigating Joshua Reynolds' death, showing Taylor her warrant card, and told him

that although he would be interviewed as a witness, not a suspect, she would like to record the interview. Taylor said nothing
but nodded in agreement. Anna was about to introduce Dewar
as a US detective on work experience with the Met when the
agent produced her FBI badge and cut in.

'I'm Jessie Dewar, a supervisory special agent with the FBI
and—'

'Fucking FBI! What they doing here?' Taylor shouted at Anna
in a broad London accent.

'I'm working the case with Detective Travis,' Dewar replied.

'Well you can fuck off back to where you came from!'

Anna was livid. Dewar had managed to upset Taylor before
she had asked a single question. She wanted to give Dewar a
piece of her mind but knew it was totally against protocol to
chastize a fellow officer in front of a prisoner. Instead, Anna
gave Dewar a stare that made it quite clear how she felt and
quickly calmed the situation by explaining to Taylor that the
agent was merely an observer benefiting from work experience
with the Met.

'Good, because I ain't talking to no Yank,' Taylor said. Anna
was pleased that he had made his position on the matter quite
clear and hoped that it would curtail any further disruption by
Dewar. Anna informed Taylor that she had been told that he
had information concerning Joshua Reynolds' death and asked
him to tell her what he knew and give some background detail
of his association with the dead man. Taylor told them that
everyone called Reynolds by his preferred name of Josh and that
he had worked as a bouncer at his club.

'Josh was a real nice geezer, everyone liked him. Not like his
tosser of a partner Marcus Williams. He was ripping Josh off
left, right and centre. I'm sitting in this shit-hole because of
him.'

'You're awaiting trial for robbery and serious assault on a
police officer. Are you saying Williams was involved in that?'
Anna asked.

'No. Williams had me set up for thieving from the club tills so Josh would sack me. With no job I soon ran out of money and had no choice other than do a robbery.'

'You were armed with a gun at the time.'

'The gun was fake and the assault was a fucking accident. I ran out the building society straight into the copper and the money went flying everywhere. Knocked the poor bloke straight on his arse and he split his head open on the pavement. I legged it with what I could pick up, which was only a few hundred, yet I got charged with nicking over two grand.'

'That was nearly six months ago. Why do you want to talk to us now?'

'No, the robbery was, but I went on the run to Liverpool and only got nicked two weeks ago, me mum of all people turned me in. Anyways I only heard about Josh's death in here when I saw an old workmate so that's why I had to speak with you. Tell you what I knew.'

Anna chuckled inside. Although Taylor came across as a very fit and hard man he made a rather inept criminal. She asked him to get to the point regarding Josh's death.

'Williams had a prostitution set-up going on in the Trojan with high-rolling Arabs, foreign millionaires, film and TV celebs. They paid big money. Five hundred a wank, a grand a blowjob, two grand for sex and those who will do it three K for anal. Williams pocketed seventy per cent.'

'Did Josh Reynolds know about this?' Anna asked.

'Not until I told him, which was a day or two before he died. He was shocked – he'd worked hard to turn the Trojan into a decent club.'

Anna leaned back in her chair to take in what Taylor had just said. She looked at Dewar, who smirked at her as if to say, 'I told you it was a murder and the suicide note was fake.'

'So how long had this been going on?' Anna asked.

'A couple of months or so.'

'Tell me, what are you expecting for this information?'

'My solicitor told me that helping the police about other crimes could be beneficial to my sentence.'

'I think your solicitor was actually referring to other crimes you may have committed,' Anna pointed out.

'I haven't done any, but you can tell the judge that I helped in a murder inquiry, can't you?'

'I'll be investigating what you said and if it turns out you have deliberately wasted police time you could find that heaped onto the charges you already face.'

'I swear on my mum's life that I'm not lying.'

'Not convincing, seeing she's the one who shopped you to the police.'

Taylor sat back, unable to meet Anna's eye after she had questioned him about the truth behind his information.

She looked at Dewar, who had been writing notes furiously throughout the interview.

'I wonder if I could ask you a couple of questions as part of my work experience?' Dewar asked, glancing pointedly at Anna.

'May as well, 'cause she ain't listening to me no more,' Taylor said, clearly angry with Anna.

'Donna Reynolds, Josh's wife, did you know her?'

'Yeah, nice girl.'

'So why did she leave the club?'

'I think she got tired of dirty old geezers squeezing her arse and tits. They treated her like she was still dancing.'

'Dancing?'

'Yeah, she was a lap dancer at the Trojan – that's how her and Josh met. She wasn't very good and Josh didn't like her dancing so he made her the head hostess. Better with her lips than her hips,' Taylor said with a loud guffaw.

'Was she overfamiliar with the customers?'

'If it meant a bit of flirting to get a punter's money out of his pockets then yeah. She knew how to play the game.'

'So their relationship was strained. They argued a lot?'

Anna knew exactly where Dewar was going with what was clearly a leading question.

'I heard them argue sometimes but all couples—'

'What about? Was it her flirting?'

'He didn't like it but he put up with it.'

'Did they argue about money?'

'I know they didn't have much in their pockets. Everything was invested in the club and their flat. Donna was the one who watched the pennies, checked all the cash tills against the receipts every night.'

'What about Donna and Marcus Williams?'

'What about them?'

'Was there anything going on between them?'

'You havin' a laugh? She was too good for that bastard. Donna wasn't that kind of girl.'

'Did Josh think she was having an affair with any of the VIPs?'

'He never asked me if she was.'

'Did he slap her around?'

'I never saw her with a black eye if that's what you mean.'

'Were you and Donna lovers? Did she need you to do her dirty work?'

'What the fuck are you on!' Taylor screamed at Dewar and stood up.

'Delon, please calm down. You misunderstood Agent Dewar,' Anna said, trying desperately to calm the situation.

'No, he didn't. His reaction made that quite clear,' Dewar said confidently.

Taylor banged his hands down on the table.

'Fuck you, you bitch. Josh and Donna Reynolds are good people. I told Josh about Williams and now he's dead. It ain't rocket science, not even for the fucking FBI.'

'Sit down and don't speak to me like that,' Dewar said firmly.

'I ain't no murderer and I'll speak to you how I fucking like.'

Taylor began to shout for the prison officer, who rushed into the room. Taylor claimed that Dewar was 'doing his head in' and asked to be taken back to his cell, at which point Travis held her hand up, indicating to the prison officer that the interview was over.

'Well, that's the end of that then. All in all, I thought it went pretty well,' Dewar said, then flipped the cover of her notebook closed and jumped to her feet, smiling at Anna.

Anna was completely taken aback by Dewar's remark and her method of questioning a witness. Not only was it, in her opinion, a poor technique, but the agent was also trying to put words into Taylor's mouth to reinforce her own suspicions. It seemed that Dewar was convinced Donna Reynolds was involved in her husband's murder even though Taylor was insinuating Marcus Williams was responsible. Anna suspected Taylor was lying, but the reality was that the interview with Taylor, like the suicide note, had raised further unanswered questions.

They walked back to the car in silence. Anna, out of Dewar's hearing, rang the office and asked Joan Falkland to make an appointment for her to meet with Donna Reynolds and not to mention the murder squad, but just say it was to do with the current owner of the Trojan. She also left a text message on Paul Simms' mobile asking him to contact her regarding Joshua Reynolds' suicide.

As they pulled out of the prison car park, Anna asked Dewar what she made of the interview with Taylor.

'I thought you handled it reasonably well, but if you'd drawn him out more you'd have got the intended reaction I did.'

'You wanted him to let rip at you?' Anna asked in disbelief.

'Yes, it's about reaction and gauging the truth. I made a false accusation, he reacted with anger, thus from his tone, demeanour and other facial expressions he is telling the truth.'

'If Donna wanted to kill Reynolds then making it look like a robbery gone wrong at the flat or Trojan would have been a better option. Plus, there's no insurance pay-out on a suicide.'

'She'd still get the apartment and his share of the Trojan.'

'So what's Williams' part in this great conspiracy then?'

'Hard to say until I've spoken with him. I doubt he and Donna were lovers but they both had reason to want Josh dead,' Dewar said with great assurance.

'So now you think it was either Donna or Williams that killed Josh.'

'No. I think Donna wanted him dead and maybe she got Williams to do it or arrange it.'

Anna felt it would be a waste of time to contradict any of Dewar's varying and conflicting opinions, as once again, she seemed to have an answer for everything. One thing she knew for certain was that Dewar would inform Langton of the day's developments and her skewed beliefs as soon as she had a chance to contact him.

Chapter Six

Anna completed her report at home and handed it to Joan the next morning to upload onto the Reynolds computer file. 'Any luck with Donna Reynolds, Joan?'

Joan replied that she had rung Donna Reynolds' mobile yesterday evening, claiming to be from the vice squad, and that a DCI Travis wanted to come and see her regarding the Trojan club. Anna sensed that Joan was rather anxious.

'Was there a problem?'

'Well, yes and no: I didn't realize her mother Gloria had answered the phone. She said Donna was having a swim in the pool, so I arranged through her for you to meet with Donna at four p.m. She started asking questions and I just said I didn't know, but I think she knew I was lying.' The constable clearly wasn't happy.

'Don't look so worried, you salvaged a tricky situation.'

'But she kept pressing me and I said she'd have to speak with you so I had to give her your mobile number.'

'Well, she hasn't called me yet.'

'Donna's living with her mum in Weybridge, Surrey,' Joan said, handing Anna the address on a piece of paper. 'Langton's in your office with Agent Dewar, I had to tell her about the meeting with Donna.'

'Why?'

'I had no choice – she asked me for Donna's mobile number as she wanted to arrange a meeting with her. I said you had already done so.'

'How did she take that?' Anna grinned.

'Mumbled something about being left in the dark again and stormed off.'

'After her performance with Taylor, DI Barolli and I will be speaking with Donna,' Anna assured her, heading towards the DI's door.

She popped her head around it and told him to be free for a four-p.m. meeting with Donna Reynolds in Weybridge.

Entering her office, the first thing she noticed was that her desk was yet again littered with Dewar's papers, and enlarged photographs of the Reynolds crime scene were laid out on the sofa and floor.

'Good morning, Travis,' said Langton. 'Jessie here was in at half seven drawing up further lines of enquiry for your investigation.'

'Well I've been busy completing my notes on the interview with Taylor.'

'Interesting interview. Jessie was just telling me about it and her observations concerning the suicide note being fake. Opens up a can of worms, doesn't it?'

'Depends how you look at it,' Anna said.

'How do you mean?' Langton asked.

'Taylor could be telling a pack of lies and the suicide note could be genuine. As you've often said yourself, there can be many sides to a story.'

'True. But I have to say Jessie has raised issues that DI Simms should clearly have considered at the time. If he made the wrong call at the scene then everything that followed is a total fuck-up. We could have a murderer out there who thinks they've got away with it.'

'Hindsight is a wonderful thing but Paul Simms never knew about Delon Taylor back then,' Anna replied.

'He might have done if he'd dug a bit deeper and made some in-depth enquiries at the Trojan,' Dewar remarked.

'Why do you think Taylor's lying?' Langton asked Anna.

'There may be elements of truth in what he said but that

doesn't mean Reynolds was murdered. He could be trying to use circumstances for his own benefit. He never came forward until he ended up on remand for robbery and assault.'

'If I may interject, Jimmy,' Dewar said.

Every time she called him 'Jimmy' it grated on Anna's nerves, but she knew it was perfectly possible that Dewar could have read the list of issues about her attitude to discuss, and was now attempting to turn things to her advantage. Anna was sorely tempted to give Dewar a piece of her mind, but with Langton on the FBI agent's side she decided it was better to keep quiet and just let her drone on.

'In my experience the behavioural actions of the person being interviewed can help to detect whether or not they are lying.'

'Are you referring to Taylor?' Langton asked.

'Yes. I focused on his micro-expressions. I wrote a chapter about it in my published paper, "The Language of Lies".'

'So what exactly are micro-expressions?' Langton asked, intrigued, and Dewar clearly knew it.

'Movements that flash up on a person's face for a fraction of a second. When someone is lying their eyes will move to the left or they may blink more rapidly.'

'How interesting,' Langton remarked.

'We still don't know what Taylor was actually thinking,' Anna said, annoyed that Langton of all people was fooled by Dewar's drivel.

'It takes experience and understanding to spot the signs, Anna. Emotions that betray a liar are fear, guilt about lying. Taylor showed none of those signs and that is why I believe he was telling the truth.'

'What about his emotional outburst and banging the table when you accused him of being Donna's lover and doing her dirty work?'

'I already told you I wanted to draw him out and see how he reacted to a statement that I had no evidence to support.'

'I was going to update the team about our interview with

Taylor but I wondered if you would like to do it. I'm sure they would be interested to hear about your micro-expression observations,' Anna said, trying to force Dewar into an awkward situation.

'As much as I'd love to I really don't have the time at the moment. They can read the report I prepared.'

'I think your next step should be an interview with Donna Reynolds,' Langton said.

'I agree, Jimmy. I found out this morning that Donna Reynolds is now living with her mother. Anna and I have an appointment to see her this afternoon. I also think we first need to revisit the flat where Reynolds died. Get a better feel for the scene before we interview his widow.'

Frustrated that Dewar had just assumed she would be interviewing Donna and keen not to let Barolli down again, Anna decided to speak up. 'I've told Paul Barolli that he can do the Donna Reynolds interview with me, so I think he should also come on the scene visit.'

Dewar ignored the comment. 'I had all the scene photographs blown up to assist us. As I said earlier, Jimmy, there are some things that don't quite add up regarding the position of the gun and the blood distribution.'

'Barolli's got plenty to do here, so you two visit the scene then interview Donna,' Langton ruled. 'It seems more sensible as you both did the Taylor interview. Travis can ask her the questions while you observe her micro-expressions. See if there's anything that indicates she's lying.'

Anna was unsure if Langton was having a joke, but felt she had been forced into a corner by Dewar and now had no choice but to agree, offering to ask Joan to get details of the new occupant of Reynolds' old flat. Dewar said that she had already made some enquiries, and that the new owner was leasing the property. A Mr Dobbs from the letting agents would meet them there at midday.

Desperate to get away from Dewar, Anna went to break the revised plan to Barolli. He was not pleased at yet again being left out of an important witness interview because of Dewar.

'You have every right to be upset, Paul, and I should have been more forceful with Langton and Dewar.'

'Don't worry about it – while you and Langton are gone and I'm SIO, she'll have to do as she's told,' Barolli, resilient as ever, remarked with a smile.

Still keen to avoid Dewar, Anna then went to the ladies' room. Having washed her hands and brushed her hair she was just opening the door to go back into the corridor when she caught sight of Langton and Dewar, with their backs to her, standing by the lift talking. Anna stepped back and held the door slightly open so she could eavesdrop on their conversation.

'I'd like to speak with the forensic scientist who attended the scene and the pathologist,' Dewar was saying.

'That's fine by me but let DCI Travis know as well,' Langton instructed her.

'Also, I'd like to sit down with DI Simms and go over everything in his report or more importantly, what he's failed to put in it.'

'I agree it wasn't an in-depth investigation.'

'A rookie could have done a better job.'

'Go easy on Simms; he's a delicate lad and as Travis said, hindsight is a wonderful thing. Don't belittle him – that will only alienate everyone and you need the team on your side, not against you,' warned Langton.

'Well, I've not found it easy so far and Travis isn't helping matters.'

'In what way?' he asked, clearly wondering what Dewar was implying.

'Well, nothing directly other than a little hit list of things to discuss with me.' Dewar tossed her head in irritation.

'What did she say?'

'She hasn't as yet. I think she deliberately left it on her desk for me to find rather than confront me.'

'Believe me, she's not frightened of speaking her mind when she wants to,' Langton said ruefully.

'Her body language doesn't help and the rest of them in the office can sense that.'

'What about her micro-expressions? Langton asked, trying to make light of the situation.

'Not funny, Jimmy. I made a casual quip about the prison staff yesterday and she nearly bit my head off.'

'What the bloody hell did you say?' Langton asked sharply.

'I jokingly referred to them as pain-in-the-ass bureaucrats.'

'She was engaged to be married to a prison officer who was murdered by one of the inmates,' Langton said, clearly annoyed with Dewar.

'She never said . . .'

'She doesn't talk about it but it still hurts her.'

'I need to tell her how sorry I am.'

'No. If she wanted you to know she would have said something there and then. As for her attitude, she wouldn't bad-mouth you to the team, it's not her style. Travis keeps things to herself because she sometimes doubts her own abilities, but she's one of the best detectives I've ever worked with.'

Dewar, obviously embarrassed, was clearly wishing she hadn't said anything about Anna's attitude. 'I didn't realize you were so close.'

'It's more mutual respect now. She's helped me through hard times and defended me when the top brass were breathing down my neck. After Ken was murdered she changed. The job became her lifeblood.'

'She sounds like a good ally to have on your side,' Dewar said sheepishly.

'She is, and you can learn a lot from her, even in a short space of time,' Langton said as he stepped into the lift.

Anna closed the door quietly and stepped back to the washbasins. With mixed emotions she stood and took a good look at herself in the mirror. Although proud that Langton had spoken so highly of her abilities, she felt tainted with guilt. She knew when Langton mentioned her defending him against the top brass he was referring to Deputy Commissioner Walters' internal investigation into the Fitzpatrick case, and she was only too aware that her old boss still had no idea that she had betrayed his trust. It pained her to think, Walters' slyness aside, that she was part of the reason he had still not made Commander.

'Hi, Anna. Paul Simms here.' Anna had been on her way back to her office when her mobile rang. 'Sorry I didn't get back to you earlier. Brian and I have moved into a new house together and it's been a bit of a nightmare trying to decide where to put everything. You'll have to come to the house-warming.'

'Thanks. Bring a bottle, I take it,' Anna said.

'Bring a man as well, if you like. He may never get out alive with half the gay police association here!'

Anna laughed. Although she hadn't spoken with Paul Simms for a long time he was still as cheerful as ever.

'What can I do for you?'

'It's about the Joshua Reynolds case you dealt with last November ...'

'The guy who shot himself — it's all done and dusted now. The Coroner's verdict was suicide.'

'I know, but I need to sit down and speak with you about it.'

'Is there a problem?' Simms asked, apprehensively.

'There's a remand prisoner who's making spurious allega-tions about Reynolds' death,' Anna said, keen not to cause alarm.

'So why's the file with you and not back on my desk?'

'It's complicated, but nothing to worry about. What about I buy you breakfast tomorrow morning? You can choose the venue.'

'In that case the Wolseley in Piccadilly. I'll book it for seven a.m.'

As Anna hung up she knew that going over Paul's original investigation was going to be a delicate situation and that a delicious breakfast wouldn't be enough to prevent her old friend and colleague getting hurt.

Chapter Seven

Anna decided it was her turn to drive as she and Dewar made their way to Reynolds' old flat at Kingsborough Terrace, Bayswater. During the three-mile journey Dewar was noticeably subdued and didn't speak. Anna wondered if she was thinking about the words of advice that Langton had given her or just feeling sorry for herself. Either way she just hoped there would be a change for the better in Dewar's attitude towards her, the team and the investigation.

Anna parked the car at the rear of the block of six flats. As they walked around to the front of the building Anna remarked that the flats looked fairly new and that property in the Bayswater area of London was very expensive. On approaching the entrance on the main road, they saw a man in his mid-forties, neatly dressed in a grey double-breasted pinstripe suit, repeatedly looking at his watch. Dewar asked him if he was Mr Dobbs from the letting agents. He confirmed he was and commented that they were late and he had a strict schedule to adhere to as he had other properties to show prospective tenants around.

'I'm Special Agent Dewar from the FBI and this is DCI Travis. We are reinvestigating the death of Joshua Reynolds and we want to familiarize ourselves with the layout of the apartment. We will be here for as long as it takes,' Dewar said, putting Dobbs in his place.

Dobbs got the message and led them through the communal entry door, which was operated by an electronic keypad and intercom system. Flat two was on the ground floor and the front door opened into a short hallway off which there was an en-suite master bedroom on the left, a second small bedroom-come-study on the right and a guest shower room with washbasin and toilet next to it. The door at the end of the hallway led to a large living room with a four-seater sofa, matching armchairs, dining table and six chairs. Double-glazed bi-folding doors opened out onto a railed terrace area. Just beyond the terrace there was a grassed area and the residents' parking bays. To the right side of the living room, behind large sliding doors, there was a modern fully appointed kitchen with integrated appliances. The property had new hardwood flooring and pristine white walls throughout. It was very modern and obviously well maintained by the letting agents.

'When and for how much did Mr and Mrs Reynolds purchase the flat?' Anna asked.

'October 2011, for five hundred and fifty thousand pounds. The new owner paid five eighty for it four months ago,' Dobbs answered.

'So Mrs Reynolds made a profit,' Dewar remarked.

'Not really, as the price included all fixtures and fittings and it was sold at the current market value. Mrs Reynolds' mother dealt with the sale due to her daughter's distressed state at the sudden loss of her husband.'

'It doesn't appear to have changed much,' Anna said.

'The bloodstained carpet was replaced with hardwood flooring throughout and other than a new settee and armchairs the premises are in the same condition as when Mrs Reynolds left it,' Dobbs said and looked at his watch.

Dewar had brought with her the enlarged scene photographs in a long cardboard tube, and now took them out and laid them on the dining table. The top picture was of Joshua Reynolds lying in a pool of blood. Dobbs, visibly shaken, put his hand to his mouth and moved away.

'Oh, my goodness, that's awful. It makes me feel sick.'

Apologizing to Dobbs, Dewar turned the photograph face

down and suggested to Anna that he could go and deal with his other viewings. They could always lock the door after them and return the keys to the lettings agents' office when they had finished. Dobbs said that was fine by him and he was out of the door like a shot.

Dewar asked Anna to help her move the sofa and other furniture into the same positions they had been in when Josh's body was found. Having done this, Dewar said that she had a copy of Donna's statement and suggested they re-enact her arrival home and her discovery of Josh's body. Anna agreed it was as good a place as any to start.

They went back into the hallway and stood by the front door. Dewar started to go through the statement.

'Donna returned home and used the Yale key to gain entry. There's also a Chubb lock but no mention was made of it in her statement,' Dewar observed.

'Could be it was already unlocked therefore she only needed to use the Yale key,' Anna suggested.

'If it was unlocked then surely she should have expected Josh to be in – her statement says that whenever they went out their door would be double-locked.'

Dewar had made a good point but Anna was worried that her sole intention was to find fault in Donna's statement.

'Do you mind me suggesting alternative propositions as we go along? It will help to prevent cognitive and confirmation bias,' Anna asked, recalling Dewar's earlier comments.

'Not at all.'

They walked down the hallway and into the master bedroom on the left. Dewar placed the photograph of the room down on the bed and looked at the statement. The furniture was still laid out as it had been at the time of Reynolds' death. Upon entering, the bed was on the left with the fitted wardrobes and en-suite bathroom to the right. A chest of drawers and vanity table were up against the opposite wall.

'In the photograph, the left door of the fitted-wardrobe door is open,' Dewar said and slid open the left wardrobe door, revealing an electronic-key-coded safe, which was bolted to the wall.

'In this close-up, the clothing on hangers had been pushed to one side, clearly showing the safe. Strange, isn't it?'

Anna looked at the photograph, 'I'm not sure what you're getting at.'

'Donna walks into the bedroom, unpacks her case, gets the dirty laundry from the basket in the bathroom yet never noticed the wardrobe and safe were open?'

Anna checked the photographs again. 'The makeup bag, evening gown and other stuff from her case are scattered on the bed so maybe she didn't go near the wardrobe,' she suggested.

'Or she already knew what had happened to Josh and staged her actions to look like she was behaving normally,' Dewar said, walking out of the bedroom into the living room and turning towards the kitchen on the right. She suddenly stopped then took two steps backwards and stood by the living-room door. Anna, who was following behind and writing notes at the same time, swerved to avoid bumping into her.

'Question for Donna. Was the living-room door open or closed when she returned home?'

Dewar then went into the kitchen and, glancing at the scene photographs, opened the integrated-washing-machine door and the cupboard under the sink.

'She puts the dirty clothes in the machine then gets the laundry liquid and softener from under the sink. After starting the machine she walks back towards the bedroom,' Dewar said, re-enacting Donna's movements then stopping by the door to the hallway. 'Only at this point do we get the shock and horror of finding her husband dead in a pool of blood.'

'Why would she do all that if she already knew he was dead? It seems to me she was acting perfectly normally and wasn't expecting to find Josh dead,' Anna remarked, but Dewar said nothing.

Anna watched fascinated as the agent walked around the living room deep in thought and talking to herself. She laid the blown-up photographs of Josh's body and the blood distribution on the floor and on the sofa. It worried Anna that Dewar still seemed to have it fixed in her mind that Donna was in some way culpable. Anna felt that suggesting Donna left the Savoy, murdered her husband and then returned to the hotel in the early hours was clutching at straws.

'Simms' report said that Donna's alibi checked out. She went to the Savoy charity ball with her mother and sister and stayed there overnight,' she observed.

'I think Simms took Donna on face value as the grieving widow. She totally hoodwinked him,' Dewar said.

Anna turned back through the pages in her notebook, looking for references she had jotted down regarding the forensic pathology. The pathologist had stated Josh had died between eight to twenty hours before midday on the sixth of November. She did a quick calculation in her mind.

'Dr Harrow, the pathologist who attended the scene, estimated time of death anywhere between four p.m. on the fifth and four a.m. on the sixth of November. Donna was at the Savoy,' Anna said firmly.

'Maybe she didn't kill her husband,' Dewar replied.

'But you just insinuated as much,' Anna said, surprised by Dewar's ever-changing theories.

'No. I was insinuating that Simms never regarded her as a suspect because he thought it was a suicide. Although she may not have pulled the trigger I now think she knows who did.'

Anna disagreed. 'There were no signs of forced entry to the flat and the pathology report said no injuries consistent with a struggle before death. All of which surely points towards suicide?'

'Or someone Josh knew and let into the flat.'

'Who unbelievably overpowers him, gets the gun out of the safe—'

Dewar interrupted Anna: 'How do you actually know that the gun was in the safe or even belonged to Josh Reynolds? His killer could have brought it with him.'

'Forensics said there were heavy traces of firearms residue in the safe. There were four bullets still in the safe and they matched the single one loaded and fired from the gun.'

'I know it sounds far-fetched, Anna, but please hear me out.'

'I'm listening,' Anna said despairingly.

Dewar then produced a gun from her jacket pocket, explaining that it was a plastic toy. She handed it to Anna then lay down on the floor on her right-hand side in the semi-foetal position that Reynolds was found in. Dewar then eased herself up onto her knees and explained that she was working backwards to try and assume Josh's posture at the time of the fatal shot. She asked Anna to hand her the gun and held it to her right temple.

'BANG!' Dewar shouted loudly, making Anna jump back. She fell slowly forward, rotating her body slightly and moving her right arm so she landed on her right-hand side with her right arm, hand and the gun outstretched above her head. Her left arm was lying across her hip at a right angle.

'Am I in the same position as Reynolds is in the photograph?' Dewar asked while still on the floor.

Anna told her that she was and Dewar then asked her to place the close-up photograph of Reynolds' right hand and the gun underneath her right hand. Anna did as she was asked and Dewar then eased herself up onto her knees again. She held the gun to her right temple and once more shouted, 'BANG!' Although Anna was expecting it this time it still made her jump. Dewar started to fall forward again, rotating slightly to her right, but now her right hand and the gun ended up under her right breast.

'Even allowing for some recoil when a gun is fired this end position or something similar would be more natural. It's hard to see how his right hand could be outstretched above his head. Unless . . .' Dewar remarked before sitting up on her knees again and handing Anna the toy gun. The agent then held her hands in the air and asked Anna to hold the gun against her right temple. Anna was about to ask, jokingly, if Dewar would like her to go bang this time but never got the chance. 'BANG!'

Dewar shouted and fell forward. As she did so her left arm hit the side of the sofa and ended up across her left hip and her right arm was outstretched above her head.

'Now place the gun in my hand.'

'I understand what you're trying to show me, Jessie, but surely there must be many variables to consider. We don't know if he died instantly, had a muscle spasm or some other involuntary reaction. Any of which could have resulted in his end position,' Anna said as Dewar got to her feet and picked up the close-up photograph of Reynolds' hand holding the gun.

'Agreed, but there is something else that points towards him not having a gun in his right hand when he was shot. Can you see what's missing in this photograph?'

'If I can't see it how do I know it's missing?' Anna asked, frustrated that after three re-enactments, Dewar was still not getting to the point.

'Look at the back of his right hand – there's no blood.'

Anna pointed to the picture of Reynolds on the floor. 'There's some on his left arm, hand and plenty on the floor.'

Dewar replied that she was not a blood distribution expert but she knew a bit about guns and firearms injuries. She told Anna that the blood distribution and brain debris on his left arm, hand and the sofa would have come from the forward spatter as the bullet exited his head and embedded itself in the woodwork of the sofa.

'Think of a pebble being dropped into water and the upward splash it causes at the point of impact,' Dewar said, keen for Anna to understand. 'A bullet has a similar effect. It enters the head, causing blood to exit back towards the gun. It's called back spatter. The closer the gun the more back spatter you get,' she explained, and picked out a photograph from the bundle she had prepared and held it up. 'Look on this close-up photo. There's some blood on the floor in line with his right knee. The direction and position is away from the body. Assuming it's back spatter then there should be blood on the back of his hand.'

Anna recalled the pathologist's report mentioning powder

burns around the entry wound, which indicated the gun was held close to the head of the victim. She realized that Dewar had hit on something that was critical to the scene assessment and wondered if it had been looked into at the time and was yet another thing Paul Simms had omitted to mention in his report.

'I have to say, Jessie, your scene re-assessment is not only very professional but also very interesting. You've raised some thought-provoking questions about how Joshua Reynolds may have died,' Anna conceded.

'Thank you, Anna. I know it was a bit long-winded but I tend to envelop myself in my own world trying to figure out every possible scenario.'

'Why didn't you tell me your concerns about the scene before now?'

'Because I needed to come here and get a real feel for the place and put it all together piece by piece.'

Anna understood, she often got a gut feeling herself and never said anything until she could confirm her own suspicions. She wondered if her bias towards the Reynolds case being suicide, coupled with her eagerness to go to Quantico, had clouded her judgement.

'There are obviously serious issues concerning the blood distribution,' Anna said, wishing she had taken more time to examine the scene photographs herself.

'Simms' report doesn't even mention a blood distribution expert attending the scene,' Dewar remarked.

'Pete Jenkins was the forensic scientist who dealt with the stuff sent to the lab so I assume he also attended the scene. Simms' report said a Crime Scene Manager and Dr Harrow the pathologist did.'

'We really need to speak with this guy Jenkins and the pathologist as soon as possible,' Dewar insisted.

'Leave it with me and I will arrange a meet with them both.'

However, Anna was apprehensive about Dewar discussing her thoughts and theories with Pete Jenkins. The agent, convinced she was right, was on a real high and Anna knew she would not let go easily. It worried her that no matter what Pete said she would try and force her opinions on him. Anna knew he was one of the best forensic scientists in the lab, as she'd reaped the benefits of his forensic knowledge and expert opinion on a number of murder investigations. If Pete Jenkins disproved Dewar's scene assessment, Anna thought it would be better coming from her, albeit second hand. That way she could tell Dewar calmly and objectively that she was wrong. She hoped that her breakfast meeting with Paul Simms might help to clear up some of her concerns before she made contact with Pete.

Arriving back at the station, Dewar went to the canteen to get them each a sandwich. As Anna made a beeline for Paul Barolli, her mobile rang.

'I'm Gloria Lynne, Donna's mother, and I'm sorry to bother you, Detective Travis, but there's a bit of a hiccup with this afternoon's agenda. It's Donna, you see. Poor darling has got herself into a bit of a tizzy.'

Anna immediately noticed how well spoken Gloria was, with a distinct upper-class voice.

'About my wanting to speak with her?' Anna asked.

'Oh, it's not that at all, I haven't even told her you're a vice-squad detective. I simply instructed her to be here at four as I had someone coming for afternoon tea that I wanted her to meet.'

'I see,' Anna said, not exactly sure what the problem was.

'Donna is still very emotional about the loss of Joshua, so the mention of police, or anything or anyone connected to him is quite distressing for her. So, I thought it best you came along unannounced.'

'So what's the hiccup, Mrs Lynne?'

'Donna forgot that she had a three-o'clock appointment at Michaeljohn.'

Anna had heard of Michaeljohn and knew that it was a very

expensive Mayfair salon frequented by royalty, Hollywood actresses and other A-list celebrities.

'I can come tomorrow,' Anna offered.

'Don't, please. I was merely wondering if it would be possible for you to come to my house a bit later. Say about six. Donna will be home by then.'

Anna said that would be fine and ended the conversation, unsure of what to make of the caller. She wondered how Gloria would react when she found out that Anna was actually reinvestigating her son-in-law's death as a possible murder. She wondered if it might have been better to tell her the truth from the outset, but at least she could now fall back on the excuse that she hadn't wanted Donna to become overstressed at the thought of speaking to a murder-squad detective.

Dewar returned with a chicken sandwich and coffee for Anna, apologizing for the delay and saying that she got stuck in the canteen talking to Barbara. Anna remarked that once Barbara got going she was a bit hard to get away from.

'She rambled on about being single and needing to lose weight if she wanted to "pull a fit bloke",' Dewar went on, 'although I have absolutely no idea what that means.'

Anna told Dewar about the phone call from Gloria Lynne and the rearranged interview time with Donna.

'It's going to be a late finish, so to save us both returning to the station, I'll take my car to Gloria's house and you can follow me,' Anna suggested.

'That's fine, but I'm wondering, now we've got time to kill before seeing Donna, if it might be worth paying a quick visit to the Trojan first?'

'Why?'

'To get the feel for the place, like the Reynolds scene. We'd be discreet.'

'Basically, you want to see how Marcus Williams reacts when we say were reinvestigating his partner Josh's death. I believe you Americans say "put the squeeze on him".'

'You see, Anna, you're thinking like me already.' Dewar laughed.

'No. I know what you're thinking and I'm not so sure it's a good idea quite yet.'

'We don't mention the interview with Donna. Then we can check Williams' mobile, see if he calls or texts her after we leave.'

'I'm becoming a soft touch,' Anna said.

Dewar wagged her finger. 'No. You like the thrill of the chase.'

Anna put her notebook in her bag. 'I'm still not convinced Reynolds was murdered.'

'You will be. Trust me.'

'As long as you promise to hold back on Donna Reynolds, treat her as a witness, not a suspect, until we have hard evidence to prove otherwise,' Anna replied, although she knew that this was unlikely to happen.

Chapter Eight

By the time Anna got to her car, Dewar was already in hers, slamming her door shut. As she started up the engine she lowered the window and told Anna she'd meet her outside the front of the Trojan club in Rupert Street. Anna watched, impressed by her enthusiasm, as she drove out of the underground car park too fast and on the wrong side of the arrows.

On her way to the club, Anna took the opportunity to put in a quick call to Pete Jenkins at the forensics lab, but his assistant said he was out at a scene. Anna left a message that she would be at the lab between eight-thirty and nine a.m. and needed to discuss the Joshua Reynolds suicide with him.

As usual there were no parking spaces to be had along Wardour Street, and so Anna resorted to the multi-storey car park in Poland Street. Walking through the neon alleyway of Walkers Court, once home of the infamous Raymond Revuebar strip club, Anna realized how little the area had changed over the years. It was still the heart of London's adult entertainment industry with its sex shops and clip joints fleecing tourists who were looking for a 'good time'. It struck Anna a lap-dancing club like the Trojan would fit in perfectly in the area and no doubt be a very profitable business.

There was no sign of Dewar as Anna reached the main entrance of the club, where large metal security gates in front of the doors were firmly closed and padlocked. Anna traced her way around to the rear-mews entrance, passing large industrial-waste bins filled with rubbish. She could see Dewar's car parked in the mews with a police vehicle sign on the dashboard to ward away any passing traffic wardens, making her even more irritated that the agent had not waited for her at the front as they had agreed. She noticed a tall black man in his mid-fifties emerging from the open rear fire doors of the club. He was carrying two crates of empty bottles, which he stacked on others that were already outside the premises. He was wearing a dark blue zip-front boiler suit, which was paint-stained, a black wool hat and workman's safety boots.

'Hi, I'm looking for the lady who was driving that car,' Anna said as she pointed.

He turned to her, his face shiny with sweat. 'Is she the FBI lady who's come to see Mr Williams?' he asked.

'That would be her,' Anna said, thinking so much for Dewar's idea of a discreet approach.

'He's on his way back from the wholesalers and said you's to wait for him. His office is straight along the corridor through the doors to the dance area. Go across it to the "Staff Only" door then up the stairs, and his office is on the right.'

'Thanks,' Anna said.

'I'd take you like I did the other lady but I gotta wait for the collections. Can't leave the empties unattended out here cause the winos come and drink the dregs.'

The thought of the winos finishing the dregs made Anna's stomach turn as she headed along the corridor, which smelled strongly of beer and wine, and into the main area of the club. It was dimly lit and her eyes took a few seconds to adjust. It was a large room with a number of supporting pillars. There was gilt everywhere, fringed red drapes on the walls and a raised circular stage, with lap-dancing poles in the middle. The stage itself was surrounded by bar stools allowing the clientele to get up close to the dancers. The thought of the place filled with sweaty groping men made Anna cringe.

On the far side of the room there was a door with a VIP GUESTS ONLY sign on it. As there was no one around, Anna opened the door to have a quick look inside, to discover it was lavishly furnished and had its own bar and private dance cubicles.

Anna thought the club felt dirty and seedy and as she went through the 'Staff Only' door, she wondered what on earth would attract someone to the premises. Upstairs she found Dewar sitting on a leather-backed chair in Marcus Williams' office.

'Thanks for waiting for me, Jessie.'

'I didn't have any choice. I parked up out the back and the next thing I knew this big black guy was telling me it was private parking. I had to tell him who I was and he called Williams, who told him to show me up here.'

The office was tidy, very elegant and well lit with recessed halogen ceiling lights. On one side were floor-to-ceiling mir-rored-glass windows which gave a one-way view out onto the main floor and stage below. At the far end there were a large modern writing desk, desktop computer and leather-backed executive chair. Behind the desk was a sideboard, on top of which were crystal glasses and decanters filled with brandy and whisky. Above the sideboard, wine racks contained bottles of Dom Perignon, Krug and Cristal champagne. Beside the desk a row of two-drawer wooden filing cabinets were placed neatly along the wall; above them there were photographs of celebri-ties entering and leaving the club. Anna took a seat beside Dewar.

'Nice place, isn't it?' Dewar remarked.

'I find it seedy and hate the smell of stale alcohol,' Anna said.

'Ah, the rich and famous like to get down and dirty. They have topless waitresses, pole dancers and as we know from Taylor anything goes in the VIP rooms ... if you've got the money. Sex, drugs and rock'n'roll. Haw-haw.'

'I'm beginning to wish we'd asked Williams to come to the station,' Anna groaned.

'I got chatting with Curtis.'

'Who's Curtis?'

'The black guy who showed me up here – he's the general

handyman. Worked here since it opened and knew Josh well. Be a good man to interview with when we have time.'

Anna got up from the chair to look over the array of photographs. She was amazed by the number of celebrities, both male and female, that frequented the club. A number of film and television stars and musicians were in the photographs with a handsome mixed-race man who she assumed to be Marcus Williams. There was one picture of Josh and the same man together standing outside the club under the neon Trojan sign. They were holding a jeroboam of champagne with filled glasses and toasting each other.

Anna was still examining the pictures when the door banged open, and both she and Dewar turned as the man in the picture with Josh walked in carrying a briefcase and a box of Cristal champagne, which he put down beside the desk.

'Sorry to keep you waiting. I'm Marcus Williams, owner of the Trojan.'

He could have made a good entrance anywhere. He was at least six feet four, exceptionally handsome, with Afro hair braided and tied back with a black band. His skin was light brown, and he had very chiselled features and blue eyes. He was wearing a grey suit, white collarless shirt, and a cashmere navy coat.

Dewar smiled, stood up to shake his hand and introduced herself. He had long tapering manicured fingers, with a large gold ring on his left little finger. He turned to shake Anna's hand as she walked over and introduced herself, then tossed his coat over the back of his executive chair before he sat down to face them. Anna explained that Special Agent Dewar was on attachment to the Metropolitan Police and working with her team.

'How can I help you ladies?' Williams asked.

'We are from the murder squad and it's been alleged that Josh Reynolds may not have committed suicide,' Anna said, getting straight to the point and before Dewar could say anything. Williams looked shocked as Anna continued, 'There are certain issues from the information we have received that raise concern, however that does not mean he was actually murdered.'

Anna noticed that Dewar was looking around the room impatiently, chewing her bottom lip, clearly frustrated that she was not the one asking the questions. To add insult to injury Anna asked Dewar to take some notes and then wondered if Williams could go over the events of the day when he last saw Josh to when he was informed of his death.

Williams took a deep breath. 'It's hard to remember now. He came into work about twelve noon and was organizing the food-and-drink delivery for the VIP event that evening.'

'How did he seem?'

'Okay, but to be honest, he'd not been himself after his mother died. He'd also lost his father the previous year.'

'What do you mean by not been himself?'

'Looking back he must have been suffering badly from depression. I just wish he'd told me so I could have helped him through it. Who knows, maybe even have stopped him from taking his own life,' Williams said emotionally.

'So did his mood worsen that day?' Anna asked.

'I'd been out to get some lemons and limes for the bar and he was walking out the back as I returned. He looked like he was really upset about something.'

'Did he say if anything was wrong?'

'I asked but he just mumbled something about having to go out and see someone on business.'

'What time was that?' she pressed.

'Half-three, maybe four, I can't be certain now.'

'Did you see or speak to him again that day?'

'He rang me at about seven and said he was going home as he had a stomach upset and felt sick. It hurts that the last time we spoke I was annoyed with him.' Williams paused and ran his hand across his face. 'I felt he was leaving me in the lurch with the VIP do that night.'

Anna asked Williams how he had heard about Josh's death and he told her that when Josh didn't turn up for work the next day he just assumed he was still ill. It was about six in the evening when Donna's mother Gloria phoned the club and told him that Josh had been found dead in his flat by Donna. Gloria had also said that as a result of the post mortem, and a suicide note left by Josh, the police thought that his death was not suspicious.

Anna asked Williams how he and Josh had met and the partnership formed. Williams told her sadly that he and Josh had been friends since grammar school and went to the same university. On graduation, Josh went to work in the City and moved up the ladder quickly, earning good money and big annual bonuses. Williams said he himself had worked for a business risk management company and he and Josh had remained best friends and regularly went 'out on the town' together.

'Josh saved and invested his money wisely, but about two years ago he got made redundant by the bank and got a good payoff. He wanted to start up a small drinks club in central London, but I suggested a lap-dancing club.'

'Why was that?'

'Look around outside – it's all sleazy clubs and sex shops. There was nothing upmarket slap in the middle of Soho. This place was a rundown shit-hole and going cheap. Josh was worried he might go under before he even got off the ground, so I said I would like to be his partner.'

'You saw its potential to make money?' Anna asked.

'Yes.'

'Were you equal partners?' Anna continued.

'No. Josh put more money in than me so we split the profits sixty-forty. He dealt with all the club's finances and we shared the day-to-day running. We trusted each other and worked well together.'

'Did he ever say anything about wanting to pull out or sell the club?'

'Never, Josh was very keen to make the club work, we both were, and the pair of us put in hours of hard graft. Reality is, it has only just taken off, and if part of the reason Josh committed suicide was because he thought the club was going to fail then he couldn't have been more wrong.'

Having got the pleasantries out of the way Anna felt it was now time to bring up Delon Taylor. She paused briefly and Dewar took the opportunity to jump in.

'Did a Detective Simms ever take a statement off you?' she asked.

'Erm, Simms, no. We only spoke on the phone.'

'Why doesn't that surprise me,' Dewar remarked and looked at Anna.

'How did Josh get involved with Donna?' Dewar asked.

'She was one of the first dancers we hired. Josh made a bee-line for her; she didn't stay on the poles for long. They got engaged and then married and he made her the head hostess. Josh never really liked her working here, used to get very protective as she was a very sexy lady and had a lot of admirers.'

'How did that affect their relationship?'

'Josh told me it caused arguments. Mixing business with pleasure is never easy.'

'Did he force Donna out?'

'No. Josh adored Donna and they wanted to start a family. Donna didn't like the long days, finishing work in the early hours. She left here of her own accord and went to work for her mother.'

'Were you one of Donna's admirers?' Dewar demanded.

'She's a special lady, everyone here liked her.'

'How much did you like her?'

He stared at Dewar and shook his head.

'Listen. Josh and me were like brothers and I'd never shit on my own doorstep.'

'Delon Taylor said you did,' Dewar remarked, hoping the mention of the man's name would be like a red rag to a bull.

Anna knew what Dewar was trying to do and was surprised when Willams leaned back in his chair and laughed.

'Oh, I see. Taylor's your red-hot informant, is he?'

'You framed Taylor because he found out what you were up to—' Dewar accused but Williams interrupted.

'You've got it all wrong, lady, Josh caught Taylor stealing money from the tills and I sacked him. And hypothetically speaking, if I murdered Josh, why didn't I kill Taylor as well?'

'Suicide or murder, you still benefited from his death,' Dewar insisted.

'No, I didn't. I had to pay for the final refurbishment. I thought Josh had arranged the finances before he died but he hadn't.'

'How much did you pay Donna for Josh's share of the club?'

'I never approached Donna about selling Josh's share. She shut herself off after his death. I saw her at the funeral but we haven't spoken since then.'

'So how did you come to buy the Trojan outright?' Dewar wasn't prepared to let go of this line of questioning.

'Donna's mother called and told me that her solicitors were handling Donna's affairs and they wanted a quick sale so Donna could move on with her life.'

'How much did you pay?'

'I don't see that's any of your business,' Williams observed.

'I can always ask Gloria.'

'That's up to you but the sale was all above board. I don't deny I got a good deal, but I still had to pay fifty K out of my own pocket after the final refurbishment.'

'Did you use money from a prostitution racket to pay for the club?' Dewar said, leaning forwards.

'No, I did not. I can't believe you've been taken in by a scumbag like Delon Taylor.'

'How did you know it was Taylor who said that?' Dewar asked, obviously thinking Williams had slipped up.

'Because it's the same lie he told Josh. Do you think he would have kept me on as a partner if it was true that I was risking the business to line my own pockets?'

Dewar glanced at Anna as if looking for support, but Anna said nothing, feeling that the agent should have been more thoughtful and cautious in her line of questioning.

*

Stepping out to the rear mews of the Trojan club, Dewar said nothing as she got straight into her unmarked car and started the engine. Anna shouted that she would meet her in the road outside Gloria Lynne's house, and watched as Dewar drove out, skirting around crates of empty wine bottles and refuse bins. A sweating Curtis appeared from the exit carrying a four-foot bronze statue of a Trojan soldier holding a sword and shield. He placed it down and removed a tin of metal polish from his pocket.

'Curtis, isn't it?'

'Yep. Curtis Bowman. Bloody statue – unlike me, you have to polish and buff it up once a week so it keeps its colour,' he said, guffawing at his own joke while pulling a duster from his back pocket.

'Have you worked here for a long time?'

'Yes, I was the handyman when it was called Doobies. Mr Reynolds kept me on when he and Mr Williams bought the place. They did it all up and renamed it – Mr Reynolds said they named it after me because I work like one,' Curtis said with a proud smile as he started to rub the polish into the statue.

'You must miss Mr Reynolds being around?'

'Couldn't believe it when I was told. He was the quiet type, you know, but always friendly and got things done. Mr Williams is a good boss as well but different from Mr Reynolds.'

'How do you mean?'

'Well, firing and looking out for fingers in the tills was always down to Mr Williams, he'd not take any thieving and in a place like this you got to watch out. He was the tough one of the two. Not afraid to go head-to-head with punters that got out of order with the girls. Strict look-but-don't-touch policy.'

'Funnily enough he mentioned that Delon Taylor was sacked for stealing.'

'Bad 'un he was, with a short temper. Best rid, I say.'

'Did you see Mr Reynolds the day he died?' Anna asked.

'A few times, but only when he asked me to do something round the place.'

'How did he seem to you that day?'

'Fine. That's why I can't believe he shot himself like that.' He shook his head.

'Neither could his wife. She used to work here, I believe?'

He pursed his lips and nodded.

'Was she friendly like Josh?'

'I don't want to speak bad about her, but she started work here as a pole dancer, then she hooked Mr Reynolds and married him. She was always a bit hoity-toity. When she became head hostess she started throwing her weight around a bit, said she was taking over running the club. To be honest she couldn't run for a bus, and she put a lot of people's noses out of joint, mine included. The girls didn't like her.'

'Maybe they were a bit jealous she'd been promoted?'

'I heard Mr Reynolds and Donna having a real row about her working here. I don't think he liked the way she dressed and flirted with the VIPs.'

'Was it just flirting?'

He hesitated before answering. 'I really don't know. I try to mind my own business, but I didn't like her for personal reasons. She'd park her car here in the yard and tell me to give it a wash, and to keep an eye out for the traffic wardens. She must have had Christ knows how many tickets and would blame me. I only got one pair of eyes and can't stand out here until six p.m. every day.'

A large rubbish truck began to back into the small yard, Curtis jumped into action, gesturing for it to move slowly towards him. Realizing she needed to get a move on, Anna left him to get on with his work.

Chapter Nine

Anna drove down a narrow lane flanked on either side by hedgerows and fields of rapeseed with blazing-yellow flowers that brightened up the countryside. It was such a contrast to central London, with its exhaust fumes and stop–start traffic, and she could feel herself beginning to relax. At first, she thought the satnav had directed her to the wrong location until she saw Dewar's car parked up on the nearside of the road. Anna pulled up behind her and looking out of the window saw a set of large decorative wrought-iron gates tipped with spikes. A plaque on one of the gate pillars read LYNNE HOUSE and below it was a CCTV intercom system and lockable mailbox built into the stonework. On the other side of the gates there was a long tree-lined gravel driveway that rose gradually upwards to an imposing Georgian manor house. Anna got out of her car and approached Dewar, who was still in her car.

'Some place, isn't it. I may as well leave my car out here and go in with you.'

'We're a bit early. It's only five-thirty.'

'I'm sure they won't mind,' Anna said, going over to the intercom as Dewar pulled up in front of the gates. Anna held her warrant card up to the camera, the gates slowly cranked open and they drove up the long gravel drive to the house. Once out of the car, they stopped to take in the breathtaking view across the front of the house down to a large lake and surrounding woodland.

'It's not just a house, it's a country estate!' Anna breathed.

'Wonder how much it's worth,' Dewar remarked.

'In this area, with all the land ... millions!'

'Those cars are worth a few bucks as well,' Dewar said, drawing Anna's attention to a four-bay detached garage. There were three cars parked in front and a man in his mid-fifties was washing one of them.

'That's the new Bentley Mulsanne he's cleaning. Costs over a quarter of a million. The others are a Maybach 62 and a Mercedes McLaren 722. They're not far off a million put together.'

'Didn't have you down as a petrolhead, Jessie.'

'It's not just boys with toys. My dad was a head mechanic on the Indy-car-race circuit and then he opened his own repair shop. Used to help out whenever I could.'

Anna nodded in approval at Dewar's skills.

The front door was opened by a stocky middle-aged grey-haired woman. In broken English with an eastern European accent, she said that she was Katrina the housekeeper and Mrs Lynne had asked that they make themselves comfortable in the library. Katrina escorted them through the vast entrance to the library, giving them little time to take in the large marble-floored hall with its T-shaped stairwell, emerald green carpet and oak banisters. Katrina asked if they would like a drink and they both said water would be fine.

In contrast to the hall, the library was much brighter as natural light streamed through the multi-paned sash windows. Oriental rugs covered parts of the polished wooden floor and there were two red leather armchairs, a matching sofa and small coffee table in the middle of the room. The two end walls were covered by elegantly ornamented bookshelves that had been positioned to avoid the direct sunlight. The shelves nearly touched the high ceiling and contained hundreds of old and new books.

'The rooms like something out of Sherlock Holmes,' Anna remarked, taking a couple of steps up the library ladder to view the books.

'Olde-worlde isn't my kind of thing. Don't mind a bit of art but those two paintings either side of the fireplace don't go with the room,' Dewar said.

Anna turned to where the agent was pointing. One picture with a black background was of three sepia-coloured, very old and haggard-looking women. Two were in the foreground of the picture standing side by side, one leaning from behind on the shoulder of the other, their heads turned towards each other as if engaged in whispered conversation. Dressed in head-scarves and shawls they looked similar, as if sisters. The third woman was in the background with only her face showing, floating like an eerie shadow while watching the two women in front.

The other painting was different: light, colourful and vibrant, it depicted a dreamlike scene with blue skies and wispy clouds. There were also three women in it but they were young, cur-vaceous and sensual. Two floated like angels above the third, who was lying on her side upon a stone table.

'I think they are meant to contrast each other. You think they might be originals?' Anna wondered.

'Original crap more like,' Dewar said.

'Do you think the old women in that picture on the left are beggar women or witches?' Anna asked.

'I think one's a psychopath and the other's Spider-Woman. The one at the back with the duster is obviously the cleaner,' Dewar said.

'What on earth are you talking about?' Anna asked, looking closer at the picture. 'Oh, I see what you mean.' She laughed as she noticed that the woman in the background was holding a bundle of sheep's wool on what appeared to be a cone-shaped spindle. One of the women in the foreground of the painting had in her hands a pair of shears while the other woman held two strands of fine thread. The strands did indeed look like silk from a spider's web.

Anna was about to examine the picture more closely when Katrina came into the room carrying a silver tray with litre plastic bottles of both still and sparkling mineral water, crystal glasses, a bucket of ice and lemon slices in a bowl.

'Have you worked here long, Katrina?' Dewar asked.

'My husband Dawid and I been here a few months now.'

'What's he do?'

'He Mrs Lynne's driver and look after nice cars.'

'Was that him outside washing the "nice cars"?' Dewar asked.

'Yes. He always wash them at end of day. Clean and ready for tomorrow.'

'Will Mrs Lynne be with us shortly?' Anna asked.

'I no know, she busy in greenhouse.'

'I noticed there are a lot of books on horticulture and botany,' Anna said. 'Plants,' she added, noticing Katrina's confused expression.

'She love her plants and no like to be disturb when working in greenhouse.'

Dewar suddenly stood up.

'Well, we are here on official police business and have had a long day. If you'd show us to the greenhouse we'll disturb her for you.'

'I'm not sure if good thing . . .'

'Well I am,' Dewar said bluntly, and raised her hand in an ushering motion for Katrina to show them the way.

The woman led them from the library, through a pantry-style kitchen and out to the rear of the house. The view was even more spectacular than from the front, overlooking further woodland and fields. The vast lawn was the size of a football pitch and had diagonal lines of freshly cut grass, the scent of which filled the air like a perfume. At the far end, on the left of the garden, there was an enormous Victorian-style greenhouse with a domed roof.

Approaching the greenhouse, they could see someone with their back to them, dressed in hooded green overalls, moving in and about the array of plants and flowers. A Doberman bitch suddenly sprang to her feet and stood her ground. At first, she snarled, revealing her sharp teeth, then began barking and growling ferociously as they approached. Anna, Dewar and Katrina stopped in their tracks. Dewar took a step backwards behind Anna.

'I forget say, dog no like be disturb also.'

'Great, now you tell us,' Anna replied, trying to make light of the situation.

'Don't give it direct eye contact. That makes it worse,' Dewar said nervously.

The door of the greenhouse opened abruptly, revealing the person in the green hooded overalls wearing a respirator mask that covered their nose and mouth.

'Somebody get this dog under control!' Dewar exclaimed.

The figure swiftly pulled the mask away and a female voice commanded, 'Atropa, heel,' and the Doberman instantly sat down and gave an obedient whimper.

'I've told you, Katrina, not to disturb me when I'm in the greenhouse!'

'It wasn't her fault. We asked her to bring us out here,' Anna said, and then introduced herself and Dewar.

'As you can see, the sign I have on the door clearly says in large letters, "Beware Poisons". When I'm spraying pesticides it's highly dangerous to enter. That's why I wear protective clothing.'

'We'll go back and wait in the house,' Dewar said, not wanting to be near the dog.

'I've finished spraying now. I just need to change and then I'll join you,' the person said. So this was Gloria Lynne – but it was hard to make out her looks as she still had the overall hood up.

Anna and Dewar returned to the library and sat waiting for the woman to reappear.

'She was very rude to her Australian maid Katrina,' Dewar remarked.

'She's Polish, from Poland, and it was you who insisted she take us out to the greenhouse. I think she was mad because of the safety implications.'

'It's only a bit of insect spray – no big deal if it gets on you, just wash it off,' Dewar said dismissively.

'How do you clean your lungs if you breathe it in then?' Anna asked sarcastically.

Dewar just raised her eyebrows and sighed. Unscrewing the top of the still water, she poured herself and Anna a glass and added some ice and lemon.

The door to the library burst open and Gloria Lynne entered. It was an astonishing transformation from the woman they had met in the garden. She looked to be in her mid-forties and very elegant in a tight-fitting black sleeveless dress and patent black high-heeled shoes. Her ash-blonde hair had a centre parting and was swept into a stylish French pleat, revealing mother-of-pearl earrings. Her light blue eyes with large pupils were piercing yet sensuous thanks to very thick mascara, deep eye shadow, and kohl around their inside rim. She had a matt foundation, with blusher and rouge, and her lip gloss was lined in dark crimson. Anna noticed she was wearing a large diamond ring and gold band on her wedding finger.

'We'll start again, shall we?' Gloria said, beaming, her teeth flashing like white light bulbs. She looked towards Anna and held out her hand, palm slightly curved to the ground as if she were royalty. A heavy gold chain bracelet with dangling charms swayed at her wrist and jingled as Anna did the polite thing, shaking the tips of Gloria's fingers. She felt as if Gloria expected her to curtsey.

'I'm Gloria Lynne.'

Anna introduced herself and then Special Agent Dewar, explaining that she was on attachment to the Met. Gloria proffered her hand to Dewar while Anna, unnoticed, switched on the Dictaphone that was in her jacket pocket. Although she felt it was a little underhand as she sensed the woman wouldn't approve of the interview being recorded, she didn't want to annoy Mrs Lynne by writing notes as they spoke.

'I do apologize for keeping you waiting. I'm an avid horti-culturalist and quite religious about keeping to a schedule. I have to feed, water and spray my plants at the same time daily and we agreed to meet at six o'clock, as I recall.'

'We were a bit early and your housekeeper kindly let us in,' Anna remarked.

'I see she brought you some water. Would you like coffee as well? Goodness me. Why can't she put the water into a cut-glass jug – we have enough of them!'

She frowned with distaste at the plastic bottles, and sighing, crossed to a tall antique corner cabinet. She moved like a dancer, her slim legs and delicate ankles enhanced by the sheer black stockings and high-heeled shoes. She took a crystal glass and poured a gin and tonic for herself, returning to the coffee table for ice and lemon.

'It's a lovely room, beautifully decorated. I was just remarking to Detective Travis on the wonderful oil paintings,' Dewar said, much to Anna's surprise.

'You like art?' Gloria asked Dewar as she turned towards the paintings.

'Yes. But I have to confess I don't know much about it.'

'They're both original oil paintings of the three Moirai. Greek mythologists say they were the daughters of Zeus and often described them as ugly, lame old women who were severe, inflexible and stern. The picture on the left depicts them in this manner. It's by Francesco Salviati, a sixteenth-century Italian painter. The picture on the right is seventeenth century, by Sebastiano Mazzoni, also an Italian.'

'They're very contrasting,' Dewar said.

'Yes. That's what attracted me to them. However, I prefer Mazzoni's Baroque style, much more appealing to the eye,' Gloria said, settling herself in the centre of the leather sofa. Anna had the opportunity to really take in the very glamorous woman in front of her. She exuded confidence and sophistication, and was very charming as she carefully placed her drink down on the small side table. Her speech and manner were both elegant and refined.

'Anyway, I am sure you didn't come here for an art lesson.

Donna should be home soon but before she is, I would like to know why detectives from a murder squad need to speak to her?'

Anna was taken aback that Gloria knew they were not from the vice squad and had to think quickly for an appropriate answer.

'I'm sorry, I didn't tell you before, Mrs Lynne. We were worried that revealing who we were in a phone call to your daughter could cause her undue distress over information that may turn out to be totally malicious.'

'As much as I'd like to say I appreciate your concern, you have been very underhand. However, I am willing to listen to what you have to say, but please don't feed me a load of flannel again, DCI Travis.'

Anna apologized again and said that they were reinvestigating her son-in-law's death due to an allegation made by an ex-employee of the Trojan. She took care to explain that he was not a reliable informant and was currently awaiting trial for armed robbery.

'I think it's best to wait for Donna,' Dewar said.

'You sound like my husband. He always thought he knew what was best for me!' Gloria said sharply, giving Dewar a stern look before continuing: 'What's the name of this ex-employee?'

'Delon Taylor,' Anna said.

'Never heard of him, and I doubt there is anything Donna can add to what she told the officers at the time.'

'We have read over her statement. However, the original inquiry covered very little about Josh's role at the Trojan club or his partner Marcus Williams,' Anna replied.

'Donna hadn't worked in that disgusting place for some time before Josh committed suicide,' Gloria said, tight-lipped.

'I appreciate that, but Delon Taylor has said that Mr Williams was running a prostitution racket in the club. It's possible Josh may have found out.'

'Good God, how despicable. I told her that working there would end in tears,' Gloria exclaimed.

'You didn't approve?'

The red lips tightened further, and she reached for her gin and tonic. She sipped her drink, not answering until she had replaced the glass back onto the table.

'Of course I didn't approve. Young girls will always be difficult, especially Donna, she's always been very strong-minded and, dare I say it, enjoyed the fact that it was shocking for me to find out.'

'How do you mean, strong-minded?' Dewar asked.

'I've always been quite strict with both my daughters and kept them out of the tabloid limelight, for their own safety of course. Donna became the rebellious one, whereas Aisa, her sister, has always enjoyed being spoilt.'

Gloria went on to explain that before Donna met Josh they had had a furious row about Donna's attitude. During the argument, Gloria had blurted out that Donna was incapable of looking after herself and behaving like an adult. As a result Donna packed her bags and stormed out of the house, saying she would prove her mother wrong and didn't need her or her money. Gloria said she was not at first aware Donna had taken up exotic dancing for a living but had found out through Aisa. Gloria suspected that Donna had deliberately told Aisa, knowing it would get back to her.

'I said nothing at first as I felt Donna was purposely trying to upset me. But when I discovered that Donna had married Josh Reynolds in Las Vegas after a whirlwind romance, well I couldn't believe it. You know a mother always dreams of wedding plans for her daughters and making it the most special day of their lives, what with arranging the celebrations and bridesmaids and choosing the wedding gown together, but sadly that was not to be.'

'Did you like your son-in-law?' Dewar asked.

'I only ever met him once and that was when I went round to their flat in Bayswater just after I heard about their marriage. As you can imagine, it wasn't a social visit. He tried to keep the peace between myself and Donna, but it was quite horrible and she demanded I leave.'

'So you and Donna patched things up after his death?'

'No, shortly before – Donna said Josh told her life's too short and persuaded her to see me and sort out our differences. I don't wish to speak ill of the dead but I have to admit that I had hoped Donna could have perhaps made a better choice. I was not that impressed with Josh being a strip club owner; but it would seem that he was surprisingly very pleasant and well educated. I only wish I'd had the opportunity to get to know him better.'

'How is Donna now?' Anna asked.

'She's getting there, but still takes things day by day. Donna works for me, so that helps to occupy a lot of her time, looking after various charities and organizing fundraising events with Aisa.'

'That's very commendable,' Dewar said dryly.

Gloria frowned. 'I can empathize with my daughter, as I know what it's like to lose someone you love dearly. My husband Xavier died when I was very young and both my girls were still babies really.'

'I'm sorry for your loss. It can't have been easy raising two young girls on your own,' Anna said quietly, keen for Gloria to continue, even though she seemed to love the sound of her own voice and didn't need much encouragement.

'It wasn't easy at first, but seven years later I fell in love with my beloved Henry and we married. He treated the girls as if they were his own – truth be known he spoilt them terribly.'

'How did he feel about Donna's behaviour?' Anna asked.

Gloria grimaced. 'Had he been alive I've no doubt he would have been as upset as I was. He passed away some years ago now. Blessing in disguise really, he'd been seriously ill for a long time.'

'I'm sorry, I noticed you were wearing . . .'

'My engagement and wedding ring – I've stopped grieving but I've no intention of remarrying and they remind me of everything Henry meant to me.' Gloria held up her left hand and gently placed a kiss on the rings before taking another sip from her gin and tonic.

'You arranged for Marcus Williams to purchase Josh's share of the club, at a very reasonable price—' Anna began.

Gloria looked annoyed and cut in: 'In my daughter's best interests – the share in the club became Donna's after Josh died, as did the flat they lived in. I felt Donna needed to move on so I had my solicitors deal with Josh's will and the sale of his assets. It's not as if Donna needed the money. Both my daughters have been well provided for and have substantial trust funds for when they reach thirty.'

'Hello, Mummy, it's me, where are you?' a voice called from the hallway.

'In the library, darling,' Gloria replied.

'Wait till you see my hair. Pierre's done a fantastic job with new extensions and highlights, you'll love it,' Donna said as she entered the library with a flourish. 'Ta-dah!' she said, striking a pose and shaking her head in a circular motion so her long blonde hair tumbled around her shoulders.

'Absolutely gorgeous, my darling, don't you agree, ladies?'

'Oh, I'm sorry, how embarrassing, I totally forgot you were having guests over, Mummy,' Donna said, red-faced.

The young woman looked very much like her mother. She was perfectly made-up, her large blue eyes enhanced with deep brown eye shadow and false eyelashes, but not in any way over-done. She had glossy lipstick, was very tanned and at about five foot ten was much taller than Gloria, with long legs, a small waist and large breasts. She was wearing Armani jeans, a white T-shirt and a purple blazer with rolled-up sleeves. She walked very upright in her high wedge shoes and her hips swayed like a model's.

'Don't go, darling, these ladies are here to see you,' Gloria said as she patted the space on the sofa next to her.

'See me? Why?' Donna asked as she sat down next to her mother.

'About Josh's death, they're detectives. It appears someone has been saying he was murdered.'

'What? I don't understand,' Donna gasped, shocked.

'It's Delon Taylor, Donna. At the moment there is no evidence to support what he says but we just need to ask you some questions,' Anna quickly explained.

'He worked at the Trojan. Josh sacked him for stealing money.' Donna had fake nails with white square tips and now waved her hands in a flurry of gestures.

'Did Josh say anything about Delon Taylor telling him that Marcus Williams was using the club as a front for prostitution?' Anna asked.

'No. Delon's lying, he's a hideous man, and Marcus wouldn't do something like that to Josh and risk the club being closed down. They were friends, they respected each other.'

'I didn't get the impression Taylor was lying,' Dewar interrupted.

'You're American. Why are you here?' Donna wafted her hands towards Dewar.

'I'm with the FBI and—'

'FBI? Josh murdered? This is really crazy. Detective Simms and the Coroner said it was a suicide. Mummy, what's happening? I don't understand why they're here.' Donna was growing visibly distressed.

Gloria edged closer to her daughter and put her arm round her. 'Don't worry yourself, my darling. The officers have a job to do and with your help they can show that this horrible little man Taylor is an inveterate liar.'

'I made a statement to Detective Simms. I told him everything.' Donna's voice was becoming very high-pitched.

'Did you tell him anything about Delon Taylor?' Dewar asked.

'No. He never asked me anything about him.'

'He never asked you if Josh had any problems at work? Anyone he didn't get on with? Stuff like that?'

'I can't remember now. Should he have done?'

'If he'd treated the death as suspicious at the outset, we wouldn't be sitting here now,' Dewar said frankly as she leaned slightly forward and looked directly at Donna.

Gloria wagged her finger at the agent. 'My daughter is hardly responsible for how Detective Simms should have conducted his investigations. She spent a considerable amount of time making her statement under a great deal of stress. You seem to forget that she had just found her husband dead with a gun in his hand.'

Anna could see that Gloria was becoming annoyed and wondered if she should interject, but Dewar continued.

'Yes, I read your statement, Mrs Reynolds, and it must have been awful for you. You'd just returned from a charity ball in the Savoy Hotel where you'd also stayed the night.'

'Yes, I'd been with my mother and Aisa. We organized it.'

'So you were in each other's company all night?'

'Yes, I shared a room with my sister Aisa. I told Detective Simms all this at the time,' Donna replied and looked at her mother.

Gloria patted her daughter's hand and her bracelets jangled. 'I also told Detective Simms my daughters shared a room and Aisa was unwell during the evening. Poor thing looked terrible when I went to check on her, she'd been sick a number of times,' Gloria added.

'Can you remember when you got home if the Chubb lock on the door to your flat was open or locked?' Dewar asked.

'Oh, for heaven's sake!' Gloria exclaimed.

Donna paused and closed her eyes, trying to recall her exact movements when she opened the door that morning. 'I don't know.'

'If Josh was in would it have been open and just the Yale lock on?' Dewar persisted.

'Yes . . . Probably, I think.'

'Were there any spare sets of keys that you gave out?'

'No.'

'Did you ever lend your keys to anyone?'

'No.'

'You said in your statement that you then went to the bedroom. Sorted out the washing and took it through to the kitchen.'

'Yes.'

'Are you a neat and tidy person?'

'What do you mean?'

Dewar kept on firing her questions at Donna, trying to unsettle her. 'House-proud, neat and tidy.'

'Yes.'

'But you didn't notice the wardrobe door and safe were open?'

Donna paused again to think.

'Why on earth are you asking my daughter these questions?' Gloria interjected.

'I'm considering the possibility that Josh may have let in someone he knew and that that person then shot him and set it up to look like he had committed suicide,' Dewar said.

Gloria jumped to her feet. 'Are you insinuating that that someone was my daughter?'

'Not at all, you already confirmed that your daughter was with you at the Savoy all night.'

A flustered Gloria pursed her lips and smoothed her tight pencil skirt. Anna thought Dewar was treading a fine line but was impressed with both her tact and direction.

'Try and think, darling, answer the question,' Gloria said. 'The sooner this is all over with the better.'

Donna nodded and then hesitantly answered. 'If the wardrobe was open I never noticed. I did have a bad hangover that morning.'

'Did you know what Josh kept in the safe?'

'No. He never told me so I assumed it was personal stuff. Obviously, I now know it was the gun.'

'So we don't know if anything else was missing from it or if the gun was actually his for that matter,' Dewar said quickly.

'I never used the safe. I didn't even know the code.' Donna looked pleadingly towards Gloria.

Dewar changed her tack to one of concern, 'Was your husband upset at the recent loss of his mother?'

'Yes. Yes, he was.'

'Anything else that troubled him?'

Donna hesitated. 'He always worried about the club being a success and repaying the cost of doing it up.'

'Clearly though, he must have been severely depressed if we are to believe he took his own life.'

'Yes, I think so, yes.'

'But he never discussed his depression with you? There were no signs, nothing untoward?'

'Well, he'd been quieter than usual.'

'What is your point, Officer Dewar?' Gloria barked as she opened a cigarette box and lit one.

'Please, Mummy, don't smoke,' Donna said.

'You know it relaxes me, darling,' Gloria said as she sucked in a lungful of smoke and then exhaled, shaking her head.

'It's Special Agent Dewar and I was just wondering if there were any problems between Donna and her husband. Any reason he shouldn't confide in her if he was feeling depressed.'

Again Donna looked to her mother. 'We had been going through a bit of rough patch and—'

Gloria stamped her foot. 'I've had enough of this. I find your questioning and treatment of my daughter intolerable. How dare you lie your way into my house and make such outlandish accusations? So they were a young couple and things weren't always perfect, but they could not be described as having problems.'

Anna decided to try to calm the situation.

'We are not accusing your daughter of anything. Agent Dewar is merely trying to ascertain Josh's state of mind at the time.'

'What do you mean by a rough patch, Donna?' Dewar asked, determined to put pressure on the young woman.

'It was due to work and—'

'Enough, Donna! She thinks Josh was murdered and is trying to make you look complicit in his death. I want you both out of my house now. I have never witnessed such underhand behaviour by a police officer.' Gloria aggressively stubbed the cigarette out in the ashtray.

Dewar would not let go. 'Did you return home already knowing your husband was dead?'

'Why are you saying these horrible things?' Donna burst into tears and reached out to her mother for comfort.

'GET OUT! Get out of my house now before I call the Chief Constable!'

Dewar was about to ask another question but Anna grabbed her arm and whispered to her to shut up and that it was time for them to leave.

'We'll need to speak to you again, Donna, but it may be at the police station next time!' Dewar snapped.

'You will be hearing from my solicitor!' Gloria shouted as she ushered them to the door and slammed it shut behind them.

As Anna removed her Dictaphone from her jacket pocket and switched it off, she caught sight of Katrina talking to her husband, who was washing a Mini Cooper Convertible with the registration DON4L. Anna assumed it was Donna's car, but could barely think straight as she was absolutely livid with Dewar. The interview had been going well until the agent had attacked Donna so unnecessarily.

They drove out of Lynne House and Dewar pulled up by Anna's car. Anna got out and leaned in the passenger window to let Dewar know she had an appointment in the morning and would be in the office a little later than usual.

'Mother's a bit up her own backside, isn't she? I know she's only trying to protect her daughter but it's unbelievable she can't see the spoilt little brat is lying. Hate those fake square-cut nails, wafting them around as she told lie after lie.'

'How do you know she's lying? Micro-expressions all over the place, were they?'

'You noticed them as well then?'

Anna shook her head. She couldn't believe how thick-skinned the woman was.

'LOOK OUT!' Dewar suddenly screamed. Anna stood bolt

upright as Dewar reached across and grabbed the waistband of Anna's skirt, pulling her tight up against the car.

Anna looked over her shoulder to see a bright yellow Lotus sports car hurtle past, the wing mirror narrowly missing her. She focused on the number plate and started to repeat it over in her mind as the car's back wheels screeched and skidded through the gates to Lynne House and up the driveway at speed. Anna grabbed her pen from her jacket pocket and wrote the number on the back of her hand: A1SAL.

'Could you see who was driving?' Anna asked.

'No, you were in the way,' Dewar said, making light of the near-serious incident.

Anna thought about the number plate for a second and then the penny dropped. Almost in unison she and Dewar said, 'Aisa Lynne!'

'Should we go in and have a word with her?' Dewar asked.

'No. We can find out where she works.'

'Why not pursue it now?'

'Because——' Anna began, clearly exasperated.

'I'm just kidding. I'm not that tactless,' Dewar said with a laugh and drove off, leaving Anna to get into her car, thinking that tactless just about said it all.

Chapter Ten

Anna got home just after eight-thirty, feeling physically and mentally exhausted after such a long working day. Too tired to even cook herself something to eat she ordered a Chinese home-delivery of Peking duck, Kung Pao beef and special fried rice. She had just stretched out on the sofa in front of the television when the doorbell rang. Anna went to her handbag and got some cash then opened the door, only to find Langton standing there with her Chinese takeaway in his hand, paying the delivery man.

'You owe me fifteen quid,' he said, handing her the food, and stomped past her into the living room. She had a feeling that his unannounced visit was to do with the fractious events at Gloria Lynne's house.

'It didn't take you long to start pissing the public off, did it?' he said, removing his jacket and throwing it down on the sofa.

'Sorry. I don't know what you're talking about.'

'Don't bullshit me! You know it's Gloria fucking Lynne I'm talking about.'

Anna was far too tired for a stand-up argument.

'What about her?' she asked as she took the bag of food into the kitchen and Langton followed her.

'She's got friends in high places. No sooner had you left her place than she was on the phone to the local Chief Constable. And, guess what? He's ex-Met and the Commissioner's bloody golf partner.'

'What's his handicap?'

'Don't take the piss, Travis!'

'Actually, I was about to take some red wine. Would you like a glass, or the Scotch is in the cupboard on the left.'

'I give you a simple suicide case that needs a few casual enquiries and you turn it into a witch hunt against Donna Reynolds,' Langton said as he removed the whisky bottle from the cupboard and poured himself a large glass, which he promptly downed in one before pouring another.

'What did the Commissioner say?'

'He called Walters, who took great delight in biting my head off because of your behaviour.'

For Anna, the mention of Walters' name put a whole different perspective on Langton's visit.

'What did he say?' she asked as she removed two clean plates from the dishwasher to avoid eye contact with him.

'He wasn't happy. He was tempted to scupper your trip to the FBI Academy until I persuaded him otherwise. What on earth made you accuse Donna Reynolds of murder?'

'I didn't.'

'Well that's not what Gloria Lynne said.'

'I mean, I didn't personally.'

'Come on, Anna. I thought you were better than that. Don't put the blame on Jessie. She's only shadowing you.'

'I'm not blaming her but she's fixated on the idea that Donna Reynolds had Josh murdered. She makes everything fit her theory and has an extremely aggressive manner.'

'I think she's a bit more experienced than that.'

'You've never worked with her. She's more interested in her own opinion and proving herself right.'

'Sounds like someone I know.'

'You know full well I consider all aspects of the evidence before I voice my opinion. As you said to her, you need the team on your side, not against you.'

'She told you I said that?'

Anna realized she had inadvertently revealed that she had eavesdropped on Langton's conversation with Dewar.

'Do you want some of this Chinese?' she asked, trying to change the subject.

'You listened in on our conversation, didn't—'

'Okay. Yes, I did, but it wasn't deliberate.'

'Just as well I was singing your praises then.'

'Thanks for putting her straight about Ken.'

'Why didn't you tell her?' Langton asked.

'I don't really know her, let alone like her, and my personal life is none of her business.'

'Understandable, but I've always found her very pleasant.'

'When she wants something to be to her advantage, she is. Look at all you've done for her,' Anna hit back.

'Do I detect a hint of jealousy?'

'No. You detect someone who's not prepared to be blamed for Dewar's mess.'

'She's got a good track record,' Langton pointed out.

'In a classroom maybe, but I don't think she's very experienced at investigative street work. Not a clue about how to talk to people.'

'She could just be nervous working in a strange environment.'

'You need to sit down and listen to the interviews I taped with Delon Taylor and at Gloria Lynne's house and rethink your opinion of her.'

'You only have to put up with her for a few more days before we leave for Quantico. So do me a favour and give her a break.'

'Patience as you know is one of my virtues,' Anna said with a wry smile.

'Good. While we eat this, you can tell me about the investigation so far. Warts and all.'

'I thought we'd just covered Dewar,' Anna said as she put the plates of food and a bottle of soy sauce down on the kitchen table.

'Don't push it,' Langton said, and smiled.

Anna gave Langton a run-down on the investigation so far, going over the interviews with Delon Taylor, Marcus Williams,

Donna and Gloria Lynne. Anna told him that although Gloria
struck her as someone who was full of her own importance she
was a very protective mother when it came to her daughters and
Dewar's line of questioning didn't help.

'Everything seems quite straightforward to me. If you've
shown Taylor to be a liar then it should be case closed,' Langton
remarked, having listened to everything Anna had told him.

'I'd like nothing more than to agree with you but Dewar has
raised some valid questions that are as yet unanswered.'

'Hang on a minute, you said earlier that she was coming up
with wild theories.'

'I said, I think she makes things fit the way she perceives them
to be. You've always said to expect the unexpected, but never
try and explain it until you find the evidence that proves or
disproves a theory.'

'So what's the problem?'

'I know Dewar's interpersonal skills leave a lot to be desired.
She likes to be confrontational, but I have to say she was very
impressive during her crime scene re-enactment at the
Reynolds flat.'

'She should be. As a Behavioural Adviser crime scene analysis is her bread and butter.'

'She went through the scene very methodically, even acted
out being shot three times and let herself slump to the ground
as if she was Josh Reynolds in his death throes.'

'A tad dramatic, but her conclusion was?'

'Dewar said if Reynolds shot himself there should have been
blood spatter across the back of his right hand. There wasn't any
and the position his body ended up in didn't seem natural.'

'It's not natural to shoot yourself in the head,' Langton
observed.

'If Dewar's right then the scene had to be staged to look like
a suicide. I've arranged to see Pete Jenkins at the lab tomorrow
morning to discuss her theory.'

'Didn't he attend the scene at the time of Reynolds' death?'

'It doesn't appear that Pete was ever asked to and I suspect

that once the post-mortem was over it was in effect case closed.'
Anna raised her eyebrows.

'The original file would have been checked and signed off as
suicide by one of the Homicide Directorate Superintendents,'
Langton said.

'They can only go by Paul Simms' report.'

'Have you spoken with Simms?'

'Meeting him for an early breakfast before going to the
lab.'

As Langton got up and helped himself to what was left of the
Chinese food, Anna looked at the kitchen clock. It was nearly
eleven. She was really tired and had an early start in the morning. As a hint to Langton she gave a loud yawn and stretched
her shoulders and neck.

'I'd like to listen to the Donna Reynolds interview tape. If
you're tired, get off to bed and I'll see myself out when I'm
done,' Langton said, offering her little choice in the matter.

Anna got the Dictaphone from her handbag, handed it to
him and went off to her bedroom. She set her alarm and lay in
bed mulling things over in her mind as she drifted off into a
deep sleep.

Anna was unexpectedly awoken by a hand on her shoulder. In
panic, she wondered where she was and sat bolt upright.

'Sorry, didn't mean to wake you,' Langton said.

Although annoyed that he had done so, Anna was relieved
that it was him.

'You been here all night?' she asked, thinking it was the early
hours of the morning.

'It's only midnight. Bit of a humdinger, that interview at
Gloria's house. Dewar did push it to the limit and—'

'Good night, Jimmy,' Anna said, deliberately using Dewar's
name for him.

'I hate being called that.'

'Please. I just want to go back to sleep!' Anna pleaded as she
pulled the duvet over her head.

'Well I just wanted to apologize for my earlier outburst. You were very polite with Gloria Lynne and tried to diffuse the situation. I shouldn't have doubted you.'

'Apology accepted,' she mumbled from under the duvet.

'I'll be off then.'

Hearing the bedroom door close, Anna pulled the duvet back down as her mind went back to the time when they had lived together. Even then, he had an annoying habit of waking her in the middle of the night to discuss or seek her opinion on some aspect of a case that was irritating him. She was glad that the breakup of their relationship had never marred their respect for each other.

Since it was so early in the morning, Anna easily found a parking bay near the restaurant where she'd arranged to meet Paul Simms. Although she knew of the Wolseley and its famed breakfasts, she had never been to it before. It had been built as a showroom in the 1920s by the famous Wolseley car company, subsequently became a bank, and then in 2003 was turned into a café-restaurant that retained many of its original features and its Venetian-style design.

The restaurant was already bustling with customers as Paul Simms waved to her from his table at the far side of the room. He was smartly dressed in a light grey woollen pinstripe suit, lilac shirt and matching silk tie. When the handsome maître d' bade Anna good morning, she told him that she was meeting a friend who was already seated.

Paul, as ever the gentleman, stood up to shake her hand and then gently pulled her chair back for her to sit down. The waiter flicked open Anna's napkin, handed her the menu and poured her a glass of water.

'Posh, isn't it?' Paul said.

'It's amazing.'

'Glad you like it. It's a bit expensive though.'

'My treat, so don't worry about it.'

Anna perused the menu and thought to herself that for a

central London location with such stunning decor the food prices were not that extortionate, though the caviar omelette was out of her price range.

'What do you fancy?' Anna asked.

'The maître d'. He's drop-dead gorgeous,' Paul replied with a cheeky grin as he peered over the top of his menu.

'I thought so too,' Anna said, imitating him with her menu.

'I saw him first, girlfriend.' He winked.

'It's good to see you, Paul. You always brighten up my day.'

Paul ordered the full English breakfast with poached eggs. He also asked for a pot of Earl Grey tea. Anna thought she'd be a bit more adventurous and opted for haggis with fried duck eggs and a Macchiato coffee.

'Got a bit of a hangover,' Paul confided. 'I was out with Brian last night at the G–A–Y club in Soho.'

Anna smiled. 'Celebrating the new house?'

'Well, that and our engagement.'

'Congratulations, Paul, I'm really pleased for you both.'

'We've been together a year now and I'm still crazy about him. We want the full monty – morning suits, marquee in the gardens of a stately home. Our sisters have agreed to be brides-maids. I'll send you an invitation.'

'Thank you, I look forward to it.'

'So what's the problem with Joshua Reynolds' suicide?'

'It's more a case of someone causing problems by questioning your original investigation.'

'Don't tell me, bloody DCS Langton?'

'No. An FBI agent called Jessie Dewar. She's a behavioural adviser at their Academy in Quantico.'

'What's the FBI got to do with Reynolds' death?'

'Langton arranged for Dewar to be attached to my team on work experience.' Anna paused before continuing. 'She thinks Reynolds was murdered and the scene was staged to look like a suicide.'

'That's ridiculous. The Coroner and all the experts said it

was suicide,' Paul said, clearly upset by what Anna was telling him.

Anna was about to say more when the waitress interrupted them as she served their breakfasts.

'When I spoke to you on the phone yesterday, you mentioned a prisoner making "spurious allegations",' Paul prompted her.

Anna outlined Delon Taylor's background at the Trojan, why he was awaiting trial and his allegation that Reynolds might have been murdered by his partner Marcus Williams.

'Then why didn't the file come back to me to interview Taylor? That's normal procedure, isn't it?'

'This is off the record, Paul, and just between us ... okay?'

Paul nodded as he ate a mouthful of his breakfast. Anna sipped her coffee and explained that Langton had deliberately allocated her team the reinvestigation as he wanted to secure them the new office at Belgravia.

'So why do you think Taylor is telling the truth?'

'I don't.'

'Then why are we having this conversation? Why isn't it case closed?' a worried Paul asked, pushing his food round the plate in an agitated manner.

'Dewar's made some observations about the blood distribution at the scene and the suicide note on Reynolds' laptop.'

'So she's a jack of all trades. Blood-distribution expert, a forensic linguist as well as a behavioural shrink! If she's got a problem with my investigation, why can't she speak to me face to face?'

'I'm on your side, Paul, but ...'

'Have you told Langton and Dewar that?'

'Of course. Look, both Langton and I have assured Dewar that you're a competent and respected investigator.' Wanting to be discreet in a public area, Anna showed him some small pocket-sized photographs she had in her briefcase of the Reynolds death scene. She explained Dewar's observations on the blood distribution and the interviews they had had with Marcus Williams and Donna Reynolds.

'I don't know if Dewar's right, Paul, but I need to make sure that everything is done by the book to support your original investigation. I'm seeing Pete Jenkins later this morning but I need to go over your actions concerning the scene before I do. I'm being straight with you and that's all I ask in return.'

'I'll be as straight as I can be.' He laughed nervously, giving a camp flick of his wrist.

'I'm serious, Paul. If, God forbid, Dewar's right, then it's a question of damage limitation.'

'My investigation report was signed off as suicide by Detective Superintendent Mike Lewis – you know him, don't you?'

'Yes, of course I do, but for the time being I don't want him to know we've met and discussed the case. He's got enough on his plate as his daughter was involved in an accident, so let me just try and iron all this out.'

'Anna, I'm not sure what more I could have done at the scene,' Paul protested. 'I was guided by the pathologist Dr Harrow and by John Freeman the Crime Scene Manager.'

'I noticed in Pete Jenkins' report that he never attended the scene. Why was that?' Anna asked, taking the opportunity to enjoy some more of her breakfast.

Paul explained that he had been advised by Freeman to call the pathologist and was present while the two of them discussed the position of the body, bullet injuries to the head and the blood distribution. Harrow had said that if the body was removed to the mortuary within a couple of hours, he would 'as a favour' handle it as a late-afternoon post-mortem as he was off on holiday the next day.

'So Freeman never suggested a firearms or blood-distribution expert should attend?'

'I did ask but Freeman said that the distribution all fitted with a suicide and if Harrow's examination concluded the same then there would be no need for further investigation at the scene,' Paul explained.

'I'm sorry, Paul, but you were badly advised and their opinions influenced your judgement. Pete Jenkins should have been called to the scene. Freeman has a reputation for being self-opinionated and cutting corners. I don't know Harrow but . . .'

'He said he'd been a pathologist covering the Lancashire and Yorkshire areas for over twenty-five years and had only recently come to London. He looked to be in his late fifties and seemed to know what he was talking about,' Paul said, looking tense.

His breakfast was only half-eaten as he placed his knife and fork together on the side of his plate and poured himself another cup of tea from the silver teapot. She knew that his nervousness had ruined his appetite.

'Sometimes experience can lead to overconfidence. Pathologists are there to examine bodies and give cause and manner of death. Not pass comment on blood distribution at a scene.'

'Well I didn't know that, and even if I did I'd hardly have felt in a position to argue the point.'

'The scene is ultimately your responsibility, Paul. Who do you think they are going to blame if this all goes pear-shaped?'

'Me. Will I get demoted to sergeant?' Paul was now very distraught.

'You acted in good faith, Paul, but inexperience has let you down. I suspect though you may be given some strong words of advice by Langton about your actions and report, but not demoted.'

'What's wrong with the report?'

'It's not very thorough or detailed. You need to cut your teeth on these kinds of cases. Always treat them as a possible murder, be thorough, trust your own judgement and challenge others.'

Paul was close to tears. Anna knew that he had always been a bit of a sensitive soul and felt she needed to reassure him, but was unsure what to say.

'I'm sorry I let you down, Anna.'

'You've let yourself down, not me. Whatever happens, I will support your actions in light of what Freeman and Harrow advised. Put it down to inexperience for now.'

'What about this Dewar woman?'

'Leave her to me,' Anna insisted. 'Now cheer up and finish your breakfast. I'm not paying for good food to go to waste.'

Paul seemed somewhat reassured by Anna's comforting advice and he managed to take a couple more mouthfuls of his breakfast. She decided not to tell him that Gloria Lynne had complained to the local Chief Constable. Undoubtedly, that would leave him a nervous wreck.

'I'm off to the FBI Academy in Quantico in a few days on a ten-week course,' Anna said, attempting to take Paul's mind off his predicament.

'So who's going to cover the Reynolds case while you're away?' he asked anxiously.

'Don't look so worried. I hope to have the case resolved before I go. Even if I haven't, Paul Barolli will be deputizing for me. He shares my views about Dewar and he's on your side.'

'Will you get him to keep me in the loop while you're away?'

'Of course, and if you've any problems or worries you can always ring me – just check the time difference first,' Anna said, and Paul laughed.

Anna finished her breakfast before asking Paul anything further about his investigation.

'What did you make of Donna Reynolds?'

'I interviewed her at length. Obviously, she was very distressed, but there was nothing that made me feel she was lying,' he said thoughtfully.

'Was her mother Gloria present?'

'Yes, she was a bit of a mother hen, very concerned for Donna, but understood that I had a job to do.'

'Did you meet Marcus Williams?'

'No, I spoke to him on the phone and sent a detective to the Trojan to speak to him about Josh. He thought Josh had been very down since his mother died, as did Donna.'

Anna touched on Josh's financial situation and Paul told her that he had seized and viewed his bank statements from the flat and that there was nothing untoward.

'Did you look at the Trojan accounts?'

'No, but I had an off-the-record chat with the bank manager and he said that a loan had been taken out by Josh when he first bought the place and that the monthly repayments were being made.'

'Anything about a further loan for renovation work?' Anna asked.

'No.'

'What about Josh's mobile phone for calls and texts on the day he died?'

'I had his and Donna's phones checked and again there was nothing untoward.'

Anna observed to Paul that he appeared to have made many more enquiries than he had given himself credit for in his report. Paul explained that he had wanted to keep it brief and that as none of his enquiries had brought up anything to suggest Reynolds' death was suspicious he had not included those details. He added that he had kept the notes, along with the forensic submission forms and other assorted documents and copies of the bank statements and phone records. Anna asked him to drop them off at Belgravia as soon as possible and reiterated that his report should have contained details of all the enquiries he had made.

'You always need to cover your own back, Paul,' she stressed.

'Shit. I didn't, did I?' he said with a forlorn look.

Outside the restaurant, Paul thanked her for her support and sound advice. As she put her hand out to shake goodbye, Paul came forward and took Anna by surprise, giving her a big hug.

'Would you be a bridesmaid at mine and Brian's wedding?'

'I'd look a bit like the old matriarch standing next to that age group, so an honoured guest will do fine,' she hurriedly assured him.

'Not true, you're looking good, so no more excuses, Anna, you're in as chief bridesmaid.' Paul smiled, hailing a cab.

'We'll see.' Anna laughed.

The cab pulled over and as she waved, Paul waved back and Anna could see the concern on his face. They both knew his situation could become serious – Anna just hoped she could protect him. That and avoid being a bridesmaid.

Chapter Eleven

A nna arrived at the forensic lab in Lambeth just after eight-thirty, only to find Pete Jenkins was not due in until nine, so she took the opportunity to grab a coffee in their canteen and phone Joan in the office. She knew that if she wanted to speak to Donna Reynolds again, or her sister Aisa, Gloria Lynne would most probably get on her high horse and object.

'Hi, Joan.'

'Morning, ma'am. How'd the enquiries go yesterday?'

'Nothing surprising but it's a day I'd rather forget.'

'Dewar?'

Anna avoided giving Joan a direct answer.

'I am at the lab this morning seeing Pete Jenkins and I need you to do some discreet research on Gloria Lynne and her two daughters Donna Reynolds and Aisa. I'm assuming Aisa uses the surname Lynne but that may not be the case,' Anna said. She gave Joan details of the Mini Cooper Convertible and Lotus she had seen at Lynne House and asked her to do a registered keeper's check on both cars.

'I'll do what I can and leave an intelligence file on your desk,' Joan promised.

'No, don't do that. Keep it to yourself for now and we'll speak when I get back. Tell Barolli I want him to get warrants issued and served on the banks for Reynolds' personal accounts and the Trojan's business accounts.'

'Has something interesting turned up?'

'Not as yet. Just some loose ends from the original inquiry that need tidying up.'

'Anything else?'

'Tell Barbara to get cracking on the house-to-house enquiries in Bayswater. She can go with Barolli to the court and then they can do the house-to-house together. You got all that?'

'Yes, ma'am.'

Anna found Pete Jenkins in his office. He was his usual affable self, gave her a warm hug and took out photographs of his baby daughter before he got round to asking exactly why she had come to see him. She did not mention Dewar, but said she was reinvestigating the Joshua Reynolds case, and wanted to go over the forensic examination and results with him.

'Seems strange that we both work for the Met now,' Pete said, making reference to the closure of the Forensic Science Service in March of the previous year.

'Oh, yeah, right, great shame about the FSS. How're you finding things now?'

He shrugged. 'Met took over our labs and renamed it Specialist Forensic Services, but the transition's not been an easy one.'

'Why's that?'

'Problem with police "in house" forensics is it's all too often about cost-saving and cutting corners and that means an investigation can be compromised.'

'Change is inevitable, Pete, and it takes time for things to settle. As for cost-saving and budgets, that's something we're all up against,' Anna pointed out.

'I know, but at times I feel like my skills and expertise are being ignored.'

'Well I'm interested in your opinion on the Josh Reynolds case.'

He shook his head. 'That case is a prime example of what I'm talking about.' He went over to a filing cabinet and removed the Reynolds case file.

Pete explained that on the afternoon of the day Josh

Reynolds' body was discovered he received a phone call from John Freeman, the Crime Scene Manager, saying that he was at the scene of a suspected suicide and was sending up a gun that had been found in the victim's right hand and a bullet retrieved from the sofa. Freeman wanted a fast-track comparison of the dead man's fingerprints against the gun and also for Pete to examine the recovered bullet to see if it came from the gun.

'I offered to attend but Freeman said as CSM he decides who to call to a scene and if he needed me he'd let me know.'

'What about the scene and post mortem photographs, did you get to see them?'

'No.' Pete shook his head in frustration. 'The only other exhibits I received for examination were after the post mortem. That was Reynolds' clothing, blood and urine samples for DNA and toxicology, and some bullets and firearms swabs from a safe at the scene.'

'What about the laptop with the suicide note on it? And Reynolds' mobile phone?'

'They would have gone to Technical Support at Newlands Park.'

She was stunned. 'They didn't come to you first for fingerprints or DNA work?'

'Nope, and full fingerprint treatments were never done at the Reynolds flat either.'

'I've got a copy of the scene and post mortem photographs on a memory stick,' Anna told Pete as she took it out of her handbag. 'Would you mind having a look at them for me?'

Pete loaded the scene photographs into his computer as Anna told him about her visit to Reynolds' old flat with FBI Agent Dewar and Dewar's re-enactments of how the shooting might have occurred. Anna chose to make no mention of the fact that she thought Dewar was prone to making the scene fit her theories, as she wanted an unbiased opinion from Pete.

'I'll have a look but it's never easy doing blood-pattern analysis from photographs,' Pete said, beginning to get anxious. He pulled out a picture from his case file of the gun recovered from the scene.

'It's an old Enfield number two mark one revolver developed in the late thirties for the British Tank Corps.'

Anna was taking notes of Pete's comments as he tapped the photograph.

'Firing tests proved the bullet that passed through Reynolds' head and lodged in the settee was fired from the Enfield.'

'What about the bullets in the safe?' Anna asked.

'Same, point thirty-eight with 178 grain and by the worn look probably issued with the gun. Firearms residue from the safe, gun and Reynolds' hand all matched as well.'

'You know something, we don't even know if the gun actually belonged to Josh Reynolds,' Anna sighed.

'If it's any help you don't see this type of gun being used by street gangs or professional criminals. These tend to be family heirlooms. Relative who fought in the war, kept it after demob then passed it down.'

'Do you think Reynolds shot himself?'

'From what Freeman sent me to examine all I can say is he was shot with the Enfield revolver.'

'That's not what I asked.'

'I know, but for me to offer an opinion on whether Reynolds pulled the trigger or not would have been dependent on a meticulous on-scene examination of the blood and brain tissue distribution.'

She pressed on but could feel Pete was getting uptight.

'Could you commit yourself when you've examined the scene photographs?'

'I'll need to spend time examining the entire scene and post mortem photographs in minute detail,' Pete told her. 'For now let me have a quick scan through them and see if there's anything blatantly obvious. You can put the kettle on in the meantime.'

Anna thanked Pete as she went over to the corner of the room and started making the coffees, conscious that she was beginning to get an ominous feeling about the Reynolds case. It was the first time she had sensed real doubt about his death being a suicide. If all the initial lines of enquiry and loose ends had been thoroughly investigated at the time then she wouldn't be in the position she was now. Delon Taylor's allegation had opened up a can of worms and the chances of resolving the inquiry before she went to the FBI Academy were rapidly fading.

Anna took the coffees over to Pete's desk.

'Agent Dewar has made some well-founded observations,' Pete said.

'I was hoping you wouldn't say that.'

'Although there's no blood on the back of Reynolds' right hand and the body position is . . . let's say awkward as opposed to unusual, there are many variables that come into play.'

'Such as?'

'The exact position of the hand, distance between the gun and the victim's head, and of course the recoil when it's actually fired,' Pete told her.

'There were powder burns around the injury.'

'Yes, I noticed the stippling pattern on the post mortem photographs. Can you send me a copy of Harrow's report?'

'Weren't you sent it?' Anna asked, amazed.

'Nope, I did phone Freeman and asked for a copy but he just said cause of death was a self-inflicted gunshot wound to the head.'

She threw up her hands. 'Even the pathologist's report didn't say *self*-inflicted! Didn't you complain about Freeman withholding information?' Anna asked emphatically.

'I'd only been working for the Met for a few months, Anna, and the last thing I wanted to do was upset the apple cart.'

'Bloody Freeman's got a lot to answer for,' Anna fumed.

'As I said, I need to do more work from the photographs on the blood distribution. I can get started on Monday . . .'

'Monday?'

'It's Saturday tomorrow, and as much as I'd do anything for you, I'm afraid working weekends is a no-no.'

'The week's gone so fast I'd totally forgotten,' Anna admitted.

Pete paused. 'There is something that struck me as unusual in the scene photographs.'

'What?'

'Reynolds' toxicology results showed no trace of any drugs but his blood-alcohol level was high.'

'So he was drunk.'

'He was over the legal limit but alcohol affects people's behaviour in different ways. In Reynolds' case it would have been seen as a mitigating factor towards suicide: emotional instability, loss of judgement and comprehension, those sorts of things.'

'But what's that got to do with the scene?' Anna demanded.

'There are photographs of all the rooms and in none of them is there an open bottle of booze or a glass. So where had he been drinking before he got home?'

'You're right.' Anna began to flick back through her notebook, looking for the interview with Marcus Williams. 'Williams never said Josh had been drinking but then again I never specifically asked him that question,' she said.

'Question is, then, where and with whom had he been drinking?'

'Pete, your observations are bloody brilliant, but they leave me with more unanswered questions and work to do,' she groaned.

'Just doing my job.' Pete smiled. 'But until I do an in-depth study, my observations are strictly between the two of us.'

'Of course, but you realize that if the Reynolds case does end up being a murder there will be an internal investigation and possible disciplinary action concerning the original investigation.'

'I've kept records of everything, including my conversations with Freeman. I did my job, Anna, with limited information, and I suggested lines of enquiry that were ignored,' he said defensively.

'Believe me, I'm on your side, Pete, but people like Freeman will try and shift the blame. Right, I'd best be off. I'm going to Fulham mortuary to see if Dr Harrow is available.'

'I'd tread carefully where he's concerned,' Pete warned.

'Why, what's the problem?'

'General Medical Council recently suspended him for four months for misconduct and bringing the profession into disrepute in a murder and suspicious death case.'

'My God! This case goes from bad to worse. How did you find out about it?'

'One of my old colleagues who moved up North was the lead scientist on a case Harrow was disciplined for.' Pete opened his desk drawer and produced a newspaper article that he had printed from the Internet. He read a line from it to Anna before handing it to her to keep. 'The panel found Dr Harrow had "deliberately ignored the guidelines" for his own convenience.'

'Well, I guess I can give Fulham mortuary a miss then.'

'He should still be there.'

'You said he's suspended.'

'Only from working on suspicious death or murder cases – if it's natural causes he can still cut them open and get his hands dirty,' Pete said cynically.

'Why didn't you tell me about him earlier?' Anna asked, glancing at the article.

'You know me. I always like to save the best for last.'

In the lift down to the lab car park, Anna read over the article on Dr Harrow, noticing from the dates that he had about a week or so to go before he had served his suspension. She anticipated that the man would be difficult to interview, as he would be on the defensive. Another case of misconduct could result in his licence to practise being permanently withdrawn, leaving him with no job at all. Anna had just got to her vehicle when she saw Dewar parking in a nearby bay. Her first thought was to avoid her by ducking down behind her car but she quickly realized how silly it would be if Dewar had already seen her. The only thing to do was to approach her first and as Dewar got out of her car Anna could see from the look on her face that she was in a foul mood.

'I thought you said you were going to tell me when you were going to see the scientist.'

'I live down the road and popped in on the off-chance. His secretary said he went straight to court from home this morning,' Anna lied, wanting to leave Pete to get on with his examination of the scene photographs.

'Then why did you tell Joan and not me that you were seeing Pete Jenkins?'

Anna realized that she had neglected to warn the constable not to mention that she was going to the lab.

'I think Joan misunderstood me. I told her that I was going to pop in to see if Pete was there. Sadly, as I just said, he's not.'

'You've been here for quite some time. Were you seeing the pathologist as well?'

'He doesn't work here. His office is at the mortuary in Fulham. We could go there now, if you like.'

'On the off-chance he's there, I suppose?'

'Yes.'

'That'll have to do for now. What's the address of the mortuary?' Dewar said tetchily.

'It's not far. I can leave my car here and go with you.'

As Anna got into Dewar's car, she remembered that she still had the newspaper article in her hand, and quietly folded it up to place it in her jacket pocket.

'You can go over Dr Harrow's report with him if you like, explain your theory about the case being a murder,' Anna suggested.

'Yes. So, you still think it was a suicide?' Dewar asked.

'As yet I'm undecided. Anyway, you're more experienced at behavioural analysis than I am.'

'True.'

At the mortuary, Dewar hurried to press the entry buzzer and waited impatiently for someone to come out and greet them. Eventually, a young female assistant dressed in blue overalls and white clogs approached and opened the locked door. Anna

introduced herself, as did Dewar, who then asked if Dr Harrow
was available. The assistant told them that he was just completing a routine post mortem and showed them to his office where
she said they could wait.

The office was rather shabby and stank of stale cigarette smoke;
the stained red carpet and curtains looked tatty and threadbare, as
did the furniture. The ashtray on top of the old wooden desk was
full of dog ends and beside it was an unwashed coffee cup with
cold dregs in it. To one side of the desk was a pile of pathology folders, the top one of which was bloodstained. Balanced on
these was a small plate with the remnants of a sandwich. A dust-
covered X-ray viewer was hung on one wall, opposite which
was a line of dented and rusty filing cabinets. The only seats
for visitors were two plastic hardback chairs arranged to face
Harrow's desk. Both Anna and Dewar decided to stand while
they waited.

'Somebody really fucked up the feng shui in here,' Dewar
remarked, looking round the room and shaking her head.

'The last time I was in this office, Doc Jennings was the pathologist. Like him, it was immaculate,' Anna replied.

'Please say you've got a wet wipe in your bag so I can clean
those two chairs if we have to sit down?' Dewar asked.

Anna told Dewar she hadn't but gave her a couple of tissues.
She wondered if the room was a reflection of Harrow's work
ethics.

'If he walks in with blood and guts all over him I'll be sick,'
Dewar said.

'Right, ladies, what can I do for ya,' asked a voice in a broad
Yorkshire accent as a man who could only be Harrow entered
the room still dressed in his mortuary overalls, the sleeves of
which were spotted with blood. He had a cup of coffee in one
hand and was lighting up a cigarette, which hung limply from
his mouth. Harrow was a short man in his late fifties, bald and
overweight with a large beer belly. His half-moon reading glasses
teetered on the edge of his nose.

As he sat down in the worn leather chair it sagged a few

inches under his weight. He opened his desk drawer and took out a packet of digestive biscuits then picked up the plate with sandwich crusts and tipped it into the bin. Using his nicotine-stained fingers he took six biscuits out of the pack, put them on the plate and invited Dewar and Travis to have one. Shocked by his lack of hygiene, they in unison said, 'No, thank you!'

Dewar made the introductions and said she was on work experience with DCI Travis's murder squad.

'I doubt there's much the bloody Met could teach your lot. FBI already know everything, don't they,' Harrow said and chortled at his joke, causing a lump of ash to fall from his cigarette onto his stomach. Dewar sat stone-faced, as did Anna, who felt quite repulsed by the man.

'We need to speak to you about the Joshua Reynolds case,' Dewar began.

'Joshua who? Names mean nowt to me, they're all dead when I get to them. What were his injuries and where was it?'

'Gunshot wound to the head in a flat in Bayswater, November sixth last year.'

'That were chap who owned a fanny club up town. Suicide job, as I recall.'

Harrow got up from his seat and shuffled over to the filing cabinets, blatantly ignoring the 'no smoking' sign above them.

'Joshua Reynolds, you say?' he said as he removed a file and took it back to his desk. 'So what's problem?'

'I think that Reynolds may have been murdered and the scene staged to look like a suicide,' Dewar said.

Harrow leaned forward, peered over the rim of his glasses, frowned and then took a bite out of his digestive biscuit.

'You must be bloody FBI, cummin' out with crap like that. There weren't a single mark on his body to show a struggle.' Crumbs from the biscuit dropped from his mouth onto the table as he spoke.

'Would you argue if someone held a gun to your head? The position of the body and the blood distribution were wrong for his death to be a suicide. I think he was kneeling on the ground, holding his hands up in the air when he was shot.'

'Can I ask you, what exactly do ya do in the FBI?' Harrow asked as he opened the file and spread his notes and photographs around the desk.

'I'm a supervisory special agent in the Behavioural Science Unit. I study offenders and their behaviours at crime scenes, advise on interview strategies . . .'

'But ya don't go out and get yer hands dirty, do ya?'

'Admittedly, it's rare that I actually attend a scene as I work from Quantico and cover the whole of the United States. Most of my work is with unsolved murders.'

'Well, let me tell ya, young lady, I've been ta more crime scenes than you've had hot dinners. I draw me conclusions by looking at dead bodies, not bloody pictures!'

Harrow pushed forward a picture of Josh Reynolds' body on the floor and close-ups taken at the post mortem of the entry and exit wounds to his head. The entry wound was smaller and quite symmetrical in comparison to the exit wound and the stippling effect from the hot gunpowder burning into Reynolds' skin was clearly evident. Bits of skull bone and brain tissue protruded from the ragged exit wound on the left side of his head. Another photograph showed the skin of his head peeled back, revealing the holes in his skull. A metal rod ran from the entry to the exit wound to show the trajectory of the bullet. Harrow lit up another cigarette and took a large puff, exhaling the smoke in Dewar's direction.

'Right, so you think he had hands up in t'air.'

'Yes, I do.'

'So how come there's not a large mass o' back-spatter blood on his upper right arm?' Harrow demanded, using his index finger to point to the exact position on the photograph.

'There is some blood there.'

'Yes, but it's downward, having arced backwards from entry wound.'

'There's no blood on the back of his right hand and there should be,' Dewar pushed.

'So bloody what, that proves nowt. Although this were a close-range gunshot, barrel were not pressed right up against his head.'

'How do you know that?' Dewar asked indignantly.

''Cause if gun was touching victim's head, you'd get an abrasion ring, and also a clear imprint of the weapon's barrel on victim's skin.' Harrow made the shape of a gun with his right hand and held it to his head to demonstrate what he meant, then continued.

'So say gun is inch or two away from head. He pulls trigger, bang equals recoil equals shooting hand moving back away from body so blood back spatter doesn't reach it. Simple as that.'

'Well, you're not a blood-pattern expert so I think that is an opinion best left to a scientist.'

Harrow glared at Dewar. 'Neither are you, Miss Fancypants. We have a saying where I'm from: "If tha knows nowt, say nowt an 'appen nob'dy'll notice."'

Anna couldn't believe how restrained Dewar was being but felt she needed some support against the unsavoury Harrow.

'There's no need for you to be so rude to my colleague,' she objected.

'RUDE, me bloody rude! You're the ones who came in here making out I'm some incompetent bloody idiot. You've read me report and the Coroner agreed with me so that's t' end of matter.'

'I also have some concerns about the Reynolds scene and the lack of forensic examination,' Anna said firmly.

'I don't have to talk to you. Now get out of my office.'

'As the DCI in charge of the case, I am considering asking for a full independent disciplinary inquiry to be made concerning every detail of the original investigation.'

Harrow sat back in his seat and looked directly at Anna, who knew the mention of such an inquiry would get his full attention.

'I'm sure that's the last thing you would want at the present time,' Anna continued, as Dewar looked perplexed, wondering how the DCI had got Harrow to back off so quickly.

Harrow said nothing as he stubbed out his cigarette and instantly lit another one, tilting his head upwards and blowing the smoke away from Anna.

'Josh Reynolds' stomach contents – I didn't see any mention of them in your report,' Anna observed.

Harrow looked through his report. 'That's because there were none.'

'None recorded or none in his stomach, Doctor?'

'I've got down here "stomach empty".'

'His blood-alcohol level was very high so he'd been drinking on an empty stomach.'

'Yes.'

'Can you be any more specific on the time of death.'

'No, too many variables like the empty stomach, intoxication and the central heating was on.'

'You said Reynolds had been dead between eight to twenty hours.'

'That's right.'

'We believe he made a phone call at seven p.m. on the fifth.'

'Entirely possible – as I said there were many variables, so I could not be more specific.'

'Did you voice any opinions about the scene to the Crime Scene Manager, Freeman?'

Dewar glanced at Anna, as Harrow let the smoke belch from his nose. 'We were both there, discussed it and agreed.'

'What did you agree?' Anna was keeping her voice quiet and controlled.

'That it *could* have been a suicide. We kept an open mind until I completed the post-mortem.'

'So if it *could* have been a suicide, it could also have been a murder. Did you advise Freeman to call a forensic scientist to the scene?'

Harrow scratched his head. 'That's not my responsibility –
you'd have to ask him.'

Anna had got the exact measure of Dr Harrow and he knew
it. He pursed his lip angrily.

'Thank you for your time, Dr Harrow. We will see ourselves
out,' Anna said.

Returning to the car, Anna asked Dewar to drop her at the lab
so she could collect her own vehicle. Dewar nodded but had a
puzzled look on her face as she turned round.

'Have you got something on him?' she asked, and Anna
nodded.

'Spill the beans on the big fat toad,' Dewar said, grinning at
her.

Anna took out the newspaper article from her pocket and
read it aloud.

'Why didn't you tell me that before we went in there?' Dewar
demanded.

'Because I didn't want you to attack his ability from the get-
go. I'd rather you formed an opinion from meeting him in the
flesh.'

'The article doesn't do him justice. He's far worse than that,'
Dewar said, and they both laughed.

Chapter Twelve

Back at the station, Anna found Joan and Barbara sitting together in the canteen when she went to get a coffee, so she went over to join them. Barbara was tucking into a slice of steak and kidney pie that was smothered in brown sauce, with mashed potato and baked beans. Joan had a cheese salad and was much more refined in her eating, taking steady bites and chewing slowly, whilst Barbara appeared be in a race against the clock. Anna asked Barbara how the house-to-house enquiries had gone.

'I haven't done them yet,' Barbara said indignantly.

Anna was about to ask why not when Joan spoke up on her colleague's behalf.

'Dewar told her that she urgently wanted timelines for both Josh and Donna Reynolds' movements covering a thirty-six-hour period before Josh's body was discovered.'

'With details of every phone call and text message Donna and Josh made and received,' Barbara added.

'Did you tell her I'd asked you to do the house-to-house?' Anna asked Barbara.

'I didn't get a chance because she stormed off, saying she was going to the lab. It's a lot of work for one bloody person to do. Who is in charge of this case anyway, you or Dewar?' Barbara wanted to know.

'I am, Barbara, and as it happens timelines will be very helpful. So if not for Dewar, then kindly do it for me.'

'What about the house-to-house, who's going to do that then?' Barbara moaned.

'If you could get it completed in the next couple of days that will be fine. Take Joan with you – be a nice change for you to get out from behind your desk, Joan.'

'Thank you, ma'am, that's really kind of you,' Joan said with a beaming smile.

'So what else has Dewar asked to be done?' Anna enquired.

Joan told her that she had asked for a copy of Donna's 999 call when she reported finding the body of her husband and Barolli was going to collect it after getting the banking warrants.

Barbara finished her pie and announced she fancied some sponge pudding and custard for dessert. She got up from the table and joined the short queue at the counter.

'She's obviously off her diet again! Oh, the yellow Lotus you asked for an owner's check on. The keeper is Aisa Lynne, but the vehicle's registered address is the Lynne Foundation, which is based in Mount Street in Mayfair. The Mini Cooper is Donna's but still registered to the old flat in Bayswater,' Joan whispered to Anna.

'Why are you whispering?' Anna asked.

'Because you told me to make "discreet" enquiries and Barbara's got big ears. She can hear a pin drop fifty feet away.'

Anna looked over at Barbara who, although standing with her back to them, was twisting her head to one side in an effort to listen in on their conversation.

'So what have you got for me?' Anna asked quietly.

'I didn't realize it was Lady Gloria Lynne you went to see yesterday.'

'Lady Gloria Lynne? Lady! Are you sure?' Anna asked, surprised by the revelation that Gloria was titled.

'Yes. Her husband was Lord Henry Lynne, a multi-millionaire businessman, philanthropist and life peer. He died six or seven years ago while they were on holiday in Egypt. Lady Lynne helped him set up a foundation that supports charitable causes around the world.'

'How did you find all this out so quickly?'

'Recent magazine article, bit of Internet searching. My mum

subscribes to *Tatler* and *Country Life* magazines and I usually read them too. I phoned her up and she's checking through all the old copies, cutting out articles and pictures for you about Lady Lynne. I told her to be discreet as well.'

'Good work, Joan. Don't put your mum to too much trouble though, okay?'

'It's no trouble at all, we've only got about a hundred and twenty-odd copies and, like me, my mum's a good speed reader,' Joan assured Anna.

'So Lady Lynne has friends in high places. That would explain how she knew I was murder and not vice squad.'

'She organizes some of London's biggest charity events. Attends the summer garden parties at Buckingham Palace and is very big in the horticultural world, with exhibitions at Chelsea and other major flower shows.'

'You're an asset to the team, Joan, and thorough in your research as well.'

'Sorry I haven't got more for you at the moment. Barbara's coming back so I'll tell you later,' Joan whispered as Barbara sat down at the table with her sponge pudding and informed Anna that she had put the surveillance team's report and overtime sheet on her desk.

'What are you talking about, Barbara?' Anna asked.

'The undercover operation you requested on Donna from her mum's house last night. They dropped the forms off just before lunch.'

'I never requested a surveillance team, let alone authorized any overtime.'

'Well, they said you had, so if you didn't then that only leaves you-know-who.'

Dewar was reading the surveillance report when a very annoyed Anna walked into their office.

'You know anything about a surveillance team being put on Donna Reynolds last night?'

'I do apologize. I totally forgot to mention it this morning,'

Dewar said, holding up the report and handing it over to Anna before continuing: 'You'll never guess where Donna went within half an hour of us leaving her mother's.'

'I'm more interested in why you saw fit to ask for a surveillance unit without consulting me first. I have to pay for it out of my budget – they're not a free commodity.'

'I've apologized, what more can I say?'

Anna asked Dewar how she managed to get a surveillance unit out to Weybridge, implying that she had posed as her in some way. Dewar explained that she had used the unmarked car's police radio and sought advice from the central control room. She had simply stated she was an FBI agent working with DCI Travis and needed assistance to urgently tail a suspect in a murder inquiry.

'Langton will be bloody livid,' Anna said, feeling stressed.

'Jimmy rang a few minutes ago, said he was coming over later this afternoon. I told him everyone was at lunch and about the result of the tail on Donna.'

'Well, I hope you told him it wasn't me that requested it?'

'Of course I said it was me. He seemed very happy, particularly when I told him that she went to the Trojan and was in there for nearly an hour.'

Anna was finding it hard to control her anger. 'Did you tell him about the eight-hundred-pound overtime bill?' she asked, looking at the surveillance file.

'No. Is it an issue?'

'Langton said there was no overtime budget on this inquiry!'

'I can't see it being a problem. Anyway, when Donna left the Trojan, a man matching Marcus Williams' description walked her to her car. She kissed and hugged him before leaving on her own,' Dewar remarked excitedly.

'And that makes her a murder suspect?'

'Don't you find it rather strange?'

'You accused her of being involved in her husband's murder, which totally shocked her and resulted in floods of tears, so to be honest I don't find it strange that in a state of distress she would want to talk to Williams.'

'She knows I'm on to her, they were just crocodile tears for her mother's benefit,' Dewar asserted.

'Well, I'm not so sure.'

'She then went to Notting Hill, parked her car, and didn't return for nearly half an hour?' Dewar sat back smiling.

'So who did she go to see?'

'I don't know — the surveillance team lost her when she walked off on foot. They waited for her to come back to the car and then followed her back to Weybridge.'

'She could have been visiting a friend for all we know.'

'Or realized she was being followed. If she was distressed like you suggest then why didn't she just stay in with her precious mother?'

'Her precious mother is in fact Lady Gloria Lynne, whose deceased husband Henry was a life peer and member of the House of Lords,' Anna said grimly.

'Well, well, I suppose that explains her airs and graces then.'

'And it also explains why she complained to the local Chief Constable about our visit. He in turn called the Met Commissioner and it ended up with Deputy Commissioner Walters giving Langton an earful.' It was Anna's turn to sit back with a tight smile.

'He's not in trouble, is he?' Dewar asked anxiously.

'I nearly got pulled off the FBI course, so your attachment must have been in jeopardy as well. Langton managed to diffuse the situation but be prepared for some words of advice from him.'

'That aside, Donna needs to be interviewed about her movements last night,' Dewar persisted.

'I agree, but we need to tread carefully where Lady Lynne is concerned. Everything needs to be above board, with every action and result recorded in detail on the computer. If she complains again the top brass will be all over us like a rash. Before we do anything else we need to write up the interviews we've done so far.'

Anna proceeded to inform Dewar that DCS Langton had

agreed that while she was on the FBI course, Paul Barolli would oversee the case as acting DCI. Dewar was unimpressed and pointed out that Barolli had only just been promoted to Inspector.

'Paul Barolli has years of experience, especially when it comes to investigating murders. I've worked alongside him at every rank and I trust him implicitly. He'd lay his life on the line for you, as he did for Langton and other members of this team.'

'How do you mean?' Dewar demanded.

'He tried to stop an armed suspect who was shooting at us but ended up getting shot himself. He's been recommended for the Queen's Gallantry Medal, the highest award a police officer can get.'

'No shit.' Dewar shook her head. 'He took one for the job. I'd never have guessed.'

'That's because Paul is a modest person and doesn't pretend to be something he's not,' Anna said, hoping that Dewar would pick up on the underlying implication. 'Anyway, I'm going to see if he's in his office now to check how he got on with obtaining the bank warrants.'

Anna's luck was in, as Barolli had just sat down at his desk, so she took the opportunity to bring him up to speed. In return, he told her that the warrants had been issued and served on the banks. He added that there was unrest in the main office as Dewar tried to stamp her authority on the team in a less than polite manner. Anna admitted to Paul that Barbara and Joan had also complained about Dewar, and that she'd dropped enough hints and even been direct with Dewar on a number of occasions but it was as if the agent didn't care and enjoyed being argumentative and upsetting people.

'I'm sorry to be leaving you in the lurch, Paul, but I have confidence that you'll do a good job overseeing the case while I'm in the States.'

'Thanks, Anna. I'll keep you updated by phone while you're away and if the shit really hits the fan I might run away and join you.' He grinned and Anna smiled. 'Meanwhile, I've got hold of the copy of Donna Reynolds' 999 call that Dewar requested.'

'Might as well have a listen to it before she does, then,' Anna suggested cheerfully as Barolli reached across to place the CD in his computer and turned on the speakers.

The recording opened with an operator announcing that the caller was through to the emergency services. A clearly distressed Donna asked for the police and was forwarded to their call centre. She was asked to give her name, address and the number she was calling from. The panic in her voice was clear, and she was crying profusely, gasping for air and just about audible.

'It's my husband Josh . . . he's been shot . . . there's a gun and blood everywhere . . . oh, God, please help him . . . I think he's dead.'

'Where has he been shot?'

'In our flat. He's not moving.'

'Where in the body has he been shot?'

'The head . . . please help him, please.'

'Are you with him now, Donna?'

'I've just come home . . . I don't know what to do.'

'The police and an ambulance are on their way, Donna. Please stay on the phone while a paramedic speaks to you.' The police operator then transferred the call, giving the paramedic details of the incident. Donna now seemed to be in a state of hyperventilation, causing her speech to become slightly slurred. She sounded as if she was about to faint.

'Can you tell me if he's breathing?'

'I think he's dead, please hurry . . .'

'Is he bleeding?'

'There's blood all over the floor and his face.'

'Can you feel for a pulse?'

'I'm scared . . . please, please help him.'

'The ambulance and police are on their way, Donna.'

They listened to the rest of the call, which mostly consisted of the paramedic trying to calm Donna down and reassure her help was on the way. Eventually, a police officer could be heard

telling the paramedic that the victim had a severe gunshot wound
to the head and there was no pulse.

'Did that sound like someone who had arranged her husband's murder?' Anna asked.

'No, that sounded like pure uncontrolled panic. I felt her fear,
it was like being in the room with her,' Barolli said.

'Dewar needs to listen to this,' Anna said, as Langton walked in.

'Joan said you were in here, Jessie not with you?'

Anna told Langton that Dewar was in her office writing
up notes and she was bringing Barolli up to speed with the
investigation, adding that Gloria was actually Lady Lynne as her
former husband was Lord Henry Lynne. Langton told her that
he too had only just been made aware of that fact.

'I spoke with Walters this morning and lucky for you Lady
Lynne doesn't wish to take the matter any further. However, he
stipulated that if you want to go near her again you run it by
him first. Is that clear?'

Anna nodded and handed Langton the CD of Donna's 999
call, asking him to take it through to Dewar as she still had some
stuff to go over with Barolli.

'How have you two been getting on today?' Langton asked
her.

'Okay, I guess, but she's been rubbing the rest of the team up
the wrong way, demanding this and that without a please or
thank-you, so I think a word from you . . .'

'Point made, I'll speak with her. She mentioned something
about a surveillance team following Donna last night,' Langton
said.

'I didn't know anything about it.'

'Sounds like it was worth it though.'

'Hard to say yet, but it cost nearly a thousand pounds in overtime.'

'How much?' Langton exclaimed in a raised voice before he
turned and stormed out of the room, slamming the door behind
him.

'I thought it was eight hundred quid?' Barolli remarked.

'Yes, but figuratively speaking that's nearly a thousand, whereas if I said just over five hundred that's not nearly eight hundred.'

'There's a method in your madness, isn't there?'

Anna smiled and nodded her head in agreement.

Dewar was still busy writing up her notes when Langton stormed in.

'Why the fuck is the surveillance overtime bill a thousand pounds?'

'It was in fact eight hundred pounds,' she replied, nonchalantly.

'I assumed the late shift did the surveillance as there's no overtime budget and anyway you're supposed to ask me to authorize it first.'

'DCI Travis had not made me aware that was the case, and if I'd known I would have done the tail myself.'

'Anna mentioned that Gloria Lynne had made a complaint. I'm sorry if it caused you any problems, Jimmy,' she went on.

'It was something and nothing really. I'm used to Walters having a moan, but I know how to handle him so don't lose any sleep over it.'

'That makes me feel better, I'd hate to let you down, especially when you've done so much for me.'

'Please be on your guard when dealing with Lady Lynne in the future. Same goes with the team,' Langton warned.

'Have I done something to upset them?' Dewar asked, looking concerned.

'To them you're a stranger; they're not used to taking advice or instructions from outsiders. You need to ease your way in, let them get to know and appreciate your skills.'

'I like to be thorough and see a job well done. If anything, I feel I've been very helpful. Anna and I are making progress and working well together. It's actually a shame she has to go to the States but I'm looking forward to working alongside DI Barolli.'

'Good, onwards and upwards then,' said Langton. 'But here, take this CD. I'd like to listen to this with you.'

Dewar played the CD through once, hurriedly jotting down shorthand notes as she went. Before Langton could say anything, Dewar restarted the recording from the beginning, pausing and replaying bits as she went along and writing further notes. Langton found it rather irritating and wondered what she was picking up on.

'Is there something interesting in the background?' he asked.

'No, I'm listening to her voice inflection,' Dewar remarked, leaving Langton even more puzzled. 'The alteration in pitch or tone can be very revealing. When telling a lie, people tend to speak in extremes; either monotone or with great energy.'

'She just found her husband dead so her voice will be all over the place.'

'Listening to this tape, I think she may have known he was dead even before she walked through her front door. We need to get Travis back in here to discuss this.'

Langton went to fetch Anna, observing that Dewar had picked up on something important in Donna's voice inflection. Anna raised her eyebrows, suspecting that Dewar was just trying to impress Langton with more psychological mumbo-jumbo. When Barolli said he'd like to join them, Anna looked at him as if he were mad.

The four of them sat in Anna's office and Dewar replayed the whole recording then asked if the others had picked up on any-thing unusual in Donna's tone of voice or answers to the operator. Anna blandly replied that Donna seemed to be in a state of emotional shock, having found Josh with a bullet through his head and lying in a pool of blood. Dewar said she would take them through the call again step by step, and explain her reasoning about its inconsistencies as she went. She played the opening where Donna was asked which emergency service she required and stated 'the police'. The connection made, the sound of Donna's pleading voice was heard: 'It's my husband

Josh ... he's been shot ... there's a gun and blood everywhere ... oh, God, please help him ... I think he's dead.' Dewar paused the CD.

'After asking for the police she said: "He's been shot," and "I think he's dead." She *thought* he was dead, ergo she must have considered he might still be alive, yet she never asked for an ambulance at any point!'

'So that's why you think she knew what to expect when she walked in the room?' Langton asked, intrigued by what Dewar was saying.

'Not just that, there's quite a bit more actually. Let's look at the voice inflection on the last bit of her phrase: "I think he's dead."'

'Can you explain what you mean by voice inflection, please?' Barolli asked.

'Certainly. Put in simple terms it's the alteration in pitch or tone of the voice which in turn can change the form and tense of the word or words,' Dewar told them.

'Which words are you talking about?' Langton asked.

'"He's dead." If I walked in and told you that your best friend had just been killed, how would you feel?' Dewar asked, looking at Barolli.

'Shocked,' Barolli replied.

'Exactly, the tone of voice in stating "He's dead" should be one of surprise, but if you already knew that your friend was dead and someone asked you how he was, what would you say?'

'He's dead,' Barolli uttered in a forlorn voice.

'The inflection changes because it's an occurrence that happened in the past and you already know it. The instantaneous surprise is absent.'

'You could also express it in a happy way if you were glad someone was dead,' Barolli pointed out, causing Langton to frown at him.

Dewar continued: 'The inflection in Donna's voice in "he's dead" is wrong. It's very subtle and unless you really focus you will miss it. "I think he's dead" is said both at the outset and when the paramedic speaks with her.' Dewar fast-forwarded the CD to where the paramedic's voice could be heard along with Donna's reply: 'Can you tell me if he's breathing?' . . . 'I think he's dead, please hurry.'

She paused the CD once more.

'Again the surprise is missing.'

Anna couldn't believe what she was hearing. Her personal and professional experience had taught her that people in shock reacted and spoke in many different and strange ways. She was about to voice her objection when Dewar held up the crime scene photograph of Reynolds' body and continued.

'I believe that Donna knew that Josh was already dead and saying she "just got home and found him" is an attempt to distance herself from the crime. Her reactions, like the scene, were staged,' Dewar said smugly.

Anna could contain herself no longer.

'This is all a matter of opinion based on something you've read about. It wouldn't even be allowed as evidence in our courts. We all react and say things in different ways when we are under emotional stress, which Donna Reynolds clearly was.'

'My opinion is based on my research. It is objective and unbiased and strengthens my case that Josh Reynolds was actually murdered and Donna was involved.'

'What about the fact Donna didn't notice the wardrobe and safe door were open and also put the washing on before finding the body? That shows she was unaware he was dead,' Anna argued.

'Staged, to make it look as if she wasn't expecting to discover the body.'

'You twist everything to suit your flight-of-fancy theories and your methods are totally unethical,' Anna said in a slightly raised voice.

'This is my field of expertise, I know what I'm talking about and that's why I'm a senior agent in the BSU,' Dewar said, puffing out her chest.

'You've never been to a real crime scene. You're a desk jockey who only looks at pictures!'

'I resent that remark, Travis.'

'I think you mean resemble, not resent!'

'What?' Dewar said.

'Donna had no motive to murder Josh. Your psychobabble is worthless crap!'

'Half the value of the club, sale of their marital home, mad at him—'

Anna stood up and banged her hands on the desk. 'She's already rich so why would she want her husband dead?'

'Who gives a fuck; the fact is she had him murdered and I know my gut instinct is right!' Dewar said, and banged her own fist on the table.

Langton and Barolli looked at each other in astonishment as the heated exchange between Dewar and Travis grew in intensity. Eventually, Langton stood up and shouted at them. 'Enough! Grow up and behave like the senior investigators you're supposed to be.'

Dewar and Travis were instantly silent, as Langton continued.

'God knows what that lot in the main office must think. They can't have failed to hear you two bickering like spoilt schoolgirls.'

Both women apologized to Langton, but not to each other, and sat in stony silence, avoiding eye contact.

'Be warned, I could pull you both off this investigation right now if I wanted to. But there are clear issues concerning the case that need to be investigated and further interviews that will have to be done.'

'Shouldn't we arrest Donna Reynolds?' Dewar asked.

'I am not taking sides here but my answer for now is NO, and that will remain the case until you have some hard factual evidence against her.'

'Yes, sir,' Dewar and Travis replied together.

'You two have different skills and experience to bring to this inquiry so you need to sit down, sort out your differences and get on with the job. Do you understand me?'

'Yes, sir,' they both repeated.

'Go home, calm down and take the weekend to reflect on what idiots you've been then start afresh Monday.'

'We were going to update the team,' Dewar said.

'Travis, have you fully updated Barolli?' Langton asked.

'Yes, sir.'

'Good, he can bring us up to speed. Now, the pair of you clear off while Barolli and I have an adult conversation.'

Anna and Dewar picked up their belongings and headed off towards the station car park, feeling rather sorry for themselves. Although they were in the lift together, they didn't speak. But after some moments of reflection, Anna came to the realization that their standoff was pointless and was the first to break the ice.

'We really let ourselves down in there, Jessie.'

'Yes, I know. The problem is we both think and see things differently and I'm all too often the Devil's advocate.'

'We're not that different, Jessie.' Anna sighed. 'God knows how many times Langton's called me headstrong.'

'I get frustrated at times, especially back home,' Dewar admitted. 'The FBI is very male-dominated and I'm the only woman on my team. Many of the men still support the view of J. Edgar Hoover.'

'What's that?'

'Women can't handle the physical rigours of being a special agent and shouldn't be in the FBI.'

'The Met's not much different on some squads. Equality is slowly improving things but working on "man-turf" is never easy.'

'I know, but why should we have to work so much harder to prove ourselves and succeed?'

'So one day we can rule the world of policing,' Anna said with a wry smile.

'I'll drink to that,' Dewar said.

'Good idea – fancy something to eat as well? We don't have to discuss the case but I'd like to know more about the FBI course.'

'Only if you let me pay.' Dewar smiled, and so did Anna.

'Fine by me. You doing anything over the weekend?'

'I'm going up to Norfolk to visit an old college friend who married a Fakenham farmer.'

Anna broke into a laugh. It was contagious, and as Dewar giggled, they left the lift together.

Chapter Thirteen

Anna woke on Monday morning looking forward to going into work. She had spent a pleasant weekend visiting her gym twice, shopping for clothes, sportswear and trainers for her FBI course and generally lazing about watching DVDs she had rented. Unusually for her, she had not even looked at or thought about anything to do with the Josh Reynolds case. Her Friday-evening dinner with Jessie Dewar had been very pleasant. Anna had suggested a Venetian-style bàcaro restaurant off Regent Street where they had enjoyed sharing tapas-sized portions of cuttlefish in squid ink, spinach and egg pizzette and meatballs. They had also shared a bottle of Pinot Grigio and a tiramisu dessert that was to die for. As she got dressed for work, Anna smiled, recalling that whilst they were eating their food, Jessie had asked why she had chosen that venue for dinner. Anna had pointed to a blue plaque on the wall, commemorating the fact that the premises were once the home of the famous Venetian painter Canaletto.

'Having heard you tell Gloria Lynne how much you loved art, I thought you'd feel right at home here,' Anna had said, causing them both to laugh loudly and Jessie to ask, 'Is that what you Brits mean by "taking the piss"?'

Anna had been keen to know more about the forthcoming course, and Jessie immediately stressed that the name of the game was to make friends and contacts. Everyone would be referred to by their first names, rank was immaterial and all participants would be treated as equals. The course classes were made up of about two hundred US law-enforcement officers and fifty from foreign police organizations. The physical fitness programme on the course was very intense and reflected J. Edgar Hoover's belief that physical fitness could be the difference between success and failure, even life and death.

'Best I remember my running shoes,' Anna remarked.

Jessie laughed. 'I'd take two pairs as they wear out quickly, especially on the Yellow Brick Road.

'What's the Yellow Brick Road?'

'I can't tell you as it would spoil the surprise,' Jessie said, with a wag of her finger.

The best thing about the dinner was that during the whole evening was they hardly discussed the investigation.

As Anna drove to work, she reflected that by the end of the evening she had got to know Jessie a lot better and respect her more. Not once had she boasted about herself; on the contrary, she had admitted that she was 'occasionally' wrong, overzealous and in her own words 'a pain in the ass'. She had been polite, funny and enjoyable company and her knowledge of serial killers and their psychological behaviour was both fascinating and informative. Anna wondered if Jessie's argumentative, bull-in-a-china-shop manner was some sort of front to prove that she could stand up to anyone, particularly men. Anna recalled her saying in jest that she never mixed work with sex, but lived in hope of finding Mr Right. It struck Anna that Jessie, like her, might be very much alone outside her professional world. She didn't know if Jessie had family, friends or work colleagues that she was close to or confided in. After Ken's death, Anna had discovered what it was like to be lonely, trapped in a world where you felt empty inside, where nobody listened to you or showed you compassion. Anna was also very aware that you didn't have to lose a loved one to feel like that and hoped, having seen the other side of Jessie Dewar, that loneliness was not something she suffered from.

*

The first thing Anna did on arrival at the station was to go straight to Barolli's office and apologize to him for her and Jessie's behaviour.

'Did you take her for a lobotomy on Friday?' Barolli asked.

'What's happened now?'

'Nothing – Dewar's full of the joys of spring, singing your praises and being pleasant to everyone.'

'Well that's good news.'

'But will it last?' Barolli raised his eyebrows.

'I hope so, especially as you will be working closely with her in a few days' time.'

'Paul Simms is in your office with Dewar. He brought over a load of paperwork and stuff to do with the Reynolds case.'

'Oh, shit!' Anna exclaimed and raced off, regretting she had not said anything to Jessie at dinner about meeting Paul for breakfast. She feared another argument as she entered her office and saw the two of them talking.

'I'm really sorry, Jessie. I was going to tell you at dinner but I didn't want to spoil the evening,' Anna said.

'Tell me what?'

Anna looked at Paul Simms, whose alarmed expression told her that she was about to drop them both right in it.

'I, um, well . . .' Anna was racking her brains to come out with something plausible to cover the delicate situation.

'Do you know what Anna wants to tell me, Paul?' Dewar asked inquisitively. Paul shrugged his shoulders.

'Please don't tell me you two have already met in secret and discussed the case?' Dewar asked in mock surprise.

'You knew?' Anna asked, somewhat taken aback. Paul's head fell forward and he half raised his hands in the air in surrender.

'Your micro-expressions and inflections gave you away when I asked you if you'd spoken with him. Same when I asked you about Pete Jenkins.'

'You knew I'd spoken with him as well?'

'Not for certain but I do now.' Dewar grinned.

'Why didn't you say anything?'

'I understand in both instances why you didn't tell me. I was quick to blame DI Simms for all the errors in the initial investigation and had we met before today I'd probably have given him a mouthful.'

'And Pete?' Anna enquired.

'I wasn't certain, so it wasn't worth arguing about.'

'I'm sorry, Jessie. I promise from now on you'll be in the loop on everything.'

'Slate's clean as far as I'm concerned. I've been going over DI Simms' investigation and he was clearly badly advised by Freeman and Harrow.'

Anna told Jessie and Simms about her meeting with Pete Jenkins when they had discussed the scene and items that were submitted to him for forensic examination. She said that Pete was still working on the blood-distribution analysis from the photographs and would take his time, but sadly any opinion he might have would not be definitive, as he was never asked by Freeman to attend the scene.

Paul Simms was shocked that Freeman had failed to pass on any of Pete Jenkins' comments to him and had been so dismissive when Pete offered to attend the scene, and he grew more and more subdued as Anna spoke. Dewar told him about their meeting with Dr Harrow and his recent four-month suspension.

'Neither Freeman or Harrow ever said anything to me about the scene being anything other than a suicide. I can't believe I was taken in like that.'

'You weren't, Paul, you relied on their experience, and they let you down,' Dewar said reassuringly. 'Together, they formed a conclusion of suicide at the scene. They should have taken a step back, challenged their thoughts and considered competing theories.'

'Freeman was lazy and failed to carry out a proper scene examination and Harrow was gung ho,' Anna added.

'Yes, but ultimately, I'm responsible for not treating Reynolds' death as suspicious,' Paul said.

'I can't say you shouldn't have done more at the time, but we all make mistakes and in turn learn from them,' Anna remarked.

Paul was close to tears. 'I'll be disciplined and demoted, won't I?'

'We don't know what the outcome of our reinvestigation will be, but whatever happens, Agent Dewar and I are on your side. Aren't we?'

'It goes without saying,' Dewar replied firmly.

Paul looked so dejected that Anna felt it was not the time to begin examining the documents he'd brought over, and so told him that she and Jessie would look through everything and get back to him if they needed to. Paul thanked them for being so understanding and hurriedly left, clearly embarrassed and hurt.

'Thanks for going easy on Paul Simms,' Anna said.

'He's a nice guy. Will he have to face discipline proceedings?'

'I hope not, but the final decision may well be out of my hands.'

Anna and Jessie were interrupted by a knock at the door. It was Joan, come to tell them that Langton wanted everyone gathered in the main office for a half eleven meeting as he was on his way with the detective superintendent who would be taking over the Reynolds case. Anna looked at her watch and saw that they had just over an hour to get things prepared. She asked Joan if Langton had said who it was; typically, he hadn't.

Anna suggested to Jessie that it would be a good idea if they had a look through the documents that Paul Simms had brought over in case there was anything that needed urgent attention or would be useful to bring up at the meeting.

They sat by the coffee table in their office and opened the box.

'What first?' Dewar asked.

'Forensics and post-mortem exhibits would be a good place to start,' Anna replied as she took out the exhibits list from the box, which was written and signed by Freeman. Jessie had her notebook and pen to hand.

'Items from deceased: bloodstained white shirt, black trousers, socks, leather shoes and underwear, Rolex watch and one St Christopher pendant – nothing exciting there then,' Anna remarked.

'No wallet?'

'Yeah, from his right pocket – it contained credit cards, Oyster travel card, cash and some receipts. In the left trouser pocket were three keys on a fob and some loose change.'

'I don't suppose it says make or type of keys?'

'No. I'm sure there's a photo in the case file of all the property laid out on a white sheet at the mortuary,' Anna said as she went over to her desk to get the folder containing the photographs.

'I don't suppose there's any recorded detail about the receipts? They might be helpful in tracing Reynolds' last movements,' Dewar suggested.

'No. Freeman is bloody useless.'

'Have we still got any of the exhibits you just mentioned?' Jessie enquired.

'Apart from the bloodstained clothing, everything was restored to Donna after the Coroner's inquest,' Anna commented as she spread the mortuary and scene photographs on the coffee table.

Among them was the picture showing the contents of Josh's trouser pockets, which she handed to Dewar. The agent looked at it closely and then picked up a close-up of the bed. She asked Anna to look at the exhibits list from the scene and see if any keys were recovered from the bed.

'Yes, two keys on a fob,' Anna said, as Dewar got a jeweller's loupe from her handbag to scrutinize the closeup of the bed and then the keys recovered at the mortuary.

'Probably Josh's house keys – he may have thrown them on the bed with the mobile before opening the safe.'

'Or they could be Donna's. Remember, she went straight to the bedroom and unpacked when she got home,' Dewar said.

'Good point.'

'The apartment door locks were one Chubb and one Yale

and the keys on the fob recovered from his trouser pocket are a Chubb a Yale and what looks like a locker key. The keys on the bed are a different shape from those in Josh's pocket at the mortuary,' Dewar remarked.

'They could be the keys for the Trojan,' Anna suggested.

'If they're not, then what were they for? Donna's statement and Paul Simms' notes never make any mention of the origin of any of the recovered keys. Strange Donna never noticed them when she unpacked the washing.'

Anna was impressed with Dewar's powers of observation and told her so, commenting that it would be worth having the pictures of the keys enlarged to show to Williams and Donna. She checked her watch. 'So, do you reckon we're ready for the office meeting?'

Jessie didn't hesitate but stood up. 'You bet your sweet ass we are. Let's go for it.'

Chapter Fourteen

As there was still some time to spare before Langton was due to arrive, Anna decided to give the team a quick run-down on Lady Gloria Lynne. She emphasized that here was a powerful woman who got instant attention by merely lifting the phone and dialling the likes of chief constables and the Commissioner, so if the eyes of God were upon them then they needed to make sure that everything was done by the book and totally above board. As much as she didn't like politics mixing with policing, it was a fact of life.

As Langton entered the room, DC Ross was adding his contribution, that 'poli' in Latin meant 'many' and 'tics' were 'bloodsucking creatures'. Anna didn't object when everyone laughed loudly and Langton, having missed the joke, commented that he was glad to see the team in such good spirits. A few seconds later, the door opened and Mike Lewis walked in. Everyone looked round, not sure if the popular detective superintendent just happened to be accompanying Langton or if he was, in fact, to be his replacement.

'Well, aren't you going to welcome Mike Lewis, your new superintendent?' Langton asked. The team, many of whom had worked with Mike Lewis on previous murder investigations, all smiled and gave an approving round of applause. Anna was pleased, but wondered if Langton was aware that Mike had signed off the Reynolds case as suicide, even as Mike gave her a warm smile, saying it was good to see her. Special Agent Dewar stepped forward to be introduced, and Anna watched as

Mike smiled and said he looked forward to working with her. Mike then approached Barolli, shaking his hand firmly whilst patting him on the shoulder, and congratulated him on his promotion to DI. The strong bond of friendship between them was obvious to everyone in the room. It had been Mike, as DCI on the Henry Oates case, who had recommended Barolli for the Queen's Gallantry Medal, and Langton had also approved and countersigned the recommendation, the result of which would not be known until August. Greetings over with, Mike stood with Langton by the large plasma screen and addressed the officers.

'Good morning, it's nice to see so many familiar faces. Some of you may know I already have a personal interest in the Reynolds case.'

Members of the team looked at each other, wondering exactly what Mike Lewis meant.

'I signed off DI Simms' report as suicide. My decision at the time was based on what was put before me, and whether I was right, or wrong, will be borne out by this new investigation. If mistakes were made then we need to rectify them, so all I ask is that you carry out your duties with professionalism and integrity.'

Anna, as ever, was impressed with Mike Lewis's frankness and honesty. He had never been one to blame others for his mistakes. It was clear that Langton had fully briefed him on the current state of the investigation and had probably assigned him the case because of his 'personal interest'.

Anna asked Barbara to go over the timeline, calls and texts she had drawn up for Josh and Donna Reynolds, whereupon Barbara explained that she had compiled the timelines from statements and phone billing enquiries made during the initial investigation. She had where possible shown not only calls received but also those made. For ease of reference, and where appropriate, she said, she would refer to the two timelines together, starting from the morning of the 5 November 2012.

Barbara read aloud: 'November fifth, Donna left the flat in Bayswater at 7 a.m., where Josh was asleep in bed. Donna spent the morning at her mother's where along with her sister Aisa, they were preparing for the Lynne charity ball at the Savoy. At noon, Donna drove to the Savoy and checked in with Aisa just before 1 p.m. to set up for the ball. Barbara continued, stating that Josh Reynolds usually left his flat between 11 and 11.30 a.m. on working days, which were Monday to Saturday. Two calls to the Trojan's drinks suppliers were made from Josh's mobile at 11.40 a.m. and 11.57 a.m. The suppliers confirmed these calls. A call was made from his office phone to food suppliers at 12.10 p.m, so this would fit with his usual arrival time of midday, as given by Marcus Williams.'

Barbara went on: '1.10 p.m., Donna, as confirmed in her statement, rang Josh on his mobile to tell him that she would be staying the night at the Savoy and probably wouldn't be home before he left for work on the sixth. This was the only call made from Donna's mobile on the fifth and the next was on the sixth when she dialled 999. Between 3.30 and 4 p.m., Josh left the club and spoke briefly with Williams, stating he had to go out on business. Williams said Josh 'seemed upset'. At 4.15 p.m., Josh phoned the Savoy Hotel on his mobile. It was not known whom he spoke to on the reception desk but it had been assumed that he rang for Donna. The call lasted thirty seconds. Josh also made another call to the Savoy at 4.30 p.m., lasting just short of a minute.'

Mike Lewis asked if there were any other calls, texts or messages to Donna from Josh's mobile. Barbara replied that there weren't but that Josh also phoned the Savoy at 6.45 p.m., and the call lasted nearly two minutes, though again it was not known whom he spoke to. Jessie asked why the reception desk staff were never asked who the calls were put through to and Barbara said that they were but that incoming calls were not monitored so there was no way of knowing to which room or to whom the calls had been transferred. Anna recalled Donna saying in her original statement that she had her phone on silent when she was at the Savoy preparing in the afternoon and had left it in her room during the ball. Mike remarked that he thought it strange that Josh did not at least try and call Donna on her mobile or leave a voice message or send a text.

Barbara continued that at 7.10 p.m. Josh phoned Marcus Williams and told him he was not coming back to work as he had a stomach upset and felt sick. From this point on there were no other calls made from Josh's mobile.

Mike asked Anna what the pathologist's report said about time of death.

'Anywhere between four p.m. on the fifth to four a.m. on the sixth, but Reynolds was clearly alive at 7.10 p.m. as he phoned Williams,' Anna said.

'So an obvious question and one we need to find the answer to is where Reynolds was from when he was last physically seen alive by Williams to the time he was murdered in his flat,' Mike observed.

Barbara raised her hand and Mike nodded to her.

'I considered that when I was doing the timelines. I contacted Josh's mobile phone company this morning and asked for a cell site analysis on all his calls. It will take a day or two but should help to narrow down his movements through the call locations.'

'Good work, Barbara,' Mike said, and Joan now raised her hand.

'I hope I'm not being rude, and I may be wrong, but there is something that appears to have been overlooked,' she began nervously, as everyone turned to her as if to say, 'This had better be good.'

'Speak up, Joan, your input is always valued,' Langton said reassuringly.

'Cell site helps with movement and location but can also assist as to whether someone was on foot or in a car. I just wondered if we know whether or not Josh Reynolds owned a car?'

Everyone looked at each other, realizing that it was something they had all overlooked.

'That, Joan, is an excellent observation. Anyone have an answer?' Mike asked, looking round the room.

'There were no car keys recovered from his flat or personal possessions at the mortuary, however there was an Oyster travel card in his wallet,' Anna said.

'I'll check with London Transport for an Oyster usage history,' Joan offered.

'We can also ask Marcus Williams, and there's Curtis Bowman, the odd-job man at the Trojan. He said something about washing cars at the back of the club,' Anna said.

Mike moved on to ask about any CCTV and Barolli said that there was none found as of yet. Nothing at the Bayswater flat itself or the street outside, and nothing from the surrounding streets either.

Barolli sucked at the end of his Biro. 'We're now so many months on since last November that most of the hard drive storage systems have been reused, so we're not having much luck. We know the Savoy Hotel CCTV was seized and a copy taken by Tech Support but as yet it hasn't been examined as Donna had a confirmed alibi from her mother and sister for her movements that night.'

'But we don't know if Josh went there on the fifth, do we?' Langton said flatly and swallowed a yawn.

'I will get on to it and make sure a twenty-four-hour period is fully viewed. I know a team joker who will be just the man for the job,' Barolli said and Detective Dan Ross slid down his chair in mocking submission.

There was a slight pause before Mike moved on to the intelligence files on Josh and Donna. Barolli told him that there wasn't anything that stood out as such and that what little information they had obtained came from either Donna or Marcus Williams.

'Any family on Josh's side we can speak to?' Mike asked.

'His father John died in 2011 and his mother Esme in August 2012, and according to Donna's original statement there is no other family in the UK but possibly some in Jamaica,' Barolli replied.

'So when his father died I assume that what he had was left to the wife Esme, and in turn when she died it all went to Josh then passed to Donna when he died. Any info on what Esme's estate was worth?'

'I don't think that's ever been looked into,' Barolli said, somewhat embarrassed that he hadn't considered it before.

'I know you have all been very busy but let's make it a priority,' Mike suggested tactfully.

'Might have to tread carefully there – Lady Lynne's solicitors dealt with Josh's last will and testament,' Dewar informed Mike. He glanced towards her, as she had so far remained silent.

'Yes, DCS Langton mentioned she has friends in high places and that's the main reason I want this reinvestigation to be watertight.'

'Joan has been doing some background work on Lady Lynne and her daughters for me, which I'm sure will be of interest to us all,' Anna chimed in, and Mike asked Joan to tell everyone what she had discovered so far.

Joan, always nervous when the 'spotlight' was turned on her, flushed and clasped her notebook as she said that there was very little about Lady Lynne's personal life on the Internet and even less concerning her daughters Donna and Aisa. She added that it would seem Lady Lynne did not talk about her daughters in public, other than to say that they helped her in the running of the Lynne Foundation. Anna added that Gloria was clearly protective of her daughters and kept them out of the public eye due to her vast wealth and fear for their safety.

Joan nodded her head in agreement and continued that she had found an old *Country Life* magazine in which Gloria had been interviewed, five years ago, after winning a gold medal at the Chelsea Flower Show for her Caribbean tropical garden. The article, Joan explained, gave an insight into Gloria's background and her love of horticulture, her main interest being cultivating and improving the quality of her plants, along with their resistance to insects and diseases. Barbara, impatient as ever, whispered to Joan to get to the nitty-gritty. Joan paused, causing Anna to give Barbara a disapproving frown.

'The article said Gloria's father David Rediker was a Cambridge graduate in Botany, who in 1975 with his wife Mavis and ten-year-old daughter Gloria, went to work for the Jamaican Natural History Museum in Kingston. Both Gloria's parents died of cancer before she was twenty and she then married Xavier Alleyne, a banana-plantation owner. Hurricane Gilbert destroyed the plantation in 1988, and Xavier died of a heart attack brought on by the collapse of his business. They had two children, Donna and Aisa. In 1992, Gloria returned to the UK with her daughters and, in her own words, faced adversity head-on and forged a life for herself and her daughters, by setting up a florist shop in Weybridge. In 1997, she met Lord Henry Lynne when he went to her shop to buy flowers and a year later they were married. Together they set up the Lynne Foundation, a charitable organization that is one of the biggest in the country with a total financial endowment in excess of a billion pounds. Lord Lynne, who was suffering from bowel cancer, died aged eighty-six while on holiday in Egypt with Lady Lynne.'

'When was that, Joan?' Anna asked.

'2006.'

'So Gloria must have been about thirty-three and Henry seventy-eight when they married,' Anna remarked.

'How gross,' Barbara commented.

'Each to their own, Barbara, we're both getting on in life and still single,' Joan replied.

'Yes, but not everyone who gets close to me pops their clogs, do they!'

Mike gave Barbara a cold look to shut her up. 'There's not much you can do once cancer has a strong hold. My wife and I were blessed that her chemotherapy treatment worked,' he said, bringing to an end any further remarks about Gloria or Henry Lynne's age. 'Anything more you can tell us about Donna?'

Joan shook her head and Mike asked Anna to go over the scene reconstruction and forensics.

Anna took them through Dewar's observations about the scene, then added that Pete Jenkins was working on the blood distribution and that the Enfield revolver might be a family heirloom. Mike pointed out that this was another reason to try to trace other remaining members of Josh's family and that Marcus Williams should be asked about the gun.

There was another pause, before Mike decided that he wanted Barolli and Agent Dewar to do the house-to-house in the morning and Anna to re-interview Williams at the Trojan and put some pressure on him. Joan looked dejected at this, and Barbara spoke up to say that DCI Travis had asked her and Joan to do the house-to-house. Mike was quick to point out that their overall knowledge of the case, from uploading the computer with everyone's notes and information and the timelines, was very important and he needed her and Joan in the office. He then asked DCS Langton if there was anything he'd like to add.

Langton pulled at his loose tie knot, then straightened and tightened it before standing up to address the team.

'If Josh Reynolds was murdered, then the Met as a whole has failed him and his family and serious questions will rightly be asked by the press and public. The top brass will be looking for scapegoats. Mistakes may have been made, however your job is not to cover up but to rectify any mistakes through a competent investigation, compiling the evidence and presenting it to the Crown Prosecution Service.'

Langton then said that on that note he wished them all the best but now had to return to Scotland Yard for an urgent meeting on other matters. Anna could not rid herself of a growing suspicion that he was hiding something, and wondered if there was more behind his trip to the States than working at Quantico.

An hour later, Mike Lewis, Barolli, Jessie and Anna gathered in Anna's office. Mike told them that although it was clear Donna

Reynolds had to be re-interviewed, they would have to choose the time and the place wisely.

'Inviting Donna to attend the station to make a further statement would be the most formal route,' Anna suggested.

'Why not just arrest Donna on her way to work or at the Lynne Foundation office?' Dewar asked.

'Lady Lynne would arrange a top-notch solicitor who would request disclosure of the evidence against Donna. On what we have so far, he would probably laugh and advise Donna that she's not obliged to make a further statement or answer any questions,' Mike pointed out.

'At the moment, Pete Jenkins' results on the blood distribution are crucial to the investigation. If he concurs with Dewar that the scene was staged to look like suicide then we have evidence that Josh Reynolds was murdered,' Anna said.

'And Donna is the prime suspect,' Dewar added.

'That may be so,' Mike said, 'but the case against her is still weak. Clearly, her being at the Savoy all night means that if she was involved, she either hired or colluded with someone to kill Josh.'

'Sounds like we need to find some hard evidence against Donna then,' Barolli said.

'Press on with the house-to-house and other enquiries I raised at the meeting. Also, go through every piece of evidence again, look for anything that suggests she is lying and build up a case against her.'

'Then we can arrest Donna and confront her in a formal interview?' Dewar asked, chomping at the bit.

'Yes,' Mike said.

Dewar rubbed her hands together in anticipation. 'What about Donna's sister Aisa.'

'You want to arrest her as well?' Anna asked, baffled.

Dewar laughed. 'No, Anna. I mean what about speaking with her now, as there was no statement taken from her in the original inquiry.'

'We don't know how close the two sisters are and it could cause more problems where Lady Lynne is concerned; however,

DCI Travis will decide if and when she feels it is necessary and appropriate to speak with Aisa,' Mike replied, and Dewar agreed. 'Right, let's get to it, write up your reports and review all the evidence so far, so you're well prepared for tomorrow.'

'Would you like to help me draw up a questionnaire for the house-to-house tomorrow, Special Agent Dewar?' Barolli asked in a deliberately overpolite manner.

'That would be spiffing, thank you, Detective Barolli,' Dewar said, and everyone laughed as Dewar and Barolli left the room.

Mike opened his briefcase and took out a blue A4 folder that was filled with papers.

'I forgot to give you this earlier,' he said to Anna. 'It's the syllabus and pre-read papers for the FBI course.'

'I feel like I've robbed you of a golden opportunity,' Anna said ruefully.

'There's always next year and you deserve my place better than anyone else I know. You'll be at the top of the ladder long before me.'

'I'm only where I am now because I've had you and Langton to guide me.' Anna looked at her old boss with affection.

'It seems strange taking up Langton's role and overseeing the old team,' Mike admitted. 'Quite daunting really. Am I doing all right so far?'

Anna gave him a warm smile. 'Yes, sir, you are doing just fine.'

Chapter Fifteen

W hen Anna arrived at the office the following morning, Dewar and Barolli had already left to go and do the house-to-house enquiries in Bayswater.

'I checked out Josh's Oyster-card usage – trips here and there on the Underground and bus but nothing on the fifth of November,' Joan said.

'I rang Marcus Williams yesterday and arranged to see him at the Trojan today,' Anna told her. 'I asked about Josh owning a car and Williams said he cycled to work and only used public transport if the weather was atrocious.'

'Interesting, there's never been any mention of a bike before,' Joan observed.

'And there's no bike in the scene photographs taken at Josh's flat.'

'Could it still be at the Trojan? Williams said Josh left on foot the last time he saw him.'

'I'll ask Williams about it later,' Anna assured her, looking up as a uniform officer carrying two large security-sealed folder bags entered.

'Bank courier just delivered these for DI Barolli,' he said, gazing around the room. Anna introduced herself as the team DCI and the officer handed the bags to her.

Settling herself at Barbara's desk, she proceeded to cut the ratchet tags off the bags and opened them. Inside one were two folders, marked JOSHUA REYNOLDS – TROJAN ACCOUNT

STATEMENTS and JOSHUA REYNOLDS – PERSONAL ACCOUNT STATEMENTS. The second bag contained bank statements for Donna Reynolds, Marcus Williams and the Trojan club. Anna decided to concentrate on the six-month period prior to Josh's death. She opened Josh's personal account folder, noting that his account was eight thousand pounds in credit at the time he of his death and that there appeared to be nothing out of the ordinary.

As Barbara came into the room, Anna started to pick up the folders to move to another desk but the sergeant said it was fine and pulled up a spare chair so that she could see everything as well.

'On the twelfth of September, there was a debit-card payment for a hundred and thirty-three pounds at the BP service station Park Lane,' Anna said, making a note then turning to Joan. 'Look up Donna's Mini Cooper, I need the exact model and engine size.'

Joan typed the registration DON4L into the computer and discovered it was a manual 1.6 Sport. Anna, sensing they were on to something, entered the Mini's details into the search engine on Barbara's computer. 'Is it a petrol or diesel?'

'Petrol,' Joan replied.

'Thinking of buying one?' Barbara asked.

'Have you got a calculator?' Anna asked and Barbara got one out of her top drawer.

'Put in fifty times one point three eight. What's that come—'

'Sixty-nine,' Joan answered before Barbara had even hit the equal button on the calculator. They both looked at Joan, Anna impressed and Barbara surprised.

'I love the numbers game on *Countdown*.' Joan shrugged.

'If Josh was using Donna's Mini, which costs about seventy quid to fill with petrol, why is he spending a hundred and thirty-three at the garage?' Anna wondered.

'He could have got some groceries as well if it was one of those express shopping garages,' Barbara said.

'Good point,' Anna agreed.

'In that case,' said Joan, 'I'll phone them and ask exactly what they sell there.'

Turning back to the folder, Anna saw that on 5 October, at the same service station, there was a transaction for £110.

'That place is on a direct route that Josh could use to travel to the Trojan,' Barbara said as she checked the exact location of the service station.

Anna went further back through the records. 'Looking at this, Josh and Donna's average weekly spend for food was sixty to seventy pounds and nearly always in the Tesco supermarket near the Bayswater flat.'

Barbara leaned over Anna's shoulder to look at the figures, which Anna found irritating, but forced herself to say nothing, realizing Barbara was just being inquisitive.

The sergeant suddenly tapped on the statement. 'Look there, just after the debit of one hundred and ten pounds. October eighth, a payment to National Car Parking of nine hundred and twenty-eight pounds!' she exclaimed.

Anna looked closer and realized that in concentrating on food and petrol she had missed the National Car Parking debit. 'It could be Josh paid for a NCP parking account for Donna's Mini when she went to work at the Lynne Foundation office in Mayfair,' Joan suggested.

Anna shook her head. 'The Foundation would probably have its own parking, or pay for it through the company accounts.'

Further down the statement there was a payment of £308 to F1 Services on 10 October, so to get Barbara away from her shoulder, Anna asked her to phone the NCP head office and get full details of the account and car park to which Josh's payment referred, and to find out who F1 Services were.

Meanwhile, Joan had ascertained that the Park Lane BP did have a mini-market but sold a limited selection of everyday products like milk and bread.

Turning the page, Anna was excited to find a debit dated 5 November that read Tesco Extra UPT, Beverley Way, for £125. As Barbara was on the phone, Anna showed this to

Joan to see if she knew what the initials meant, but she
didn't.

Barbara put down the receiver. 'NCP can't give us an answer
right away so I've given them all the details and they'll get back
to us asap.'

Anna thanked her but she hadn't finished.

'Unattended Payment Terminal, UPT for short – it's when
you pay at the pump by debit or credit card for your petrol. It
baffled me on one of my statements so I checked it with my
bank,' Barbara said smugly.

'Tesco Extra, Beverley Way, is in New Malden on the A3 ,'
Joan observed, turning to her colleagues.

'Donna had the Mini that day. Josh had to be filling up with
petrol and either has a car we don't know about or borrowed
one,' Anna said.

'If Donna was at the Savoy, could Josh have borrowed her car
in the afternoon without her knowing?' Barbara asked.

'Possible but unlikely – a Mini takes roughly sixty to seventy
pounds to fill, not a hundred and twenty-five.'

'So whatever car he was using must be big, like an SUV
maybe,' Barbara suggested.

'I'll check Josh Reynolds' name on the motor-insurance
database,' said Joan. 'If he was insured to drive they'll be able to
give us a make and model of the car.'

'Thanks, Joan. Run Donna Reynolds and Marcus Williams as
well,' Anna added.

For a short while the room fell silent except for the tapping
of fingertips on keyboards.

'Right,' said Joan. 'Nothing recorded for Josh, and Donna is
just insured for the Mini with Josh listed as a named driver.
Insurance runs out in September this year. Williams is insured
for a Bentley Continental GT as from January this year.'

'So no fresh leads there,' muttered Anna, frowning as she
returned to the private account statements to see if there was
anything she had missed. She thought it most strange that neither Donna nor Marcus Williams seemed to know anything

about Josh having or borrowing a car, and realized this made it all the more important to find out exactly where Josh had gone on the afternoon of the fifth.

By mid-morning, Barolli and Dewar had completed their enquiries at the Bayswater flats. They had spoken with all the residents except the occupants of flat three, who were, according to a neighbour, away on a cruise holiday and not due back for two weeks. No one they spoke to had seen or heard anything unusual and only ever recalled seeing the Josh and Donna in a blue Mini convertible. Some added Josh had a silver racing-style bicycle that he often used.

'Well, that wasn't very productive, was it?' Dewar remarked nonchalantly as they stood inside the communal area of the flats.

'I'll have to come back to speak with the cruise couple in flat three,' Barolli said as they went to leave and return to the office.

'Hold the door there, me old china!' a male voice shouted.

'Is he talking to us?' Dewar asked, confused.

'He means me – china plate means mate,' Barolli explained as he looked up to see a white man in his mid-forties pacing towards him, carrying a ladder in one hand and a toolbox in the other. He had short black hair, which was receding, a pierced left ear with a small loop earring and was wearing blue jeans, T-shirt and black V-neck jumper with a handyman's toolbelt buckled around his waist.

'Excuse me, darlin',' he said as he squeezed past Dewar and then Barolli, nearly hitting him with the ladder. 'Sorry 'bout that, getting meself in a right two and eight with me crown jewels here.' He gave a broad apologetic smile.

Barolli called to Dewar to wait, as he wanted to have a word with the man.

'I can't understand anything he's saying,' Dewar complained.

'It's Cockney rhyming slang, crown jewels means tools. He might be the caretaker who looks after the building, so a quick chat might be worthwhile.'

'If you say so,' Dewar said unenthusiastically.

'Excuse me, Mr . . .?' Barolli asked.

'Gorman, Ken Gorman,' the workman replied.

'Born within the sound of Bow bells, were you?' Barolli asked, wanting to appear casual and knowing this to be the origins of a true London Cockney.

'Me old man was, south London boy me, Bermondsey born and bred. You're cozzers, ain't ya?' Ken asked, putting down his ladder and toolbox.

Barolli produced his warrant card, introduced himself and asked Ken if he was the caretaker for the flats.

'Nah, work for the company that has the maintenance contract, so I looks after other buildings as well as this one.'

'What sort of jobs do you do?' Barolli asked with intentional interest.

'Communal plumbing, electrics, water supply, them sorts of things. Anything that goes wrong inside a privately owned flat is the responsibility of the owner unless the premises are leased, cos me company is also under contract wif the all the landlord's agents for this building.'

Barolli asked if he knew Mr and Mrs Reynolds who used to live in flat two.

'The geezer who topped himself?' Ken asked and Barolli nodded, 'Yeah, nice bloke and so was his missus, she made a great mug of Rosy.'

'So you'd been in their flat for a cup of tea,' Barolli remarked for Dewar's benefit. 'Did you do any work for them?' He noted a look of unease on Ken's face. 'I'm not worried if you were doing a bit on the side for cash in hand,' he said reassuringly.

'Definitely off the record?' Ken asked, looking around to make sure no one else was listening. Barolli insisted that there was nothing for him to worry about.

'I did some odd jobs for them – leaky tap, blown fuse, fixed some kitchen cupboards, that kind of thing. Terrible, him topping himself like that. I mean, blowing your own brains out – what a mess it left on the carpet and sofa. Not to mention his poor missus,' Ken said, shaking his shoulders in abhorrence.

'You saw his body then?' Dewar asked, suddenly taking an interest in the conversation.

'Nah, the letting agents called me to clean up so I binned the sofa and carpet then laid a new wooden floor. Rest of the place looked okay cos it had just had a fresh lick of paint before he shot himself,' Ken explained.

'Did you do the painting?' Barolli asked.

'No. Some black geezer did and to be honest it was a bit of a slap in the face, but what really pissed me off was when he tried touting for business with the other residents.'

'What do you mean?' Dewar asked.

'Knocking on doors, asking if they wanted any odd jobs done. Don't think he was even qualified like me, I'm registered to do gas, plumbing and electrics, it's all about health and safety, you know what I mean, like,' Ken said, producing his official 'Gas Safe' and registered electrician's cards. 'I've got me plumber's card here somewhere,' he continued as he fumbled in his pockets.

'Do you know his name?' Dewar pressed.

'Nope, never met him, must have left me plumber's card in the van.'

'So who told you about him touting?' Barolli asked.

'Old couple at number three, Mr and Mrs Braun, they's on a Saga cruise at the moment. Anyways, he knocked on their door but bless 'em they told him I does the jobs round here and said they'd report him so he cleared off.'

'Do you know if he came back?' Dewar asked.

'Mrs Braun told me they'd seen him going into Mr and Mrs Reynolds' a couple of times but, as far as I know, he didn't bovver any of the other residents. I spoke with Mr Reynolds, he apologized and said he was just a family friend doing some painting work for him.'

'Do you know when Mrs Braun last saw him or when he was doing the painting in the Reynolds flat?' Dewar asked.

'It was around late October time last year,' Ken said.

'Did they describe him to you?' Barolli asked.

'Mrs Braun said he was tall, black, probably in his fifties, and wore a Rasta hat and blue overalls,' Ken told them, picking up his toolbox and ladder once more, clearly keen to get on.

Back in the car, Dewar wondered if the black man that Ken Gorman was referring to might be Curtis Bowman, the odd-job man at the Trojan. Barolli agreed that it was a strong possibility.

'There's something not right here,' Dewar continued, reaching for her seatbelt. 'Josh told Ken that the decorator was a family friend. Curtis was friends with both Josh and Donna, so if it was Curtis doing the decorating why hasn't he or Donna said anything about it?'

'What are you thinking?' Barolli asked, turning the ignition key.

'I'm thinking decorating the flat allows you to become familiar with the layout.'

'You mean Curtis could have seen the safe, wanted the contents and then murdered Josh?'

'Yes, or . . . he may have been allowed to keep any money in the safe as a payment for killing Josh . . .'

'Then making it look like a robbery gone wrong would have been a better option,' Barolli said, as he checked his mirrors and pulled out to drive them back to the station.

'Okay, okay, let me think this through. Josh's perceived suicide got the attendance of an inexperienced DI, plus a CSM and pathologist, both of whom, as chance would have it, are incompetent.'

'Inexperienced, incompetent or whatever, why stage the scene?' Barolli asked, unable to understand Dewar's thought process.

She licked her lips. 'Because it had to look like a suicide so that it wouldn't get the full works. The killer or killers knew that. And the insurance payout becoming invalid so not going to the loving wife is even better. It only helps her cause – you understand what I'm saying? If it was an obvious murder you'd get the likes of Langton overseeing the case and a full forensics.'

Barolli sucked in his breath, still uncertain.

'I know I'm right, I'm certain, and that caretaker's description fits Bowman. Reynolds knew him, would open the door to him, maybe he went round to get payment for painting and decorating, safe open stashed with money . . . bang!'

'Okay, it's possible. If Donna and Curtis Bowman were in it together then we need to call Anna before she gets to the Trojan,' Barolli said. He didn't want to curb Dewar's enthusiasm but he couldn't believe how quickly her theories and suspicion changed from one suspect to another.

Chapter Sixteen

Anna was already en route to the Trojan when she received Dewar's anxious phone call about the conversation with Ken Gorman. Barolli, who was driving, had put his mobile on speakerphone so they could both listen.

'Your point about the scene being made to look like a suicide because it would attract less police attention is valid, Jessie,' Anna said, 'but it's still all conjecture at the moment and we need some strong factual evidence.'

'It has to be Curtis Bowman who did the decorating: he fits the description Mr Gorman gave,' Dewar insisted.

'Did Gorman actually see him?' Anna asked.

'No, but Mr and Mrs Braun at number three did and they told Gorman.'

'They're away on holiday for another two weeks,' Barolli chipped in and Dewar frowned at him.

'Donna must have known Bowman was doing the decorating yet she never mentioned it to Simms or us,' she continued. 'The only reasonable explanation is she hired him to kill Josh.'

'At the moment, all we can do is either wait for the Brauns to return from holiday or ask Curtis Bowman outright if he was the decorator,' Anna told them.

'Your being naïve, he'll deny it and tell Donna then you've played your hand and blown it. I think we should arrest Bowman, offer him a plea bargain as an incentive and see if he will give Donna up,' Dewar said anxiously.

Anna could hear the frustration in her voice, but felt obliged to explain that in the UK legal system anything that could be interpreted as coercion or a threat to intimidate a suspect could end up with the whole case being thrown out of court.

'Leave Curtis Bowman to me – and don't worry, I will be discreet,' Anna told Dewar.

'Well, don't say I didn't warn you,' Dewar replied.

Feeling that the agent was becoming rather petulant, Anna asked to speak with Barolli, who pulled over to the side of the road and switched off the speakerphone, taking the mobile Dewar begrudgingly passed him. Anna told him that if Donna and Curtis were involved in Josh's death then Dewar was right to be concerned about what they might do if they suspected police were on to them.

'I want more investigation done on Donna and Josh's relationship,' Anna said. 'He's no family in the UK that we know of and Marcus Williams is not totally reliable. Aisa could, if approached in the right way, shed more light on the relationship.'

'We could do that if you like,' Barolli suggested.

'Okay, go to the Lynne Foundation reception, and if Donna's not there go and speak with Aisa,' Anna said. 'Approach the visit from the angle that you're merely confirming everyone's alibis for the night of Josh's death then casually work the conversation round to Donna and Josh's relationship.'

Barolli promised he would ring her if there were any problems before switching back to speakerphone as Anna gave them a run-down on Josh's personal bank account statements and the costly petrol receipts, suggesting they read through the bank documents when they got back to the office.

'I'm sorry for implying you were naïve and I'll accept a meeting with Aisa as consolation for not arresting Bowman!' Dewar shouted and Barolli explained that she had been leaning up against him and listening in on their conversation.

'Just as well I didn't say anything derogatory then,' Anna remarked dryly.

Dewar laughed and shouted back, 'You're beginning to warm to me!'

'Slowly but surely,' Anna replied, and they all laughed. 'Just please, tread lightly with Aisa, we don't want to provoke Gloria. I'll catch up with you back at the station,' Anna said and then hung up.

Barolli remarked that it was very interesting about the petrol receipts. 'A car that takes over a hundred and thirty quid to fill must have at least a ninety-litre tank. My Ford holds about seventy, so something—'

Dewar interrupted him. 'What's that in gallons?'

He pulled out once again, heading towards the station. 'Seventy litres is just over fifteen gallons.'

'That's about the same as my Ford gas tank holds.'

'You got a Mondeo as well then? Reliable and cheap to run, aren't they,' Barolli quipped, stopping for a red light.

'No, a 67 Ford Mustang Convertible,' she replied nonchalantly, making Barolli feel slightly embarrassed at his assumption.

'Is it the GTA?' he asked with an air of authority, which aroused Dewar's interest.

'As it happens, yes, with a V8 engine.'

'They're a bit of a rare beast. I was told that Wilson Pickett's song "Mustang Sally" was inspired by the GTA.'

The light turned green and Barolli pressed the accelerator.

'Close, it was actually the 65 Fastback he wrote about. You like classic cars?'

'Absolutely love them. I go to the festivals when I can. Brooklands in Surrey has an American classics day in September. I can take you, if you'd like,' he said, glancing towards Dewar.

'I'd love to but I'll be back at Quantico by then,' Dewar said, genuinely grateful. 'The Mustang belonged to my dad. He smashed it up when I was a kid and it just got left under a tarpaulin. Years later, when he opened his own repair shop, we rebuilt it together.'

'Now that's something to be proud of,' Barolli said admiringly.

'I am, but sadly Dad died before we finished it, so I completed it myself. I don't drive it all the time but when I do it feels like he's sitting there beside me and keeping me safe along the way.'

Visibly moved by the fond memory of her father, suddenly she reached into her bag to open a small leather photo wallet and showed Barolli a photograph of herself sitting proudly on the bonnet of the car with a beaming smile on her face.

Barolli glanced over. 'Two American beauties,' he said, focusing again on the road, but he could see that Dewar was flattered – she grinned and looked away, but she couldn't hide the red glow that came over her face.

As Anna parked in the rear mews she could see Curtis Bowman washing a blue Bentley Convertible.

'That's a nice car, Curtis. Must cost you a fortune in petrol though,' she remarked, tongue in cheek, as she walked round the vehicle in mock admiration.

'Oh, it's not mine; it belongs to Mr Williams,' Curtis replied, taken aback at the very idea. Anna smiled at him and the penny dropped.

'You was joking with me, weren't ya, officer,' he said, wagging his finger at Anna who smiled.

'Mr Williams will have you decorating his house for him next,' Anna said, wondering if Curtis would take the bait.

'No way. I don't have time for that as well as all the stuff I have to do here.'

'I'm surprised you've never been asked, as the handyman work you do in the club is so good. I'd have thought you'd be a first-choice decorator for anyone who knew you,' Anna remarked disingenuously.

'Mr Reynolds, God rest him, asked me once but I had to say no.' Curtis shook his head.

'What, to decorate his flat?' Anna asked.

'No, his mother's place after she died. Said he wanted to do it up and sell it. He was so down when she passed.'

'Pity, you'd have done a good job,' Anna said.

'My wife wouldn't stand for it; I hardly sees me kids as it is. I'm in bed when they get up for school and here when they get back.'

Anna couldn't be a hundred per cent sure that Curtis was telling the truth, but there was something about him that put her at ease. His reaction, demeanour and straightforward approach made her sense that he was an honest and forthright man who simply got on with his life and did as he was asked to the best of his ability, which made her feel it was safe to ask him questions that were a bit more probing.

Curtis began to wipe the Bentley down with his shammy leather.

'You said Mr Reynolds asked you about decorating his mum's place – do you know if he found anyone to do the job?' she wondered.

'Well, when I asked him, he said he had.'

'Did he say who it was?'

'I can't recall exactly – let me think back.' Curtis paused for thought and held his chin. 'That's it, bloke called Sam, Sammy or Samuel, something like that.'

Again, Anna didn't get the impression that Curtis was lying as she moved on to ask him if he knew whether the decorator had ever done any work at the flat Josh shared with Donna. Curtis said he didn't and Anna casually asked him if he used to wash Mr Reynolds' car for him as well.

'He didn't have a car, sometimes used Donna's.'

'What about a bike?'

'Yes, he used to leave it inside the back door.'

'Did he use it the day you last saw him?' Anna pressed.

'No. I remember he hadn't been on his bike for a while and I asked if he'd sold it and he said it was at home with a broken pedal. I said I'd fix it but he never brought it in to me.'

'Well, thanks for your time, Curtis,' Anna said, and started to walk off.

'There's something I remembered about the last day I saw Mr Reynolds.'

Anna stopped instantly, eager to hear what Curtis had to say.

'You asking about the decorator man just brought it back. The same day Mr Reynolds died, there were a man walking through the club. I ask him what he was doing and he said he come to see Josh and he was his uncle.'

'Did he give his name?' Anna asked, but Curtis shook his head.

'Can you describe him?' Anna asked, trying to hide her excitement.

'About my height, black, fifty-five maybe, with a Rasta hat and dreadlocks. The thing was, he was wearing the same type blue overalls as me, but his had a lot of paint splashes on.'

'Had you seen him here before?'

'No, just the once and never since. I told him where Mr Reynolds' office was and he went up the staff stairs.'

'Can you recall what time this was?'

'Afternoon sometime, I think, just before he left the club though. I knows that 'cause I saw him speaking to Mr Williams and then walk off.'

Anna thanked Curtis for his help. She didn't think he was trying to pull the wool over her eyes and felt increasingly certain that Dewar was totally wrong about any involvement the handyman might have had in Josh Reynolds' death. The hard part would be getting Dewar to accept the fact.

Marcus Williams, smartly dressed in a blue linen suit and matching shirt, was in his office working at his desk when Anna walked in, and immediately invited her to take a seat opposite him.

'So what can I do for you this time, DCI Travis?' Williams asked.

'Did Josh ever use your Bentley?' Anna asked without preamble, taking her notebook out of her bag.

'No, I've only had it a couple of months. I had a Saab Convertible before that. He used it occasionally to pop out to the wholesalers or—'

'What about the day he died?' Anna interrupted, getting to the point.

'Definitely not, it was off the road then being re-sprayed after some little shit keyed it all along one side.'

'Did he have access to any other cars?'

'Only Donna's Mini, as far as I know; beyond that it was like I told you on the phone, public transport or his bike.'

'Curtis Bowman said he stopped using his bike in October.'

'That could be the case. I never asked or kept an eye on how he got to and from work,' Williams said, leaning back in his chair.

'Did Josh have any other family left after his mother died?'

'His Aunt Marisha or Marsi as everyone called her. She was Esme's sister and lived in Brixton but the family fell out with her donkey's years ago. Esme had a brother and maybe other sisters in Jamaica but I'm not sure.'

'Do you know Marisha's surname or where she lives?' Anna asked.

'No. I went to see her with Josh a few times, when we were about fourteen.' Williams grinned. 'I remember she was a large woman who had a big smile and really infectious laugh. She used to make a mean fish stew.'

'What about Esme or Josh's funerals – didn't any family attend?'

'At Esme's, yes. Josh introduced me to her brother who had flown over from Jamaica. I think his name was Samuel but I only spoke with him briefly and he wasn't at Josh's funeral. Actually, come to think of it, Josh did say that he thought his Aunt Marisha would have made the effort to attend her sister's funeral,' Williams said.

'Did his Uncle Samuel ever visit him here?'

'Could have done but I never saw him.'

'Do you know anything about Josh having either his own flat in Bayswater or his mother's flat redecorated before he died?' Anna asked.

'He said he was going to do his mum's place up and either lease or sell it but I don't know if he did or about redecorating his place.'

Deciding to gauge Williams' reaction to the mention of financial matters at the club, Anna asked if he or Josh had ever got involved with loan sharks.

Williams was clearly offended as he gave a firm, 'NO.'

'So, no problems paying off legitimate loans, tax returns—'

Williams jumped up from his seat, went over to a corner cupboard and withdrew two large cardboard boxes. He thumped them down on his desk, declaring that all the Trojan's renovation invoices, business receipts and accounts for the last two tax years were inside. Anna thought his reaction was overly defensive.

'Everything you need is in there, including a dealer's receipt for the Bentley as it's my company car, so feel free to take the boxes with you,' Williams said, flippantly pulling out his mobile phone to check a text.

Anna, irritated by his attitude, stood up, got her handcuffs out of her handbag and held them up to Williams as she spoke.

'Personally, I don't give a toss if you're fiddling the books, but this is your last chance to answer my question or I will arrest you for fraud and let the tax man loose on you,' Anna said firmly, making it clear she was in no mood to be messed about.

Williams let out a sigh of defeat. 'Okay, okay, we paid cash for the renovation work. The invoices were drawn up by the builder to look like different companies had done some parts of the work and ...'

'I'm here because Josh Reynolds may have been murdered and your lying to me doesn't help you or my investigation.' Anna set the cuffs down on the table in front of her and reached into her handbag, removed her Dictaphone and placed it on the table next to her handcuffs. 'You're going to tell me the truth and I'm going to record the rest of this conversation, right?'

Williams, clearly worried, nodded as she switched on the tape.

Anna had been growing more and more convinced Williams was hiding something else, and it occurred to her that there might be something to Delon Taylor's allegation after all. She looked Williams straight in the eyes and he turned away.

'Look at me, Mr Williams,' Anna said, leaning further forward, and he glanced at her briefly. 'Delon Taylor was telling the truth about you making money out of illegal sexual activities, wasn't he?' He said nothing in reply, making her increasingly sure she was on to something. She glanced again at her notes from the Delon Taylor interview. 'So, if Taylor was telling the truth about the illegal sex then he also told Josh about it. Josh found out and confronted you.'

Williams leaned on his desk with his hands covering his face, his breathing growing erratic. Anna, sensing he was becoming upset, changed tack, convinced an aggressive stance was not the way forward now she was so close to the breakthrough. 'The truth, Marcus, that's all I want. You owe it to Josh.'

Williams looked up at her as he took a deep breath, and then in an unsteady voice he confessed that it was true that Taylor told Josh about the sex-for-money scam, but Taylor was stealing money.

'Josh spoke with some of the girls and then confronted me. We'd been friends so long Josh would know if I lied so I admitted it.'

'Why risk everything and do it in the first place?' Anna wondered, shaking her head.

'Gambling debts,' he replied succinctly.

'When did he confront you?'

'In here on Halloween night last year. It was surreal as I was dressed as Count Dracula and Josh as Van Helsing, the Count's nemesis.'

'So that was it – he just accepted your apology, forgave you and let you keep your ill-gotten gains?' Anna remarked dismissively. Again, Williams leaned on the desk and put his hands to his face, now turning his head from side to side. Anna knew his own overwhelming guilt was about to break him

'I gave him fifty grand in cash and said to use it to pay off the final renovation.'

'When did you give him the money?'

'Two days before he died.' Williams looked at Anna, as if pleading for sympathy.

'What did Josh do with the fifty thousand?'

'Took it home with him in a cash bag and put it in his own safe. We never kept large sums on the premises.'

'Did you still have gambling debts at the time?' she demanded.

'Yes, but only ten grand. It's paid now.'

'So you had a motive to kill him. Get the money back to pay off your debts.'

'Then I wouldn't be telling you this now, would I?' he appealed in his own defence.

'You must have considered that if the police didn't find the money in the safe then Josh may have been murdered for it?' Anna asked firmly.

'I didn't know what to think – I'd just lost my best friend.'

Anna asked Williams if he knew where Josh's mother Esme had lived. He said it was in Notting Hill, wrote down the address on a piece of paper and handed it to Anna: flat two, Brandon Walk on the Lancaster West Estate, which Anna estimated was probably no more than a mile from Josh's Bayswater address.

'Why did Donna come to see you here last Thursday evening?'

'She said that you and that American FBI agent had been to see her at her mother's house and virtually accused her of murdering Josh,' Williams replied.

'So what did she want from you?'

'To know more about what Delon Taylor said and if it was true. I had to tell her it was all lies.'

'Well, we both know differently now, don't we.' Anna raised her eyebrows. 'Anything else she wanted to know?'

Williams went on to say that Donna had asked him if he knew what Josh kept in the safe at the flat. He had told her he didn't know and Donna had then asked him if Josh was having an affair.

'Was he?' Anna asked.

'I did sort of suspect something was going on just after his mum died. I asked him but he said it was only a bit of fun and he was going to end it anyway.

'Do you think it was one of the girls working here?'

'No way, and besides, they're not his type,' Williams replied instantly. 'Donna can be a bit of a rich bitch but she's classy, and kept him on a tight leash, so I reckoned it was just what he said – a bit of fun, nothing serious and already over by the time I'd mentioned it.'

Anna suddenly remembered her heated exchange with Dewar about the surveillance unit tailing Donna and losing her on an estate in Notting Hill. She unfolded the piece of paper with Esme's address on it and saw it was indeed the same place; she could have kicked herself for not reading the full location on the surveillance report. She abruptly asked Williams what happened to Josh's Trojan keys after he died, and learned that Josh had left them on the office desk on the day Williams last saw him. Anna grabbed her mobile, excused herself and went over to a corner of the room and discreetly rang Joan.

'Where was the estate they lost Donna?' Anna asked anxiously.

'Lancaster West, Notting Hill.'

Anna ended the call and then picked up her handcuffs.

'Marcus Williams, I am arresting you on suspicion of the murder of Joshua Reynolds and attempting to pervert the course of justice,' she told him, as she picked up her Dictaphone and turned it off.

'I didn't kill him. I swear before God, I didn't,' he protested, all trace of his earlier attitude long gone.

'You'd better get yourself a solicitor,' Anna said, leading him out of the office.

Chapter Seventeen

Barolli and Dewar finally found an empty parking bay at the Berkeley Square end of Mount Street. On the way over from Bayswater, Dewar had made a fictitious business call to the Lynne Foundation offices, asking to speak with Donna Lynne, only to be informed that she had been off sick since last Friday and it was not known when she would be returning to work.

As they walked down Mount Street with its array of high-end establishments selling couture fashion, jewellery, art, antiques and even shotguns, Dewar kept stopping to window-shop. Barolli indulged her by stopping as well.

'Some of the country's finest fashion and shoe shops are in this road. Very pricey though,' he told her.

'I could never work on this street,' Dewar remarked matter-of-factly.

'Temptation?' Barolli enquired.

'Yeah, I'd never be in the office. Marc Jacobs, Chanel, Lanvin – it's every woman's dream and even a gun shop for the American tourist,' Dewar replied as she paused to stare at the Louboutin display.

'Come on.' Barolli took hold of her arm and playfully dragged her away. 'The Lynne Foundation is over the road,' he said, as he pointed to a nineteenth-century Renaissance-style building and Dewar stopped so abruptly he almost bumped into her.

She stared across at the impressive red-brick four-storey

building, with its ornate pink terracotta façade, floral motifs and statue of a head above the front entrance.

'Wow! Is that a bust of Henry Lynne above the door?' she asked, causing Paul to laugh.

'That statue is actually part of the building, which is well over a hundred years old,' he said, unable to contain his smile.

'Then it could be Henry Lynne,' she remarked glibly with a grin.

Barolli showed the guard his warrant card and informed him that he had come to see Aisa Lynne, who was expecting him. The guard, instantly co-operative, said that Aisa was in her office on the fourth floor, and that the lift was down the corridor.

Dewar followed Barolli to the old cage-style lift with its metal scissor-gate entrance and exposed mechanics revealing an antiquated cable system.

'I'm not getting in that,' she said, visibly concerned.

'It looks perfectly safe to me,' Barolli told her as he pulled the gate and it opened with a loud rattle. 'After you.' He gave a bow and wave of his arm whilst politely holding the lift gate open for her.

'I'm taking the stairs.'

Barolli got into the lift then let go of the gate, which sprang closed with a loud crash. He pressed the button for the fourth floor. The cables creaked and the lift suddenly jolted and took off like a spring-loaded jack-in-the-box.

'Bloody hell!' Barolli shouted, as Dewar laughed.

Barolli reached the top floor in seconds and arrived at a chestnut-and-oak panelled open reception area, which was furnished with Georgian leather armchairs, a sofa and coffee table. To one side there was a secretary's desk and opposite it an office with open double doors of oak and Aisa Lynne's name on a plaque. A little further down was another office bearing the name Donna Lynne Reynolds.

Two women emerged from Aisa's office, one was white,

plump with chubby cheeks and aged about thirty, her brown hair tied back in a ponytail. The other lady was mixed race and noticeably younger. She had a slim athletic figure with shiny dark hair that was cut short in a gamine hairstyle. She wore little makeup; she didn't need to due to her radiant olive skin tone, and was elegantly attired in a short floral print dress and red kitten heels. Neither noticed Barolli as they went over to the secretary's desk. The mixed-race lady sat down, looked through the tray of paperwork, picked up a large file and held it up.

'For chrissakes, I told you I left it on your desk. Tell me, Jane, do I have to do everything for you?' she asked in a public-school accent, but the plump lady, close to tears, said nothing.

'Excuse me, I don't mean to interrupt you but I'm looking for Miss Lynne,' Barolli said as he held up his warrant card.

'Which one?' the mixed-race lady asked.

'Aisa,' Barolli replied.

'You're talking to her,' she said with a cheesy smile.

Barolli looked surprised. 'Sorry, I didn't realize . . .'

'The colour of my skin threw you, did it, cos it's different from my mother and sister's?' Aisa said in an offhand way.

'No, not at all.' Barolli blushed.

Aisa laughed. 'Don't worry, officer, it happens all the time. So, what do you want?'

At that moment, Dewar came through the stairwell door.

'Is she in?' the agent asked before Barolli could say anything.

'This is Miss Aisa Lynne,' Barolli said, noticing that Aisa was not impressed with the repeat of his own mistake.

'Sorry, I assumed you'd be white,' Dewar said nonchalantly and without malice.

'From your accent I *assume* that you must be the FBI lady, though strangely enough you appear very different from the way my mother described you,' Aisa said, sharply enough to make her point. Aisa walked towards her office, followed by Dewar and Barolli.

'I wasn't being racist,' Dewar protested.

'I wasn't implying you were. I know what it's like to be the butt of racist remarks. Even the upper classes are not immune from ignorance when it comes to skin colour. Donna and I were referred to as the Salt and Pepper Sisters at school,' Aisa said casually.

Dewar couldn't help thinking to herself that although upper class, Aisa, like her mother, was rough round the edges. Gloria's first husband, Xavier, must have been black or mixed race, hence the genetic difference in skin colour between the sisters.

'Looks like you and Donna had the last laugh, successful businesswomen from a wealthy family,' Dewar said.

'You sound like Mummy, who by the way, would not be very happy that you have come here without an appointment.'

'We didn't want to worry her unnecessarily,' Barolli said.

'Rubbish, you really pissed her off the other day and didn't want to incur her wrath again,' Aisa remarked, and then sat at her desk, pressed the intercom, and without a please or thank-you, asked Jane to bring in a pot of coffee.

Barolli and Dewar looked at each other, neither of them quite sure how to begin the interview, but Barolli decided to take the lead. 'Do you mind if we ask you some questions about the night Josh died? It's routine to go over everyone's movements.'

'There's no need to beat about the bush: you mean Donna's movements – that's why you're here, isn't it?' Aisa said, kicking off her red shoes and walking over to the leather sofa. She invited Dewar and Barolli to sit in the armchairs opposite as she flopped down and swung her outstretched legs onto the sofa cushions. Her floral dress slid up to mid-thigh and Barolli couldn't help but notice her very shapely legs.

'If you're worried about Mummy, don't be, as I'm not going to tell her about your impromptu visit. She's naturally concerned for Donna and so am I. If Josh was murdered, I can assure you my sister had nothing to do with it.'

'We are continuing with our enquiries and don't as yet know if he was murdered,' Barolli said, nervous that Dewar may say something to the contrary.

Jane, the secretary, entered the room carrying a tray with a cafetière of coffee, cream and two cups, which she put down on the table. Aisa, again without a please or thank-you, told Jane to get her a glass of fizzy water, ice and lemon. Jane obediently went over to the drinks cabinet, did as she was told and then asked Aisa if there was anything else she needed.

'Book me a manicure at Harrods, my Chanel dress needs to go to the dry-cleaner's and don't disturb us unless it's urgent,' Aisa, said, pointing to the dress, which was hanging on the coat rack.

Dewar could see that Jane was clearly hurt by this treatment, as Aisa swallowed a large mouthful of her fizzy water, promptly belched then remarked that champagne had the same effect on her.

Barolli asked Aisa to go over her and Donna's movements on the day and evening of the Savoy charity ball.

'We left Lynne House around noon and went in Donna's Mini to the Savoy. The day was spent with the hotel functions manager and other staff preparing for the ball.'

'Did you have your own rooms at the Savoy?' Dewar asked.

'No, we shared. The ball started at eight, but the lobster and prawn tian with beluga caviar dressing made me ill so I went upstairs for a lie-down and returned to the party for the late-night firework display.'

'So you didn't see your sister for a few hours?'

Aisa, plainly disliking Dewar's implication, was firm in her reply: 'No, but Donna was with my mother and hundreds of guests downstairs. We went to bed at around three a.m. and Donna was very drunk.'

'And in the morning?' Dewar asked.

'I got a lift home with Mummy in the Rolls and poor Donna returned to her flat, where she discovered, erm, she . . . she found Josh's body,' Aisa said, clearly moved by the thought of what that moment must have been like.

Dewar took out her notebook and flicked it open to her

meeting with Donna. 'Your sister said she and Josh had been going through a bit of rough patch. Did she tell you about any problems or disagreements they were having?'

'Nope, she never even mentioned anything like that. Donna only told me things that she knew would annoy Mummy, like them running off to Las Vegas to get married. If they were having marital problems then she'd never tell me.' Aisa took a sip of her water followed by another belch.

'So Donna used you to annoy your mother. Do you have a good relationship with you sister?' Dewar asked.

Aisa frowned, lifted her legs off the sofa then set her glass of water down on the coffee table with a thud, causing some of it to splash over the rim of the glass.

'Donna and I have always been close, looked after each other and consider ourselves true sisters. Even though we are not blood sisters. Gloria is not my real mother. I was adopted by her and Xavier Alleyne in Jamaica.'

Barolli and Dewar looked at each other, surprised.

'It makes no difference to us or our inquiry,' Dewar replied, in an effort to ease the tension.

Aisa picked up her water and took another mouthful, this time without a belch. She placed her hands on her knees and took a deep breath to compose herself.

'I don't bear a grudge about being adopted, but I do get annoyed when people make assumptions about who or what I am,' she said calmly.

Dewar didn't feel that she had said anything that could be taken in such a way. As much as she would have liked to know more about Aisa's background she realized it was a sensitive subject and not the time or place to ask about it, so she steered the conversation back to the investigation.

'How did you get on with Josh Reynolds?'

'I never really got to know him. Josh was a quiet man who kept things to himself.'

'Can you think of any reason he would take his own life?'

'No, but I can tell you one thing for certain. My sister Donna had nothing to do with his death. They were very happy and I more than anyone know how badly his death affected her. She was just coming to terms with her loss when you reignited all the pain by implying that Josh was murdered and Donna involved. That was why Mummy was so livid.'

'Your mother is obviously very protective of you and Donna,' Dewar remarked.

'That's only natural after the life she's had. She knows more than most what it's like to lose the people you love and face hardship, but look around you at all she's achieved in creating the Lynne Foundation,' Aisa said with obvious pride.

At that moment the desk phone rang. Aisa stood up sharply and strode to her desk.

'I thought I told you not to disturb us, Jane,' she snapped and then paused. Barolli and Dewar saw a look of panic come over the young woman's face as she shouted, 'Fucking stall her!' She turned around to them. 'Shit, Mummy's on her way up. She'll go ape-shit if she finds you two here. You stay where you are until I've got her away from here.'

Dewar and Barolli sat in stunned silence as they watched Aisa react like a startled gazelle in fear of an approaching lion. They had to curtail their amusement as she stumbled across the room whilst trying to get her shoes on, grabbed her coat and handbag and was out of the open office door in no time. They could hear the sound of the lift scissor gate opening.

'Hello, Mummy, what are you doing here?' Aisa asked as she noisily kissed her mother on the cheeks.

'I was up this way so I thought I'd pop in and—'

'Surprise me, how nice. I was just going out for lunch,' Aisa interrupted.

'Tell me, Aisa, why does pleasure always come before business with you?' Gloria asked disapprovingly.

'Don't be silly, Mummy, you know I work very hard. China Tang at the Dorchester okay with you?' Aisa said, evidently leading her mother back towards the lift as their voices began to fade.

'Am I expected to pay as well?' Gloria demanded.

'If you insist, Mummy, that's fine by me.'

Back in the car once more, Barolli rang the office to let the team know that the meeting with Aisa had not been very productive. Barbara responded by asking if he and Dewar would make some enquiries at somewhere called F1 Services in White City. Barolli entered the postcode into the sat nav and the two of them set off again.

It was immediately apparent that F1 Services specialized in servicing, repairing and supplying parts for high-performance sports cars such as Porsche, Aston Martin, Mercedes and Ferrari. Graham Smith, the owner of the premises, was a portly man in his late fifties and from the state of his greasy overalls and oil-stained hands it was obvious that he liked to run his business from the workshop floor. He was initially offhand and not very helpful, saying he'd never heard of a Josh Reynolds, couldn't recall the specific transaction shown on Josh's bank statement and couldn't help them further.

Smith's attitude quickly changed when Dewar told him that they could either get a search warrant to go through his books or he could assist them by looking for the documentation himself. Picking up on the threat behind Dewar's remark, he asked again for the date of the transaction and started to look through the company files on his desktop computer.

'Right, found the job sheets for that day,' he said. 'Only one job for three hundred and eight pound for a Mr J Reynolds.'

'Can I have the car model, registration and home address he gave please?' Barolli asked as he got out his notebook and pen, eager to take down the details.

'Sorry, but I don't have them,' Smith said apologetically.

'Why not?' Barolli enquired, deflated that he and Dewar had hit another dead end.

'Because the work was only for the re-fit of a new rear offside tyre – it's a twenty-minute in and out job. We just deal with sports and high-performance cars if that's any help,' Smith said, trying in some way to be helpful.

'Not really, but thanks for your time,' Barolli said as he stood up to leave and put his notebook and pen back in his pocket.

'What was the make and spec of the tyre?' Dewar asked casually.

'Goodyear Eagle F1 GS-D3, spec 285/35R19 run flat,' Smith replied in a manner that suggested he thought it would mean nothing to her. As she paused to think, Smith asked her if she would like to write down the details and he pushed a pen and Post-it pad across the desk.

'Developed as a factory fit for the Maserati Quattroporte and Ferrari F430. So if he was replacing an original tyre, as like for like, the car would be registered from 2004 onwards,' Dewar said, with a wry smile as she pushed the pen and pad back towards the garage owner, who sat in stunned silence.

Dewar got up also and thanked him, with more than a touch of sarcasm, for giving up so much of his valuable time and walked out of the door.

Chapter Eighteen

Having booked Marcus Williams in at the station, Anna got Barbara to help her carry the boxes of Trojan receipts and documents up to the squad office, where Joan was waiting to inform her that Mike Lewis had called and he would be at the office meeting later with Langton, and Pete Jenkins was also attending. Joan went on to say that she had some information regarding Josh's payment of £928 to NCP.

'His account was with a car park that's a ten-minute walk from the Trojan. They don't require details of vehicles but issue a swipe card to open and close the barrier. The last entries recorded against his card were the fifth of November, eleven thirty a.m. entry, and exit at three fifty-eight p.m.'

'There was no NCP card in his wallet, but he must have owned or had access to a car the day he died. Sad part is we've no idea of its make, model or colour or where it is,' Anna added as she handed Joan Esme Reynolds' address, asking her to find out if the premises had been sold or were being leased. She also wanted Joan to ascertain Esme's maiden name and then run a Brixton voters' register search using the maiden name and the first name of Marisha, Esme's sister.

Joan, already working her socks off, glanced over at Barbara, who was ringing her hairdresser to book an appointment.

As Anna went into her office, Barbara finished her call, picked up the boxes of the Trojan receipts and put them down on Joan's desk.

'What's all this?' Joan asked, annoyed. Barbara told her they were the receipts from the Trojan.

'It's obvious DCI Travis put them down on your desk for a reason,' Joan said sharply.

'Don't get your knickers in a twist, I'll help you go through them,' Barbara huffed.

'Fine, but please leave it there,' Joan said as she pushed one of the boxes back over to Barbara's desk. Barbara pushed it back, causing it to knock the pile of Reynolds' bank statements to the floor. Suddenly the box itself toppled over and as it fell the contents poured out, mixing with the bank documents. Joan tried to grab the fluttering papers but only succeeded in making matters worse.

'Oh, my God, were they in date order?' she wailed, and her cheeks flushed red as she angrily crawled around the floor picking up the papers.

'I don't know, just stuff them back into the box,' Barbara said apathetically as she knelt on the floor to help.

'It wasn't my fault, you know. If you hadn't put them on my desk in the first place—'

'All right, it was an accident,' Barbara interrupted, then nudged Joan. 'We can sort them out later so just shove them back for now. I'll get some paper clips for all these loose receipts.'

'I haven't got time to do all these receipts as well as the phone and laptop stuff,' Joan said, frustrated with her colleague's nonchalant attitude.

Anna was rigging her Dictaphone up to the computer speakers ready for the morning meeting when she heard the beep of her mobile. It was Pete Jenkins, letting her know he was running late. Langton, who had now been brought up to date with the latest developments, shook his head and insisted they make a start anyway, and so Anna played the tape of her interview with Williams. When it had finished, everyone acknowledged what a good job she had done and Langton praised the way that she had skilfully utilized, yet adhered to, the rules of evidence.

Mike Lewis went over to the large low-tech whiteboard that he had asked Joan to get for the office. He picked up a black marker, then wrote down the salient points as he addressed the team.

'Two days before his death, Josh Reynolds took home fifty grand to put in his safe, so where did it go?'

Joan said that she had looked through Reynolds' personal bank statements and there were no deposits or withdrawals that tallied with this amount. Mike was about to continue when DC Ross came into the room and apologized, claiming he had been so engrossed in viewing the CCTV footage he hadn't realized the time. The team gave him a slow handclap, whereupon he held up a DVD and told them they would be really applauding him after they watched it. Mike said he'd have to wait his turn but the team knew that when Dan Ross was being serious it had to be something good. Mike gestured to the whiteboard.

'This is a team effort and I'm not here to do it all for you, so come on, speak up,' Mike encouraged them. Anna could see how much Mike had learned from Langton, yet his approach and style of delivery were completely different, unassuming yet a natural motivator and leader. Joan held up her hand.

'Yes, Joan,' Mike said.

'Well, we now know his mother Esme's home address. I've checked it out and it's not been sold or leased so we might find something there,' Joan suggested, and Mike gave her a nod of approval as he wrote down SEARCH ESME'S. 'Next point.' He turned back to face the room before continuing.

'Unknown black male/decorator at Josh and Esme's flats.'

'The decorator needs to be traced and interviewed. He could have known about the money in the safe and therefore had a motive,' Mike pointed out.

'I think your quite right, sir, and the decorator was Curtis Bowman, the Trojan's handyman,' Dewar said

Mike was about to ask Dewar why but Anna interjected.

'It wasn't and I'd go as far as to say that Bowman is as clean as a whistle. The decorator was most likely Josh's Uncle Samuel who came over from Jamaica for his sister Esme's funeral and returned there.'

'Do you know for certain he returned?' Dewar asked

'No, but he didn't go to Josh's funeral,' Anna replied and Joan said she would make enquiries with the UK Border Agency.

Mike Lewis said they couldn't just assume it was Samuel who did the decorating, but he wanted it resolved quickly. Anna briefly added Samuel might have a sister Marisha who lived in Brixton, but enquiries were still ongoing.

Dewar mentioned that there was a set of keys recovered from Josh's body at the mortuary and maybe they were for Esme's flat.

'Anyone know where these keys are now?' Mike asked.

Anna said that they had been restored to Donna. There was an air of restlessness around the room as everyone recognized the significance of the information and Mike wrote down ESME'S KEYS + DONNA? on the board.

Barolli speculated that if Josh was having an affair then he could have been using his mother's flat as a love nest, which meant a jealous husband or boyfriend could be involved.

No one spoke, as if mulling over this new possibility, and eventually Langton said that if that was the case, making the scene look like a suicide didn't really fit with a crime of passion.

Dewar looked over to him. 'I disagree because it would fit with a jealous wife who wanted it to look like something other than a crime of passion.'

Mike wrote quickly on the board, trying to keep up, and asked for just one point at a time before inviting Dewar to continue.

'The surveillance unit lost Donna near Esme's block of flats and she may well have Josh's keys for the premises. Donna also suspected Josh of having an affair. These are all things that she never told DI Simms or us, for that matter.'

Anna turned to Dewar.

'Hang on a second. To be fair, Donna was never asked about

Esme's flat when we spoke to her, or if she thought Josh was
having an affair.'

Dewar, thinking Anna was challenging her opinion, folded
her arms. 'So you don't think she was in any way suspicious or
jealous of Josh?'

Anna sighed and everyone could feel the undercurrent
between the two women.

'I'm not saying you are wrong, I'm simply suggesting that
Donna could have a reasonable explanation for—'

Dewar interrupted her. 'It's clear Josh was having an affair
and Donna suspected that to be the case. Whatever way you
look at it, *jealousy* is motive,' Dewar said, plainly suggesting that
Anna's own comments stemmed from pure envy.

'There is nothing on his mobile, laptop or e-mails to suggest
he was having an affair,' Anna said curtly, refusing to back
down.

Mike could see that Langton was annoyed at their squabbling.
He was about to interject when the DCS spoke up.

'Let's move on, shall we. DC Ross, surprise us all with your
CCTV revelations,' Langton said gruffly, making it clear he was
yet again unimpressed with Dewar and Travis's behaviour.

Ross walked over to the DVD player and put a disc into it,
bringing up the CCTV footage on the large screen. He pressed
Pause.

'As you are all aware, I was given the enviable task of
viewing a shedload of CCTV footage from the Savoy, where
the Lynne Charity Ball was held. I have of course produced
and edited this DVD on my own and I hope that you enjoy
the—'

'Get on with it, Ross!' Langton barked.

'This is the entry and exit barrier at the hotel's underground car park and as you can see the time clock shows
10.05 p.m. on the fifth of November.' Ross pressed play on
the DVD.

The guard in the security kiosk could be seen watching TV,
then, without looking, he raised his hand and pressed a button.

The barrier moved upwards and a brown Mini Cooper appeared in the CCTV as it left the car park.

Ross paused the tape. 'As you can see, the registration is DON4L and that plate is registered to Donna Lynne.'

Ross then played a further section of CCTV footage that showed the Mini returning to the car park at 11.50 p.m.

There was complete silence in the room as everyone took in the importance of what they'd just seen. Anna looked over at Dewar, who, she thought from the smile on her face, was revelling in the moment.

'Aisa said that Donna drove her in the Mini to the hotel,' Dewar said, raising her eyebrows at Anna.

Fearing the two of them were going to argue the point, Langton stood up. 'Good work, Ross.' He smiled and then nodded at Dewar. 'It would seem that your suspicions about Donna Reynolds were right, Jessie.'

'Thank you, sir, but I believe I was wrong about someone being hired to kill Josh. Donna's clearly an accomplished liar who planned everything down to a tee and used the charity function as a cover to go and kill her husband.'

Members of the team nodded or voiced their agreement, although Anna felt Dewar was being self-righteous and milking the moment and wanted to comment on the fact that due to the reflection of light on the vehicle's windscreen it was not exactly clear who was driving. But she held back, fearing any remark would just be seen as sour grapes.

Pete Jenkins came in and sat down, shifting uneasily as he noticed that everyone was looking at him.

'Have I done something wrong?' he asked.

'Not at all,' said Mike. 'In fact, you are right on cue. We have evidence that Donna Reynolds lied. She left the hotel between ten and twelve the night of the fifth. So your crime scene report and blood distribution is now critical to the investigation. Do you want to share your findings with us?'

Pete stepped forward and said that he believed there was evidence to support the theory that Josh Reynolds was murdered and the scene staged to look like a suicide. The room filled with an air of anticipation, everyone eager to hear what the forensic scientist had to say.

Pete played a short animated video of what happens when someone is shot in the head, giving them all a running commentary.

'Notice as the bullet enters the head we get the back spatter of blood towards the gun and as the bullet exits so we get a forward spatter of blood away from the head.'

He brought up a picture of Reynolds' body and, using a laser pointer, drew everyone's attention to the bloodstained carpet by Josh's right knee.

'This blood is back spatter and I believe that someone was standing by Reynolds' right side as the bullet entered his head.' Pete superimposed an 'A' shape onto the carpet. 'The area below the cross line of the A is a void, meaning that the back spatter blood landed on someone or something at the time the bullet entered Reynolds' head.'

Pete next brought up a close-up picture of Reynolds' right hand holding the gun. The room was silent as everyone absorbed the importance of what he was telling them.

'As Agent Dewar correctly observed, there is no blood on the back of his trigger hand. This could however be due to the recoil from firing the gun, which can cause the hand to move upwards and away from the head.' Pete demonstrated what he meant whilst holding his thumb and forefinger like a gun.

'Wouldn't that leave back spatter on the underside of his right palm and little finger?' Langton asked, demonstrating his knowledge and experience of investigating gunshot cases.

'It could well have done, but as there were no individual photographs taken of this area we will never know,' Pete said, and Langton shook his head in disbelief at how poor the scene examination had been.

'Reynolds' right arm must have been moved so the gun could be placed in his hand by the killer,' Langton remarked.

'It's possible, but having his hands up in the air at the time he was shot would also account for an outstretched right arm,' Pete said.

'So he was in effect executed?' Langton asked and Pete nodded.

'What about fingerprints and DNA on the gun?' Langton asked.

'Only found Josh Reynolds',' Pete informed him, and added that there was something else that was strongly indicative of the scene having being disturbed after death. He brought up an enlarged picture of the sofa showing the blood and brain debris that had spurted from Reynolds' head as the bullet passed through.

'The blood and tissue matter here is forward spatter from the exit wound. If you look at the upright of the settee there is blood on it and some across the front edge of the seat area. There is no staining between these two areas of blood, yet they physically align with each other,' Pete said, leaving the team wondering how they could align when there was nothing there. It became clear what he was talking about as he slowly super-imposed a moving image of blood spatter, which followed a linear path from the blood on the edge of the sofa to the stain-ing on the upright.

'At the time the bullet exited Reynolds' head there was something on the settee that his blood spattered onto. I cannot say what it was but there was nothing submitted from the scene that would account for the void on the settee.'

'Could it have been a money bag or something similar?' Dewar asked.

'It's possible.' Pete paused. 'But my concluding observation is that, interestingly, the width of the void is the same as a piece of A4 paper.'

Everyone in the room applauded him loudly but Pete pointed out that if it weren't for Dewar the questions about the crime scene and Josh's death would never have been raised. The team all congratulated the agent who, as far as Anna was concerned, was revelling in the attention and looking at her rival as if to say, 'I told you I was right.'

Barolli was next up to address the team and opened by saying that he and Dewar had spoken with Aisa Lynne, who was mixed race and had been adopted by Gloria, and seemed rather prickly about it. He reported how she was insistent that her sister had nothing to do with Josh's death and had said Donna was at the hotel all night.

Mike Lewis asked if they thought Aisa was deliberately lying to protect Donna. Before Barolli could reply, Dewar said that although Aisa was rude and a spoilt brat, she didn't think so as the younger sister, feeling ill, had left the ball after dinner and returned just before the firework display. Taking that into consideration, she would have been unaware that Donna had even left the hotel.

Dewar then related what had happened during the visit to the F1 Services garage, when they'd learned that Josh Reynolds had a tyre re-fit for a Maserati Quattroporte or Ferrari F430 registered between 2004 and 2009.

Langton asked Dewar how on earth she could narrow down the car from a tyre? Barolli, leaping to her defence, told them all that she had rebuilt a 67 Ford Mustang and was very knowledgeable about sports and classic cars, so much so she even left the garage owner speechless. Dewar blushed, smiled at Barolli and then emphasized that nevertheless it was just an educated guess that could help to narrow down the search until more reliable information was made available to them. She also added it would take in the region of £130 to fill either car with petrol.

Mike was starting to wind up the meeting, telling them that the new evidence that had come to light was down to everyone's hard work and diligence and had cast strong doubt on the Coroner's verdict of suicide. DC Ross's discovery of Donna leaving the hotel in her car showed that she was lying and her alibi was a lie. Mike promised that she would be arrested but not until the following day as there were a couple of loose ends that he wanted tidied up that evening.

DC Ross asked if that meant there would be some overtime for working late.

'Against my better will and judgement, but because the investigation requires it, overtime authorized,' Langton said with a
smile, causing a cheer round the room.

'Okay, everybody let's keep up the good work,' Mike said
enthusiastically. 'DC Ross, I need you to continue viewing the
CCTV footage and find out what time Donna left the hotel in the
morning. Me, Barbara and Agent Dewar will execute a search
warrant at Esme Reynolds' flat,' he continued. 'Pete, would you
mind coming along, in case we need your expert advice?'

Mike wanted a quick team meeting at six a.m. the following morning, but before that they were to sort themselves into
two surveillance groups, one to watch Lynne House and the
other the Foundation offices. Mike then made it clear that if
possible he wanted Donna arrested in the street, well away
from Gloria the volatile mother hen. Langton said he would
inform Deputy Commissioner Walters of the evidence against
Donna and the necessity of arresting her and searching Lynne
House.

Mike glanced over at Barbara, who was checking the time as
she was going to miss her hair appointment.

'Barbara!' he shouted, making her jump.

'Go to the magistrates' court and get search warrants for
Esme Reynolds' flat and Lynne House.'

Langton suggested that Agent Dewar go with her and get
an insight into the process used to obtain the warrant and
then asked to speak with Mike Lewis and Anna in Anna's
office.

Langton reminded Mike that Travis's last full working day
would be tomorrow as they were flying out to Washington on
Thursday morning. Anna assured him that she and Barolli
could deal with Williams tonight and then she would be free
for the arrest and interview of Donna Reynolds tomorrow
morning.

'I'm sorry, Anna, but I want Barolli and Dewar to interview
Donna,' Mike said.

'I really think you're making a mistake, Mike,' Anna protested, clearly upset. 'Dewar is already convinced Donna is guilty and will approach the interview from the wrong angle.'

'The interviews with Donna will need continuity and I don't want to chop and change the interviewers,' Mike explained.

'Well, let me do the first one with Dewar then,' Anna suggested.

Langton gave a sigh as he shook his head in frustration. 'You are allowing your feelings towards Dewar to cloud your judgement. Mike is right and anyway you've got Williams to deal with.'

'There's no evidence against him for murder now we know about Donna—'

Langton raised his hand for Anna to stop. 'A night in the cells will teach him not to lie in future. If we've nothing on him, get the vice squad in to deal with him in the morning.'

'I can call them now then I'd be free to deal with Donna's arrest,' Anna said, becoming even more impatient.

'If you want to arrest and interview Donna, then fine,' Langton said calmly, then paused just long enough to make Anna feel that he was agreeing with her. 'But you stay here in London and see the job through to the end. You can also explain to Walters why you have thrown away the opportunity of a lifetime and wasted thousands of pounds of taxpayers' money.' Langton glared at her.

For a moment, she sat in stunned silence, realizing that he was being deadly serious, before gathering her things and storming out of the room.

Langton was in two minds to follow after her. He knew that it wasn't just her feelings towards Dewar that influenced the way she was thinking. She was so dedicated to the job and her team that sometimes she just didn't see the wood for the trees. Mike Lewis could sense that although the DCS was annoyed, he didn't really enjoy going head to head with Anna. He knew that she had always been Langton's protégée, but the problem was that many of the master's traits had rubbed off on the pupil.

'Have a look in Travis's filing cabinets and see if she's got any Scotch,' Langton said to Mike, before slumping back in his chair.

Mike searched through the cabinets and found some glasses and a nearly empty bottle of Scotch.

'I'd say there's enough for a couple of large singles here,' Mike said, holding up the bottle and handing Langton a glass.

'You can't go out to do a search smelling of booze,' Langton said, taking the bottle from Mike. He unscrewed the cap, took a large swig, then gave a long sigh and leaned forwards.

'Why does Travis drive me so fucking mad, Mike?'

'I don't know, guv. You could ask her before you get on the plane, and then discuss it during the eight-hour flight.'

'Piss off to your search'

'I'll keep you posted,' Mike offered as he made to leave the room.

'No. I don't want to hear another word about Gloria fucking Lynne or her spoilt daughters. I'm perfectly happy to read about it in the papers on the plane.'

As the door closed behind Mike, Langton swigged down the rest of the bottle, and then placed it carefully in the centre of the desk. It was a long flight and he knew he and Anna would be together for an even longer period at Quantico. He didn't really need an answer to why Travis drove him mad. When she was angry, when she was trying to keep a lid on her temper, she had two pink spots that appeared on her cheeks, and her beautiful eyes flashed. He still loved her, he also admired her, and the attraction he had initially felt all that time ago had never disappeared. It was buried, but sometimes, out of his control, it rose to the surface. He would need to keep a firm lid on his emotions at the FBI Academy.

Chapter Nineteen

It was early evening by the time Barbara and Dewar met up with Mike Lewis, Pete Jenkins and two uniform officers at Esme's flat on the Lancaster West Estate in Notting Hill. Barbara had possession of the search warrant, which had been issued by the magistrate at the Horseferry Road court. On arriving at flat two, Brandon Walk, they could see there were no lights on.

Mike knocked on the door and waited for an answer; when none came he knocked again and after a further minute of waiting instructed the uniform officers to use 'the enforcer'. Dewar asked Barbara what Mike was talking about and she explained that this was a steel battering ram that was used to open doors. Dewar remarked that they call it the 'big key' back home and then hurriedly stepped back as the uniform officer removed the ram from a zipped holdall and positioned himself in front of the door. He swung the ram back and then smashed it into the door, causing it to fly open with a loud bang. The Chubb and Yale locks buckled under the impact as wooden splinters from the doorframe flew into the hallway, which was littered with unopened post and flyers.

Hearing the noise made by the ram, the neighbour from flat three came running out armed with a baseball bat, but he apologized on seeing the uniform police officers, adding that he thought someone was breaking in. Mike explained that they were executing a search warrant and asked if he knew Esme Reynolds or her son Josh. The neighbour said that he had only moved in five months ago but was told that the lady next door had passed away and her son was looking after the place. Dewar asked if he ever saw anyone coming or going from the premises and he replied only once, which was last Wednesday evening around eight-ish when he was on his way out to the pub. Asked to describe the visitor he said that a very attractive woman with long blonde hair, wearing tight jeans and a purple jacket, came out, locked the door behind her and walked off.

Mike thanked him for his assistance and promised they would try not to make too much noise. Dewar observed that the description fitted Donna.

'The plot thickens,' Mike said as he stepped into the flat, which had a musty damp smell. Putting on a pair of protective gloves he flicked the hallway light but nothing happened. He bent down and picked up some of the post from the top of the pile, glanced through it and opened a letter from the electricity supplier npower.

'Non-payment – they must have cut the electrics off,' Mike said, handing the letter to the other uniform officer and asking him to get an engineer out to switch the electrics back on and a carpenter to fix the door and fit new locks. Meanwhile, there was still a couple of hours of daylight left so they might as well crack on and if needs be they could call for some arc lights and generators to be brought to the flat.

Dewar and Barbara went into the kitchen, which was covered in dust. The linoleum floor was old-fashioned, with worn areas in front of the cooker and beside the sink unit. The mould-covered interior of the fridge smelled putrid from remnants of unidentifiable rotting food. In the cupboards were a few tins of chopped tomatoes, baked beans, and packets of rice and pasta. A plastic-lined shelf holding wine glasses and tumblers had been put up above a wine rack that was filled with fine red and white wines along with bottles of Bollinger champagne. Dewar commented that the costly collection seemed out of place in the overall surroundings. There was nothing that looked as if it had been used recently, nothing in the pedal bin, and the dishcloths and towels were neatly folded.

Mike Lewis checked out the living room with Pete Jenkins but found nothing of interest, then put his head around the kitchen door.

'Bit of a dead zone, isn't it?' Dewar remarked.

'This place is privately owned and being close to the nobs in Notting Hill Gate is probably worth in the region of three fifty to four hundred grand,' Barbara said, surprising the agent.

Mike observed that it looked like Josh had indeed been having the place redecorated as the living-room walls had been painted and there were stacked picture frames that had yet to be re-hung. They went through the hallway and checked the cupboard beneath the stairs. It contained a number of different coloured tins of paint, rolls of woodchip wallpaper, brushes, a pasteboard and dust sheets. Dewar remarked that it was strange that the decorator hadn't taken his stuff with him and Mike suggested that if it had been Josh's Uncle Samuel, and he'd returned to Jamaica, then that would explain the decorating materials being left behind.

Next, they went upstairs, where there were three bedrooms, the smallest of which was filled with cardboard boxes, some with OXFAM written on them. On looking through these, it appeared they were mostly filled with Esme's clothes. One box contained old photograph albums, Josh's old sports trophies and schoolbooks. Barbara found an old address book in one box and on the off chance flicked it open to the Ms, finding what she was looking for: Marisha and a phone number. Barbara rang the details through to the office, where Joan said she would check it out, get an address from the phone number and inform DCI Travis.

The second bedroom was slightly bigger, with a single bed and Chelsea Football Club wallpaper, quilt cover and pillowcase. An old computer desk stood by the window, the curtains above it a sun-damaged blue.

'This must be Josh's old room,' Mike said, and opened the fitted wardrobe, which had nothing in it other than mothballs and some dirty shoeboxes. Barbara noticed an old black-and-white picture on the computer desk, of a uniformed army offi-cer standing next to a British World War Two tank. The butt of his service revolver protruded from its holster.

'I'd say this chap could be the original owner of the Enfield revolver,' Barbara said as she put the picture into a property bag.

'God, this place is so old-fashioned it's hideous. I doubt Josh Reynolds would bring a woman back here for sex,' Dewar sneered as Pete Jenkins walked into the room.

'I'm not so sure,' he said. 'Come and have a look at the boudoir next door.'

They all squeezed through into the main bedroom. This had been painted white and had thick cream curtains edged with dark red bands and draped back with matching rope ties. The bed was king-sized, with a cream duvet and white Egyptian cotton pillowcases. There was a pine chest of drawers and a fitted wardrobe. A zebra skin rug was positioned along the foot of the bed; there was no carpet, but the floorboards had been painted white.

'My, my, maybe this was where the liaison took place: up the stairs, lights out and into bed,' Dewar said, opening the chest of drawers, which was empty.

Mike eased the wardrobe open but only hangers were left on the rail.

'I can take the bed sheets and pillowcases back to the lab for DNA,' Pete suggested as he put down his large forensic case and proceeded to pull back the quilt.

As she started to cross the room Barbara stepped onto the zebra skin rug which promptly slid from under her feet, causing her to topple backwards. Mike managed to grab her before she fell.

'Bloody thing hasn't got any slip grips on it,' Barbara mut-tered, embarrassed at her near mishap, and she bent down and repositioned the rug.

'Wait a minute, the zebra skin, pull it back,' Dewar exclaimed excitedly.

Barbara pulled the rug away and Dewar stepped slowly onto the floorboard, making it creak. She pressed her hand flat against it, and then straightened to use the heel of her foot. The floorboard was loose.

'I wonder what's hidden under here?' Dewar smiled.

Pete Jenkins got down on his hands and knees and discovered that the nails were missing from this particular board. He tried to ease it up, but soon realized he would need a screwdriver to prise it open. Dewar waited impatiently for Mike Lewis to retrieve an implement from downstairs; she was starting to doubt they would find anything. The odd thing was that unlike the other boards, which were all flush, the loose board had been sawn slightly shorter. Mike returned with a kitchen knife and handed it to Pete, who slid it into the narrow gap and slowly lifted the twelve-inch piece of loose floorboard away.

'Anything?' Dewar asked, bending down over Pete as he blindly felt around with his hand.

'Nope, nothing,' he replied and then lay flat on the floor so he could get his hand further along the space underneath. 'Hang on, there's something here, feels like cloth of some sort.'

He asked Barbara to get a large paper exhibits bag from his forensic kit and lay it out on the floor beside him. He then eased his body back and slowly withdrew a cloth money bag.

Dewar was now kneeling beside him, eager to see what it contained. With his gloved hands Pete eased the bag open and removed wads of fifty-pound notes, tied with elastic bands. He flicked through a bundle.

'There's a grand in each of these. There may be more down there, this one was stuffed so far back,' he said, dusting himself off as Dewar started counting the bundles of cash.

'I can do fingerprint examinations on the top and bottom notes of each bundle to start with, but as they're used notes and untraceable, any Tom, Dick or Harry could have left their prints,' Pete said.

'There's just short of a hundred and sixty thousand here,' Dewar breathed, causing Mike to give a long, low whistle of surprise.

Barbara gestured to Mike. 'Guv, it doesn't make sense that Josh Reynolds would hide the money under floorboards when he had a safe.'

'Well we know from the neighbour's description that Donna had keys for this place. She may have taken the money from the safe after she murdered Josh,' Dewar suggested.

'You might be right, Jessie. There's plenty for you and Barolli to put to her in interview now,' Mike said.

Finally, the engineer arrived and reconnected the electricity while a carpenter put new locks on the door. Meanwhile, Pete Jenkins bagged up the money, the bed sheets and the decorator's paint tins, hoping they might yield some DNA or fingerprints. Mike Lewis asked the neighbour about garages that were owned by the residents. The man said that there was a row of twenty round the back of the flats but he had no idea as to who owned which one, except of course his own.

Mike Lewis, Dewar and Barbara went over the premises with a fine-tooth comb, checking for more hidden cash or anything else that might prove useful to the inquiry. However, they found no keys or paperwork related to a garage. Mike knew that he could not force open all the garages, nor did he have the time to knock on every resident's door asking which garage they owned. He would just have to wait and hope that the arrest of Donna would result in the recovery of the keys and the discovery of the garage and maybe Josh's car. The last thing he did was to take the Chubb and Yale locks that had originally been in the front door as they made their way out.

On the journey to Marisha Peters' flat, at 51 Clarendon House, Radley Street, Brixton, Anna hardly spoke a word. Barolli, who was driving, tried to engage her in conversation about Quantico and the FBI course but her replies extended to nothing more than a simple 'yes' or 'no'.

Barolli attempted to reassure her. 'If you're worried about Dewar, don't be – I can keep her in check while you are away.'

'You think so, do you?' Anna remarked glibly as she stared out of her passenger window.

Barolli couldn't let that go without comment. 'You're like a pair of squabbling schoolgirls pulling pigtails and it looks bad in front of the team. What was it you said about earning respect?'

Anna turned and looked at Paul, saying nothing, but the look on her face told him he had hit a nerve.

It was another ten minutes of silence before they reached their destination of Clarendon House, a 1950s concrete tower block of council flats. The estate looked as if it suffered from the anti-social behaviour of bored kids, and signs of drug use and graffiti were rife, mostly tags from the local gangs.

Barolli pressed the lift button and the door opened, whereupon the strong smell of urine hit them as they noticed the wet floor.

'You'd think the council would clean up the place,' Anna said, disgusted.

'They probably do, but it's a lost cause,' Barolli sighed. 'This is one of the most notorious blocks, lot of gangs around, and at night it's shut the door, close the curtains and put your telly on at full volume.'

Anna said she would rather walk up the fire escape stairwell, Barolli agreed, and together they trudged up the ten flights of stairs, which didn't smell much better. The long stone corridor on floor ten was covered in graffiti. Barolli knocked at the door of flat 51 and waited.

'Who's there, mon?' a female voice asked in a strong Jamaican accent.

Barolli said that it was the police and they needed to speak with Marisha Peters about her nephew Joshua Reynolds.

'You is talkin' to her but I don't seen Joshua in years, so I can't help yer.'

Anna looked at Barolli, whispering to him that she obviously doesn't know that Josh was dead, then called out that she was DCI Travis and it was important that they spoke with her privately.

The flat door slowly opened to reveal a very overweight black woman who looked to be in her late fifties. She was wearing a red calico skirt, light top, blue cardigan and Ugg boots. A tight red cotton headscarf covered her hair and the front of her fore-head. Anna and Barolli showed Marisha their warrant cards and she invited them into the flat.

'Go on in dere, I won't be a minute, got a stew fish on for me tea,' Marisha said as she pointed to the small living room.

The smell of fish was overpowering, but the flat was rea-sonably clean and the living room with its worn carpet and furniture was tidy. There was thick-flocked wallpaper, and the curtains were tied back with stockings. In front of the electric three-bar fire stood a clothes airer on which there were wet, dripping underclothes drying. An oversized LCD 3D TV dominated the room and on the stand below it there was a Bose surround sound system, Blu-ray DVD player and Sky+HD box. On top of an old wooden dresser there was an iPad and docking system with a set of tabletop speakers.

'Likes the mod cons, doesn't she?' Anna remarked.

'Knowing this estate, it's probably all nicked gear bought from the local fence,' Barolli said with a sly smile.

Marisha came into the living room carrying a tray with three coffees, milk and sugar. She put the tray down on the small table by the sofa and briefly went out again, returning with a half-full bottle of spiced rum in her hand. She held the bottle up, inviting Barolli and Anna to have a drop with their coffee.

'Just a tiny one,' said Barolli, not wanting to appear rude. Marisha was about to pour some into his coffee cup, but Anna was not happy about it.

'Thank you for the offer, Marisha, but we are both still on duty,' she said politely.

As Marisha lifted the bottle away, Anna noticed a splash of rum fall into Barolli's cup. Anna frowned at him and he shrugged his shoulders. Not wishing to appear offensive, she told Marisha she was welcome to have some with her own coffee if she wanted, but the woman shook her head, explaining she was teetotal. 'It's me brother's rum anyways, he's been drinking it since he was a baby, and I'se thought youse may like a tipple with de coffee.'

Marisha left briefly to put the bottle back in the kitchen and Anna looked at Barolli as he sipped his drink.

'It was only a tiny drop by accident,' he said, pleading innocence. Anna chuckled and said she'd forgive him this time.

Marisha shuffled back into the room. 'So what trouble is me nephew Joshua in?' she asked casually as she eased herself down into an old wingback chair.

'I'm sorry to have to tell you that he's dead,' Anna said.

There was a look of shock on Marisha's face as she held her hand to her mouth in disbelief at the news.

'When, what happened to him?' she asked in a trembling voice and began to cry. Her whole body was shaking so Anna consolingly placed her hand on Marisha's.

'He passed away last November,' Anna told her.

Marisha squeezed Anna's hand tightly and wiped her nose on the sleeve of her cardigan. 'November! Oh, my, so soon after Esme. He was such a lovely boy.' Marisha again wiped her nose on her sleeve.

Anna looked in her jacket pocket and handbag for a handkerchief but didn't have one. Barolli asked Marisha if she had any tissues and she said that there was a box in the kitchen. Barolli got up to find it.

Anna continued, 'It was believed that Josh was suffering from depression and committed suicide.'

'Suicide, oh, my, he done it hisself, how terrible.' Marisha burst into more tears.

Barolli returned with the box of tissues and a glass of water and gave them to Marisha, who wiped the tears from her eyes, blew her nose loudly and gulped down the water.

As she hadn't asked how Josh died Anna didn't go into details but explained that as a result of some new information Josh's death was being reinvestigated as a murder. This caused Marisha to cry and shake uncontrollably. Anna had to wait for several moments before she could continue, saying that they had come to see her as they wanted to know more about Josh's family background.

Marisha, sniffing and blowing her nose, said that she had not seen Josh since she fell out with her sister Esme over fifteen years ago.

Anna glanced at Barolli, waiting for the tears to stop, before telling Marisha that she didn't want to pry but wanted to know why she and Esme had fallen out. It transpired that Esme had caught her husband John and Marisha kissing each other and was convinced they were having an affair. Marisha said it was just a drunken one-off incident at a party but Esme banned her from coming anywhere near her family again and poisoned Josh against her.

'It were just a friendly kiss, John was a good faithful husband. It was all in Esme's mind, but she was so worked up she go and tell my boyfriend Dexter and he left me.'

She starting sobbing once more and asked for another glass of water, and so Barolli duly went off to the kitchen for a refill.

'Josh didn't invite me to the funeral and I didn't dare go for fear he'd turn me away. Now I've not paid my respects to him either. I feel so bad, so bad,' Marisha said, shaking her head and blowing her nose.

'How did you know about Esme's death?' Anna asked.

Marisha hesitated and Anna assumed she was composing herself before answering.

'From ma brother Samuel, he call me after Josh had rung him to say Esme had died.' Marisha explained that Samuel had always lived in Jamaica, but kept in touch with her and Esme, calling them three or four times a year.

'Did Samuel come over for the funeral?' Anna asked.

'Yes, he couldn't afford de flight so Josh paid for his ticket and he stayed with me. It was good to see him after thirty years but so sad it was because of Esme's passing.'

Anna was about to ask Marisha more when the woman became very agitated.

'Samuel, oh, my, he don't know about Josh's death!' she exclaimed, visibly distressed.

Anna said she would be happy to make a call to him on Marisha's behalf if it would help. Marisha refused as if insulted. She pursed her lips, thanking Anna for her kind offer, but said that it was something she must do herself, as Samuel would take the news badly.

Anna wondered what Barolli was up to as he was taking so long. When he eventually returned from the kitchen, he claimed that he had let the tap run so the glass of water was a bit cooler this time, but Anna suspected he'd been having a quick snoop around.

She wanted to ask more about Samuel's visit, but due to Marisha's state of shock, knew she'd have to proceed delicately.

'Did Samuel say how Josh was when he met him?'

'He said he was a handsome young man, very successful and owed a big nightclub in da West End. Do ya know where he's buried as I'd like to visit his grave and lay some flowers?' Marisha asked, becoming emotional again.

Anna told her that his body had been cremated but she would try to find out where his ashes were. She pressed on and asked Marisha how long Samuel had stayed with her.

'Only for about four weeks, then he had to go back home to look after his fishing business.'

Anna calculated that Samuel must have returned to Jamaica in mid-September.

'Do you know if he did any decorating work for Josh?'

'Yes, Samuel say he done some work on Esme's place for him as Josh was going to sell it. I tink he also done some work at Josh's flat, you knows – to earn a few pennies as he don't have much money.'

'I may need to speak with Samuel about Josh so could I have his phone number please?'

'He don't have a phone, he go to one of them phone cafés to call me.'

Anna handed Marisha Barolli's details and asked her to tell

Samuel to ring the DI next time he called, before thanking her for her time and wishing her well.

'Are the 3D TVs any good?' Barolli asked Marisha as he got up to leave.

'They is okay but de glasses give me a bit of a headache.'

'I was thinking of getting one but they're quite expensive, aren't they?'

She proudly folded her arms, standing in front of the huge screen. 'Samuel bought me it as a present when he was stayin' as my old TV went on de blink. He had a big win on a horse race, came in at fifty to one.' Marisha paused and gave Barolli a sly smile, wagging her finger. 'I know why you're askin'.' She went over to the dresser and opened the top drawer.

'This was a legitimate purchase, sir, I've got the receipt here somewhere with the price on ...'

'It's okay, I can have a look at the price online,' Barolli said, somewhat embarrassed that Marisha had seen right through his ploy.

As they made their way back to the station, Anna wondered aloud why on earth he had asked Marisha about the TV.

'I thought it might be nicked,' Barolli explained.

'Well considering the state of shock Marisha was in over Josh's death, I thought it was inappropriate.'

'The kitchen was like something out of a cookery programme — new cooker, fridge and a host of other modern appliances. I took down the serial numbers,' he said, holding up his notebook.

Anna frowned. 'She said Samuel had a big win on the horses so she probably had receipts for the lot.'

Barolli shrugged his shoulders. 'Well at least we got to the bottom of the decorator problem.'

'That's if Samuel finished the work himself,' Anna observed.

'Maybe Dewar's right about Curtis Bowman — Josh could have got him to finish it.'

'Dewar's wrong. Bowman is telling the truth,' Anna said firmly.

Barolli, realizing he had upset her, changed the subject.

'Fancy stopping off for something to eat?'

'I'm not that hungry and to be honest I just want to get home.'

'Do you mind stopping so I can get a takeaway?' he asked.

'No,' Anna said, rather begrudgingly.

She pulled up outside a shabby-looking chicken joint that Barolli liked the look of and waited for him while he got some fried chicken and chips. The smell stank the car out and made Anna feel queasy for the remainder of the journey to the station. She was heartily glad that they were not in her own car.

Chapter Twenty

The next morning, Barolli rang in to say he was running late as he'd been sick in the night.

'Serves him right for eating that disgusting takeaway,' Anna said, and winced, recalling the horrible smell in the car.

'That's exactly what he said,' Joan giggled.

'How did the search of Esme's flat go?' Anna asked.

'You didn't hear?' Joan said with surprise. 'Agent Dewar spotted a loose floorboard and they found nearly a hundred and sixty thousand pounds hidden under it! And they've got a witness who saw Donna there the night the surveillance team lost her.'

'Good,' Anna said apathetically, realizing her thoughts about Donna being innocent had just taken a big nosedive. She'd already been informed that officers were preparing to arrest the young woman that morning.

'Oh, I nearly forgot, my mum said that her current issue of *Gardeners' World* says that the next one, which is out tomorrow, has an interview with Gloria about her latest flower-show display.'

'Your mother and you don't have a garden,' Anna said, bemused.

'No, but we have a lovely collection of pot plants on the balcony of the flat.'

Shaking her head, Anna went to ring the vice squad, who agreed to come to the station to deal with Marcus Williams.

Some time later, a subdued Barolli walked into her office and apologized in a croaky voice for being late.

'You look like death warmed up,' Anna observed, surprised at his dreadful appearance.

'I feel like it. I think it was the fried chicken.'

'You're lucky it wasn't full-blown salmonella poisoning.'

'Make me feel better, why don't you?' he groaned.

'You've only yourself to blame.'

'I've had food poisoning before but this was so much worse. Had a rash all over me last night, my heart was palpitating ten to the dozen, temperature hit the roof then the room was spinning round and round in a psychedelic blur. I was hot but not sweating and to top it all I couldn't pee or sh—'

'Enough! Too much information!' Anna cut him off.

'I hope I don't fall asleep when we interview Williams.'

'I've rung the vice squad and they're coming over to deal with him so you can have a lie-down on the sofa there while I go for some breakfast.'

'Oh, thank God.' He was lying on his back with a cushion over his face within seconds.

'Gold to silver, any eyeball on red yet?' Mike Lewis asked over the surveillance van radio.

'Negative, negative,' came the reply from Barbara, who was maintaining observation at Lynne House while Mike Lewis was near the Foundation offices with Dewar.

'We'll just have to arrest Donna in the house if she doesn't come out soon,' Dewar said, folding her arms in a cantankerous manner.

'Be patient,' Mike said calmly.

'Patient! We've been here for two hours.' Dewar sighed.

'Eyeball on white leaving premises in yellow Mike Victor,' Barbara said.

'Is that Gloria, is she going out?' Dewar asked, leaning over Mike to check the coloured code sign names.

'No, white is Aisa. Mike Victor means motor vehicle and yellow is the car colour. Gloria is blue and Donna is red.'

'This colour stuff is driving me nuts,' Dewar grumbled.

'Correction on last transmission: red is with white and units on tail,' Barbara said and Dewar came to life.

'Received. They can keep tail and you stay at current location and await instructions to search premises,' Mike told Barbara, who acknowledged him.

Dewar asked what he was going to do now and Mike said he'd decided to arrest Donna in her office and search it at the same time.

Dewar looked surprised. 'Without a search warrant?'

'Don't need one. We have a legal power to search after arrest for serious offences like murder.'

'That's good to know,' Dewar said, yet again confused by the different laws in the UK.

As the surveillance team followed Aisa's car, they kept in continuous radio contact but it was nearly an hour before Mike and Dewar saw the vehicle go into the underground car park at the Foundation offices.

Five minutes later, Mike Lewis, Dewar, three other members of the team and a uniform officer burst into Donna's office to find her sitting at her desk. Mike produced his warrant card, introduced himself then told Donna that he was arresting her on suspicion of the murder of Joshua Reynolds, cautioned her and asked if she understood.

A startled Donna started to cry, saying she didn't understand as she had done nothing wrong. She repeatedly proclaimed her innocence and childishly begged to speak with her mother.

Dewar crossed over to Donna's handbag and went through it for a set of keys to match those in the mortuary photograph, which they suspected to be for Esme's flat.

'What are you looking for?' Donna asked, tears rolling down her cheeks.

Dewar looked up at Mike and shook her head, just as Aisa barged into the room and demanded to know what was happening. On recognizing Dewar, she realized what was going on.

'Don't worry, Donna, I will call Mummy, she'll sort this out.'

Aisa then turned to Dewar. 'People like you just like to humil-
iate us because we're wealthy and better off than you are.'

'I suggest you keep your insinuations to yourself, Miss Lynne,
or you may find yourself being arrested as well,' Dewar said
coldly.

'Fuck you!' Aisa pushed Dewar out of the way and stormed
out of the room.

Dewar smiled. 'Told you she was a bit rough round the edges.'

Mike radioed Barbara and told her to execute the search warrant at Lynne House and to make sure they looked in Donna's
car for any keys that might fit Esme's flat. Meanwhile, he and
Dewar would take Donna to the station while the other officers
searched her office and seized her desktop computer.

Pleased that events were moving, at least, Barbara spoke
on the intercom with the housekeeper, who opened the gates.
Pulling up at the front of Lynne House, the DS caught sight
of a woman in green gardening overalls standing by the front
door. She had never met Lady Gloria Lynne but recognized her
from a picture Joan had shown her from a magazine cutting. As
Barbara stepped out of the car she could see that Gloria was on
the phone and had a face like thunder. Approaching Gloria, the
search warrant in one hand and her warrant card in the other,
Barbara said who she was and why her team were at the house.
As she handed Gloria a copy of the warrant she told her team to
start on the house while she searched Donna's Mini, which was
parked by the garages.

'Just one minute!' Gloria said sternly as she examined the
warrant. Barbara stopped and the rest of her team followed suit.
Gloria proceeded to read out the details of the warrant over the
phone.

'My solicitor would like a word with you,' Gloria said as she
handed Barbara the phone.

The solicitor suavely informed her he was Mr Charles
Leicester and he represented the Lynne family. Barbara recognized his name and was aware that he was a top London

solicitor 'I'm sure your search of Donna's bedroom and car shouldn't take you too long.' He laughed. Barbara was puzzled by his remark, as Lynne House was enormous.

'We will be here for some time, sir, so I need to get on.'

'From what Lady Lynne said was on your warrant, I suggest you look at it again, officer,' Leicester said in a condescending tone.

Barbara reread the search warrant and it hit her like a ton of bricks. In her rush to get it authorized, she had inadvertently typed LYNNE HOUSE, WEYBRIDGE, PROPERTY OF MRS DONNA REYNOLDS, making it invalid, as Gloria owned the property. Gloria had a smug smile on her face as Barbara handed back the phone.

'On my solicitor's advice, and not wishing to be obstructive, I am willing to allow you to search Donna's bedroom and her car,' Gloria said, as she screwed up the warrant and tossed it to one side.

Barbara knew that she should call Mike Lewis there and then but she wanted to search the car first. On looking in the Mini's glovebox, she was highly relieved to find a set of three keys, which when compared to a close-up photograph of those recovered from Josh's pocket at the mortuary appeared to match. She was certain they were the important set and that the smallest key was for a garage. Taking a deep breath, Barbara phoned Mike, who was understandably very annoyed, brusquely informing her that he would book Donna into custody and she was to meet him with the recovered keys at Esme's flat.

A short while later, DC Ross came down from Donna's bedroom to report that apart from seizing a laptop and iPad they had found nothing of any interest. Gloria had shown them the evening dress that Donna was wearing on the night of the charity ball and they had packed it in an evidence bag.

Lady Lynne came back out to the front of the house and approached the two officers.

'You are here as a minion, carrying out the orders of DCI

Travis and that objectionable FBI woman. You can tell them
that I will not allow my daughter Donna to be their scapegoat
and will do everything in my power to make sure their careers
are over.'

'I will let her know that your solicitor Mr Leicester will be
attending the station to represent Donna,' Barbara replied.

'He is arranging for Ian Holme QC to attend. No doubt
you've heard of him, officer,' Gloria said with a smirk as she
turned and walked into the house.

Barbara knew the name Ian Holme very well. He was one of
the most feared defence barristers around and nicknamed
Andrex by police officers. Not because he was soft, but because
by the time he'd finished with you in the evidence box, you felt
like you'd been torn up and used as toilet paper.

Just over an hour later, Mike Lewis and Dewar met up with a
somewhat deflated Barbara and DC Ross in the garage area at
the rear of Esme's flat. Dewar had the set of locks taken from the
flat. There was an anxious look of anticipation on all their faces
as Barbara removed the recovered keys from the plastic property
bag, took the Yale lock from Dewar and held the most likely
key against it.

'Bit like the Prince testing the shoe on Cinderella,' DC Ross
remarked.

'Well, if it fits, I'm not marrying you, Ross,' Barbara replied
as she eased the key forward and slid it gently into the cylinder.
Everyone was leaning over her as she turned the key and the
lock moved to and fro.

'Bingo,' Barbara said with a sigh of relief, and everyone smiled.
She then tried the other key in the Chubb lock with the same
success.

'Two down, one to go,' DC Ross said and pointed to the third
key on the set in her hand.

Dewar bent down and examined the T-lock handle on one of
the garages. 'All these doors have the same type of lock and that
third key looks the right shape and size.'

'Shall I pick first?' DC Ross said, gazing down the row of twenty garages.

Mike told Ross to shut up and for them to start at one end. Barbara got to the eighth one along when finally the key slid into the lock and opened it.

'Here goes,' Mike said as everyone stepped back so he could lift the heavy metal door open. As he did so the others in unison impulsively crouched down to try and get a better look as the lower rear of a car was exposed.

'Low suspension, rear diffuser and two sets of dual exhausts. It's a Ferrari 430 Spider,' Dewar predicted, even before any identification badges or registration plate came into view. Mike lifted the door fully open to reveal the car, which was a 2009 Ferrari Convertible with its roof up. The length of the vehicle only just fitted into the small interior of the seemingly bare garage. Mike flicked the light switch on the wall and nothing happened, but with the door open the daylight filled the space and they could see a bike mounted on a wall bracket.

'You were right,' Barbara said, impressed with Dewar's knowledge.

'Unusual to see a blue one – that shade is known as Azzurro California,' Dewar said in admiration.

'How much is it worth?' Mike asked

'In English pounds, in the region of ninety-five to one hundred grand,' Dewar told him.

DC Ross whistled as he looked at the dusty car.

'Ninety-five fuckin' thousand, bloody hell, I'd be scared shitless to drive it out of here, never mind around the West End.'

Dewar wafted her hand towards him to shut him up.

'If Josh Reynolds' business was in difficulty where on earth did he get the money to buy a Ferrari?' Mike demanded.

DC Ross, eager to make an impression as usual, suggested that maybe Josh had got into debt with loan sharks and that was why he was murdered. Mike doubted that would be the case as they usually paid a visit first and beat the crap out of you or at the least would have taken the car off him.

Barbara pointed out that there was nothing in Josh's, Donna's or the Trojan's bank statements that indicated a purchase or loan for such a vast sum of money.

'Now we've got the car registration, we can interview the previous owner and see how they were paid for the sale,' Mike said.

'Donna Reynolds had easy access to large sums of money,' Dewar remarked and the others looked at her, eager to hear her thoughts. 'The Lynne Foundation charities – Donna looks after some of the accounts which have millions of pounds in them. A missing hundred grand here and there probably wouldn't even be noticed.'

'A drop in the ocean,' DC Ross agreed, smiling, and yet again he was rewarded with a cold glance from an irritated Dewar.

She tapped the bonnet. 'Let's check out the charities, see if we come up with a nice round wedge going out.'

Mike phoned Joan in the office and told her to get someone over from Tech Support asap to examine Donna's office computer and in particular the charity accounts she handled. They were to pay particular attention to the 2012 transactions for the six-month period before Josh died and to work backwards from 5 November. He also asked Joan to get a vehicle transporter sent down to the garage for the removal of the Ferrari to the lab. Joan in turn told him that Ian Holme QC had arrived, Barolli had served the disclosure and Holme was now in a private consultation with Donna.

Mike pointed out that without the keys to the Ferrari there was not a lot they could do until the car was taken to the lab and opened.

They could however check along the walls in case there were any loose bricks to hide the keys behind, but none were found. The garage was bare apart from the bike, old bits of newspaper and oily rags.

DC Ross looked up to the ceiling and it struck him as rather odd that there was no light or even wires for one.

'A switch, but no lights,' Ross mused, but everyone ignored

him, thinking he was trying to be funny. He asked Barbara for the set of keys recovered from Donna's car. Taking the small garage key, he inserted the tip into the top of the light switch box, then used the tip as a lever, at which point the front of the box came open revealing a hidden compartment with keys to the Ferrari.

'Am I good or am I good?' Ross said, taking a bow.

'Irritating . . . but good,' Mike conceded.

A cursory search of the car revealed no driving, insurance or registration documents or anything else of value to the investigation. Nobody was inclined to continue beyond that, so as not to destroy possible evidence from fingerprints and DNA.

Mike and Dewar departed to head back to the incident room, leaving Barbara and DC Ross waiting at the garage for the arrival of the tow truck.

'Imagine it, nearly a hundred thousand quid, you could put that down on a mortgage for a house, or a flat,' Ross said wistfully.

'Yeah, but if you've got the money, it's a different thought process – young rich City blokes have all got Bentley's and Porsches. Me, I'd be happy with a convertible Mercedes but I would need a sugar daddy to get one.'

'Maybe he had a rich girlfriend,' Ross said, yawning.

'He had a rich wife and his mother-in-law is loaded, she was left millions.'

Ross turned to look back at the Ferrari: even with a light film of dust it had a gleaming power, far out of his league, but given the choice he would have had a red one.

Chapter Twenty-One

Paul Barolli was still fast asleep on the sofa when Anna got back from the canteen, his mouth wide open and making a snoring noise that sounded like a log being slowly sawn in half. Anna went over and shook him gently but Barolli, clearly still disorientated, rolled off the sofa, hitting the floor with a thud. Anna couldn't stop herself laughing as she helped him up, asking if he was okay. He rubbed his eyes and confessed he still felt really rough. Anna suggested that he go home and sleep it off but Paul said he'd be okay and slowly went to his office.

Anna decided it was time to pack up her files and paperwork into plastic boxes so Dewar could use her desk while she was away without disturbing everything. As she checked over her desk she noticed Dewar's copy of Donna Reynolds' bank statement. Anna was forced to admit to herself she still had mixed feelings about Donna's involvement in Josh's death but everyone else on the team seemed convinced that they'd 'got their woman'. A gut feeling was no argument against the weight of evidence that had accumulated against Donna. Anna knew that if she were still on the case she would have gone over everything with a fine-tooth comb and certainly more than once. The problem was, she didn't have the time, and if she was honest with herself she was ready to walk away.

The desk phone rang, and when she picked it up it was Pete Jenkins.

'Hi, Anna, I expected Dewar. I thought you'd be off on the big bird by now.' He chuckled.

Anna told him that she was just tying up loose ends and her flight was in the morning.

Pete said he'd miss her and she was to send him a postcard of the FBI Academy so he could put it on his wall and say he'd been there. Anna laughed. Pete asked her if she had a pen and paper handy, as she might want to write some information down, but that he would also e-mail a report for the team later.

'The money we recovered from Esme's last night, I've got some results.' He explained that Mike had taken Donna's fingerprints after arresting her and they were now loaded onto the live scan computer system, while a courier had just delivered her DNA swabs. He had so far managed to look at the fingerprints on the top and bottom note in each £1000 bundle.

'As expected, Josh Reynolds' fingerprints are on lots of the notes. On one bundle I found both Josh and Donna's prints and on others Josh and Marcus Williams'.'

'Evidence-wise that doesn't prove anything against Donna,' Anna remarked.

'No, but from firearms residue on the cash bag that match the Enfield revolver and fibres that match felt matting in the safe, it's reasonable to conclude that the bag was in Josh Reynolds' safe at some point.'

Anna recalled that Marcus Williams had said Josh put the fifty thousand in a cash bag.

'It just doesn't make sense that Josh would take the money from his safe and hide it under floorboards at his mother's,' Anna reasoned.

'I agree, but however you look at it, to open the safe you need to know the code. Josh obviously knew it, but do you really believe that Donna, his own wife, wouldn't know?' Pete asked, and Anna knew there was sense in what he was saying. Still, something niggled her as she sought to make sense of Donna's actions.

'But if she went to Esme's last Thursday, why not take the money then? We'd been to see her that afternoon and Dewar as good as accused her of murdering Josh.'

'Unless she had a torch she wouldn't have seen a thing. The power had been cut off for some time,' Pete said with a touch of sympathy.

'She could have gone back in daylight,' Anna said.

'Anna, I'm a forensic scientist not a detective, so I can only present you with my results. I've got a lot to do, so I need to crack on.'

'Thanks, Pete, I'll pass the results on to Mike Lewis.' Anna sighed, frustrated that she couldn't put her finger on what was wrong.

There was a knock and Joan came into the office with the news that she had the results of the cell-site analysis for Josh Reynolds' phone for 5 November, which were very interesting. The constable held out the paperwork but Anna said to leave it on the desk for Dewar and Mike Lewis to look at, as they might want to use it in the interview with Donna.

'They found a Ferrari in a garage at Esme's flat, apparently just like the one Dewar thought it would be,' Joan continued. 'She wants Donna's work computer examined as she suspects Donna was stealing money for Josh from the Lynne Foundation charities.'

'I know you mean well but I really don't want to hear any more about Dewar and the bloody Reynolds case. As far as I'm concerned, my part in the investigation is over,' Anna snapped, exasperated with Joan's continual need to drip-feed her information.

Joan's lower lip began to tremble as she apologized for being a nuisance. She picked up one of the plastic boxes, saying she would put it in the storeroom and come back for the other.

Anna could have kicked herself – as scatty as Joan could be, she was one of the last people Anna would ever want to offend. She called Joan back and said she was very sorry and she hadn't meant to be rude.

'I know you didn't, ma'am, you've a lot on your plate, what with your FBI trip and everything.'

'When it's just the two of us, please call me Anna. You are one of the lifelines of this team, Joan: every statement, every enquiry result goes through you to be uploaded. More than anyone your finger is always on the pulse and I respect you for all the hard work you do and especially the little details you so often spot that the rest of us miss,' Anna said with genuine honesty.

'Thank you, Anna. Do you mind if I say something else about the Reynolds investigation?' Joan asked, and Anna told her to speak her mind.

'I think you're right about Donna. I have gone over everything and as far as I can see the evidence against her is all circumstantial. Agent Dewar seems to have convinced everyone she's right and I'm frightened to say anything to the contrary in case they laugh at me.'

'Never be afraid to speak your mind, Joan; your opinion should be valued as much as anyone else's,' Anna insisted.

Joan said that she would miss her while she was away. Anna gave her a friendly hug and told her that if ever she needed someone to speak to then just call, but to check the time difference first. Just as the constable was about to leave, Mike Lewis and Dewar came in. Mike handed Joan the registration number of the Ferrari and asked her to check on the national computer for the current and previous owner. As she hurried off, Joan said it would be a pleasure.

'She looks like the cat that just got the cream,' Mike observed.

'And so she should,' Anna stressed. 'She's one of the hardest workers out there and sometimes it's good to let her know how much she's appreciated.' She paused and straightened up. 'If it's okay with you, I'll head off home now I've sorted my desk out, and get everything ready for tomorrow.'

Mike said he would be in touch, they shook hands and he gave her a kiss on the cheek then left the room as Dewar stepped closer to Anna.

'I know we haven't always seen eye to eye, but I just wanted to say that it's been an honour working with you, even though it was for such a short time,' Dewar said.

Anna was unsure whether the agent was being genuine, but politely she returned the compliment and put her hand out. Dewar took a firm hold as they shook on it.

'No hard feelings?' Dewar asked, and Anna replied with the same words, even though she couldn't help but wonder if Dewar was actually glad to see the back of her.

'If you need any help or advice on the course, just ring me. It's not cheating, just mutual assistance between two damn good investigators,' Dewar said, surprising Anna, who told her she would, but had no intention of doing so.

'I've told Don Blane, your course instructor, all about you. He's the guy I spoke about, remember?' Anna recalled her making an inappropriate remark that Don could get a virgin to open up in interview. 'He'll look after you, so anything you need just ask him. I might be back at Quantico while you're still on your course so it would be great to go out and have a few beers together. I'll take you for a spin in my 67 Mustang and you can stay a weekend at my lakeside condo.'

'That would be nice,' Anna said, trying to sound sincere.

As Dewar left the room to join Mike Lewis for Donna's interview, she couldn't resist a parting shot: 'If I'm right about Donna, I'll let Mike Lewis tell you.'

Anna wondered how Dewar would feel if she was wrong.

Anna put the last of her personal belongings in her briefcase and closed it, but as she lifted it from her desk, she caught sight of the cell-site analysis report for Josh's phone. All the calls made by Josh on the 5 November were listed, and the positions of the phone masts that the calls were linked to. Curiosity got the better of her and she sat down to check through the calls from the time he was believed to have left the Trojan. At 4.15 p.m., he rang the Savoy Hotel reception and the mobile mast was in Wells Street. The next call, again to the Savoy reception desk, was at 4.30 p.m., and Anna suspected Josh must have been collecting the Ferrari from the NCP or driving it when she saw the mast was on the Marylebone Road. The call lasted for nearly two minutes and passed cell masts on the Harrow Road flyover, Westway on the A40 and finished at Acton. This meant Josh had to be travelling in a vehicle and at a considerable speed. The next call was not made until 6.45 p.m. and originated from a mast in Malden Way on the A3, then thirty seconds later the mast changed to Beverley Way for the remainder of the call. Joan had noted that the £125 petrol purchase shown on Josh's bank statement was made at Tesco Beverley Way at 6.50 p.m. The last call Josh ever made was to Marcus Williams at 7.10 p.m. and the mast was near Esme's flat. As Josh's bike was recovered with the Ferrari he would most probably have walked back to his flat, which Anna estimated would have taken him at least half an hour from the garage. She thought it strange that he had left the bike and wondered if it was because he had been drinking. The cell-site information was helpful in narrowing down the time of death but Anna had no idea why Josh should travel out of London via the A40 and then return on the A3. There was a two-hour period during which his location could not be accounted for. He could have been to see a secret lover, but why when he clearly used Esme's as a love nest? Who was this mystery woman? More importantly, Anna wondered why she had never revealed herself since Josh's death.

Anna turned to Donna's bank statement, concentrating on the month before Josh's death. None of the withdrawals and payments seemed untoward until on Friday, 2 November, Donna withdrew £1000. Anna suspected this was a cash-over-the-counter transaction and recalled Pete Jenkins saying he had found Josh and Donna's fingerprints on one of the bundles of money. Knowing that Dewar and Mike had gone downstairs to interview Donna, Anna highlighted the transaction then wrote a note for Dewar: DID DONNA GIVE JOSH 1K – WHY – AND WHAT FOR?

Once more, Anna picked up her briefcase and grabbed her handbag and coat and was about to leave her office when Joan came in to say goodbye. She was almost in tears as she shook Anna's hand.

'I know you've finished with the Reynolds case but would you like me to keep you updated?' Joan asked.

'As it happens, yes, I would, but keep it just between you and me, okay?'

'Mum's the word,' Joan said, and touched her nose.

'I'd like to listen to a copy of Donna's interview, so I'll e-mail you a password for my Dropbox account and you can load the file and anything else of interest onto that.'

Joan looked terribly depressed.

'Cheer up, I'm not going for good,' Anna told her. 'I'll be back before you know it and whatever case I am allocated I'll ask for you to come on board.'

Joan was becoming more tearful, which only made Anna more eager to leave, sadly reflecting that as often happens with the Joans of this world, they just step that bit too close for comfort.

Donna Reynolds looked composed and quite glamorous, in a Chanel suit, large pearl earrings and matching necklace – not at all like someone who had just finished a long consultation with her lawyer. Ian Holme QC, who had come straight from court to represent her, was in his late fifties, had piercing blue eyes and a large head with a wave of swept-back grey hair. He was tall and thickset with big broad shoulders and large hands, and, in his black court jacket, matching waistcoat and grey pinstripe trousers, created a tremendously imposing impression.

Donna nervously looked at her wristwatch as Mike Lewis and Dewar entered the room and sat down opposite her and Mr Holme. Mike noticed Donna's watch was a diamond-encrusted Rolex and thought it was probably worth more than his family estate car. He introduced himself and Special Agent Dewar, explaining that she was on work experience with the Met. Mr Holme looked over the rim of his half-moon glasses and remarked that Lady Lynne had made him more than aware of exactly who Agent Dewar was and he hoped her conduct would be more professional this time round. Dewar had been warned by Mike about the lawyer's fierce reputation and thought it best not to respond.

Mike switched on the DVD recorder and recited the caution to Donna, who listened intently, clenching her hands together on her lap. Mike said that he would firstly like to go over the statement she made to DI Simms back in November 2012. Holme confirmed that he had discussed the statement with Donna during their consultation.

'So you were at the Lynne Foundation Charity Ball all night on the fifth?' Mike asked her.

'Yes, and I stayed in the hotel overnight.'

'You never left it?'

'No, except to go to the ladies' room and eventually bed,' Donna said, confused by Mike's insinuation.

'This was also verified by Lady Gloria and Aisa Lynne,' Mr Holme interjected.

'That's not true, is it, Donna?' Mike looked Donna in the eye.

'Are you suggesting that Lady Lynne and Aisa are lying?' Holme asked.

'No, Mr Holme, I'm suggesting Donna is, and they were totally unaware she left the hotel.' Mike opened the case folder and got out a CCTV picture of Donna's Mini leaving the hotel car park. It had been edited to remove the date and time stamp. He placed the photograph on the table and turned it round for Donna to see, pointing to the vehicle's number plate.

'Is that your car?'

'Yes,' Donna said nervously.

'Do you know where and when this picture was taken?' Mike continued. Donna stared at the picture and shook her head.

Mike took out a duplicate photograph with the time and date stamp on and placed it on the table for Donna and Holme to see.

'Ten o-five p.m. on the fifth of November 2012 leaving the Savoy underground car park,' Mike said and then placed another picture on the table, again pointing to the time and date stamp.

'Eleven fifty p.m., your car returning to the same car park.' Mike was expecting Mr Holme to object that he had not had access to the pictures before the interview, but he didn't.

Donna looked startled as she turned to Holme. 'I swear it wasn't me driving.' Holme raised his hand for her to stop and explained that the police were not obliged to disclose all their evidence prior to the interview.

'My client has said it was not her and I notice that the driver is not visible in any of your pictures. Do you have any CCTV footage that clearly shows Donna Reynolds driving the vehicle in and out of the car park?' Holme said in a calm and precise manner.

Donna began to shake and was close to tears. Mike pressed her, asking if it wasn't her driving then who was it, to which Donna replied she didn't know. Holme leaned over and whispered to his client, who nodded to him repeatedly during their hushed conversation.

Holme tapped the table with his pen. 'I was at the Charity Ball that night and as I recall the hotel had a valet parking service. Are you aware of that fact?'

Mike looked at Dewar. She shrugged her shoulders and shook her head.

Holme continued: 'I'll take that as, no, shall I? My client used the valet service and her car keys were not back in her possession until she left the hotel on the morning of the sixth.' He smiled smugly.

'You got the car keys from reception, drove to the Bayswater flat, murdered Josh and then returned to the hotel, didn't you, Donna?' Mike quickly countered, staring her in the eye.

'Do you have anyone from the hotel reception who can confirm she asked for her car keys that evening?' Holme interjected.

Mike admitted he didn't and was annoyed that the car-park evidence was now less compelling. It irritated him that Holme was guiding Donna and not letting her answer the questions, but he had no choice but to move on. Next, he produced the set of keys for Esme's flat.

'These keys were found in your car—' Mike began, but Holmes leaned over and had another whispered conversation with Donna, eventually nodding for her to answer.

'They are keys for Josh's mother's flat. I was given them by DI Simms after the post-mortem,' Donna said, fumbling for a tissue from her pocket to wipe her eyes.

'Why did you go there last Thursday evening after visiting Marcus Williams at the Trojan club?' Mike demanded.

'You had me followed?' Donna asked, crying.

Holme again leaned towards her.

'Mr Holme, would you please allow Donna to answer my questions,' Mike said, and the steely-eyed QC glared at him.

'As you never disclosed any of this to me, I need to advise Donna accordingly. She is being cooperative and I do not want her to give an answer that may be taken out of context and made to fit your wild theories,' Holme said calmly and then, turning to Donna, told her to continue. He reached over to a box of tissues on the table and plucked one out, handing it to her. She blew her nose and sniffed.

Donna then said quietly that after Agent Dewar and DCI Travis had been to speak with her at her mother's house she couldn't believe that Josh might have been murdered. She felt as if she was left in the dark, and in that very distressed state she went to see Marcus Williams. Donna insisted she had wanted to find out what Delon Taylor had said and if there was any truth in it. She blew her nose again, crumpled the tissue, swallowed hard and took a deep breath before continuing.

'Before Josh died, I had suspected he was having an affair. At the time he was acting strangely and I became a bit paranoid about it, but I never found anything that confirmed my fears. I thought Josh had sold Esme's flat to pay off some of the Trojan bank loan and renovation work. After Agent Dewar came to see me at my mother's, I wondered if he did have an affair and was using his mother's flat.

'You must have realized he hadn't sold Esme's flat when DI Simms gave you the keys?' Mike said sharply.

'No, I did not. I was given all his belongings in one plastic bag. My mother sorted through it and put his personal belongings in a box for me. I never looked through the box until after DCI Travis and Agent Dewar came to see me.'

'Why then?' Dewar asked.

'Because your questions made me suspicious again, of Josh having an affair. I found the keys in the box and wondered if they were for Esme's flat so I went there.'

Mike placed some photographs of the recovered money down on the table.

'There's one hundred and fifty-eight thousand pounds here in bundles of a thousand. It was found in a cash bag under the floorboards at Esme's flat. Do you know anything about it?'

'No, nothing at all,' Donna said, clearly shocked.

Mike asked her if she knew the combination for Josh's safe and she said she didn't and neither did she know if he'd had any money in it.

'Can you explain then why your fingerprints and firearms residue matching the gun were on some of the money we recovered?'

Donna looked stunned and she turned to Holme, trying to make sense of what she had just been told.

'Josh phoned you at the Savoy and said he was ill and was not going into work. It was the perfect opportunity so you sneaked out from the ball.'

'No, I swear I didn't,' Donna pleaded.

'Josh was in the living room asleep so you quietly opened the safe, got the gun, made him kneel in front of you and then you shot him,' Mike said firmly.

Donna sat shaking her head in disbelief as Holme impatiently drummed his large fingers on the table and rolled his eyes.

'I really must object, Superintendent Lewis. Nearly every question you have asked is based on evidence that was not disclosed to me. You are trying to entrap my client, so I would like full disclosure and a further consultation with Mrs Reynolds before any more questions are put to her.'

Mike knew he had no grounds to object to Mr Holme having a consultation break, and decided that he would disclose further information regarding the recovery of the Ferrari beforehand. As he looked through the case file for a photograph of the car, Dewar took the opportunity to question Donna.

'You faked the suicide note that Josh left on his laptop, didn't you?'

'No, I never even knew it was there, the police found it,' Donna whimpered and again wiped her eyes with the tissue.

Mike Lewis began to explain to Dewar that as Mr Holme has asked for a consultation break, they were obliged to allow it, but Holme interjected, saying that he had been served with a printed copy of the suicide note and he was interested to hear Agent Dewar's reasoning why she thought Donna had written it.

Holme patted Donna's hand. 'Are you happy to continue?' he asked, and she nodded.

Mike knew that the validity of the suicide note would have to be put to Donna at some point so he let Dewar continue.

The agent asked Donna to look at the copy of the note.

'Let me just point something out to you, Donna. The design of the note is wrong for someone about to commit suicide. It's set up for an audience, written in the past tense and full of grammatical errors. It is clearly fake.'

'I don't understand. I swear to you I didn't write it. I never even knew about it until DI Simms spoke to me,' Donna wept.

Mr Holme leaned forward, resting his elbow on the table and his chin in his hand as he looked at the suicide note.

Dewar was about to continue but the lawyer interrupted her: 'A very astute observation, Agent Dewar. Tell me, are you a recognized expert in the field of forensic linguistics?'

'I have studied it and written a paper on the subject,' Dewar replied smugly.

Holme shook his head and raised his eyebrows, clearly not impressed with Dewar's reply.

'Are you a recognized linguistics expert under the United

States Supreme Court "Daubert" test? Or a mere dabbler in the subject?' Mr Holme asked disapprovingly, neatly demonstrating his knowledge of American law.

Mike could feel Dewar tensing up beside him as she clenched her hands together. 'I am conversant with the "Daubert" test, however—' she started to say but Mr Holme interrupted her and remarked that 'being familiar' was not good enough, so he would refresh her memory and enlighten Superintendent Lewis regarding the "Daubert" test.

The way Holme took over the interview was beginning to make Mike tense as well, as the arrogant man removed his half-moon glasses and swung them round in his hand.

'The expert must have sufficient knowledge, skill and experience of the subject matter and acknowledged stature in an academic or other peer community.'

Dewar's cheeks flushed red as she realized she had been found out and her opinions would count for nothing in a court of law. Although she had also wanted to ask Donna about her 999 call to the police, she realized it would now be futile as Mr Holme would again challenge her reliability as an expert. Her embarrassment turned to resentment at being belittled in front of Mike Lewis.

'Do you always believe in a client's innocence?' Dewar challenged Holme, who sat back in his chair and wafted his hand.

'Good Lord, no,' he replied honestly with a chuckle, then deliberately paused before continuing: 'But I do believe Donna Reynolds.'

Mike Lewis took control of the interview and asked Mr Holme if he had read Pete Jenkins' forensic report about the blood spatter. The lawyer confirmed that he had and remarked that it was interesting that the report was made from photographs many months after Josh Reynolds' death and not as a result of observations made at the time.

Mike knew that Holme was implying that the original scene investigation was a total farce. Feeling the pressure, Mike pressed on, glancing towards Donna.

'The conclusion of the report is that your husband did not shoot himself and was in fact murdered, then the gun was placed in his hand to make it look like a suicide.' Mike took a calculated risk and put a photograph of Josh's dead body down on the table in front of Donna. She looked briefly at the picture then began to tremble uncontrollably and burst into a fresh flood of tears.

'I didn't kill Josh. I swear it. I didn't kill him. I loved him. I loved him!' As expected, and hoped for by Mike, a very angry Mr Holme objected to Donna being shown the photograph.

Holme raised his voice. 'Forensic science, like your interview tactics, can be wrong. Your behaviour is underhand and oppressive. I demand a break for consultation.'

Mike quickly turned off the recording equipment. He then stood, picked up his case file and the photographs and told Mr Holme to let the custody sergeant know when he was ready to recommence the interview.

Dewar followed Mike out of the room, racing to catch up with him as he strode down the corridor.

'You had her on the ropes there, why stop?' Dewar asked but Mike said nothing. 'The tears and sniffling are a big act, just like her sham 999 call. You should have kept going at her or allowed me to.'

Mike stopped in his tracks.

'If I want your opinion I will ask for it. I wanted Holme to break the interview before you screwed up again. He lured you right into his trap and played you for a fool. I should have listened to Anna and taken her into the interview,' Mike said with anger.

'But I'm right, the suicide note is a fake.'

'You don't get it, do you?' Mike said, shaking his head.

'Get what?' Dewar asked.

'Holme knows it's a fake, and I've no doubt he agrees that Josh was murdered, but he's saying, and making a very good job of it, that it wasn't Donna.' Mike, exasperated, continued to walk on. 'I warned you, I told you not to get in a head-to-head with Holme.'

'I'm sorry, Mike, it won't happen again.'

'Too bloody right it won't because Barolli will be doing Donna's next interview with me.'

Chapter Twenty-Two

Wanting to look her best on arrival Stateside, Anna was wearing a white silk shirt and a new black-and-red woollen pinstripe suit as she waited for the driver Langton had arranged to pick her up from the flat and take her to Heathrow. The tailoring line of the one button jacket and A-line slit skirt accentuated her curvaceous figure.

Anna had never been inside Terminal Five and was impressed by the size and design of the white-steel-and-glass structure. Staring up at the departure board, she searched for the 10 a.m. British Airways flight to Dulles International Airport, Washington.

'Bit overdressed for an eight-hour flight, aren't you?' she heard Langton's voice say from behind her. She turned to greet him and saw that he was wearing a white T-shirt, grey cotton jacket, matching cargo trousers and trainers, with a backpack slung over his shoulder.

'Good morning, sir, how nice to see you too. The FBI will be impressed by your fine attire,' Anna said with a sarcastic smile.

'Cut the "sir" crap, Travis, you know it's James out of the office,' he said, totally ignoring the rest of her remark.

'I got here early so I've checked in already. The desk is this way,' he added, and walked off without even offering to carry her case or laptop bag.

Anna told the check-in assistant that she was travelling with Mr James Langton and asked if she could sit next to him on the flight.

'I'm sorry, Miss Travis, Detective Chief Superintendent

Langton was allocated the only upgrade we had to Business Class.'

Anna turned and glared at Langton, who had appeared beside her.

'I can't believe your bare-faced cheek, using your rank and profession like that.'

'If you don't ask, you don't get,' he said, shrugging his shoulders, and casually walked off, telling her to get a move on.

After going through security to the departure lounge, Langton asked Anna if she fancied a bit of breakfast as they still had over an hour before the flight. Anna said she did and pointed to a nice-looking restaurant.

'Too stuffy and I fancy a pint of Guinness with a full English, so we'll go to the Wetherspoon pub over there,' Langton announced.

Anna was in two minds whether to tell him he could go to the pub on his own but before she could say anything he was off again.

Anna was slowly eating her bacon sandwich and Langton was at the bar getting his second pint of Guinness when a text message came up on her phone. It was Joan telling her that she had uploaded the first Donna Reynolds interview onto her Dropbox account and that Mike Lewis had thrown Dewar out of the interview. She'd added a 'PS' not to forget the latest issue of *Gardeners' World*.

'Who's that from?' Langton asked, peering over her shoulder and taking a sip of his Guinness. Anna laughed as the brown froth left a moustache above his upper lip. Realizing what she was laughing at, he went to wipe his mouth on his sleeve. Anna tutted at him and pushed his hand out of the way, then used her napkin to get rid of the froth.

'It was Joan wishing me bon voyage. She texted that Mike Lewis threw Dewar out of the Donna Reynolds interview,' Anna said as she started to download the DVD file of Donna's interview to her phone.

'I know, he phoned me last night. He didn't literally throw

her out but he refused to let her sit in on any further interviews,' Langton informed her.

'She overstep the mark again?' Anna asked, keen to hear more.

He leaned across the table and spoke softly: 'Let her cock-ups be a lesson for when you work in her world at Quantico. Don't jump in feet first. Listen and take advice. Dewar's overeager to prove herself, but you've always got to choose the moment you step forward – you make mistakes with overconfidence and you pay for it.'

'I'll remember that,' she said quietly.

'So, are you looking forward to the FBI course?' he asked.

'I am, but to be truthful I would have liked to see closure on the Reynolds case before I left.'

Langton looked at his watch. 'In essence, you have. Mike spoke with the CPS last night and they approved him charging Donna this morning.'

'A lot of the evidence is just circumstantial; she may not have done it.' Anna was taken aback by Langton's information.

'For Christ's sake, let it rest! Donna's been caught out by her lies and by forensics. The jury will decide whether or not she murdered her husband, not you,' Langton said, picking up his backpack and pointing to the departure screen. 'Our flight's boarding, I need to go to duty free, so I'll meet you at the gate.'

Before she could follow him her phone beeped and there was another text message from Joan saying she had uploaded Donna's second interview and that the *Gardeners' World* article about Gloria Lynne was very interesting. Anna reflected she was glad that she wouldn't be sitting beside Langton after all, as it would give her the opportunity to watch the Donna interview during the flight. On her way to the boarding gate she popped into the newsagent's, bought the magazine and tucked it away in the side pocket of her laptop bag.

Once in the air, Anna got out her headphones and then transferred the two files of Donna's interviews from her phone to her laptop. She pressed the Media Play button and reclined her

window seat back a little so that she felt more comfortable, just
as the flight attendant approached her and asked if she would
like a drink. Why not, she thought, and asked her for a gin and
tonic with ice and lemon. It felt strange, but extremely pleasant,
viewing the interview with a plastic glass in her hand thousands
of feet above land.

As she watched, the dominating presence and intellect of
Ian Holme QC was obvious; he was a master of his trade. She
knew that Gloria would be paying for his time and expertise
out of her own pocket, and estimated that his services for
representing Donna at trial would be in the region of at least
a million pounds. As she came to the section where Holme
questioned Dewar's experience she felt some sympathy for
the agent. She had not been rude or aggressive towards Donna,
or Mr Holme, but in implying she was a linguistics expert, she
had stepped outside of her field of expertise and been made to
look a fool.

Anna was about to watch the second interview when she
looked up and saw Langton walking down the aisle towards her
carrying a large glass of whisky. On seeing him she quickly shut
the top of her laptop.

'Do you mind if I join you?' he asked, and Anna patted the
empty seat beside her.

'Sorry about snapping at you earlier, I've a lot on my mind,'
he said as he sat down.

From his slightly slurred speech, Anna knew that he had been
enjoying more than one glass of whisky. It made her smile, as
she knew that he was never aggressive in drink but liked to
natter and put the world to rights.

'Want to share your thoughts?' Anna asked.

He took a sip of his whisky, leaned back in the seat and closed
his eyes. 'I don't know, I'm feeling tired.' He opened his eyes
and looked at her. 'Before I knew I was going to Quantico, I
began losing interest, started taking a back seat in the investigations I was overseeing. Strange really, win or lose I used to love
the thrill of the chase.'

'Do you think that is what our work is about, winning and losing?'

'Course it is – we win if we find the evidence and get a conviction and if a jury say not guilty we've still done our job in getting them to trial. When you can't find the evidence and a case runs out of steam, then it's depressing, but you have to let go and move on,' he said.

She said nothing but took a moment to look at him. He seemed to have aged and looked tired. Anna was surprised when he took hold of her hand.

'What are you thinking?' he asked.

'Oh, just how complicated a detective's life can be, one step forward, one step back, sleepless nights, those sorts of things.'

'Tell me, now you're a DCI, how do you like to relax and forget about work?'

She released her hand, unsure exactly why he was asking her that. He turned to face her, and again held her hand.

'You still wear your old engagement ring.'

'Yes. Is there a problem with that?' she asked somewhat curtly.

'Have you been able to move on from losing, um . . .'

'Ken,' she said, annoyed that Langton had forgotten his name.

'Right, Ken . . . it must be two or more years since it all happened.'

'Yes.'

'So have you moved on?'

'What do you mean?'

'Well, exactly what I said – have you formed any new relationships?'

'I don't think it's any of your business.'

'No, it isn't,' Langton insisted, 'but I care about you and one of the reasons I put you forward for the FBI course was because I felt that you were stagnating – maybe not the right word – but I've been very aware of you becoming a bit solitary.'

'Stagnating and solitary, don't be ridiculous,' Anna said, offended.

'No need to sound so uppity.'

The slur in his speech was becoming more noticeable.

'I'm not uppity, for heaven's sake. I also really love my work and—'

He jumped in. 'What do you love about it?'

She sighed with impatience. 'Fitting the pieces of the puzzle together, finding the evidence, tracking the criminal—'

Anna was interrupted by a long sigh from Langton as he stared ahead, his dark eyes brooding and shadowed with pain. 'The energy's going, Anna, I'm not getting any younger and I've had enough of dealing with the dregs of society. But this trip, if it pays off, will put the life back in me. If it doesn't happen then I've lost and he's won, so I'll quit, retire.'

Anna looked at him, surprised by what he had just said, assuming he was referring to Deputy Commissioner Walters preventing his promotion.

'Do you think you would feel differently if you had been made Commander by now?' she asked, knowing she had inadvertently contributed to his current position but desperate to know how much his failure to be promoted disturbed him.

'It would certainly mean more money and a very lucrative pension, but right now it's not uppermost in my mind,' he said and took another sip of his drink.

'You deserve promotion to Commander more than anyone else in the Met after all the cases you've solved.'

'I know that, just a pity fucking Walters doesn't see it that way. As far as he's concerned that fuck-up with the murdering drug dealer Fitzpatrick was the end of my career. The one that got away. Even if I'd got Fitzpatrick to trial and he'd walked I'd at least feel I hadn't totally failed.' He gave a soft laugh, and as Anna looked at him, he boyishly ran his fingers through his hair.

'Let you into a she-cret,' he said, sounding more sloshed, then leaned in very close and whispered in her ear.

'Real reason for me going to work with the FBI is to help find you-know-who, if there's anywhere in the world that bastard is hiding out the feds will get him. So, I suppose there's still a bit of life left in the old dog.' He nudged Anna with his elbow.

'I'll get Fitzpatrick this time, you can count on it, and then I can get back to Laura and the kids.'

Anna was keenly aware that the Fitzpatrick case had never ceased to eat away at his pride and all at once it dawned on her that his attachment to the FBI, purportedly to work on cold cases, was a cover for his quest to get even with the man who had humiliated him. She didn't think he was really ready to retire, far from it, but realized his decision depended on whether or not he was successful in finally tracking down and arresting Fitzpatrick. Langton tucked his empty glass into the pocket in front of the seat and closed his eyes; eventually, he started to snore. She gave him a gentle nudge and suggested he'd be more comfortable in his Business Class seat. As he got up he kissed her gently on the cheek.

'Thanks for listening, Counsellor Travis.'

As Anna watched him weave unsteadily back down the aisle she remembered the Langton she had known and loved so deeply. Since meeting Ken and then tragically losing him her feelings for Langton had changed. They were still there, but she recognized they were no longer of love, more like a deep affection. She wondered if he would have any recollection of their conversation when he woke up, and in many ways she hoped he didn't.

Anna flipped open her laptop, asked for another gin and tonic and then started the DVD file of the second interview with Donna. She could see that Barolli had replaced Dewar in the room with Mike Lewis. Ian Holme spoke first.

'My client has spent the last seven months believing her husband committed suicide. Being accused of Josh Reynolds' murder, with what can only be described as spurious circumstantial evidence, only serves to further undermine her emotional state and wellbeing. She has made a statement that I will now read to you.'

Donna sat beside him, still as he had just said in a very emotional state, crying and wiping her eyes with a tissue.

Holme said that Donna had no knowledge of the Ferrari or

where it had come from. She admitted that she had gone to Esme's flat on the Thursday night, but this was only the second time she had been to the premises, as Esme did not approve of a stripper marrying her son and had never been told that she was Lady Gloria Lynne's daughter. She claimed that when she went inside the flat there was no electricity so she was only there for a matter of seconds before leaving. She knew nothing about the money hidden under the floorboards. As for her fingerprints being found on some of the money: Josh had said he didn't have time to get to the bank and needed cash to pay a decorator so she had withdrawn a thousand pounds from her own bank account and given it to Josh on Friday, 2 November.

Mike interjected and asked Mr Holme if Donna would be willing to answer some questions to clarify the current position regarding the flat and also the identity of the decorator. After a whispered conversation Donna said she wanted to be helpful and would answer in the interest of helping the police catch the real killer of her husband.

Mike continued. 'Do you know the identity of the decorator?'

'I saw him coming into the Bayswater flats one day when I was running late for work — well I think it was him as he was carrying painting stuff and wearing overalls,' Donna said.

'Do you know his name?' Mike Lewis asked.

'No, Josh never said and I didn't ask. I think he was only at our flat for a couple of days.'

'Did you see him at Esme's funeral?' Barolli asked.

'I didn't go to the funeral as I was recovering from minor surgery in a private hospital.'

Anna noticed Donna appeared a little more relaxed.

'Do you know if he worked at Esme's flat?'

'No, but Josh did say he was going to have it done up and sell it and I thought that he had.'

Barolli asked Donna if she could describe the man and she said not really other than he was black, mid-fifties and wore a multicoloured hat.

'When did you see the decorator at the flats?' Mike asked.

'It was late October, I think.'

Anna realized that the man Donna had seen could not be Samuel Peters as Marisha had said he had returned to Jamaica in September. She wondered if Donna was lying to try and deflect suspicion away from her.

There was another pause as Mike glanced at his notes.

Donna leaned forwards. 'Do you think it was the decorator that killed Josh?' She seemed nervous and Mr Holmes latched onto her question.

'The police will investigate further, Donna, and if he had access to your flat then he would know there was a safe,' Mr Holme said reassuringly, and Donna looked pleased.

'If the decorator also worked at Josh's mother Esme's, he could have killed him, taken the money and hidden it there,' Donna said with enthusiasm and Mr Holme agreed with her. It was odd to see Donna behave almost childishly, nodding her head as if to agree with herself.

'That would be very convenient for you and an excellent proposition but for a couple of facts,' Barolli said as he leaned towards Donna, who appeared confused by his comment.

He continued: 'We know from a witness that Josh's Uncle Samuel did some decorating for him and he returned to Jamaica long before Josh was murdered.'

Holme could see where Barolli was going with this information and was quick to interject on Donna's behalf.

'My client said she was not aware of who did the decorating and if this Samuel returned to Jamaica then clearly Josh had hired someone else to decorate the flat.'

'You're lying, Donna. You saw the decorator in August or September and it suits your story to try and blame him because we both now know it wasn't a suicide,' Mike said.

'No, I'm not lying. I swear to God it was October and I didn't know any Samuel,' Donna pleaded, and began to shake nervously.

Mike looked at his notes before continuing. 'With regard to Esme's flat, did you go back there after last Thursday?'

'No.'

'Why not in daylight, especially if you wanted to know if Josh was using it for an affair?'

'My mother told me not to.'

'Your mother knew about you going to Esme's?' Mike asked, surprised.

Mr Holme again interjected and said that this fact was alluded to in Donna's statement and she had told her mother the following morning. Lady Lynne had then made enquiries regarding Esme's will and the property, became Donna's after Josh's death.

'All above board and legitimate, officer, and no doubt something you might consider strange for an alleged murderer to do. I refer of course to your opinion of Donna, and not Lady Lynne,' Holme said with a smirk, trying to be flippant.

'Do you mind if I ask Donna some questions about her job at the Lynne Foundation?' Mike looked at Holme.

'Is it relevant to your enquiries?' Holme demanded.

Mike said that it was to do with her relationship with Josh and leaving the Trojan to work at the Foundation. Holme looked at Donna, who nodded.

'You went to work for your mother after Esme Reynolds died?' Mike asked.

'About then, yes.'

'Is CCS Medical Trust one of the charities you personally look after?'

'Yes, amongst others, but that is the biggest,' Donna said proudly, and yet again Anna was struck by how childish Donna appeared to be.

'With I believe a turnover in the region of thirty million pounds,' Mike said, smiling back at her and deliberately giving an encouraging nod of respect, at which Donna smiled again.

Mike opened a blue folder and placed a computer printout of the CCS Medical Trust account in front of Donna and took out a copy for himself.

'Can I draw your attention to the highlighted section, September fourth, 2012? As you can see, one hundred thousand pounds transferred electronically from CCS Medical to an account in the name of Mr John Peters. Does that transaction ring any bells?' Mike asked and Donna peered closely at the list.

'No, it doesn't, but it could be someone who was owed monies for doing work related to a charity,' Donna said.

'The John Peters account was opened at the end of August 2012 using, as you must be aware, Esme's maiden name, her husband's Christian name and their address of flat two, Brandon Walk,' Mike said calmly.

Donna looked like a rabbit caught in headlights as she turned to Mr Holme and shook her head. She waited for his advice, but this time he didn't lean over to whisper and Anna could see that he was taken aback by Mike Lewis's revelation.

'Do you know anything about this, Donna?' Mr Holme asked, almost as if he doubted her honesty.

'No, I swear I don't. Other people have access to the account so—'

Mike interrupted Donna: 'Yes, but they don't all know Esme's address and maiden name, do they?'

'But I, honestly, I mean I didn't know her maiden name or her husband's name,' Donna implored.

Anna was amazed that Mr Holme didn't interject; she could only think that he was shocked at what Mike Lewis had uncovered and the fact that Donna might have been lying.

'Can you assist me, Mrs Reynolds, regarding the J. Peters transfer that is clearly connected to your work at the Lynne Foundation?' Mike asked and sat back in his chair, staring at the young woman.

As Donna continued to read through the document the tears started to roll down her cheeks. She pleaded and pleaded that she didn't know anything about the debit from the CCS Medical account. Mr Holme told her that it would be in her best interest at the present time to make 'no comment' to any

further questions that were put to her. A sobbing Donna said
that she wanted to tell the truth. Mr Holme sighed irritably and
said it was her choice as to whether or not she heeded his
advice.

Mike Lewis had really upped his game and it was obvious that
he knew he was now in the driving seat. Anna watched intently
as Mike placed another highlighted document down on the
table.

'September fifth, an electronic transfer for ninety-eight and a
half thousand pounds for the purchase of a Ferrari. Ring any
bells?' Mike asked and tapped his finger on the highlighted area
of the piece of paper.

Donna said nothing, but merely shook her head and looked
bewildered as Mike put a picture of the Ferrari on the desk.

'This car was recovered from Esme Peters' garage and registered in the name John Peters, flat two, Brandon Walk,' Mike
said.

'That can't be right. I never—' Donna's voice was high-
pitched with nerves as Mr Holme interrupted her.

'We can ask for a break to discuss the CCS money transfers.'

Donna nodded and said she'd like to do that. Mike Lewis
made a wide-handed open gesture, saying he was happy for a
break to take place but that there were two bits of further information he felt he should disclose first.

'A man matching Josh Reynolds' description collected the
Ferrari from the garage a few days later.' Mike looked at Donna,
inviting her to give him some form of explanation. Mr Holme
gave her a stern look and she said nothing.

'Let me tell you what I think happened. When Josh's business
began to fail and he needed money to prop it up the two of you
hatched a plan.'

Donna was shaking her head and clasping and unclasping her
hands.

'You knew that your mother would never give you money to
support Josh's business. But working for the Lynne Foundation,
stealing thousands here and there out of a multi-million-pound

account would be a drop in the ocean and never missed.' Mike cocked his head to one side as if saying 'I'm right,' but then Holme patted the table with the flat of his hand.

'So why should my client murder her husband?' the lawyer said.

'From the love nest we found at your client's mother-in-law's, it is clear that Josh was having an affair. I believe that Donna knew this and in a fit of jealousy decided to murder him and make it look like a suicide.'

Donna half rose out of her chair and then sat back down again. 'No, I never knew about any affair. I loved him, I still do, I could never kill him, never.' Donna burst into sobs, her whole body shaking, and quickly became an incoherent wreck.

Mike suggested she cut the act and confess to Josh's cold-blooded murder.

Mr Holme stood up, demanding an end to the interview. Mike Lewis then announced he would be contacting the Crown Prosecution Service to ask for permission to charge Donna with the murder of Joshua Reynolds.

Anna sat back in her seat, quite stunned by what she had just seen. She couldn't believe that Donna had managed to fool everyone, both at the time of the murder, and over the near seven months since. Was she really such an accomplished actress, or the victim of circumstances beyond her control? For Anna, it still didn't add up, because at times Donna's actions didn't make sense. Her gut feeling told her that Donna wasn't lying, but the circumstantial evidence and the woman's own naïvety had made it seem that she was. This Donna, like the distressed one in the 999 call, was in Anna's eyes, telling the truth.

Anna recognized that even if Donna stole the CCS charity money it didn't mean she killed Josh. There was also now the clear possibility that someone other than Samuel decorated their flat and could be the real killer. Anna mulled it over: what if Samuel did decorate Josh's flat? It meant Marisha was lying or mistaken about when her brother left the UK. If Samuel had been the decorator Josh would probably have given him keys for his own and his mother's flats, especially as he was one of the family. What didn't make any sense was why he would be involved in his nephew's murder. Anna threw her pen down, irritated that she could not make sense of the interview and all that was going round and round in her mind. 'Enough,' she said to herself, realizing that she was spoiling what should be an enjoyable flight and that her doubts could wait until later. She packed away her laptop and settled down to enjoy her in-flight meal with a glass of wine, followed by a relaxing nap.

The next thing Anna knew, she was being roused by a flight attendant asking her to fasten her seatbelt as they were about to land. She looked out of the window at the ground below, wondering if the FBI Academy was in amongst the houses, buildings and woodland she could make out. Filled with optimism at the prospect of working alongside FBI agents at the prestigious Quantico headquarters, Anna could not recall a previous moment in her career when she had felt so excited.

Twenty-Three

Thanks to the assistance of an immigration officer, Anna and Langton quickly cleared Dulles passport control and collected their bags. Langton needed to nip to the gents and Anna agreed to keep an eye on his bags. As he left, she looked at her watch and calculated it was early evening in London, so she took the opportunity to phone Joan's mobile.

After thanking Joan for the DVD files, Anna admitted that even having watched the interviews she was still not convinced of Donna's guilt and raised the possibility that there was another decorator besides Samuel or that Marisha was lying. Joan told her that Paul Barolli had said the same thing and he had made an appointment for Marisha Peters to come in to the station so they could ask her more about her brother Samuel.

'I need you to find out who the official photographer was at the Lynne Charity Ball on the fifth. Then get digital copies of all the photographs he took and upload them onto my Dropbox.'

'Why?'

Anna looked up and saw Langton returning. 'I've got to dash, I'll call and explain tomorrow.'

'Have you read the *Gardeners' World* article yet?'

'Not yet, but I will,' Anna assured her, and slipped her phone in her pocket as Langton approached, worried he'd throw another wobbly about her fixation with the Reynolds case. The result was that she didn't hear what Joan said next:

'It's called "These Plants May Kill" – a bit creepy but very

interesting. You never know what dangers lie in a garden ...
Hello, Anna? Hello?'

Having passed through US Customs they noticed a man dressed
in a dark-blue polo shirt that had the FBI crest on it. He was
dark-haired, aged about forty, very handsome and incredibly
fit-looking with broad shoulders, large chest and muscular arms.
On seeing Anna and Langton, he came over and with a warm
smile and firm handshake introduced himself as Special Agent
Don Blane. Anna recalled Dewar saying Blane was the course
instructor and she hoped that Don would not be Dewar's clone.

'Hi. It's real nice to meet you. You look just like the photos
our London office sent over. Transport is just outside so if you'd
like to follow me,' he said as he took hold of Anna's case for her.

Outside, Don Blane opened the sliding side door of an old
weather-beaten, FBI-logo'd, minibus and put Anna's case inside.
Before Langton could add his own case, Blane told him that the
car behind would take him to Lake Ridge where he was staying.
Anna turned and saw a shiny black Lincoln with a suited chauf-
feur standing beside it. She glanced at Langton and shook her
head in disbelief, to which he retorted that he hadn't pulled
rank this time.

'So, you're not staying at Quantico?' Anna asked with raised
eyebrows, knowing that he was hiding something.

'Um, no, but I will be working from there,' Langton breezily
replied. 'By the way, what I said on the plane about Fitzpatrick
is strictly confidential. Only the Commissioner and Deputy
Walters know why I'm here. Walters tried to put the kibosh on
it but the director of the FBI spoke personally with the
Commissioner who overruled Walters.'

Anna immediately responded that she had no intention of
telling anyone, and though she didn't say it she was miffed at his
implication. 'Another thing, about the Josh Reynolds case—'
Langton started, but Anna interrupted him.

'Don't worry, I'm over it.'

'Rubbish, I came back to see you again on the flight. You

were sound asleep and your notebook was open on the seat with all your observations about Donna's interview.'

'You looked through my personal belongings? How—'

'Before you get on your high horse, just listen to me. If you really think something's wrong, find it, but be sure you have the evidence to back it up. If there's no evidence, accept it and move on. Tell Mike Lewis what's worrying you – he respects you and he'll listen.'

Langton got into the Lincoln but before closing the door, he leaned out: 'I'll see you at the FBI Academy tomorrow. We can have dinner together.' Anna nodded and he closed the door.

Don Blane informed Anna that the journey time to the Academy was about forty-five minutes and that he was the class tutor, so if there was anything she wanted or needed she should feel free to ask. Anna was struck by how pleasant and well-mannered the man was and sensed he was being genuine. Blane remarked that Jessie Dewar had told him Anna would be the one to watch out for. Anna asked what Dewar had said and Don explained that she had been singing Anna's praises and thought she could well be the top student. Anna was extremely surprised by this and guardedly said that she had enjoyed working with Jessie.

'How did you find her?' Blane asked.

Anna said that she hadn't really had much of a chance to get to know her but she seemed okay. She paused briefly as she thought about Blane's question. 'Why do you ask?'

'Nothing really, just curious – she was telling me about your Reynolds case and what she'd uncovered and how she thought it was the wife that murdered the husband.'

'She's not slow in voicing her opinion,' Anna remarked, and he laughed.

'That sounds like the Jessie I know. She's not afraid to speak her mind, but the problem is she gets a fixation about something and she won't let it go.'

'We're all guilty of that sometimes,' Anna said, knowing that her clash of swords with Dewar came from both of them holding strong views.

'Jessie's heart's in the right place, but as I'm sure you know, there's no substitute for years of front-line investigative experience.'

'She seemed pretty confident to me,' Anna said.

'Jessie came to the Behavioural Unit with very little experience as a field agent, so she feels the need to prove herself. The problem is, she latches onto facts that support her theory and unintentionally ignores evidence to the contrary.'

Anna thought that Don Blane was very shrewd. He clearly knew that Dewar must have ruffled a few feathers while she was in London, yet he was defending her in a kind and respectful way. With a sense of relief, she began to feel that they might get along after all.

As they drove to the Quantico base, Blane gave Anna a guide to the area, telling her that the Academy had opened in 1972 and was situated on a US Marine Corps base, surrounded by over 400 acres of woodland and lakes. The Forensic Science Research and Training Centre were also based on the same site along with outdoor and indoor firearms ranges and a mock town called 'Hogan's Alley'.

They eventually arrived at a checkpoint, where two armed Marine guards examined Blane's ID and Anna's papers as well as searching the minibus before allowing them to pass. It was at least another two miles through woodland before Anna could see the honey-coloured buildings of the Academy.

Blane parked by the main building, got out and hurried round to Anna's door to open it. He carried her case and laptop bag into the reception area, where he introduced her. She handed over her course invitation paperwork and was given a room key, and an FBI badge with her picture on it hanging from a lanyard, which she was told must be worn at all times when on the Academy grounds but was not to be used or shown off the premises. Blane then took her down a long glass corridor and pointed out that similar glass corridors throughout the complex came together and met in a glass-covered quad that linked all the buildings. He explained that you didn't ever need to go outside between buildings but it was easy to get lost when you didn't know the place.

Anna followed him into the lift to the top floor of the dormitory building as he explained that the rooms were not exactly the Hilton, but adequate and comfortable. On entering her room, Anna saw that it had a threadbare red carpet and a single bed in one corner, with a small workstation-come-desk next to it and a lamp. The bed consisted of white sheets, a blanket and a grey bedspread. The wardrobe was tiny and there were only about half a dozen coat hangers. Next to the wardrobe there was a small chest of drawers and a wooden armchair that looked rather rickety. Anna told Blane that it was exactly like the rooms at the Hendon Police College in London, only with a better view, as looking out from the window the woodlands and lakes were quite stunning. She noticed an assault course that stretched as far as the eye could see into the woods. It had high brick walls, rope climbing frames and balance beams along the way.

'Is that part of the FBI training?' Anna asked, pointing from the window.

'That's the Yellow Brick Road, a six-mile obstacle-course run. It's part of the fitness regime and if and when you can complete it then you are awarded with a yellow brick to honour the achievement.'

'So what does an FBI training day entail?' Anna asked with trepidation.

'We start at seven a.m. with physical exercise, push-ups, pull-ups and a smaller assault course. Then it's into the classroom learning about profiling, latest forensics, leadership and media. Day finishes about five p.m. and then there's your case research to work on in the evening.'

Anna felt exhausted just listening to the daily routine. She had not really contemplated what the course would consist of, only that it was a good career move, but now it sounded extremely daunting. She asked Blane if there was Wi-Fi in the room, only to learn that that for security reasons it was not allowed, and the only Internet access was from the computers in the library. He suggested that she unpack and he would meet her downstairs by the elevator and take her to the supplies store to get her training uniform and other course equipment.

Having emptied her bags and used up every inch of storage space, Anna set up her laptop on the desk and put her notepad down beside it. She then went to join Don Blane in the reception area, from where he took her to the stores and supplies room. She was given a large blue holdall with the FBI logo and crest on it, a pair of brown cargo trousers and three blue FBI polo shirts to be worn during class. A grey FBI tracksuit, matching T-shirts and blue windcheater jacket were also provided, along with books relating to her course. As Blane, ever the gentleman, picked up the holdall to carry it for Anna, she glanced to see if he was wearing a wedding ring and noticed he wasn't. She really liked him and if her first impression was accurate she thought she'd like to spend some of her ten weeks at Quantico getting to know him better. Blane suggested that she drop the holdall off in her room and then they could have a bite to eat in the canteen as it closed at seven.

As they sat eating their food, Anna told him that she had expected the canteen food to consist of pizzas, hot dogs and hamburgers but was pleasantly surprised to see how healthy it actually was.

'The motto "A healthy mind in a healthy body" is a big thing here,' Blane said as he ate his chicken salad.

Anna had opted for the tuna fish with fresh vegetables.

Blane took the opportunity to explain more about the course, informing Anna that two hundred US law-enforcement officers and fifty international students would attend it and that each class consisted of twenty-five students. The name of the game was to make contacts and get to know as many fellow students as possible. He went on to say that the course would officially begin at two p.m. tomorrow afternoon in the lecture theatre where the aims and objectives would be set out.

Anna smiled. 'That's good news. I can sleep in a bit. I was naïve to think that the jet lag wouldn't get the better of me.'

They finished their meal and Blane asked Anna if she would like a look round.

'I'd really like to see the library and use one of your computers for some research,' she replied at once.

'Damn, you're keen, and I haven't even allocated you a case project yet,' he said jokingly.

'Actually, it's something to do with the Reynolds case. I'm hoping to get background and travelling details on a Jamaican citizen called Samuel Peters.'

'I might be able to help you there. I'm a good friend with a US drug enforcement agent on the island called Bill Roberts. I can have a chat with him if you like and see what he can find out.'

'Thanks, Don, that would be really helpful.' Anna smiled.

'Off the record, I take it?' he asked.

'For now, yes, but if anything comes of it, I can get one of the team back home to draw up the necessary paperwork and make it an official enquiry.' Anna took out the notebook she usually had with her and jotted down what she knew about Samuel.

'Well, it's the same time in Jamaica as here, and there's no point in hanging around.' Blane grinned, getting out his mobile to ring Bill Roberts. He turned away from her as he caught up with his friend but Anna could see from his body language that he was conveying the urgency of the enquiry.

Anna thanked him profusely before confessing that she hoped he didn't think she was being rude but she was very tired after a long day, and then deliberately added that she didn't want to keep him from his partner any longer.

'No worries, just me at home now; my wife passed away three years ago from cancer. No kids either, but I spoil my nieces and nephews something rotten.' He looked at her with amusement.

'I'm sorry, I didn't mean to pry,' Anna said, wishing she'd not been so sneaky.

'Not at all. What about you, anyone in your life?'

'Not at the moment. My fiancé passed away two years ago – he was a prison officer and a violent inmate attacked him.' Anna had never been so matter-of-fact and open with anyone about Ken's death; she didn't know why but it just felt right to be unguarded and honest with Don. There was so much about his manner, smile and the way he spoke that she felt attracted to.

Blane stood up and, looking into Anna's eyes, shook her hand. 'If there's anything at all you need, please call me,' he said, handing her his business card. 'And I was wondering if you'd like to go out to dinner tomorrow night?'

Anna's face lit up and she had no hesitation as she replied, 'That would be really nice, thank you.'

Langton couldn't believe how luxurious Jessie Dewar's lakeside apartment was. The large living-come-dining room had floor-to-ceiling windows that gave a panoramic view across the man-made lakes and golf course. The floors were real wood and the walls were pristine white with modern art hanging through-out and splashing the rooms with colour. The white leather sofa and armchairs were large and comfortable. A glass dining table and six white leather chairs were positioned near the sliding glass doors that led onto the large terrace with glass and alu-minium railings. There were two double bedrooms, the master with en-suite bathroom, and both with LCD TVs and walk-in closets. A double garage to one side was designed to fit in with the surrounding buildings.

Langton decided to take a wander over to the golf club to eat and have a cold beer. Once there, he was surprised how busy the restaurant was and didn't really feel properly attired to eat in it, so he opted for the barbecue menu on the veranda and had a T-bone steak, fries and salad. The meal was delicious and he was joined by a couple of the golf-club members who had just finished their round. One turned out to be the local sheriff and so Langton told him that he was with the Met Police in London and a visiting lecturer on a course at the FBI Academy. He and the sheriff got on very well and spent an enjoyable evening topping up each other's beer glasses whilst swapping war stories.

Langton returned to the condo quite drunk, and contemplated calling Travis, but knew she would be exhausted and well asleep by now so he didn't bother. He was looking forward to having dinner with her and wondered if he should invite her to stay at Dewar's as there were two rooms. Why not, he thought to himself as he lay on the bed fully clothed, whereupon the alcohol and jet lag kicked in and he was fast asleep within minutes.

Chapter Twenty-Four

A call from the reception-desk officer summoned Dewar and Barolli down to Witness Interview Room One, where they were greeted by the sight of Marisha Peters grinning widely and swaying slightly in her seat. Barolli introduced Dewar and said she was helping him with his enquiries into her nephew Josh's death.

'I is helping too, just like Miss Dewsi, and I can tell youse I knows a thing or two,' Marisha said, wagging her finger.

'Have you been drinking, Marisha?' Barolli asked.

Marisha shook her head, and then sucked air through her teeth in annoyance.

'I told youse, Officer Perrolli, I'SE DON'T DRINK!'

Marisha was slurring her words and Barolli knew that she was lying. Checking her eyes he noticed her pupils were dramatically enlarged.

'Have you been taking drugs, Marisha?' he pressed.

'DRUGS, no way, mon. I've not touched the ganja for years.' Marisha licked her lips and started to shake slightly. 'Can someone tern de heating down. I'se burning up in here and me mouth's no spit left,' she said, but showed no signs of sweating.

Barolli leaned towards Marisha to smell her breath and smiled at her.

'You had some of that spiced rum with your coffee?'

Marisha grinned back, giggling, and leaned in close to his face to whisper: 'Well, only a little one fer a bit of da Dutch courage, before I'se come and see ya to tell you what I knows about da rich bitch.'

Her voice was so croaky that Barolli pushed his own bottle of water across the desk. Marisha squinted, trying to focus on it, and grabbed at thin air in her attempt to pick it up. Barolli noticed her breathing was becoming heavier and there was a faint rasping sound. He picked up the bottle of water and put it in Marisha's hand, then turned his back towards her so he could have a whispered conversation with Dewar.

'She doesn't look too good to me. She's clearly had a skinful so I don't think it's appropriate to interview her at the moment.'

'You're being overcautious,' the agent insisted. 'She's only had the one rum and her wheezy breathing is down to her being overweight.' Before he could reply, Dewar started her questioning: 'I want to ask you some things about your brother Samuel.'

'De good lord knows she done for ma nephew,' Marisha said, her voice becoming more agitated as she started to rock backwards and forwards in her chair, constantly licking her lips.

'The date he went back to Jamaica is important, as I believe Donna Reynolds is trying to frame him for murder,' Dewar said firmly.

'Frame who for murder?' Marisha asked with a confused look on her face as she began to scratch her lower left arm repeatedly.

'Did Samuel ever meet Donna when he was decorating?' Dewar asked, growing exasperated.

'Decorating Donna, yes, ma'am, he also decorate Esme's real good.' Marisha again sucked air through her teeth and began to shake even more.

'Will you please answer my question?' Dewar said, becoming frustrated.

Barolli was concerned. 'Marisha, are you okay? I can get a doctor to come and see you if you feel ill.' Dewar glared at him, but he quietly told her that he didn't think it was a good idea to continue, as Marisha was clearly on another planet and due to her condition anything she might say would be ruled worthless as evidence. Dewar, latching onto Marisha's comment about Donna, ignored his advice.

'When did Samuel go back home?' Dewar asked, leaning forward, pressing for an answer. Marisha stared into space and began to sway and shake even more, as Barolli noticed that her pupils had got larger and she had scratched her arm so roughly that she'd drawn blood.

'Answer my question, Marisha, or I will arrest you for perverting the course of justice,' Dewar said assertively.

Marisha's breathing had become even more erratic.

'Samuel never steal no money, the rich bitch give it to him.' Her shaking was now uncontrollable.

Barolli could see the woman was incapable of understanding the questions and it was time to get her medical assistance.

'Stop now, Agent Dewar,' he said.

'She's lying, she knows something. Tell me why Donna gave Samuel money, Marisha.'

'Ask de lord, he knows she done for my Samuel as well!' Marisha shouted at the top of her voice.

'He helped Donna so she paid him off, didn't she?' Dewar asked loudly.

Marisha suddenly squeezed her chest with both hands and her eyes began to roll in their sockets as she bent forward, apparently in great pain.

'Where is he, where is Samuel now?' Dewar persisted.

Marisha couldn't speak; it was as if she was suddenly starved of oxygen, and she looked at Barolli as if begging for help. He jumped up, opened the interview-room door and shouted for someone to call an ambulance. As Marisha slumped to the floor, Dewar knelt down beside her and unzipped her jacket and the top button of her blouse.

'She's lying to protect Samuel and I—' Dewar started to say as Barolli knelt down.

'Shut the fuck up, Dewar, and help me with CPR.'

By the time the ambulance arrived, Marisha was unconscious, but still alive thanks to the continuous CPR that Barolli and

Dewar had given her. Having seen their witness safely off to hospital accompanied by a uniform officer, Barolli phoned Mike Lewis to tell him what had happened, stating only that they had just started to interview Marisha when she collapsed and had a suspected heart attack. Mike Lewis told Barolli that he and Dewar were to wait, as he was on his way over to speak with them both, and on no account should either of them leave the station.

Barolli paced around Travis's office, racking his brains about what to tell Mike and whether or not he should defend Dewar. He knew that the whole incident had been captured on CCTV but was somewhat relieved that being a witness interview room the system was video only and no sound.

'What are you looking so worried about, we've done nothing wrong,' Dewar remarked.

'You don't get it, do you, Jessie? We are in serious trouble here. If Marisha dies, it will be treated as a death in police custody.'

'But she wasn't under arrest,' Dewar said.

'It doesn't fucking matter, she was in a police station when she collapsed. I told you we should have got her medical attention right away.' Barolli rubbed the base of his neck, which was tight from stress.

'I only did what I thought was right,' Dewar said emphatically.

'What was right? You threatened to arrest her without a whiff of evidence that she was involved.'

'She said Donna killed Josh and Samuel knew. Marisha's trying to protect her brother. Question is, why and where is he now?'

Barolli looked at her with disbelief. 'She didn't know what time of bloody day it was. I suggest you tell Superintendent Lewis that you continued to question Marisha as you feared for Samuel Peters' safety and current whereabouts.'

'Okay, if that's the way you want to play it. I'll do it for your sake, if it will keep you out of trouble.'

*

An angry Mike Lewis informed Barolli and Dewar that Marisha was in a coma after a serious heart attack and still in a critical condition. Barolli breathed a sigh of relief as Mike told him that there would be no suspension from duty, but as a matter of course the Met's Department of Professional Standards would interview him and Dewar later in the day. Mike went on to tell Dewar that the only reason he was allowing her to stay on the team was because of Barolli, and if he didn't people might become suspicious and suspect some sort of cover-up. He also informed her that she was on her final warning, and then asked her to leave the room while he spoke to Barolli. She hesitated, glancing towards Barolli, but he wouldn't meet her eyes.

When it was just the two of them, Mike asked for the full story, off the record, and so Barolli told him the truth about what had happened and what Marisha had said whilst intoxicated.

Mike rubbed at his head with frustration. 'This bloody case has more directions than a guidebook. Do you think Samuel Peters is involved?'

'Could be, but we need to get to the bottom of exactly when and if he returned to Jamaica. There's enough to get a search warrant for Marisha's flat, might find something that's useful,' Barolli said.

'A picture of Samuel would be a good start! We should run his name with the UK Border Agency and get onto the Jamaican police, see if they can help.'

'I wouldn't hold your breath on either having any up-to-date records,' Barolli remarked bluntly. Mike glumly agreed and fell silent, thinking about the case, until Barolli voiced a new idea.

'I know Marisha was pissed and talking gibberish, but do you think Donna and Samuel could be in this together?'

'We know jack shit about Samuel, but we do know Donna's a liar and a thief, the CCS Medical theft shows that. We also know she left the Savoy in a car on the night in question. Mike paused for thought then continued: 'Get Dan Ross to go over the

Savoy Hotel CCTV to see if a man matching the description we have of Samuel was seen entering or leaving the building on the night of the fifth of November.'

'I'd say at a posh charity event like Lady Lynne's, dreadlocks and a Rasta hat would make him pretty visible, so if he was seen he'd be remembered,' Barolli said, grinning.

Anna was abruptly woken from her sleep by the sound of gun-fire and thunder flashes. Disorientated, she didn't have a clue what was going on and sat bolt upright as her eyes adjusted to the light and she realized where she was. Getting out of bed, she saw that her alarm clock gave the time as eight am, but had not rung to wake her. She went over to the window, pulled back the curtains, and could see trainee FBI agents running over assault courses, enacting hostage situations and pumping out live rounds on the firing ranges.

Dressed in her FBI uniform and carrying her notepad she made her way down to the canteen for breakfast and enjoyed some mixed fruit salad and scrambled eggs on toast. Feeling rather bloated and glad that she didn't have to do any physical exercise yet, she then went to find the library to use the Internet.

The library was an ugly two-storey concrete building, with a drab interior, extensive bookshelves, work desks and com-puters. Anna glanced out of the window while she waited for her pass card to be issued, and noticed a red Ford Mustang Convertible pull up in the car park. Looking up, the librarian spotted the car as well and commented that he hadn't realized that Agent Dewar was back from her European trip. The crafty beggar, Anna thought to herself, as she saw Langton get out of the vehicle and lift the cloth roof up. She had wondered why he was so cagey about where he was staying but it did seem churlish that he hadn't had the decency to tell her it was Dewar's place. She thought she'd have some fun with him later.

Anna found a free computer desk, went onto her Dropbox

and saw that Joan had uploaded the Charity Ball photographs. She scrolled through the files, concentrating on the time each picture was taken, and started to open the photographs taken from nine p.m. onwards.

Donna and Gloria Lynne were easily recognizable in a number of the photographs, as well as a host of politicians, film and television celebrities. Although Anna had not met Aisa, she knew who she was from the description Barolli and Dewar had given, plus there were some pictures of Gloria and Donna together with a young woman who was obviously Aisa.

Anna meticulously wrote down the file number and time of every picture Donna appeared in. She remembered that Donna's Mini was on the hotel CCTV leaving the underground car park at 10:05 p.m. and returning at 11:50 p.m. Donna was clearly in a number of photographs, either as the subject or in the background, between those times. Anna now knew for certain that Donna Reynolds could not have driven her car or murdered Josh during that time period. While there was still the possibility Donna had hired someone to kill Josh and let them use her car, she thought that unlikely. Still, the fact was that someone had driven Donna's Mini that night.

Anna returned to her room and rang the office, realizing it was four p.m. in the UK. Joan answered and Anna immediately said that she needed to speak with Mike Lewis, but Joan told her that it was not a good time as there had been a bit of an incident and DPS were interviewing Mike, Barolli and Dewar. Anna asked her what had happened and Joan said that she was not fully aware of the circumstances but that Marisha had had a heart attack whilst being interviewed by Barolli and Dewar and was now in a coma.

'Tell Mike Lewis from me that Donna did not leave the Savoy between the relevant times and the pictures from the Charity Ball prove it,' Anna said.

'Well they are now working on a couple of theories, one being that Samuel Peters knew that Donna killed Josh so she paid him to keep quiet,' Joan said.

'Joan, you're not listening – Donna did not leave the hotel

therefore she couldn't have killed Josh,' Anna insisted, wondering why Joan was having difficulty in grasping such a vital piece of evidence.

'Dewar is also considering that Donna may have actually paid Samuel to commit the crime,' Joan went on.

Anna felt like screaming but held back. 'Dewar is talking absolute crap, she makes everything fit her theories—'

Joan interrupted, saying it was not a wild theory and Anna needed to listen to what had happened since they last spoke. Joan promised she would send Anna a copy of the interview with Marisha and explained that the woman had said that Samuel and Donna had known each other and Donna gave Samuel money, which Dewar thought must have been for killing Josh.

'That's absurd. We don't even know if Samuel was in London when Josh died and why would he agree to kill his own nephew?' Anna remarked with disdain, as Joan continued, saying that they had searched Marisha's flat and found forty thousand pounds cash hidden in the freezer, but nothing to indicate Samuel Peters' whereabouts. Dewar had suggested it was even possible that Donna had murdered Samuel as well.

'How much?' Anna exclaimed, hardly able to take it all in. Joan explained that Barolli had asked her to contact the UK Border Agency about Samuel leaving the country, which she had already done, but they were about as much use as a chocolate teapot and as yet she still had to make enquiries with the Jamaican police.

'Are you all in Dewar's dreamworld back there? I really need to speak with Mike Lewis.' Anna was infuriated at what she thought were wild flights of fancy.

'He's in with DPS at the moment but he does believe it's possible – you know, Samuel using Donna's car.'

Anna felt like she was going round in circles.

'Joan, for heaven's sake, there is not a shred of evidence to support that theory.'

'Well there is now.'

'Exactly what evidence have they got?' Anna was trying very hard to keep her voice on an even level and not shout into the phone.

'Barbara found a picture of a black man on a Jamaican fishing boat at Marisha's and he fits the description of the decorator, who we now know is Samuel Peters.'

'Along with every other Rastafarian with dreadlocks and a beanie hat,' Anna snapped.

'No, Dan Ross found CCTV of the same man entering the Savoy Hotel at nine fifty p.m. on the fifth and leaving ten minutes later.'

'You are kidding me . . .' Anna shook her head.

'I wish I was but the CCTV footage also shows the same man outside the hotel and he clearly walks off round the corner towards the underground car park. Also, when they enlarged the footage it was clear he had some keys in his hand.

There was a pause as Joan waited for Anna to reply, but when she didn't she continued:

'They think that Donna gave Samuel the car and flat keys, and he returned them later that night after killing Josh.' Joan added that Pete Jenkins had found fingerprints on the paint tins at Esme's flat that matched those on the money under the floorboards and the money in Marisha's freezer. Although there was no trace on the UK database, they were believed to be Samuel Peters' prints as they also matched other prints found at Marisha and Esme's flats.

There was another pause. Anna was wondering what other revelations were to come, but Joan then apologized for being the bearer of what in effect was bad news, destroying any belief in Donna's innocence. Anna could feel Joan's impatience to end the call but she wasn't quite finished and asked if the large sum of money found in Marisha's flat was connected to the purchase of all the new electrical equipment. Joan reported that along with a new luxury bed and other household items, they were all cash purchases made a few weeks after Josh's death and totalled about ten thousand pounds.

Anna was completely taken aback by what Joan told her and couldn't believe that her uncovering of photographic evidence proving that Donna did not leave the hotel actually served to compound the young woman's guilt. Dejectedly, she realized that it was impossible to keep up with the investigation when she was thousands of miles away. She thanked Joan for all her help, adding that she would not be bothering her any more and would see her in ten weeks.

Anna lay on her bed in her room, looking up at the ceiling; she didn't feel sorry for herself, just frustrated that yet again the evidence suggested she was wrong about Donna's innocence. Her gut instincts were usually right, but she accepted that Josh's death was a complex investigation. Marisha, if she regained consciousness, or Samuel, when his whereabouts were discovered, would hopefully reveal the answers to all the questions. Even without them as witnesses the case against Donna was a very powerful one.

Her mobile bleeped and she saw that there was a text message from Langton, saying that he was going to the canteen to have some lunch if she wanted to join him. She wasn't very hungry, especially after the scrambled eggs, but she wanted to tell him what had happened in the Reynolds case and that she was taking his advice about letting it go and would concentrate on the course. She also thought it would be a good opportunity to wind him up about the car and staying at Dewar's condominium.

As she entered the canteen she saw him sitting in the far corner, so she waved and got herself a cup of coffee before joining him. Langton was eating a tuna salad with boiled potatoes.

'The food here isn't up to much, unless you're a rabbit or a health freak,' he complained, pushing the salad around the plate with his fork.

'Well you must be getting plenty of fresh air.'

'What's that supposed to mean?'

'You know, out at the condo by the lakeside, and then a quick spin round the block in the Mustang with the roof down.'

Langton nearly choked on a boiled potato as he realized Anna had figured out where he was staying.

'I didn't say anything because I didn't want to upset you.'

'Upset me? I couldn't care less where you're staying; what I don't understand is why you didn't just tell me.'

'Dewar was returning a favour as I got her a nice work flat in London. I thought you might think there was something going on between us,' Langton protested.

'Don't flatter yourself by thinking I would feel even the tiniest bit of jealousy if there was anything between you and Dewar.'

Langton winced and decided it would not be such a good idea to ask Anna to stay with him at the condo.

'I'm going outside for a cigarette,' he said, irritated by her constant ability to get under his skin, then headed off, leaving her alone at the table.

Anna found Langton sitting on a bench, smoking, and sat down beside him. He inhaled deeply, and chewed at his lower lip, before he eventually turned to face her.

'You know, Anna, I have cared for you for so many years.' He hesitated, as if unsure whether to go on.

'The time we were really close, living together, was very special. I loved you, and I know I was never able to commit myself enough for you, or for myself – call it a state of panic, whatever. You were too young, I was too old, and the time just wasn't right. It's all a question of the right timing in life, and I know that our separating was the best thing for both of us, you especially. I knew it even more when I saw you so in love with Ken, and I was truly envious of how happy he made you. What happened was tragic, and I even understood what that pain must have felt like. When my first wife died, I honestly felt that if I buried it, didn't accept what had punched out my soul, I'd maybe heal and so I buried myself in my career.'

Anna was close to tears. 'I know, I remember you telling me to make sure I took time off, not be like you and return to work straight away. I just couldn't face being without Ken, I didn't want to sit at home and think about the life he and I should have had together. Like you, I have found my career has helped ease the pain.'

'You've changed, you are losing your femininity, Anna, and I hate to see it,' Langton went on. 'There is no need for this tough exterior all the time and you are obsessed with work. I said to you, make sure you have a life outside the Met, or it'll eat you up and then suddenly you'll be ready to retire and the years have flown past and you're middle-aged, lonely and single.'

She shook her head, and then gave a light laugh. 'Stop making me out to be some kind of harridan, because I'm not. As for the Reynolds case, well I was wrong about Donna, so like you suggested, I'm here and not involved with any of it, and I'm moving on.'

'Fine, whatever,' he said casually.

'No, it's not just fine, whatever. Right now, I'm content with my personal life. Yes, I'm career-minded: I want to continue moving up the ladder, and I'm really grateful that you created this wonderful opportunity for me here at Quantico.'

He threw the cigarette onto the ground and stubbed it out with the toe of his shoe and then looked at her and said nothing. She realized he was waiting to hear what else she had to say and felt obliged to continue.

'You remarried and now have a beautiful wife and two lovely children. It makes me happy that you found a life outside the Met and I need you to understand that I will too.'

Langton stood up and suggested they go for a walk. At first, she hesitated, then sensing they had come to some kind of amicable agreement, she acquiesced.

As they walked along the edge of the wood it was as if they were good friends sharing a stroll on a sunny day. When he put his arm around her shoulder, she feared that he was about to spoil the moment.

'I've got to learn to stop worrying about you, haven't I?' he said quietly as he gave her a big squeeze and released her. They walked along together a little further before she changed the subject.

'Any news on Fitzpatrick?'

'I'll come clean with you, it's been bubbling for quite some time but even though nothing is confirmed, they wanted me here as there have been some positive sightings. You know his escape has been a constant thorn in my side, always niggling away at me, the obvious mistakes I made. God, I hope I get him this time, then I can walk away with my head held high and stick two fingers up to that arsehole Walters.'

Anna stared straight ahead, filled with the sensation that it was now or never; she might not get another chance to confess what had happened.

'I want to explain something about the Fitzpatrick case,' she began nervously, and they stopped walking. She was about to continue when Langton gently placed his index finger on her lips to stop her. He smiled down at her and stunned her with what he said next.

'You don't need to, I already know. In fact, I've known for quite some time now.'

'Known . . . known what?' Anna asked with trepidation.

'It was you. Walters deliberately dropped clues to upset me but I know how underhand he can be so I guessed he'd fooled you into letting the cat out of the bag about my screwing up.'

'Why did you never say anything to me?'

'I wasn't going to give him the satisfaction of ruining our mutual respect and friendship.'

'I have had such a guilt trip over it and I have honestly intended to come clean with you so many times, I just never had the guts to do it. I was worried you'd never speak to me again,' Anna admitted.

He chuckled and gave her one of his lovely smiles. 'Look, thanks to Walters, I was a dead duck in the water anyway and I wanted you to still think I had no idea who it was. Besides, it kept you on your toes and you were more thorough with your investigations that I was overseeing.'

Anna's head was spinning like a top, totally disoriented by what she had just learned, but no sooner had she managed to gather her thoughts to explain to him properly than his mobile rang, and he patted his pocket to take it out. He moved away from her, listening intently, then said, 'I can go now.' Immediately, he started to walk at a quick pace towards the car park.

Anna hurried after him. 'What's happened?'

'It's what I've been waiting for and the reason I'm here. FBI agents think they have new information on Fitzpatrick. They have a jet fired up and want me to go now,' he said, picking up pace. When they got to the Mustang, he unlocked it, grabbed a holdall from the back seat then tossed the car keys to Anna.

'Leave these with Blane for me,' he said as he slung the holdall over his shoulder.

'It's all so quick; are you sure you're ready for this?' she asked with concern.

He tapped his forehead with his index finger. 'I've had his gloating face printed up here in my nightmares for too long, so you bet I'm ready. The Mustang's insured for any driver, so if you want to go for a spin I'm sure Dewar won't mind.'

'I don't think so ... Do me a favour?'

'What?'

'We already know Fitzpatrick has no qualms about killing people. If he's cornered he won't go down without a fight so please, please be careful.'

Langton walked over to Anna, gave her a kiss on the cheek and instructed her not to worry.

'Enjoy dinner with Don Blane.'

'How did you know he'd asked me out?'

'He's like a pig in a bacon factory with his nerves. Said he'd asked you out and wanted to know what food you liked, would flowers be appropriate, blah blah.'

'What did you say?'

'I said that more than anything she just likes to know you care,' Langton told her as an unmarked car with a flashing blue magnetic light pulled up in the car park. He got in and opened the window. 'Don't worry, I like him and you have my full approval!' he shouted. At first, she was sure it was just in jest but then something in his manner changed. He looked at her in that way he so often had, which always touched her, as if he was asking something from her, and his dark eyes seemed incredibly sad, but then the window glided back into position and he was gone.

Chapter Twenty-Five

The Academy's thousand-seat auditorium was like a state-of-the-art cinema, with its comfortable orange seats and a massive screen on which the FBI badge and motto were projected. The room was suddenly filled with the sound of the national anthem and everyone stood up as the US contingent belted out the verses of 'The Star-Spangled Banner' with great gusto. The welcoming address was given by the Director of the Academy, and Anna found it easy to identify who the Americans were as they rapturously applauded at every pause in the Director's half-hour speech.

Each of the course instructors introduced themselves and gave a resumé of their specialities and career achievements. Some went on longer than others and there were clearly one or two who thought they were God's gift to the fight against crime. Anna found it hard to concentrate as her mind wandered to her earlier conversation with Langton. She couldn't believe he had never said anything about her lack of discretion in discussing the Fitzpatrick case with Deputy Commissioner Walters. He had let her sweat it out for nearly two years, during which the guilt and feelings of remorse she had carried had on many occasions been all-consuming and reduced her to tears.

Her attention was brought back to the auditorium stage when she heard the voice of Don Blane, who spoke with authority and humour about his career and stood out as the most professional and humble of the tutors. When Blane finished there were further talks about the rules and regulations they were all to abide by and it was nearly four p.m. before they were to go to their allocated classrooms.

As Anna looked round her classroom, she was disappointed to see she was the only female in the group of twenty-five. Blane immediately made it clear that the object was to get to know each other, rank was immaterial and only Christian names were to be used throughout the course. The room went quiet when he pointed to the tables at the back and informed them that their weekend homework was to read through and familiarize themselves with their course case files. Every inch of the tables was laden with thick files, each of which bore a student's name. After outlining the details of the course modules, Blane ended by wishing them an enjoyable weekend and said he'd see them all by the start of the Yellow Brick Road at seven a.m. on Monday morning for a fitness test.

Anna picked up her file and went over to him, saying that his personal introduction was the most professional and best bit of the introductory session.

'Thank you, Anna. Are you still okay for dinner?' he asked, clearly worried that she had changed her mind.

'What time and where shall I meet you?' Anna replied with an affectionate smile.

'Fantastic, seven at the reception, okay?'

'Perfect. I'll see you there and I'm really looking forward to it,' she said, still smiling.

Although she still felt tired and jet lagged, Anna was eager to read the case file when she returned to her room, so she'd be well prepared for her first class. The file was very thick and contained witness statements, forensic reports, search records, maps and photographs. She settled herself at the small desk and opened the file to the first page, which contained brief details of the real incident the case study was based on.

Mandy Anderson was a fifteen-year-old girl who had gone missing two years previously during the late spring of 2011. She was the adopted only child of a very religious Catholic couple.

On the day she disappeared she had been at the shopping mall with two friends. She parted company with them at about two p.m., saying she had to be at the church by three for choir practice. There was CCTV footage of her leaving the mall, but from that point Mandy Anderson was never seen or heard of again – she had simply disappeared off the face of the earth.

The object of the exercise was to read all the statements and reports then draw up lines of enquiry for both police and forensic investigations, as well as a victimology report on Mandy Anderson and offender profiles for possible suspect categories. Solving the case was not the issue, but demonstrating astute decision-making, inductive reasoning and skilled referenced research were imperative to receive a pass mark on the case file exercise.

Anna turned to the next page in the file and saw a picture of Mandy in a missing-persons leaflet. She looked much younger than her fifteen years and very angelic, dressed in a choir outfit of red cassock, white linen surplice and a gold crucifix. There was an air of innocence about her – she wore no makeup yet was exceptionally pretty. Wide blue eyes, little tip-tilted nose and long flaxen hair. She had a beaming smile, which partially revealed her dental braces over pearly white teeth.

Attached to the file was a large map, which Anna took out, unfolded and placed on her bed to examine. She noticed a vast wooded area called Prince William Forest and was surprised to see the FBI Academy and Marine Corps base on the edge of the map. Anna then realized that Mandy Anderson's disappearance must have been a local investigation. It crossed her mind that Jessie Dewar might have dealt with the profiling on the case and she wondered if Don Blane had deliberately allocated her the file. She certainly thought there would be no harm in asking him later at dinner.

The mapped area was massive, and gridded red lines showed all the twenty-six square miles of woodland that had been systematically searched by ground teams and body dogs. Helicopters had flown over the area using heat-seeking and other high-tech equipment, but every effort to find any trace of Mandy had proved fruitless. The search had been a massive operation lasting months, with the assistance of the Marines and the Sheriff's office plus a multitude of local residents.

Anna next opened out a large street map that was marked in different colours showing the two routes that Mandy was known to regularly use between the shopping mall and her home on Hallard Drive. One route went right past the church where she sang in the choir. Also ringed on the street map were all the local areas, including drains and wasteland, that had been searched, and where house-to-house enquiries had been made.

Anna was about to read the statements of Mandy's mother and father when she glanced at her watch and saw that it was already six p.m., and so she decided she would get ready for dinner with Don and read the rest later. The cold case excited Anna, not so much the fact that a young innocent girl had gone missing and most probably been murdered, but the thought that maybe, just maybe, she could find a line of enquiry that had not yet been considered.

Meanwhile, Langton had been flown to Miami in a small private FBI jet. For security reasons, the exact destination was undisclosed, even to him, and he was only told that on arrival he would be taken to a marina where a yacht was waiting to take him to a secure observation point for suspect surveillance. Although frustrated at the lack of information, he thought that the FBI had good reason to be wary as Fitzpatrick was known to have corrupt politicians and police officers on his payroll.

On reaching the marina, he was surprised by what he saw. Moored there was a large motor yacht with a sleek black V-shaped hull, the sporting lines of a luxury speed boat and a black half-dome roof that allowed you to see out but not in. The FBI agent accompanying Langton told him that the 100-foot vessel was an Italian-built Mirage Argonaut and one of the fastest super-yachts in the world. Langton asked what it was worth, at which the agent laughed and said in the region of ten million dollars but it didn't cost the FBI a penny, as it was a seized asset from a Columbian drugs lord. As he walked up the gangplank onto the main deck, Langton was struck by the sheer opulence in front of him. A large Jacuzzi was by the stern, surrounded by white leather sofas and armchairs. To one side there was an Art Deco crystal dining table with ten matching crystal chairs and a large, circular fully stocked bar.

On leaving the main deck and entering the residential area, Langton's illusions of further grandeur were shattered. The luxury interior had been stripped bare and replaced with high-tech surveillance equipment and computers, which were manned by FBI agents. The man accompanying him explained to him that the exterior was a façade and most of the luxury sleeping quarters had been turned into offices and a conference room, and the six permanent onboard agents shared the crew's quarters at the stern.

Langton was taken to the conference room, which from its size and remaining decorations he surmised had previously been the master cabin. It had an array of LCD screens, satellite maps and PowerPoint projection equipment. The room was filled with agents and an FBI SWAT team dressed in military-style fatigues, Kevlar helmets, bulletproof vests and carrying submachine guns as well as side arms and stun grenades. Compared to what he had been used to, Langton felt as if he was going to bump into Tom Cruise and the cameras would roll for a *Mission Impossible* sequel. Despite himself he couldn't help but be impressed.

The director of the FBI's Drugs Enforcement Team, Jack Deans, introduced himself and welcomed Langton on board and introduced him to the assembled agents as a detective chief superintendent in the Met who was after Fitzpatrick for multiple murders in the UK. Deans made it clear from the outset that Fitzpatrick was a ruthless killer who would see the death of an FBI agent as another trophy on his mantelpiece. Langton realized that Deans was in effect telling his men that the object of the exercise was safety first and thereby giving them authority to shoot to kill.

Deans went on to say he had received information from a seasoned undercover agent that Fitzpatrick might be using the alias of Roger Layman. 'Layman,' he said, was trying to off-load a large shipment of a new designer drug that contained, amongst other ingredients, a high dose of fentanyl. Deans then related how Fitzpatrick had tried, unsuccessfully thanks to Langton, to flood the UK drugs market with fentanyl and although he had lain low for two years, he was still believed to be the most powerful drug lord associated with the distribution of that particular substance or any of its derivatives.

Deans informed the room that the name Roger Layman had recently been used to rent a three-million-dollar, Tuscan-style villa in an opulent waterfront community on Tropic Isle by Delray Beach, fifty-six miles north of their current position. The villa was on a canal inlet, which allowed direct access to an Intracoastal Waterway that provided a 3,000-mile navigable route between the Atlantic and Gulf coasts. Deans said it was believed that Fitzpatrick would be coming into Delray by boat the following day and that once moored at the villa's private jetty he was in effect a rat in a trap. There would be no way out as Navy gunships were to be called in to block off his escape via the waterways and the SWAT teams would approach from both the front and rear.

Deans brought up the most recent photograph they had of Fitzpatrick and Langton could see that it was one that had been forwarded to the FBI by the Met two years ago. It was a poor-quality CCTV shot taken when Fitzpatrick had entered an accountant's office in London and murdered a man by injecting him with a lethal overdose of fentanyl. Dean brought up an e-fit picture alongside the first and Langton recognized it as one that he had helped to compile. Langton knew that he had only been able to do so because Fitzpatrick had duped him into believing he was a senior FBI agent and they had sat and talked with each other for nearly half an hour.

Langton was aware of a feverish heat taking hold of him, which happened every time he thought about how foolish he had felt after realizing the man he had hunted for so long had audaciously sat with him in the station. He wondered if Walters had informed Jack Deans about the incident but realized he hadn't when Deans commented that the image demonstrated remarkable facial recall since Langton had only seen Fitzpatrick when chasing him in a car as the man was taking off in a plane. As was the FBI way, a chorus of clapped approval followed, to which Langton nodded his thanks and smiled, inwardly grateful that the truth had not come out.

Dean continued that Fitzpatrick was a master of disguise and had previously undergone plastic surgery and had his fingertips burnt with lasers to avoid detection. He then asked Langton if there was anything he'd like to add and Langton said only to agree with Director Deans and reiterate how dangerous a man Fitzpatrick was.

Deans pressed a control panel on the table in front of him and all the LCD screens in the room lit up, showing live feeds of the interior and exterior of the waterside villa. Listening devices and pin eye cameras had been secreted in the villa and the resulting pictures were transmitted onto the LCD screens. A real-time aerial satellite picture appeared on the large screen behind Deans, who used a laser pointer to indicate all the FBI surveillance positions. The only people known to be in the villa were a young boy and a Hispanic woman in her fifties, though they were currently out shopping in a black Lexus 4 × 4. The boy was believed to be between thirteen and fifteen years old, with an American accent, and the Hispanic woman was thought to be the housekeeper.

Langton did not interrupt but felt a slight hesitation about the teenager because he knew that Fitzpatrick's son had been at an English public school and would have an upper-crust accent, if anything, unless the time spent in the US had ironed it out. However it was, he felt, a possible indication that they had the wrong man.

Deans started winding down, informing everyone that the journey to the suspect's villa in Delray would be made under the cover of darkness. He instructed them all to turn their mobiles off as from that point on all ground-radio transmission would cease and contact would only be made through secure and encrypted satellite links. Deans explained he'd called in the expertise of the SWAT team, not only to take the subject out, but because they were a damn sight younger and better shots than he was. His comment resulted in a roar of laughter and heckles, the most notable of which was from the SWAT Commander, who promised his team would follow the director anywhere, if only out of an idle sense of curiosity. Everyone in the room laughed even harder, including Langton, as although he was not really at ease with their humour, he knew that the banter was a universal police thing, a way of easing the tension before the dangers that lay ahead.

Sitting in the galley with Jack Deans afterwards, discussing the operation over a coffee and sandwich, Langton froze when a dark-skinned man walked in wearing a long white cotton Arab robe and headscarf; he was accompanied by four stunning-looking women dressed in translucent white linen kaftans and skimpy bikinis. Langton wondered what on earth was going on. Deans, noticing the look on his face, grinned and informed him that they were all FBI agents and part of the undercover operation.

Langton laughed. 'Looks good, but I'm glad I don't have to wear one of those outfits.'

Anna had a slight moment of panic as she was getting ready to go to dinner with Don Blane. She had showered and washed her hair, only to discover that there was no hairdryer in the room and she had not brought one with her. Thankfully, the lady in the room next door let Anna borrow hers. It transpired that she was a Los Angeles detective lieutenant called Beth Jackson, who said that she was going into town for a drink and asked Anna if she'd like to join her. Anna thanked Beth but said that she had already made a prior arrangement. She couldn't be certain but she thought from the look on Beth's face that she took her apology as a veiled excuse to avoid her company.

Appearing well dressed and respectable had always come naturally to Anna and was never something she usually worried about. This time, however, she did feel conscious about what she should wear. She hadn't brought much with her in the way of smart clothes and decided to wear a purple sleeveless shirt with dark, straight-leg denim jeans, a knee-length white woollen cardigan and flat shoes.

Blane was waiting in the foyer with a small posy of flowers wrapped and tied neatly with a blue ribbon. He looked handsome and smart in brown chinos, a crisp white shirt and light blue sports jacket.

'You look lovely,' he said as he handed her the posy.

'Thank you, Don, they're gorgeous,' Anna said with a smile, taking in the sweet scent of the flowers.

'I thought we'd go to a seafood restaurant by the Occoquan River in Woodbridge,' Blane suggested as he led her out to his seven-seater Ford Flex car and politely opened the passenger door.

Anna thought it curious that Blane had such a large vehicle for a single man.

'This is a nice car, similar to the Ford Galaxy that they sell back home. We call them people carriers,' Anna said.

'It's handy for taking the kids camping, fishing or just out for the day,' Blane said nonchalantly. Anna recalled that he had previously told her he didn't have children and was about to ask who he meant but he continued before she had time.

'The RTC has a beaten-up old van but this car gives them a bit more comfort and makes the trip more enjoyable.'

Anna was puzzled: 'Sorry, but what do you mean by RTC?'

'Residential Treatment Centers, the modern descendant of orphanages. Many of the kids are victims of severe neglect or abuse, with behavioural and psychological problems. I help as a counsellor in my free time. It's hard work communicating with some of them as they have become trapped in a world of their own and fear outsiders,' he explained.

Anna sensed sadness in his voice and wondered if there was something in his own past that gave him a better understanding of the abuse and neglect they had suffered.

She realized that since meeting Don Blane she had seen nothing but good in him. He was a sincere and honest man who had a radiance that made her feel warm and safe. She knew that she had been denying the obvious to herself as she tried to comprehend how much he reminded her of Ken. Yet, she held back, for while she was confident that Don was exactly as he appeared to be, she feared that fate or other unforeseen circumstances, as had so often happened in the past, would never allow her life to be as happy as she wanted it to be. As she looked from the car at the beautiful woodland scenery and the reflection of the trees and clouds on the surface of the Occoquan River, she knew that her fears were unwarranted. A serious relationship with Don was never going to happen as she only had ten weeks at the Academy before returning to the UK.

A waitress showed them to their table on the veranda, which had a lovely view across the marina, river and woodlands beyond. The sun was slowly setting in the distance, the red glow making the woods seem as if they were on fire, yet it was a calm and relaxing sight to behold. Blane was attentive and thoughtful, telling Anna that if it was too cold they could go inside or get one of the patio heaters turned on. Anna assured him she was very comfortable and they sat down.

Don ordered a Californian Sauvignon Blanc and asked the waitress to let Anna taste the wine first. It had a wonderful balance and freshness and Anna nodded her approval. She decided to go straight to a main course of garlic roasted tiger shrimp and bay scallops tossed in linguine and marinara sauce, with a side salad. Blane ordered a starter of clams in beurre blanc sauce, asking for two plates so they could share, and confiding to Anna that he couldn't let her leave the restaurant without trying the clams. For his main course he chose the Maryland crab cakes with mash potato and coleslaw.

'Cheers,' Anna said, raising her glass and he clinked his to hers.

'Here's to an enjoyable and successful course.'

'I've started reading over the case file,' Anna told him.

'I have to confess, I deliberately gave you the Mandy Anderson case,' Blane admitted. 'I read your CV and saw that you successfully investigated the disappearance of a young girl who had been missing for five years.'

'That doesn't make me an expert on mispers and anyway, I had a good team behind me . . .'

'DCS Langton seemed to think differently.'

'Well, that's not unusual for him where I'm concerned.' Anna said, raising her eyebrows in disapproval of Langton's opinion.

'No, I didn't mean in a bad way. He said that your ability to think laterally and see what others can't is astounding. He doubted that anyone but you would have uncovered the evidence that led to the discovery of the little girl's body and subsequent conviction of her killer.'

Anna's look changed to one of curiosity as she began to sense there was more behind Don allocating her the Mandy Anderson file.

'Were you involved in the investigation?' she asked.

'No, they felt I was too close to Mandy's parents Peter and Sally. Jessie Dewar was given the case.'

'Can I ask how close?'

'I met them through the church just after my wife died. Mandy was fourteen then and her parents had just told her that she was adopted. She didn't take it well and went a bit off the rails, denouncing religion and becoming rather difficult. After she tried to run away, Peter and Sally asked if I would speak with her as they knew that I had been an orphan and they hoped I might be able to connect with her.'

'And did you?' Anna asked

'I like to think so, yes. She came to understand that being

adopted didn't mean your real parents hated you. I brokered an agreement with Peter and Sally that when she was sixteen she could look for her birth mother and I would help her.'

'The file said she went missing just before her sixteenth birthday,' Anna remarked and he sighed, nodding his head.

'I don't know how I can really help you, Don – I'm a stranger in a foreign land and don't know anything about the case except what's in the file.'

He cocked his head to one side and frowned. 'But you're a good detective and a pair of fresh eyes on the case. The smallest detail may mean something to you and no one else.'

'I would need to interview people, start afresh—'

For the first time since she had met him, Don interrupted her: 'All the main statements are in the file and I can ring Peter and Sally Anderson so you can meet them.'

Anna sat back in her chair and thought about what Don was asking her to do.

'Okay, but I can't promise you a successful conclusion.' She sipped her wine and in some ways wished she hadn't mentioned the case file as the mood of the evening had changed, but she didn't want to let him down.

'Thank you, Anna,' Blane said.

'From what I've read in the initial report, Mandy was last seen leaving the mall to go to choir practice.'

'A girl who Mandy didn't like joined their group at the mall. Dewar thought she used choir practice as an excuse to part company with them,' Don said.

'Maybe that was just coincidence and she'd already arranged to meet someone else,' Anna suggested.

'Then why not tell her friends that?'

'Because she didn't want them to know who it was.'

'So it could have been a man,' Don remarked.

'Or someone her age, but the question is, who and why be secretive?' Anna said.

Don twisted his wine glass by the stem and looked at her.

'Langton was right, you are the bee's knees.'

The tension that had built up whilst discussing the case evaporated as she laughed, partly pleased by Langton's compliments, but also because of the way Don looked at her. It was obvious that he was smitten, which she found she rather liked, but there was no time to respond as suddenly their waitress appeared with their starter.

Chapter Twenty-Six

Anna woke after a very restless night. The Mandy Anderson case kept running through her mind, so much so that she had stayed up until three a.m. reading the parents' and many other statements in the file. Her evening with Don Blane had been thoroughly enjoyable, especially after they stopped discussing the case. They ate their dinner and chatted about their likes and dislikes in life, and what had made them want to become investigators. It struck Anna how much they actually had in common and she had no qualms about being honest and open with him.

Anna lay in bed thinking about what could have happened to Mandy Anderson. In all the statements, she was described as being almost perfect: athletic, friendly, well-liked, good scholar, and deeply religious – this was repeated over and over again. She'd never had a boyfriend and was popular amongst her small group of friends and the church congregation. Anna sighed, baffled at how on earth Mandy could just disappear without a trace in an area where everyone seemed to know each other and crime was a rarity.

She checked her watch, and as it was just after eight a.m. she decided to get dressed and go to the shopping mall where Mandy was last seen. She wanted to get a feel for the area, meet the Andersons and walk the two routes Mandy was known to use to go home. It would also allow her the opportunity to buy a hairdryer and some other bits and pieces she needed. She checked her mobile and saw that there was a text message from

Joan, saying she had uploaded a copy of Barolli's notes from the interview with Marisha, who was still in a coma. Although she felt some sympathy for the woman she resolutely deleted the text, determined not to be drawn back in. She tried ringing Langton to see how he was getting on but his mobile cut straight to voicemail, so she sent a text message: 'Take care, hope you get him. Anna x'

That left her with the dilemma of whether to make use of Jessie Dewar's Mustang or not. 'Should I or shouldn't I?' she briefly thought to herself, before temptation got the better of her. After all, Langton had said it was insured for any driver.

Having put the convertible roof down Anna turned the keys in the ignition as she lightly put her foot on the accelerator. The loud roar from the Mustang's twin exhausts made her jump and she wondered again if she was doing the right thing in driving Dewar's treasured car. Slowly, and cautiously, she pulled out of the car park onto the road to the main gate. She was glad no one was watching as each nervous touch of the accelerator made the car lurch forward. Having reached the gate she asked one of the guards for directions to the shopping mall. He told her to take the I-95 to Woodbridge and she couldn't miss the fifty-foot-high circular sign saying Potomac Mills Mall.

Anna was relieved that it was only a twenty-minute journey, as she found herself nervous behind the wheel of the powerful Mustang. The mall itself was enormous and as it was early, she found a parking space quite easily. Orientating herself with the map from the case file she started on the walk to the Anderson house on Hallard Drive. Anna realized that Mandy's route was through middle- and upper-class residential areas, apart from a three-minute section along the side of woodland, which could be seen clearly from the main road.

Number fifteen Hallard Drive was a two-storey wood-cladded house in the centre of a winding road. The front porch was a pristine white, with a screened front door, small swing bench and a garage to one side. Anna had not noticed a church and, checking the map, realized she would pass it on the return journey to the mall.

'Hi, I'm Sally Anderson. Are you Anna Travis?'

Anna looked up and saw a woman coming down the driveway.

'Yes, I am,' Anna said, realizing Don must have rung the couple already.

Sally Anderson was a very pretty woman with pale blue eyes and dark hair with streaks of grey. The case file said she was forty-five, but she looked much older and Anna suspected that the stress of Mandy's disappearance had aged her prematurely.

'I was so deep in thought and admiring your lovely house I didn't see you,' Anna apologized.

'Please do come in, and don't worry, we're used to people stopping and staring. Thankfully things aren't as bad as they used to be,' Mrs Anderson said, and Anna presumed she was referring to the press interest their daughter's case must have brought to the community.

The front door of the house opened directly into the living-come-dining room, which was well furnished and immaculately neat and tidy. The wooden floor, cabinets, table and chairs were all old-style but looked remarkably new and were well polished and shiny. A large wooden crucifix of Jesus on the cross hung above the small log-burning fireplace. The other walls had photographs of Mandy at different ages, and her parents.

Sally explained that her husband Peter was at the supermarket but she was keen to show Anna Mandy's bedroom and took her upstairs.

'We have left the room exactly as it was when she went missing. I just dust, vacuum and keep it aired. Please feel free to have a look round while I make a coffee or would you prefer tea?'

Anna could see that Sally was distraught and still believed that one day her daughter would be back. 'Thank you very much, a coffee would be lovely.'

Anna smiled at Sally sympathetically, knowing with reasonable certainty that Mandy would never again return to the house.

Mandy's room was large and decorated with colour co-ordinated pinks. Anna smiled as she recalled her own room when she was a little girl, a princess's abode and the castle where she was safe and could be whoever she wanted to be. The bed had a soft pink quilt and pillowcases; the curtains were white with little pink rosebuds that matched the wallpaper. A silver-framed photograph of Mandy in her choir robes was on the bedside table. Anna recognized it as the same picture in the case file. She opened the white wooden wardrobe and saw stacked in one corner a pile of unopened presents, some covered in 'Sweet Sixteen' gift wrap, reminding her that Mandy disappeared a few days before her sixteenth birthday.

Anna sat on the small white stool in front of the pink, Cinderella-style dressing table on which were stacked about twenty birthday cards. She noticed that the envelopes were sealed but each one was the same pink colour. She thought this unusual and knew that it should be standard procedure for an investigating officer to check who sent every card and see if there were any from someone unknown to the parents. She wondered if this had been the case and Sally Anderson had then resealed all the cards.

In the dressing-table drawer, Anna found a small 2011 diary, which she opened and turned to the 21 May, to find that it had CHOIR PRACTICE 3 P.M. written in it, but recalled the case file said that there was no prearranged choir practice on that day. Anna was surprised the original investigation had missed the significance of this entry. There was the possibility they thought it was an error by Mandy but she wondered why Mandy would write something in her diary that was not true – was choir practice an entry to cover a secret meeting? Anna also considered it could have been cancelled or simply Mandy making a mistake. She flicked through page after page, wondering if any of the other choir practice entries might be false and if the church would still have a record of the practice times so she could compare them against the diary.

Anna went downstairs and joined Sally in the living room.

She had made a pot of fresh ground coffee and laid out some cupcakes.

'The birthday cards and presents, I noticed, are still all sealed and wrapped,' Anna remarked. 'Did the investigating officers look through them?'

'Yes, they were all from friends and relatives. I resealed them all and rewrapped the presents,' Sally said with a sad look.

'Do you mind if I take the cards and Mandy's diary with me?'

'No, not at all. Is there something in the diary — a clue maybe?'

'I don't know yet, I need to look at it in more detail,' Anna told her.

Sally began talking about Mandy's prowess on the piano and had just moved on to her singing in the choir when Peter Anderson arrived home. He was smartly dressed in a blue shirt and pleated trousers but looked aged beyond his years, no doubt from the stress caused by the disappearance of his daughter. Peter sat next to his wife on the sofa.

'From the moment we reported our daughter missing, we assisted the local Sheriff's Office in every way we could,' he explained. 'We were initially treated with sympathy and respect. After four weeks with no sightings or clues as to Mandy's whereabouts the Sheriff asked for the assistance of the FBI. Overnight, things changed dramatically, all because of the opinion and recommendations of one of their behavioural profilers.'

Anna could sense the increasing anger in Mr Anderson's voice as he went on to explain that the profiler had said that Mandy was either abducted off the street or more likely had returned home, where something untoward had happened to her. Anna, realizing he didn't know the name of the profiler, nodded and let him continue.

'The sole basis for this was that statistically parents or other family members of the victim's commit the largest percentage of child homicides,' he said, pursing his lips. 'The FBI came to OUR HOUSE, ripped it apart and desecrated OUR

DAUGHTER'S bedroom, searching for supposed clues that I was her killer. I was arrested and questioned for two days.'

'We felt so low,' Sally added, and started to cry.

'Don Blane stood by us all the way. He protested my innocence in church and told the congregation the vicious hate campaign against us had to stop. I can honestly say if it wasn't for him, Sally and I would have moved away ages ago.'

Blane's personal involvement was way beyond what Anna had imagined and she felt humbled that he had asked her to look at the case.

'Will you find Mandy?' Sally asked.

It was a familiar question for Anna in missing persons cases, but still one she dreaded and always found difficult to answer.

'I wish I could say, yes, Sally, but I can't. I can promise you that during my time at Quantico I will work with Don and do everything in my power to find out what happened to her,' Anna said quietly and sincerely. Before leaving, she asked Sally who she thought were Mandy's closest friends. The woman told her that Julie Collins was her best friend and lived at 58 Lincoln Avenue, the same street as the church.

Walking slowly along the pavement, taking in the peaceful sunny surroundings, Anna couldn't get over how pleasant the area was. Nice homes, children in the street riding bikes and playing on front lawns. Anna thought about Mandy's room and what it had revealed about her. Nothing suggested she was in any way promiscuous – if anything the decorations were childish for a girl who was nearly sixteen. Everything about her was angelic, apart from the blip when she discovered she was adopted, but that did not seem to have been a lasting problem after Don became involved.

Ahead of her was a distinctive building with a large sign saying ST COLUMBA'S CATHOLIC CHURCH. It was different from what Anna was expecting – brick built and very modern, no steeple or cross but a large glass entrance in the shape of the cross. It had a stark look to it and stood on a large plot of land alongside the priest's house and a separate community hall, with woodland at the rear. Anna could hear the sound of a piano playing 'Rock of Ages' coming from the hall next door, so thought it might be the resident priest.

As she walked over to the door the music stopped and on entering she saw a raised stage at the far end with a grand piano on it.

'Hello, Father, are you there?'

A tall freckle-faced young man with ice-blue eyes, pale skin and red hair that was gelled and sticking up came out of the backstage darkness. He looked to be around eighteen and was about six feet tall.

'I heard the piano and thought it was the priest playing,' Anna said.

'That was me; did you like it?' he asked brusquely, and sat back down on the piano stool.

'Yes, it was very accomplished indeed. Is the priest about?' Anna asked as she stepped up onto the stage.

'No, Father O'Reilly's out on parishioner visits. I'm keeping an eye on things till he's back. I'm Jack Brennan. You're not from round here, are you?'

Anna couldn't help but notice that Jack spoke in a machine-gun staccato manner and showed little facial expression, though he seemed very pleasant. His surname sounded familiar but she wasn't sure if she had seen it in the case file.

'I'm Anna Travis and I come from England.' She smiled.

'England, wow, I've always wanted to go there. I'd like to see the Tower of London and go to the Royal Opera House. Have you been to them?' he asked, suddenly full of enthusiasm. His eyes lit up when Anna said she had.

'Do you know when Father O'Reilly will be back?' she asked.

'Before five, 'cause he has a vigil mass then. Have you seen Manchester United play soccer?' he said, the tone of his voice again changing when he asked about something he was interested in.

Anna confessed that she hadn't and Jack looked a bit dejected, as if she had let him down by not having watched United play. From his reactions and behaviour, Anna wondered if Jack had some form of autism spectrum or attention disorder. He began to play 'God Save the Queen', telling Anna it was to remind her of home, and she nodded her approval at his note-perfect ability.

As he played, Anna got out her notepad and started writing down her details and mobile number for Father O'Reilly and added that she'd like to speak with him about Mandy Anderson.

Jack suddenly stopped, got up and stood beside her, towering above her as he looked over her shoulder to see what she was writing. It didn't feel to Anna that he was being rude but more something that was just part of his physical makeup and natural inquisitive behaviour.

'Don't worry, it's just a note for Father O'Reilly,' Anna said.

'Why do you need to know about Mandy?' Jack asked, causing her to stop and glance up. She noticed that there was a look of concern on his face.

'Did you know Mandy Anderson?'

He nodded. 'She was always nice to me and helped me with the piano and my singing,' he said quietly.

'Well, I'm helping to try and find her.'

'I helped as well, everyone around here did but they never found her,' he said with a sad expression. Anna moved closer.

'You must miss her.'

'We were at the same school and played piano duets in church sometimes, and we were both in the choir. She was a better singer than me, the best voice in the choir – it will never be the same again without her.' He turned away abruptly, and sat back at the piano.

Anna nodded, although she could think of a lot more to be heartbroken about than losing the best singer in the choir. She asked him if he used to hang around with Mandy and her friends and he said that he didn't as they never invited him and he didn't think they liked him. He ran his big hands along the piano keys and then blinked.

'Well everyone apart from Mandy, that is.' Anna felt quite sorry for Jack, realizing he was probably one of those kids who was teased or bullied by others because of the way he looked and acted.

'Would you do something special for me?' Anna asked.

Jack instantly stopped playing the piano and looked at her inquisitively. 'What?'

'I need to be sure that Father O'Reilly gets this note. It's important and could help find Mandy.'

Jack took it from her and placed it in his pocket. 'You can count on me,' he said with a beaming smile.

As Jack took the note, Anna noticed that the back of his hands looked red raw and scratched.

'That looks painful.'

'It is. My dad told me off, said I should have known better,' he said ruefully.

'Known better about what?' Anna enquired.

'I was clearing some bushes at the back of the church by the woods and forgot about the Jimson weed. The sap caused a bad rash,' he said, pulling up his shirt sleeves and showing Anna the front and back of his hands and lower arms, which were covered in bumps and blisters. She commented that it did look very sore, and Jack told her it wasn't that bad. Anna felt there was a sweet innocence about the young man as she reminded him to make sure the priest got her note. He gave her a thumbs-up.

As she walked down the path away from the church hall, Anna heard Jack start to play a tune that sounded familiar but she couldn't quite place it. She wanted to stop and listen some more but knew there wasn't the time as she had to get back. As she continued her journey towards the shopping mall it seemed increasingly unlikely that Mandy could have been openly abducted off the street from either route she might have taken that day. If she had got in a car willingly then it had to be with someone she knew and trusted.

There were no cars in the driveway of 58 Lincoln Avenue,

Julie Collins' house, but Anna could hear pop music coming from an open window. She guessed, owing to the volume, that Julie might well be in on her own. Ringing the doorbell a couple of times, she got no answer, so she waited until there was a gap in the music and held her finger down on the buzzer. The music stopped and a few seconds later the door was opened by a young girl in bare feet, with heavy makeup and short brown hair, dressed in a loose T-shirt, no bra and cut-off jeans.

'My mom and dad are out and I don't want to buy anything or become a Jehovah's Witness. Thanks anyway,' she said abruptly, and started to close the door.

Anna introduced herself, showed her FBI card, and said that she wanted to speak with Julie Collins about Mandy Anderson.

'I'm Julie. Have they found Mandy?' the girl asked excitedly.

'I'm sorry, she hasn't been found. I'm helping on the case and was told that you were her best friend.'

Julie invited Anna into the house, which was very similar to the Andersons', though slightly bigger and with minimal religious artefacts. She took Anna through to the kitchen, got herself a can of Diet Coke and sat down with Anna at the kitchen table. Anna asked her to go over the day she last saw Mandy and in particular if there was anything strange or different about Mandy's behaviour. Julie said that Mandy was her normal self and that they had gone to the mall at about ten, and were just hanging out looking in the shops, and talking to other friends they ran into while there. It was about two p.m. when Mandy left, claiming she had choir practice.

'You said that you went into the shops – did Mandy buy anything that day?' Anna asked.

Julie frowned, looking up at the ceiling, deep in thought, trying to remember an incident that was by now two years old. Anna waited, but Julie said nothing and tapped her fingers on the Coke can.

'It doesn't matter how inconsequential it might seem, anything you remember might just be useful.'

'There was something she was looking at, but it was just a cheap little camera gadget, a sort of secret agent spy thing.'

'Tell me what you remember about it?' Anna asked.

'Okay, she said she wanted to go to Prezzies to have a look round. It's a kind of gift and gadget shop, and she picked up a key ring that had this tiny little camera that took real pictures.'

'Did she buy it?' Anna asked.

'I remember she showed it to me. For fun I grabbed it and took a photograph of her.'

Anna couldn't recall having read about the camera in the case file. Julie finished her Coke, crushed the can in her hand and threw it into the kitchen bin.

'Slam dunk,' she said.

Anna was trying to be patient, but knew that the purchase of the camera could be vital new evidence.

'Julie, I really need to know: did Mandy buy the camera?'

Julie sighed and shrugged. 'I don't know, but she bought a birthday card in another shop.'

'Did she say who for?'

'No, and I didn't ask.'

'Could she have had a boyfriend you didn't know about?'

'You kidding? Around here you can't fart without someone noticing. We tried to set her up with a boy once at the church disco, but it was a disaster.'

'It wasn't Jack Brennan, by any chance?' Anna asked.

Julie burst into laughter. 'You gotta be kidding, even Mandy wasn't that desperate.'

'I got the impression they were friends, she helped him with the piano and singing.'

'Yeah, but only 'cause she felt sorry for him. He's kind of weird, comes and stands next to you and listens in on conversations, then starts talking about something completely different.'

Anna wondered if Julie simply resented Jack because she saw him as 'different'.

'He seemed pleasant enough to me when I met him earlier,' Anna remarked in the boy's defence.

'Oh, he's harmless but he's got no friends as such. Apparently, he's got some form of ADHD.'

Anna's earlier suspicions about Jack were right. She knew that the reality was that many kids would never give the likes of Jack Brennan a chance, or make an effort to be friends with him.

'Did you tell the police or FBI about Mandy and the key ring?' she asked.

'No, 'cause I never knew if she did buy it or not and they never asked me about what we did before she decided to go off.'

Anna realized that poor investigation skills had meant the camera key ring had been overlooked, and that if Mandy had bought the gadget for someone else then that could be the person who abducted and possibly killed her. She doubted that the killer would still have possession of it and suspected it was long since disposed of, or lay with Mandy's body, wherever it might be.

Driving out of the mall, Anna felt more at ease with Dewar's powerful Mustang as she looked for the directions back to the I-95, thinking about her meeting with the Andersons and how cruel life had been to them. She glanced down at her map to find that the I-95 was signposted as a right turn and then looking up suddenly saw the red traffic light in front of her. There was no cross traffic, and Anna could, under the local traffic laws, legally make the right turn through the red light, but she panicked and slammed on the brakes.

The driver behind had not slowed because the way was clear and was expecting the Mustang to turn right. Anna felt something slam into the rear of the car, causing her neck to snap back and then jolt forward and banging her forehead on the steering wheel. For a terrifying moment, she thought she was about to pass out.

The driver behind was a middle-aged woman who was thankfully understanding about Anna's naïve knowledge of the traffic laws, and mercifully the only damage appeared to be to the bumpers of both cars. Anna suspected she had mild whiplash and concussion, but was more worried about Dewar's Mustang and how she was going to explain what had happened. Langton, she thought, would go ape-shit. A member of the public had already called the local police and an ambulance on witnessing the incident. Noticing that she was unsteady on her feet from the knock to her head, the driver of the other car sat Anna down on the roadside.

By then, Anna was in floods of tears, completely distraught and confused about what to do and panic-stricken about the damage to Dewar's precious car. And so she phoned the only person she could think of helping her: Don Blane.

Chapter Twenty-Seven

When Blane arrived at the scene of the accident it seemed to Anna that her knight in shining armour had come. She had managed to calm herself down while the attending ambulance crew tried to persuade her that she should go to the local hospital for a check-over but she insisted that apart from a stiff neck and headache she would be okay. The local police were very understanding and knew Blane well, and after he'd had a quiet word with them they agreed not to investigate the incident any further. He also called a garage repairman that he knew who agreed to fix the bumpers on both cars, and to tow away the Mustang to repair the damage as soon as possible. The man said he'd have it done by the end of next week, though a new chrome bumper would be noticeably shiny.

The lady who had gone into the back of Anna was quite distressed but Don calmed her down, gave her the address for his friend's garage and said he would pay for the damage.

Blane told Anna he would take her back to the Academy and whether she liked it or not she was to get some stuff together and stay in his guest room so he could keep an eye on her and make sure she didn't have a relapse or dizzy turn.

'I'm fine, Don, and I don't want to put you out,' Anna protested, rubbing her neck. 'I'm sure you've better things to do with your weekend than look after me. I also need to do my profile CV and work on the Mandy Anderson case file.'

He looked at her and shook his head disapprovingly. 'No you

don't, they can wait. Some rest is what you need right now, so don't argue with me.'

Left with little choice but actually not displeased, back at the Academy, Anna went to her room and packed the FBI-issue holdall with some overnight stuff and her wash bag. She tried ringing Langton again but as before it cut straight to voicemail. At first she was concerned for his wellbeing and worried that something might have happened to him, but then considered it more likely that the silly bugger had forgotten to take his phone charger with him. Anna looked at the Anderson case file on her desk, briefly thought about leaving it behind, then put it into the holdall along with her laptop. Any attempt to pick up the now-full holdall caused her to wince at the sharp pain, so she had little option but to drag it along the floor to the lift. Waiting there, she was approached by Beth Jackson, the Los Angeles detective from the room next to her.

'Hi, there's a group of us going out tonight, we're meeting in the reception area at seven, if you'd like to join us.'

'I'm really sorry, Beth, I had a bit of an accident earlier and I don't feel—'

Beth cut her off: 'Yeah, whatever. Have a nice evening, wherever it may be.'

The detective clearly didn't believe her as she had the holdall beside her, with her pyjamas poking through the half-closed zip. Anna tried to explain but Beth ignored her and just walked off towards her room.

Blane was waiting on the ground floor. As he picked up the holdall he caught sight of the case file, looked at Anna and smiled.

'You need to rest, not work.'

'I'm sorry, I just thought if I couldn't sleep then I should do something productive.'

'Okay, here's the deal. You have a bath then relax while I cook dinner. The Anderson case can be discussed while we eat, then after dinner it's rest time.'

'Agreed,' Anna replied, and held up her hand to shake on it.

'Sally and Peter thought you were wonderful and very understanding. Thanks for being open and honest with them,' Blane said.

'They were lovely people and I can see exactly why they care deeply for you,' Anna said, deliberately making her feelings of gratitude clear. He said nothing, and Anna hoped that it was just because he was shy.

After half an hour's driving along the main road, Blane turned off onto a dirt track just outside of Woodbridge. The track narrowed and eventually cut through woodland comprising tall fir, cedar and pine trees, the fragrant scent wafted into the car filling it with a relaxing atmosphere. Rays of sunlight cut through the branches and the woodland became denser as they drove on. Soon Anna could see a clearing leading to a shoreline, with a small boathouse and jetty. As they drove into the clearing there appeared a beautiful raised two-storey red cedar log cabin that overlooked the bay.

'You live here?' Anna asked, amazed at the peaceful surroundings and stunning views across Belmont Bay and the Potomac River.

'It's sort of a home from home,' Blane said and then explained that although he had an apartment in Woodbridge he liked to come out to the cabin at weekends. Anna laughed when he said that his colleagues at work called him the weekend hermit.

Blane carried Anna's bag up the wooden steps and opened the double doors. The inside was open-plan with high A-framed beamed ceilings, and exuded a cosy welcoming charm. There was a large wood-burning fireplace with an old stone chimney, and a deep wood-framed sofa and chairs placed in front of it. The wooden floors and walls were partially covered with Native American rugs. The dining area was to one side, with a circular table made from blocks of wood that were laid together in a basket weave pattern with six matching chairs. To the side of the table, wide French windows allowed a stunning view across the bay, and led out to the deck area where there was a wooden picnic table, log chairs and a hammock.

Blane told Anna that the master bedroom was upstairs, along with an en-suite bathroom. She could see that the upstairs was also open-plan and built in a balcony style that overlooked the downstairs.

Anna noticed there was another bedroom downstairs with a bathroom beside it. Blane suggested that Anna could have the upstairs room but she told him not to be silly as she was perfectly happy to sleep downstairs. Reminding her she was his guest, he carried her bags upstairs. The bedroom was stunning and full of natural light from the windows and a door that opened out to a balcony. The four-poster bed was positioned so that you could lie and take in the view across the bay.

Anna, totally overwhelmed by the breathless beauty of the cabin and its surroundings, somehow managed to thank Blane for his thoughtfulness and hospitality.

Smiling, he told Anna to make herself at home and that although the place was very 'olde worlde', technology had caught up with it and there was hot running water, electricity and even Internet and mobile phone connections, though the signal could be weak or slow at times.

'Even better.' Anna grinned.

Langton lay in his cabin on board the FBI's converted Mirage power-yacht and looked at his watch. It was nearly six p.m. on Saturday evening. He felt completely frustrated at having spent the previous night and most of the day cooped up in the command and control room, only able to watch the outside world and the interior of the suspect's villa on an array of LCD monitors. He had tried to get some sleep during the night but the small cabin he shared was uncomfortable, and the top bunk bed he'd been given was far too small, the gap between the ceiling and his nose only about eight inches.

Try as he might he just couldn't sleep due the anticipation of finally arresting Fitzpatrick. It didn't help that his cabin was directly below the on-deck Jacuzzi, and the sound of the cavorting undercover officers laughing and splashing around kept him awake as well. Looking at his watch again he found that only three minutes had elapsed. The latest information was that their suspect Fitzpatrick was not expected to turn up until after sunset, which wasn't until eight p.m., and if anything did start to happen, someone would come and get him.

Langton thought about the events that had occurred since they had set sail from Miami. There was nothing positive or even remotely encouraging to suggest Fitzpatrick would definitely show up and there was always the possibility it was not even him. Langton knew that the FBI had tapped into the villa's landline but no calls of any interest had been recorded and no one apart from the young boy and the Hispanic-looking woman had come or gone from the property all day. They were picking up a mobile-phone signal coming from the villa but encryption equipment was being used so they could not hear the conversation. Jack Deans had told Langton this was a positive sign as it was a known method popular with drug dealers to prevent law enforcement agencies from listening to their calls.

Langton glanced at his watch again; in total eight minutes had passed since he last looked. God, was he bored. He finally had just dozed off when he was disturbed by a knock at the door, and one of the FBI agents entered. Without thinking he went to sit up and banged his head on the cabin ceiling and swore under his breath.

'Detective Langton, sorry to disturb you, but Director Deans thought you'd want to be woken. There's just been a call on the villa landline to a pizza joint. The young boy has ordered two extra-large with sides to be delivered. A big order for him and the housekeeper so we figure he's expecting company.'

'Thanks, I will be up in a minute,' Langton replied as he got down from the bunk bed and, checking his watch, saw that it was 8.30 p.m.

In the control room, the LCD screens were showing the jetty area. Langton realized that because of the darkness, the surveillance team had switched to specialist night vision cameras, which detected and amplified any available light so an image could be displayed, albeit in black and white with a green aura. He knew that this would make it more difficult for him to recognize Fitzpatrick, plus the night-camera lens would make the suspect's eyes a reflective white.

Jack Deans pointed to a screen that had a satellite view of the Florida coastline on it as he spoke into his head mike.

'Intensify earlier satellite image to close-up,' he said, as the picture zoomed inward from the skies like something on Google Earth. 'This was taken while it was still light. Can't make out who's on board but close enough to track her and she's heading our way.'

Langton couldn't believe how good the picture quality was as a large powerboat came into view, bouncing along the sea at a high speed. A navigational indicator in the top right of the screen showed the boat's speed and that its distance from them was twenty-two miles south.

'Obviously, as it turned dark the picture was lost. We've got a helicopter following them.' Deans said.

'Won't they see it from the boat?' Langton asked.

'Not unless they've got eyes like Superman – it's a Sikorsky Black Hawk, heavily modified with stealth technology and flying three miles above them. They were used in the raid to take out Osama Bin Laden. Switch to the Black Hawk's thermal-imaging camera,' Deans ordered into his mike and a multicoloured image in the shape of the speedboat came up on the screen. Deans explained that the camera picked up heat and colourized objects that emitted thermal radiation. Langton knew exactly what the director was talking about as the Met's helicopters had the same equipment. He suspected that Deans was just showing off to his men and decided to let him ramble on.

'The reds, yellow and white in the picture are heat sources and the cooler objects are the blues, purple and green. From the movement of the yellows, we think there are three people on board,' Deans explained.

Langton was amazed at what he was witnessing and shuddered to think what it all cost. 'Are you going to use the Navy to stop the boat once it enters the canal waterways?' he asked.

'No, too risky,' Deans told him. 'I want him to moor the boat and be on terra firma when we take him out. He mustn't make it into the villa; the last thing I want is a siege situation. So we're dependent on you to make the ID.'

Langton prayed that the man he blamed for destroying his promotion and making a fool of him was on board the boat. He didn't doubt his ability to recognize him again, even if he'd had more plastic surgery; it was the fact that he would have to make a split-second decision from a night-vision camera picture that worried him. He stood and waited in silence as the satellite tracked the boat's movement towards them, the distance to go now ten miles.

Langton heard the sound of a doorbell and wondered where it had come from, before he realized it was from within the villa. He looked up at the screens, one showing the boy moving towards the front door and an exterior camera showing a pizza-delivery boy ringing the bell. Deans explained that the delivery boy was one of their agents, dubbed 'Baby Face' after the notorious 1930s public enemy Baby Face Nelson. Langton wondered why on earth the FBI agents so often used nicknames. He forced a smile but in reality it was to hide his anxiety as he saw the boat had entered the inland waterway and was less than a mile away. Langton's stomach churned with the knowledge that within minutes he might hold Fitzpatrick's future in the palm of his hand. It struck him that he hoped that the SWAT team didn't shoot the dealer. He'd far rather look him in the eye, slap on the cuffs and tell him he'd been nicked, as he had done with every scumbag he had arrested over the last thirty-two years of his police service. Langton had never carried a firearm, or been on a unit that was trained to, and he was glad that was the case. He had only ever carried a truncheon and used it as a last resort.

Now he could hear a voice over the radio speaking in pho-netic code, and from the background sound he suspected it was the pilot of the helicopter giving the boat's position. Then there came the deep throbbing of a boat's engine and the gurgling of bubbling water as it taxied towards them. The control room was eerily silent, until Deans spoke.

'Teams Alpha One and Two, take positions. You go on my command.'

Langton could see out through the one-way glass onto the boat deck, to where five SWAT team officers crawled on their bellies with their weapons, while the man dressed in the Arab outfit cavorted with two girls on a sofa and the others played in the Jacuzzi. Deans beckoned Langton over to him and a close-up picture of the boat appeared on the largest screen.

'As soon as you recognize him, I'll give the command to go.'

Langton had faced many frightening situations in his career, even being close to death when he was stabbed in the stomach. But now he felt unbelievably tense as he wiped beads of sweat from his forehead with the back of his hand. He was conscious that others in the room might notice but then realized that everyone was focused on the screen as the boat drew up along-side the jetty. The man piloting the boat was Mexican-looking, as was the other man on the deck. Langton was thankful this was the case as he recalled Deans saying there were only three people on board.

A tall white man appeared on the deck of the target boat, at least six feet four, wearing a turtleneck sweater, jeans and a base-ball cap. On the night-vision camera his clothing seemed all black apart from his white trainers,

'Yes or no?' Deans asked Langton as the camera zoomed into the man's face.

Langton stepped nearer to the screen but frustratingly the peak of the man's cap was pulled low, almost touching his nose. The camera started to zoom in even closer but the man jumped from the boat onto the jetty and started to walk towards the house.

'I need an answer, Langton,' Deans said, as the camera zoomed in and out to refocus on the suspect.

'It could be him,' Langton replied.

Deans glared at him. 'Could be is not fucking good enough. I can't risk him getting inside the house.'

'Well get the fucking camera to focus on his face,' Langton retorted. He suddenly found his mind flashing back to the murder team office in London, to the moment Fitzpatrick had fooled him by posing as an FBI agent and then calmly walked out of the station. The walk, it was the walk – slightly hunched shoulders, head down and an arrogant swagger, but pigeon-toed. Langton concentrated hard as the man took another step towards the house, and in that instant he knew it was Fitzpatrick.

'Yes, it's him,' Langton said confidently as he turned and looked at Deans.

'Go go go!' Deans shouted down his mike.

Langton's attention was suddenly drawn to another screen to the right of Deans.

The ear-piercing boom of an exploding thunder flash made the FBI boat rock and at the same time a smoke bomb ignited between Fitzpatrick and the villa. But Langton was focused on what he could see on the other screen, where the young boy was at the villa's patio doors and opening them. Langton instinctively knew he was going out to greet his father. No one else in the control room had noticed as their attention was fixed on the main screen and Fitzpatrick. Like a man possessed, Langton ran from the control room, onto the deck and jumped down onto the jetty. The SWAT team were already in front of him and darkness turned to day as floodlights from the FBI boat lit up the garden. He could see Fitzpatrick on the grass verge; he was frozen to the spot. The cloud from the smoke bomb was being carried by the breeze towards the dealer and towered over him like an enormous foaming wave. SWAT team agents were screaming, 'Armed FBI, get down on the ground!'

'THE BOY'S IN THE LINE OF FIRE!' Langton screamed at the top of his voice, running as fast as he could.

Fitzpatrick suddenly pulled a gun from his rear pocket, but before he could even raise it the sound of rapid gunfire filled the air. Langton could only watch as the power of the bullets physically lifted Fitzpatrick off the ground and sprays of blood spurted from the entry wounds glistening in the floodlights.

Everyone stopped in their tracks, as smoke covered most of the area where Fitzpatrick lay, apart from his feet, which weren't moving. Warily, the SWAT agents inched forward, their guns trained on the dealer, but Langton knew he was dead. Concerned only for the safety of the son, he sped past the agents. On reaching Fitzpatrick's body he could see through the smoke that the young boy was motionless and partially lying over the top of his father. Langton turned and looked back towards the jetty, where the two Mexican men had been apprehended and Deans was walking towards him.

'You were so fucking interested in Fitzpatrick you didn't see the boy. He's dead because of your trigger happy attitude!' Langton shouted.

'We have a job to do, Langton,' Deans roared, striding forward. 'Fitzpatrick endangered the boy's life when he pulled a gun and you nearly compromised the whole operation.'

On hearing the sound of someone sobbing, Langton turned and found that the boy, covered in blood, was now kneeling on the grass. He had thought at first that the boy had been shot but he could see there were no holes in his white T-shirt and slowly it dawned on him it was Fitzpatrick's blood.

The boy stared at Langton, terrified, wiping the tears from his eyes.

'Langton? You're Langton?' he said. Gone was the American accent, his high-pitched voice was impeccably English.

Langton nodded, putting out his hand to help the boy up. The boy raised his right hand and pointed his father's gun at Langton's chest, his voice turning into a shriek.

'You did this to my father, you killed him like you did my mother!'

Langton looked at the boy and realized that his eyes had

changed from terror to total hatred. He braced himself, waiting for the bullet to enter his body.

'Put the gun down, son,' Deans said. Langton could see that all the SWAT team had their weapons pointed at the boy. The boy ignored them and with a trembling hand kept the gun aimed at Langton.

'Don't force my men to shoot you, son. Just put the gun down,' Deans said coldly.

Langton stepped closer to the boy to block off their line of fire and shouted at Deans to get his men to back off. He presumed that if the boy was going to shoot him, he would have done it by now, but more than anything he didn't want to see an innocent child killed for his father's sins.

'What's your name?' Langton asked as he slowly knelt down in front of him.

Deans, clearly furious at Langton's actions but unwilling to exacerbate the situation, ushered his men to step back and lower their weapons. The boy's lower lip trembled, his whole body shaking as Langton asked him again.

'What's your name?'

'Jonathan.'

'Listen to me, Jonathan: I swear to you that I didn't kill your mother.'

The boy was shaking even harder, trying unsuccessfully to control himself, but still dangerous because as terrified as he was he still held the gun in his hand.

'My father said you did, you were chasing her and caused the car crash that killed her. She died because of you.'

Langton knew that the truth was very different; yes, someone had tampered with the brakes on the car, but, although never proved, it was thought to have been Fitzpatrick, so he could take his son from her.

Keeping his voice steady he held the boy's attention. 'It was men who were looking for your father, they were drug dealers who he owed money to, and they rammed your mother's car off the road.'

'That's a lie, my father wasn't a drug dealer!' Jonathan shrieked, and the gun waved from side to side.

Langton raised his voice, firmly and steadily, maintaining direct eye contact with the boy.

'Look around you, Jonathan; all this wealth, the boats and planes, continually moving from place to place.'

Langton paused and he could see that Jonathan's gun hand was now beginning to drop a little as he was thinking about what Langton was saying. 'Look over there, to the boat your father came in – that's cocaine and a drug called fentanyl the FBI are unloading.'

Jonathan's eyes were welling up with tears as he lowered the gun another couple of inches. Langton realized his words were getting through to the boy, but suspected he had known the truth all along.

'Come on, Jonathan, you must have seen boxes of fentanyl before?'

'It's medicine he sold,' Jonathan said, raising the gun upwards, pointing it directly at Langton.

'Okay, it's medicine, but did you ever see him with any doctors or visiting hospitals?' Langton asked, now inching closer to the frightened, confused boy.

'My father was a good man.'

'I know that, Jonathan, and he always wanted what was best for you. He loved you and your mother very much. They both want you to be the best at whatever you choose to do.'

Suddenly Jonathan's head slumped forward and he dropped the gun to the ground as sobs shook his body and he wept uncontrollably. Langton picked up the gun, threw it behind him and then embraced the boy as if he were his own son, squeezing him tightly and stroking his head to comfort him.

Finally, Deans edged forward, picked up the gun and whispered to Langton, 'What on earth do you think you were doing. My men—'

Langton cut him off abruptly: 'I'm doing my fucking job. Policing is about saving life, not taking it!' He got to his feet and stood to one side as the boy was taken from him, catching someone muttering 'asshole' under their breath. Maybe he had sounded like one to the rest of the team, but watching as the boy threw a pitiful look towards the blood-soaked figure of his father, his attention was brutally brought back to the reason he was there. It was finally over and he could return to London with the case closed. He couldn't resist one last look at the dead man who had made such a fool of him. In death, Fitzpatrick's chiselled face remained unmarked, his blank eyes wide open, and whether the smirk on his face was out of fear or surprise, it would be remembered for a very, very long time.

After a hot relaxing bath, Anna slept for a couple of hours. When she woke, the cabin was in near darkness, lit only by the flames of the log fire. The shadows from the flames had a seductive quality, accompanied by the sound of crackling wood. She got out of bed, still feeling snug and cosy, as the cabin was toasty warm. From the indoor balcony, she could look below into the living area but Don was not there. Glancing out of the window, she saw him walking up from the river's edge, rod in one hand and a large freshly caught fish in the other.

Unobtrusively, Anna stepped back, as she wanted to watch him going about his business. As he put the fish in the sink she could see that he had already peeled some potatoes and greens, which were in pots on the stove. But before he could attend to them his mobile rang.

'Hi, Carl, what can I do for you?' Blane asked quietly.

Anna started to tiptoe back towards the bedroom, trying not to eavesdrop on the conversation.

'I arranged for her to speak with the Andersons, but I wasn't aware she met Jack,' she overheard him say, and instantly knew the call was about her.

'I know she has no lawful powers over here. She's very experienced and I simply asked her to look over the case file,' he continued calmly and politely.

'Look, Carl, I think Jack may have been exaggerating a little bit, Anna is not an aggressive person and—'

It became evident that Don was having difficulty in conveying his point of view to Carl, whoever he was.

'Telling the Academy Director will benefit no one, Carl, me included. Leave it with me. I will deal with the matter, okay?' Blane said, and there was a short pause.

'Thank you, and I promise it won't happen again.' He sighed as he finished the call, and shook his head. Then he proceeded to gut the fish.

Anna wondered if it was Jack Brennan's father on the phone or a senior FBI agent who was chastizing Blane. She waited twenty minutes before getting dressed into tracksuit bottoms and a T-shirt, worrying all the while that she had let Blane down. As she went downstairs to join him she contemplated asking him what the call was about, but dreaded him thinking that she had been listening in. In the event she decided it was best to say nothing and wait to see if he raised the subject during the evening.

Blane gave Anna a big smile as he greeted her and asked if she had slept well, with no obvious annoyance in his tone.

'That bed is so comfortable, I feel much better and my headache is gone. Now, can I please help with something?' Anna stepped in closer.

'Just relax, sit by the fireplace. I hope you don't mind seafood again. I'm going to oven-bake a freshly hooked striper. Anna giggled as she said a 'stripper' was fine. Realizing what had amused her, Blane explained that the fish was a striped bass.

All the while they waited the half hour or so before dinner was ready Blane never mentioned the phone call from 'Carl' or anything about the Mandy Anderson case. Anna was still concerned about the car accident but he reassured her she really had nothing to worry about except maybe a few harsh words from Dewar. Anna insisted that she would pay for the damage to both cars and once the Mustang was repaired she would call Dewar and explain what had happened.

Blane served the striper with vegetables and a sauce made from roasted garlic, lemon pepper, sweet basil, lime juice and butter. Anna thought it tasted delicious and complimented him on his cooking, even as she was desperate to talk about Mandy Anderson, and hoping to find out more about the phone call he had received.

'I think I may have found a new bit of evidence today,' Anna eventually said.

Blane swallowed his mouthful of food and wiped his mouth on his napkin. 'Tell me about it.'

'I met a girl called Julie Collins – she was with Mandy just before she left the mall.'

'Yeah, they were best friends. She's turned out to be a bit of a madam, total opposite of Mandy. So what did she have to say for herself?' he asked and took a sip of wine.

Anna repeated her conversation with Julie, mentioning the birthday card and the possibility that Mandy had bought a camera key ring. Blane shook his head, put his knife and fork down and sat back in his chair.

'Why on earth did Julie withhold this vital information in her original statement?'

'In fairness she was never specifically asked what happened before she and Mandy parted company.'

Anna could see that he was upset by the missed opportunity.

'Have you spoken with Peter and Sally Anderson about Mandy going to the mall to buy a birthday present for some-one?' he asked.

'No, but I think if Mandy had told her parents about it, they would have mentioned it by now.'

'I agree, but it would still be worth asking the Andersons and checking Mandy's diary for any entries that refer to birthdays.'

'I've got her diary and already looked through it,' Anna told him. 'The only birthday reminders are for family and girl-friends – her mother and father's were months away and there's definitely nothing for May or June.' She paused for some wine. 'I've also left a message for Father O'Reilly at the church. I'd really like to speak to him about the old choir practice records to see if they match up with the diary, but he hasn't got back to me yet.'

Anna was keen to raise her conversation with Jack Brennan, but hesitated; it didn't immediately add anything to the investigation but she was desperate to know who 'Carl' was. She decided to broach the subject from a different angle.

'I also met a Jack Brennan at the church – he was very pleasant.'

'He's a nice lad, suffers from ADHD,' Blane observed. 'When he was younger, the other kids bullied him and made him the butt of their jokes, but they just tend to leave him alone now. He spends all his spare time at the church, doing odd jobs and playing the piano. Did he say anything useful about Mandy?'

'Nothing useful, but he clearly liked her and missed her not being in the choir.'

'Mandy was one of the few that actually made the effort to be nice and talk to him, so he probably misses her a lot. Some of the kids, Julie Collins being one of them, even went as far as saying he had something to do with her disappearance. He was interviewed but he was with his father all day.'

'Why would they do something like that?' a shocked Anna asked, realizing she had not yet read Jack's interview in the case file.

'Spitefulness and because they see him as the oddball. I can never understand how some kids can be so cruel and narrow-minded. More wine?' he asked, holding up the bottle.

Anna smiled and nodded, hiding the fact that she was vexed that her ploy to try to discover who 'Carl' was hadn't worked so far. She decided to keep the topic of conversation on Jack Brennan.

'I noticed Jack had a horrible-looking rash and blisters on his arms and hands. It must have been causing him pain when he played the piano but he never complained.'

'Really, did he tell you how it happened?'

She nodded. 'He'd been pulling out some Jimson weed and forgot to wear gloves, said his dad was upset with him.'

'I'm not surprised – if there's anyone who knows about every dangerous plant out there it's his dad.'

Anna asked him if Jack's dad was a botanist and Blane told her that he was the Chief Park Ranger for the County and had co-ordinated all the woodland searches for Mandy Anderson. He added that Jimson weed was very prevalent in Virginia and could be a lot more dangerous than just causing a rash.

'It's a member of the Solanaceae plant family and contains atropine, which makes you very ill, causes hallucinations and can even kill you.'

'What's Solanaka . . . ?' Anna started to ask, but gave up trying to pronounce the unfamiliar word. He grinned and apologized for being too technical.

'It comes from the Latin word *solanum*, meaning "night-shade".'

'What, like deadly nightshade?'

'Yes, but the strange thing is it's also used for medicinal pur-poses, such as an analgesic during surgery.'

'So how come you know so much about plants?' she won-dered, playing with the stem of her wine glass.

Blane modestly claimed his knowledge was limited, and came from a poisoning case he'd dealt with, in which a care worker in an old people's home collected berries from a nightshade plant, crushed them and put them into the food. It was not enough to kill the residents but made them very ill and then she would give them another drug to counteract the atropine.

'Some saw her as their saviour, changed their wills and left her everything. Once the will was changed that was it and she didn't bother with the antidote. She was something else, but we got her in the end.'

'How did you catch her?' Anna asked.

'A suspicious relative, plus the sudden high mortality rate in the home. Once arrested, she delighted in telling us how she had the power to control life and death.'

Anna had been so mesmerized by what he was telling her that she hadn't realized that the conversation had slowly weaved away from the subject of Jack Brennan, and now it was too late – they had finished their meal.

She offered to help with the washing-up but Don was having none of it, telling her to go and relax by the fire and put on some music if she wanted. She wandered over to the rack of CDs and looked through them, impressed by the wide range but not really sure what to put on. She smiled as she noticed the name of one of the artists.

'I didn't take you for a Barry Manilow fan,' she said.

'That's my adopted mom's, she's mad about him.'

'Yeah, right,' Anna said, and they both laughed.

'Go ahead, put it on. I fancy a bit of nostalgia,' Blane said.

Anna put the disc in the player and the first track opened with a slow, rolling piano intro that she recognized right away as the tune that Jack Brennan had been playing as she left the church. Reaching for the CD cover she saw that the song was called 'Mandy'. It was rather eerie as she listened closely to the words of the opening verse, but she told herself she was just being silly. Then came the chorus and the references to Mandy, who came and gave without taking; he sent her away but still needed her today.

Anna, settling herself on the sofa, wondered if she was just imagining things but remembered Jack telling her 'it will never be the same again without her'. Something made her suspect that the song was more than a fond memory to the young man. She glanced over at Don, who was still washing up, wanting to tell him about the song but anxious he'd think she was just imagining things, as he seemed to have a soft spot for Jack. She was equally keen to examine Jack's original statement now that she knew that it might be vital, and so made an excuse to Don that her headache had returned and she didn't feel so good, so she thought she'd lie down. She felt bad as Don blamed himself, fearing it was his cooking or the wine that had made her feel unwell.

Anna assured him it wasn't and kissed him gently on the cheek before starting to go upstairs. Before she was midway up, he asked if she minded him changing the CD as it was getting on his nerves, to which she laughed and by the time she reached her bedroom the strains of Mozart drifted up. Yet, Mr Manilow's rendition of 'Mandy' continued playing in her mind.

Chapter Twenty-Eight

It was after midnight as Anna sat cross-legged on the bed, with statements and documents from the case file strewn all over it and the floor. She still felt bad about deceiving Don into believing she had a headache, and her dilemma now was whether or not she should go downstairs and wake him up, or wait until the morning to tell him what she had uncovered. If she was right, about where the camera key ring, birthday card and, vitally, Mandy's body could be, the Andersons might have some closure. 'Well,' she thought, 'I won't get a wink of sleep and Don wants this resolved even more than I do . . .' but first, she wanted to get her scribbled notes in order, and gather the documents from the file so she could fully explain her reasoning, which pointed to not one but two suspects being involved in Mandy Anderson's abduction and murder.

The vital information Anna had found came firstly from looking at Jack Brennan's statement. It contained the same points he had spoken about at the church, but in slightly more detail, along with his family background. His mother had left when he was very young and he was an only child who now lived with his father, the local Chief Ranger. He knew Mandy through school and the church; she was kind to him and helped him with the piano. Jack's account of his movements for the afternoon that Mandy went missing was that his father had taken him out on a long driving lesson and they had returned home late evening.

Thanks to Jack's alibi, Anna had at first thought she was

wrong about the Barry Manilow song having a deeper significance for the young man, but what she discovered next
convinced her otherwise. Jack Brennan's personal details showed
his date of birth as 21 May 1996, meaning he was sixteen on the
day that Mandy disappeared. Anna wondered if he was the
recipient of the camera key ring and card, but more worrying
was that if that were true, his alibi had been a lie. There was no
statement in the file made by a Mr Brennan, but Anna thought
it impossible that he wouldn't have been asked to confirm his
son's movements on the day in question. She had recalled Blane
saying that as the local Chief Ranger, Jack's father had led the
woodland searches for Mandy Anderson, so she had looked
through the case file for the search map and accompanying
report to find his name.

On discovering the Chief Ranger was called Carl Brennan,
Anna realized that this must have been the very same 'Carl' that
Don had been talking to on the phone earlier in the evening.
It made sense that Jack would have told his father about meeting Anna at the church, but she couldn't understand why Jack
would suggest that she had been in any way aggressive. She
appreciated, due to Jack's ADHD and his being bullied, that Carl
might be an overprotective father, but why threaten to make a
complaint to the Director of the Academy? It could just have
been an idle threat – but what if it was actually more than that,
some sort of nervous reaction in fear of being found out? If Jack
Brennan had abducted or killed Mandy and, as Anna suspected,
Carl Brennan had alibied his son then they were both lying.

She had been about to tidy up the mess on the bed when she
noticed the pile of Mandy's birthday cards and decided to look
through them, checking them properly this time. It felt strange
reading them, as the contents of the cards wished the girl a
happy sixteenth, yet she had probably died before she even
reached that age. Stranger still was the card Anna opened next,
which was signed, 'Love always, Jack xxx', and in which the
word 'always' was written in a slightly different-coloured pen, as
if added as an afterthought.

This anomaly made her recall Jack's comment that things would never be the same without Mandy. She sighed, everything buzzing around in her head, when suddenly the unexpected memory popped up of Dewar saying that the Josh Reynolds' suicide note was fake because its wording suggested it was written by someone who already knew he was dead. Anna scratched her head to ruffle up her hair. Could Dewar's theory also apply to the birthday card?

She looked again at the card from Jack and felt almost sure it was written as if he knew there was some sort of permanence about Mandy's disappearance.

'Okay, okay, now just sit back on this for a second,' she muttered to herself and then began to piece it together slowly. If Jack killed Mandy then Carl Brennan must have lied about his son's movements on that day, and he must also know where Mandy's body was.

She grabbed the search record and spread the map out over the bedroom floor. Checking the report, she could see that it had been compiled by Carl Brennan, who also co-ordinated the efforts of the Park Rangers, Sheriff's officers, US Marines and members of the public in the woodland searches.

Anna decided the best thing to do was to write down, on bits of paper, the names of the teams, including the date and time they had searched each gridded area of woodland. Having laid them out on the corresponding areas of the map, nothing struck her as out of the ordinary.

She was beginning to gather up the bits of paper from the map when she noticed something odd about the searches on 25 May. Carl Brennan had led a team of eight people searching an area of woodland in Prince William Forest at eleven a.m. Ten other searches, in different areas, had taken place at the same time on that day, but what made Carl's team stand out to Anna was that one member, a Mr J Knox, appeared to be in two places at the same time. At first, she thought that it could have been chance, someone with the same surname and initial, a relative perhaps, but as she looked closer she could see that the same thing re-occurred with the whole of Carl Brennan's team. Each member listed on his team was also listed at another site at the same time. She was certain she was right – Carl Brennan must have made up a team using real names and there could only be one reason. Mandy Anderson's body was buried in this section of woodland.

It was nearly two a.m. by the time Anna had put her notes in chronological order. Nevertheless, she pulled on a jumper over her pyjamas, went downstairs and before waking Blane laid out the statements and search map on the dining table, along with her notepad. She hesitated in his bedroom doorway, worried about upsetting him with her revelations. He was sound asleep, looking completely at peace, but her mind was made up; she wouldn't be able to sleep herself as she was far too keen to run her thoughts by him.

Anna gently touched his shoulder. 'Don, it's me,' she whispered. 'I'm sorry to wake you but I really need to speak to you.'

Don, still half asleep and not really taking in what was happening, said nothing as he moved over to one side of the bed and pulled back the quilt, inviting her to join him.

'No, it's not that, Don.'

She didn't feel affronted – had it been under different circumstances she would probably have slipped into bed with him, but now she switched on his bedside lamp. He squinted as his eyes adjusted to the light.

'I think I may have uncovered what happened to Mandy and where she's buried,' Anna said softly.

He went bright red, flipped the quilt back over the bed and scooted out the other side, grabbing his dressing gown from the end of the bed.

'I'm sorry, Anna, forgot I was buck-naked. I was half asleep and didn't mean to offend . . .'

'I'm not offended at all. I'm the one who should be apologizing for waking you at this time in the morning,' she admitted sheepishly.

*

Blane joined Anna, having had a quick wash and put on a track-suit, sitting down beside her on the sofa. She decided to get straight to the point.

'At first, I wasn't sure and I thought I might be imagining things, but I've been going over and over the case since I went upstairs. I've laid everything out for you to look at,' she said and pointed to the map and case file papers covering the dining table. 'Okay, here we go – are you ready?'

He smiled, nodding his head. There was something so girlish about her excitement, and he leaned back as she clapped her hands.

'Right, I think that Jack Brennan killed Mandy Anderson, and his father Carl, having found out, either helped him dispose of the body or deliberately made sure the area where she is concealed was not searched.'

Don looked at Anna with surprise, yet he knew from her tone of voice and demeanour that she was being serious, as she seemed calmer and focused. He was certain she would not be making such a bold statement if she hadn't found evidence to back it up.

'You won't believe this, but it was the song "Mandy" on the CD player. Jack was playing the same tune on the piano when I left him at the church. Something was niggling me about it, but I thought I was being silly and imagining things. I had to be sure before I said anything to you,' Anna said, embarrassed, feeling she had let him down by not confiding in him at the time.

He sensed the unease in her voice.

'Whatever your reasons were, I don't care. All that matters is we trust each other. Never be frightened to tell me your thoughts,' he said.

'All right, well I might as well be honest about everything. I also overheard your conversation with Carl Brennan, but I didn't know at the time who you were speaking to.'

'I knew you had heard, the floorboards creak at the slightest movement so I knew you were up. I didn't tell you that Carl was having a moan and overreacting because I didn't want you to worry. He hugged her before continuing. 'I have to say you were very good at not giving yourself away, you must have been very curious to know who I was talking to.'

Anna slowly eased back from his embrace, thinking that it was good that he could joke about her antics, but at the same time she needed to finish what she had started.

'I think Carl's reaction was a nervous one, plus he may have been fishing for information,' Anna said as Blane put his arm around her shoulders, and asked her to tell him everything that had raised her suspicions about Jack and Carl. She dived back to the table to fetch her notepad, and then rejoined him beside the fire, taking a deep breath before taking her time to explain what she thought might have happened. She said that it was Jack Brennan's birthday on the day Mandy disappeared and she suspected that the camera key ring and birthday card Mandy bought at the mall were for him. Not wanting to be ridiculed about the present, or associating with Jack, Mandy lied about choir practice as a cover to secretly visit him on her way home.

'I mean, I know all this is just supposition, and I could be wrong, but it sort of makes sense, do you agree?'

'Yeah, in a way. Do you think there was anything sexual going on between the two of them?' he asked.

'I don't know for certain, but I think Jack's feelings for Mandy may have been stronger, possibly an infatuation.'

'And hers for him?' Blane pressed.

'Well, more sort of friendly, platonic even – she respected him in some ways, like his ability on the piano, but also felt sorry for him.'

'He may not have interpreted it that way,' Blane added.

'Exactly, and that's why I believe something may have happened at his house, not premeditated but something that caused a spur-of-the-moment reaction and ended in her death.'

Blane thought about what Anna said and nodded in agreement.

'So if Mandy did die in the Brennan house then Jack and Carl are lying about being out on a driving lesson all afternoon,' he said quietly.

'Yes. Carl's involvement is where I really doubted my thoughts. I even considered that he might have abducted Mandy and persuaded or duped Jack into creating an alibi for him.'

'There's nothing wrong with that, you're right to consider every possibility.'

'Thank you,' she said, more than ever aware of what a different creature he was to Langton, prepared to listen and not constantly challenge her views or suspicions.

Anna took hold of his hand and led him over to the dining table. She pointed to the underlined names of the people apparently searching different areas at the same time. He picked up on it straight away.

'Unless these people have clones of themselves this is impossible.'

'I think Carl Brennan knew that Mandy was buried in that section of woodland and deliberately falsified the search report so she wouldn't be found,' Anna said.

'So Carl may have returned home to find Mandy's body and then moved her to the woods.'

She nodded. 'Or Jack buried her in the woods, and then told his father what had happened. Either way, Carl had to falsify the search records to conceal the crime.'

Blane spent quite a while intently studying the search record and map again. Anna, knowing he didn't doubt her, just watched him as he slowly moved his index finger across the maps and then sighed deeply as the realization of what she had uncovered set in.

'Dear God, this is unbelievable. Why did no one check over this search record two years ago?' Blane said despairingly.

'Mistakes happen, Don, we both know that.'

'The damn answers were staring them in the face and they missed what was on the surface all along. Peter and Sally Anderson suffered because of incompetence and shoddy detective work and poor Mandy deserved better as well!'

Anna could see that Don was angry yet deeply moved by how the outcome would affect the Andersons.

He had returned to the fireplace and was resting his hands on the mantel as he stared into the blazing logs.

'Why, Anna, why didn't Carl come forward if it was an accident?'

She moved closer and rested her hand in the small of his back.

'I don't have the answers, but I do know when it comes to family, or in this case father and son, the saying "blood is thicker than water" is very pertinent.'

He nodded in agreement, but she could feel his sorrow.

'We will need to inform the local Sheriff and get a warrant to search the Brennan house and the woods, but we can't do that until morning so we may as well get a couple of hours' sleep until then.' He straightened up and headed towards his bedroom. Anna very much wanted to follow him, but sensed that he wanted to be alone with his thoughts, so she began to clear up the case file papers and map from the dining table. Not feeling at all sleepy she decided to put some more logs on the fire and soak up the warmth while resting on the sofa. She had just settled herself comfortably when she heard his bedroom door open, and looked up to see him come back into the room carrying an envelope.

'Bill Roberts, the drug-enforcement agent in Jamaica, e-mailed some documents just after you went to bed. I've printed them off,' he said and put the envelope on the dining table, next to her handbag.

She knew that he was feeling guilty about the missed opportunities during the FBI investigation into Mandy's disappearance.

'If you want to talk I'm a good listener,' Anna said, moving along as he sat on the edge of the sofa.

'I'm dreading telling Sally and Peter Anderson we screwed up. It will totally destroy them.'

'You didn't screw up, your colleagues did.'

Blane leaned forward and put his head in his hands. 'If only I'd checked the statements and search records.'

'If you hadn't asked me to look at the case then I'd never have spoken with the Andersons, gone to the church or met Julie Collins. Call it fate or whatever you like, but you instigated it, not me.'

He gave a soft chuckle and then got to his feet. 'I'm keeping you up and you haven't had any sleep yet.' He leaned forward, kissing her on the cheek.

Anna grabbed his hand. 'I'm happy here on the sofa, but I'd feel even happier if you stayed with me.' She drew him towards her as she lay back on the cushions. He knelt down beside her and looked into her eyes as they both nervously savoured the moment before he slowly drew her towards him, kissing her, a kiss that was passionate yet tender. Anna had no fear – this was a man who respected and cared for her. Even though the feelings between them were intense and she wanted their embrace to go further, as she was certain he also wanted, something held them both back. He lifted her gently to sit on his knee and put his arms around her. She knew that she had finally moved on from the loss of Ken as she snuggled her face into his neck.

Smelling bacon and eggs frying, Anna sat up and saw that Don was already awake and cooking. He looked over his shoulder and on seeing her he came and leaned over the back of the sofa and kissed her gently on the lips.

'I phoned Sheriff Mitchell and the District Judge, who will do a special hearing at eight a.m. for search warrants.'

'Is it okay for me to come with you?' Anna asked.

Blane smiled and told her she would be the star of the show and moreover would have to tell the Judge what she had uncovered so that he could see that 'probable cause' evidence existed that Jack and Carl Brennan killed and/or disposed of the body of Mandy Anderson.

Everything went smoothly at the District Court and the Judge duly issued both arrest and search warrants for the Brennans and

their house and vehicles. Sheriff Mitchell went with Blane and
Anna to the Brennans' address. When they pulled up at the
house there were no cars in the driveway, although they realized
the vehicles might be parked in the double garage. Blane had
possession of the warrants and rang the doorbell but there was
no answer, so he knocked loudly. Anna, who was standing back
from the porch, noticed the net curtain of a front window move
and Jack Brennan peep out from behind it. She told Blane what
she had just seen.

'Jack, it's me, Don Blane,' he called. 'Is your father in?'

At first there was no reply and then they heard a voice from
behind the front door.

'He said I wasn't to let anyone in until he got back.'

Don glared at Sheriff Mitchell, wondering if someone in his
office had let something slip.

'Jack, you need to let me in.'

'I can't or my dad will be mad with me, like he was last night
'cause I spoke with that English lady.'

Although the warrant allowed Blane to force entry he was
loath to scare Jack by doing so. 'It's okay, Jack, I promise you he
won't be mad, but he's in a bit of trouble and you can help
him.'

The door opened and Jack Brennan appeared wearing knee-
length shorts, a T-shirt and trainers. He was visibly agitated, a
look of anxious concern on his face.

'What's happened to my dad?'

Blane took Jack through to the living room and told him that
his dad was fine but asked if he knew where he was. Jack said he
didn't but he'd gone out early in his Park Ranger's truck. Blane
knew that as Carl Brennan would never run off and leave his
son, they could just sit and wait for him to return, but he and
the Sheriff agreed it was better to be safe than sorry and put out
an APB on Carl. They also knew that legally they were treading a fine line by questioning Jack, but they needed to trace
Carl Brennan quickly.

Blane sat Jack down and calmly explained that the District

Judge had said that they could search the house and cars and held up the warrant.

'I haven't stolen anything,' Jack said defensively.

'It's not about stealing things, Jack, it's about the day Mandy disappeared. Did she come here with a birthday present for you?' Blane asked.

'No.' Jack sucked in his breath and bit down on his lips in a childlike manner.

'Is that the truth, Jack?'

'Yes, you can ask my dad, he'll tell you it's the truth. It's the truth, honestly that is the truth.'

The Sheriff was outside putting out the APB when Anna noticed that there was a kitchen to her left, which led her to wonder if there was a door that led out to the garage. Indeed there was and it was open. The garage was huge and would comfortably hold four cars. There was a sink in one corner next to a washing machine and dryer, and a door to the rear garden. Next to this was a wall rack with a range of neatly assembled garden tools hanging from it. There was one car, an old red Ford Fiesta, which was in good condition and well polished. Anna looked through the passenger window and was astonished by what she saw. The car keys were in the ignition and dangling from them was a tiny digital camera.

As Anna returned to the living room it was clear that Blane was becoming frustrated at his lack of progress with Jack.

'That's a lovely looking car in the garage, beautifully polished. Is it yours, Jack?' Anna asked.

'Yes, ma'am, my dad bought it for my sixteenth birthday and taught me to drive in it.'

Anna held up the Fiesta's car key while hiding the digital camera in the palm of her hand. 'I found this on the garage floor.' She paused as Jack peered at the key.

'That's the key for my car,' he said.

Anna let the camera fall from her palm and it swayed like a pendulum, yet Jack didn't bat an eyelid or even break his eye contact with her. She thought this strange, particularly if Mandy

Anderson had bought it for him. Blane glanced at her, as she moved a fraction closer to Jack, whose big raw hands clenched and unclenched.

'Where did you get the lovely little camera?' Anna asked.

'I found it,' Jack said, now avoiding eye contact and looking worried.

'Mandy gave it to you on your birthday and told you not to tell anyone, didn't she, Jack?' Anna asked with a cheeky smile.

Jack smiled back and nodded. 'Promise you won't tell my dad, or he'll be upset with me again.'

'Yours and Mandy's secrets are safe with me and Don. I bet she gave you a birthday card as well?'

'Yes, she did,' Jack said proudly.

Blane smiled at him. 'Have you still got it?'

Jack leaned forward to Blane and whispered, 'I hid it from my dad but you can see it if you want. It's signed, she signed it, because it is very special, she signed, "Love Mandy".'

'It must have been a wonderful surprise when Mandy came round with a card and present?'

Jack looked away from Blane and shook his head firmly.

'No, she's never been to my house, not ever. You can ask my dad.'

Blane kept his voice relaxed and smiled, saying he'd love to see the birthday card.

'Okay, I'll go and get it for you,' Jack said and dashed off upstairs.

Anna was surprised that Blane hadn't followed up on Jack's obvious lie and was about to ask why but he preempted her.

'Jack doesn't think he's lying because he's erased the memory of Mandy ever being here that day.'

'But why be so open about the camera and card?' Anna asked.

'Because you were right, Mandy wanted it to be kept a secret. To Jack they are precious keepsakes that it would seem even Carl doesn't know about.'

Anna agreed but was still confused as to whether or not Carl was involved.

'Jack knows right from wrong and is not a habitual liar,' Blane insisted. 'He and Carl may not have spoken about Mandy since the day she went missing, but they certainly did yesterday as Carl's phone call last night revealed.'

'So you think that Jack telling his father about meeting me may have relit the fuse,' Anna said.

'And it made Carl twitchy – his call was really a fishing expedition to see what was happening.'

Jack came back into the room and proudly presented the birthday card to Anna to look at, childlike and smiling as he tapped the card in his hand.

As he did so, Blane spoke to Sheriff Mitchell, and quietly suggested that Jack be interviewed at the station by a forensic psychiatrist, who might be able to jog his memory into recall, without causing an emotional breakdown.

It was a sad moment as Jack was driven away in a patrol car. He was still smiling happily, but only because he had no real understanding of what was happening to him.

'Any luck with Carl's whereabouts?' Blane asked the Sheriff as they stood in the driveway.

'Not as yet – they put out calls over his car radio but either it's switched off or he's deliberately not answering.'

'Shit. Carl's gone to dig her up. The tool rack in the garage – there was no shovel!' Anna exclaimed.

'Then he has to be at the area that he made sure was never searched,' Blane said. 'Okay, let's go.'

The three of them were in the Sheriff's car in an instant, driving at high speed down the I-95, magnetic blue light flashing and sirens on. Sheriff Mitchell recalled that there was a single dirt track road into that section of woodland and it was a mile long with a dead end, so if Carl Brennan was there he would have to come back out the same way.

It was about three minutes more before they reached the location. As they drove slowly down the track they caught sight of a Ranger's truck in the distance, at which point the Sheriff took out a pair of binoculars to get a closer look and confirmed that it was Carl Brennan's. Turning the binoculars towards the woods he reckoned that he could just about see the figure of someone walking back towards the truck carrying what looked like a black trash bag. Mitchell turned off the patrol car's engine and said that it was best to get out and approach on foot.

As they got closer to the vehicle a man came out of the woods, but he wasn't carrying anything. He was tall and dressed smartly in a park ranger's tapered grey shirt, green trousers, matching arrowhead tie and brown felt hat. On seeing them he smiled, waved and started to walk along the dirt track in their direction. Blane muttered to Anna that it was Carl Brennan, and positioned himself in front of her, saying she was to stay behind him. Anna could see that he had his right hand behind his back and was carrying a small Glock pistol, concealing it from Carl's view. Simultaneously, Sheriff Mitchell put his hand down to his right side, unclipped his holster and gripped the gun, ready to use it if he had to. Although Carl Brennan wore a holster and firearm, his hands were loosely by his sides as he approached them.

Anna started nervously as the man suddenly raised his right hand slowly upwards, thankfully past his sidearm to his hat, which he lifted and doffed politely.

'Hiya, Sheriff, Don, everything okay?' Carl said and placed his hat back on his head.

'What you doing out here, Carl?' Sheriff Mitchell asked.

'I had a tip-off about some poachers out looking for black bears, so I came to check it out,' Carl answered.

'Where's the black bag you were just carrying?' Sheriff Mitchell asked.

Carl looked uneasy and paused, obviously thinking up an answer. 'Oh that, it's a coyote carcass I just found, I'm going to put it in the incinerator.'

There was a wretched few seconds' pause, Carl's eyes flicking nervously.

'There's no point in lying, Carl. We know that you falsified the Mandy Anderson search records,' Blane said gently.

Carl's body sagged as if he had been punched and the air drained from his body. Blane stepped forward, removed the Ranger's gun from its holster and handed it to Sheriff Mitchell, who turned to face Carl and spoke as a friend. 'The District Judge has issued warrants for your and Jack's arrest, Carl, and forensics are searching the house now.'

'Oh, dear God, I knew it, one day, oh, my God . . .'

Carl Brennan now looked as if someone had just sucked the lifeblood out of him, as ashen-faced he trembled and chewed his bottom lip. Blane could see he was close to tears, not because of what he had done but for the deep love he had for his son.

'He's a good boy, Don, he loved Mandy and if anyone's to blame, I am.'

The dejected man gave a long low sigh and began to explain. He had just returned home from work that fateful day and was opening the front door when he heard Jack arguing with a girl inside the house. He went in and saw Jack at the top of the stairs and the back of the girl so he didn't know who it was at first. Carl heard the girl say to Jack that he shouldn't have tried to kiss her and she wanted to go home. Jack was pleading with her to stay and tugging her by the coat when Carl shouted out to the pair of them to stop and come downstairs immediately. Carl began to cry as he went on to say that on hearing his voice the girl turned sharply towards him and Jack let go of her coat, causing her to stumble forwards and fall down the stairs.

'I heard the loud crack as her neck snapped and she ended up by my feet with her face staring up at me. Jack stood there, frozen to the spot, not knowing what to do. I told him to go to his room and stay there.'

'He never told you Mandy had given him a birthday card or present?'

Carl looked bemused and stunned by Don's question, as he answered, 'No.'

'Why didn't you just call Sheriff Mitchell and explain what happened?'

'Because I was scared that Jack would be arrested and taken from me. Even if I told the truth I'd just be seen as a father trying to cover for his son. It was an accident, I swear before God it was an accident.'

'Was lying and disposing of her body worth all this, Carl?' Blane asked softly.

'No, but my son was.'

'Did you tell him what to say at the time?'

'Yes, but we never spoke about it again after that day. He's obliterated her fall from his mind, as if she never came to the house and it never happened.'

Carl's composure fell apart as he began to sob. He appeared to have aged twenty years in the few moments it had taken for him to explain the tragedy and kept on repeating, 'God forgive me.'

Chapter Twenty-Nine

Over at the police forensic lab, Anna and Blane watched avidly as the two digital files on the mini-camera were loaded onto a computer. The date and time stamps showed that both were taken on the day Mandy went missing. One was of her at Prezzies gadget shop timed at 1.45 p.m., and the other sitting next to Jack on his bed at 3.10 p.m. This picture was obviously taken by Jack holding the camera up towards himself and Mandy and it also appeared that he was about to kiss her on the cheek.

'Maybe that is what they were arguing about, like Carl said, Jack trying to kiss her,' Anna suggested.

'Probably, but how can a father's love for his son result in so much sadness and misery?' Blane remarked, visibly moved as he looked at the last pictures of Mandy alive.

'Are we going to break the news to the Andersons now?' Anna asked.

'No, Sheriff Mitchell will be handling the case and knows them well. I couldn't face them or know what to say right now.'

Anna could see how tired and upset he was so she put her arms around him and gave him a spirit-lifting hug as she whispered in his ear.

'We could go back to the cabin, have something to eat and then start where we left off on the sofa last night?'

Blane said nothing, but from the way he squeezed her, Anna knew his answer was yes.

Having stopped to buy some chicken, ribs and side salads for a barbecue, they made their way back to the cabin. 'Were Agent Roberts' enquires in Jamaica helpful?' Blane asked.

'I haven't had had a chance to look through the documents yet,' Anna replied as she leaned over to the back seat to get the thick envelope out of her handbag.

'By the amount of stuff in here, it looks like he's gone out of his way to help me.'

'That's Bill Roberts for you, thorough in everything he does,' Blane commented.

Anna began to read Bill's report:

Copies of all the documents that I have referred to are attached to this e-mail in pdf format.

1. August 6th 2012 Samuel Peters attended British High Commission, Kingston, Jamaica and applied for a fast-track visa to attend sister Esme's funeral. Stated he would be staying with sister Marisha Peters at 51 Clarendon House, Brixton. Biometric data, by way of photograph and fingerprints, were taken and he flew to the UK on August 8th on a six-month open return ticket. Kingston Customs could not assist me as to if or when Samuel Peters returned to Jamaica.

2. His visa application form gave occupation as fisherman living in Manchioneal Bay for last 25 years. I visited location and found it to be a small and impoverished fishing community. Samuel lives alone in a run-down wooden shack. According to friends he has not been seen since he said he was 'going to Esme's funeral'. They described him as pleasant but lazy, often drunk and sleeping long hours due to his love of spiced rum.

3. I attended Registrar General's Department to check Samuel's background further. It transpired that a Samuel Peters made Internet applications, on September 20th 2012, for certified copies of his marriage certificate to a

Gloria Rediker and birth certificate for their son Arum Joshua Peters. These were sent to Marisha's address and payment was made with her Visa card.

4. A week later Samuel Peters made Internet applications for copies of a Gloria Peters and Xavier Alleyne's marriage certificate and their daughters' birth certificates, Donna Mavis Alleyne, born 1986, and Aisa Moira Alleyne, born 1988. Marisha Peters' credit card and Brixton address again used. The Gloria Peters that married Xavier Alleyne gave a maiden name of Rediker and the certificate clearly shows that she was a widow?

5. I checked to see if another Samuel Peters with similar details was dead or existed and I could not find even a close match. Therefore Gloria Peters' marriage to Xavier Alleyne is bigamous.

6. Gloria Peters and Xavier Alleyne married in 1986 in Montego Bay, where he owned a banana plantation. After the collapse of his business Xavier died from a heart attack in 1990 aged 32. The plantation was sold to property developers after his death. Gloria allegedly moved to the UK with her daughters and obviously I will leave further enquiries concerning her whereabouts to you.

7. David and Mavis Rediker came to the island in 1975 with their daughter Gloria. David was a botanist for the Jamaican Natural History Museum in Kingston. He died in 1982 and Mavis in 1984. The current director of the museum remembered the Rediker family and informed me that David was, figuratively speaking, 'a victim of his own research'. He said David became addicted to and overdosed on atropine from the berries of the Sacred Datura plant. It is a member of the nightshade family found on the island and more hallucinogenic than LSD.

8. The Redikers lived in a house that was provided by the museum. After David died they allowed Gloria to remain at the premises to care for her mother who was dying from cancer. The director recalled that Gloria, then aged about

18, became pregnant by and married a fisherman called
Samuel whom he described as very apathetic and unsup-
portive.

9. Samuel Peters has two sisters, Esme three years older, and
Marisha one year younger, both emigrated to UK in 1984.
I can find no record in Jamaica of them having been mar-
ried or giving birth to any children.

Anna leaned back, closing her eyes. 'Lady bloody Lynne's a
bigamist and her daughter was in an incestuous relationship!
My God, this is unbelievable stuff; Josh Reynolds must be
Gloria's son. Bill Roberts is bloody amazing.' Anna sighed with
elation as she flicked through the copies of the birth and
marriage certificates. She stamped her feet and banged the
dashboard with excitement. 'There's so much information
here, and boy oh boy has it thrown a bunch of spanners into
the Reynolds investigation.'

'You can forward the e-mail to your team in London when
we get back to the cabin,' Blane suggested, hoping she would
agree.

'Not yet, I need to make sense of all this first.' She waved the
documents animatedly.

Blane was disappointed, as he'd been looking forward to a
quiet afternoon and evening together. 'Would you prefer me to
take you back to the Academy?'

'No. I'd appreciate your help in trying to make sense of all
this.'

He forced a smile, slightly relieved that she had not wanted to
return to the Academy. 'I'll do my best but I don't really know
anything about the Reynolds case.'

'Well I can tell you all about it while you do the barbecue.'

Blane resigned himself to the fact that making love by the
fireplace would just have to wait.

Making the most of the journey time, Anna phoned Joan, who
was delighted to hear her voice and wanted to know all about the

336 of her classmates

course and her classmates. Anna looked across at Blane as she told Joan that she was having the most wonderful time and her course instructor was one of the nicest and most interesting people she had ever met. He smiled as Anna continued her conversation.

'I want as much detail as you can find on Lord Henry Lynne, his death in Egypt and who his will was made out to,' she said, pausing at Joan's sharp intake of breath.

'Also, look through the documents taken from Esme's flat and see if there is a birth certificate or adoption papers for Josh. This is very important, Joan – if you find it, scan it and e-mail me a copy.'

'Can I ask why?'

'It's work in progress, but I think I may be on to something big about Lady Lynne.'

'Should I tell Mike Lewis?' Joan asked.

'No. Please don't say anything to anyone yet; at the moment it's just a gut feeling.'

'Mum's the word and I'll get on to it first thing in the morning,' Joan promised.

Anna looked at her watch and realized she'd got her time difference the wrong way round. It was five p.m. in the UK and not early morning as she thought and in her excitement she'd forgotten it was a Sunday.

'Josh's birth certificate is really important. Would you mind going in this evening?'

'I'll do what I can but . . .'

'I'll make sure you get paid double time,' Anna promised, piling on the pressure.

'Okay, my mum's visiting her sister in Bournemouth so I'm on my own anyway.'

'From the information I have in front of me Samuel Peters may not have returned to Jamaica.'

'What! He's still in London?'

'I don't know for certain, but it looks like he was up to something and if I'm right he may have paid for his meddling with his life.'

Joan gave a small gasp. 'Marisha is still in a coma, but when you think about it, could she have killed Samuel to keep the money for herself?'

Now worried that she had asked too much of Joan, Anna was eager to calm her down.

'I can't say at the moment, but finding the whereabouts of Samuel, dead or alive, will be a major breakthrough,' Anna said.

'I'll do my best to find him for you.'

'Thanks, Joan, and remember, not a word to anyone' Anna cautioned.

'Course not. By the way, did you read the magazine article about Lady Lynne?'

Anna wondered if she should be upfront and admit she hadn't, but she didn't want to offend Joan after asking so much of her. 'Um, yeah, really interesting – I'm glad you told me about it.'

'Amazing, isn't it, that so many poisonous plants are actually used as medicines. Lady Lynne created the David Rediker Trust in memory of her father who was a botanist. She's put millions into research on plants that can be used for medicinal purposes,' Joan gushed.

Yet again she could have kicked herself where Joan was concerned, Anna thought as she hung up, wishing she had read the *Gardeners' World* article on the plane as it might have heightened her suspicions long before she read Bill Roberts' report.

Anna next phoned Pete Jenkins, who, from the background sounds, was bathing his daughter.

'I need you to look at some stuff on the Reynolds case for me first thing in the morning.'

'Sorry, Anna, but Mike Lewis is now holding the purse for the forensic budget so only he can authorize further examinations.'

'I wouldn't ask if it wasn't important, Pete. If I'm right it will be crucial to finding out what really happened to Josh Reynolds.'

'I'd love to help you, Anna, but . . .'

'Samuel Peters may have been murdered as well,' Anna said as persuasively as she could.

'How did I know before you even said a word that this was going to be complicated?'

'It's a simple DNA comparison, that's all, and you already have the two samples in the lab.'

'Whose?' Pete asked bluntly.

'Donna and Josh Reynolds – I need you to tell me if they have the same maternal DNA.'

'You bloody what? You want me to do a mitochondrial test to see if Josh Reynolds was shagging his sister?'

'Half-sister would be more exact, but yes, that is the general idea.'

'I'll go stick a needle in Lady Lynne's arse for a drop of blood to compare it against, shall I?'

'That won't be necessary right now, and if she is the mother that will be my pleasure.'

'Anna, for fuck's sake get real, you're asking me to do something that you have no evidence to support and is totally unethical,' Pete said, alarmed at her outrageous request.

'I have certified copies of both their birth certificates and I believe they have the same mother.'

'Copies? How did you get them? No, no, on second thought don't tell me, I don't want to know. It was good speaking to you, Anna, but you need to talk to Mike Lewis.'

'Pete, don't hang up, there is some other stuff that is of use to you about Samuel Peters.'

'What?'

'His fingerprints were taken at the British Embassy in Jamaica when he applied for a visa so they should be on the UK Border Agency database by now.'

There was a brief pause during which Anna could practically hear the cogs turning in Pete's head.

Finally, he sighed. 'Can I ask where the hell you're getting all this information from, particularly when you're thousands of miles away?'

'Can't say at the moment, but I've no reason to doubt it's reliable and true. If I'm right, and I think I am, then politically it is very sensitive stuff.'

'But you want me to put my job on the line to see if the Lynne family have links back to the likes of Cleopatra and Oedipus,' Pete said indignantly.

'Okay, the maternal DNA can wait, it was an impetuous request and I shouldn't have asked you to take risks like that. You could say you located Samuel Peters' prints having thought about how he would have needed a visa to come to the UK,' Anna said, still hoping to win Pete over.

Again there was a pause before Pete continued: 'I'll do the fingerprints, but I want copies of the birth certificates and written authority before I do the maternal DNA testing.'

'Thanks, Pete, I owe you big-time.'

'Too right you do!' Pete said, and hung up.

Pulling in to park the car outside the cabin, Blane turned and looked at Anna and gave her a wry smile.

'What?' she asked innocently.

'When you get the bit between your teeth you really go for it, don't you?' he remarked.

'Was I a bit overboard with Pete?'

'You were asking him to put his job on the line by the sounds of it, and that is an awful lot to ask anyone.'

'I need the DNA results to solve this case,' Anna said indignantly.

'So this Lady Gloria, is she some bigwig back in England?' he asked, changing tack to keep the peace.

'Rich, powerful and very influential. She probably has a direct line to the Queen and Prime Minister, she's that important.'

'Really, to the Queen and Prime Minister?' Blane grinned.

'Figure of speech, but probably true,' Anna said, and they both laughed.

Chapter Thirty

By the time they sat down to enjoy the barbecued ribs, chicken and side salads, Anna had read the *Gardeners' World* article and given Don a run-down of the background and both investigations into Josh Reynolds' death, and played him the tape of her and Dewar's interview with Gloria Lynne. They sat at the dining table eating their food as Anna showed him a copy of the suicide note, which he took his time to read.

At last, he turned to look at Anna. 'I have to say that I agree with Dewar: it doesn't seem the type of note you'd expect someone who's about to commit suicide to write.'

'Question is, who did write it?' Anna wondered, eager for his thoughts.

'The note does reveal a possible family connection through knowledge of Esme's death.' He pointed to the line that read, 'I have felt very depressed since my mothers death.'

'Does Donna refer to her husband as Josh or Joshua?' he continued.

'Josh, why?'

'And he regularly used the name Josh himself?'

'Yes, all the time.'

Blane pointed to the end of the note and Anna picked up on his thought process.

'It's signed "Love Joshua". I'd say Donna didn't write it.'

'Your attention to detail is amazing!' she exclaimed and kissed him.

'With the certificates Bill Roberts sent you there is a clear connection between a Gloria Lynne and Samuel Peters,' Blane observed.

'Marriage certificates don't show dates of birth. It's the same with the parents on a birth certificate – only shows their ages,' Anna said, with a tinge of frustration.

'Let's do a side-by-side comparison of what we have concerning Gloria and Samuel, see what's recurring,' he suggested.

'I love working with you,' Anna said gratefully.

Blane picked up the Gloria Rediker and Samuel Peters marriage certificate.

'They married in 1983 when she was eighteen. Samuel is shown as a fisherman aged twenty-four, so age-wise that fits with Samuel's birth certificate. Gloria's father is shown as David Rediker deceased, and mother as Mavis Rediker.'

Anna leaned in closer, and pointed out that the witnesses to Gloria and Samuel's marriage were Esme and Marisha Peters. She picked up the Gloria Peters and Xavier Alleyne marriage certificate. 'Gloria's parents are shown as David Rediker and Mavis Rediker, both deceased. It's got to be the same Gloria that married Samuel Peters, Xavier Alleyne and then Lord Henry Lynne.'

He pointed to the 'condition' section of the marriage certificate, which said widow, as Bill Roberts had reported.

'That's obviously a lie to enable her to marry this Xavier guy.'

Anna's laptop pinged: there was an e-mail from Joan with attachments. One was a scanned copy of Josh Reynolds' birth certificate. In the text, Joan said that this was the only certificate of his she could find and there were no adoption papers. The other attachment, a marriage certificate, showed that Esme and John Reynolds had married in London in December 1985.

Anna read Josh's birth certificate. It showed Esme Peters as the mother of Joshua Peters, born Jamaica on 5 August 1983, with the father unknown. Blane picked up the copy of Arum Joshua Peters' birth certificate that Bill Roberts had sent and held it next to the laptop screen. The date and place of registration for the birth were exactly the same for both Arum and Joshua, but the one sent in by Bill Roberts had Arum's father listed as Samuel Peters, a fisherman, aged twenty-four, and the mother Gloria Peters was shown as eighteen at the time of giving birth, with a maiden name of Rediker.

'Okay, let me get this straight, Gloria Rediker was eighteen when she married Samuel Peters, then gave birth to Arum six months later,' he observed.

'Right, so that means Arum and Joshua have to be the same person. For some reason, Gloria must have given Arum to Samuel's sister Esme without going through the proper channels,' Anna said.

Blane followed up on her comment: 'Then Esme emigrated to England and met John Reynolds, they married and gave Josh his surname.'

'That means this birth certificate Esme had for Josh is fake,' Anna realized, resolving to e-mail Joan to get a forensic document examiner to look at it.

'All this happened thirty years ago. What we don't know is how it fits with the death of Joshua Reynolds. This is so frustrating,' Anna said, sitting back in her chair and running her hands through her hair.

Blane suggested they strip the information back to basics, as sometimes when you looked too deep you missed the obvious. 'Okay, let's go again. Nineteen eighty-three, Gloria Rediker was pregnant and married Samuel Peters in Port Morant, a small fishing village at the south-eastern tip of the island. A year later, Mavis Rediker dies then Gloria and Samuel are evicted from the house with their son Arum Joshua Peters,' he said.

Anna looked at her notes. 'By late eighty-five Esme was in the UK with her son Joshua and married John Reynolds ...' She paused before looking up at him. 'Gloria must have given Arum to Esme just after the eviction,' she said.

Blane continued: 'Nineteen eighty-six, Gloria Peters, née Rediker, is pregnant with Donna and marries Xavier Alleyne, a wealthy banana plantation owner in Montego Bay, which is at the western tip of the island. A couple of years later, Gloria and Xavier have a second daughter, Aisa.'

Anna raised her hand, causing Blane to stop.

'Hang on, Aisa is mixed race, whereas Donna is white, and she told Dewar and Barolli she was adopted.'

'Well, if Xavier was mixed race as well, then it is feasible to have one white and one mixed race child.'

'Yeah, but the only reason she would think she was adopted would be because Gloria told her she was.'

Lack of sleep and the warm room were making Blane feel tired; Anna, however, wasn't flagging in the slightest.

'I'd say that Gloria dumps Samuel, then has a bigamous marriage to Xavier, rags to riches and four years later he suddenly dies of a heart attack aged thirty-two!' she pressed on, not noticing that Blane was beginning to lose interest and yawning.

Standing up, she began to pace around the room. 'Next, Gloria sells the land to property developers, moves to the UK with the two girls and sets up a florist's shop in Weybridge. There she meets and marries the billionaire Lord Henry Lynne, aged seventy bloody eight!'

'And did they both live happily ever after?' Blane asked with apprehension.

'He lasted eight years, died on holiday in Egypt, no post mortem, no questions asked.'

'So technically, her marriage to Lord Lynne must be bigamous as well if the one to Samuel was never annulled,' he added, stifling another yawn.

'I know there's no evidence to show she murdered Xavier or Lord Henry, and I'm treading a dangerous path, but I'm convinced that it's all linked to Josh Reynolds' death.'

'I think we should just concentrate on Josh, Samuel and Gloria for now,' Blane advised.

Anna sighed. She knew he was right but she was becoming more convinced that all the deaths that surrounded Gloria were not just mere coincidence.

She sat down in front of her laptop. As she pressed the keys,

Blane leaned back out of her field of vision and stretched his arms, cocking his head to one side to watch her as she concentrated on the screen, the tip of her tongue poked out between her lips. After a couple of minutes she raised her hand and wafted it towards him, to draw his attention.

'Here, look at this article Joan uncovered where Gloria talks about her past and all the hardships she endured. She never mentions a marriage to Samuel, a son called Arum Joshua, or that Xavier's money funded the florist's shop. She clearly lies to protect herself and her image!' Anna said as she pulled the *Gardeners' World* magazine out of her laptop bag.

'I'm not doubting your thoughts, Anna, but we've been sorting through this for a long time, a short break might do us good,' Blane hinted heavily. 'It always helps me to think more clearly when I come back with fresh eyes.'

She ignored him as she thumbed through the *Gardeners' World* magazine and put it down on the table. There was a full-page colour spread of Gloria, including a picture of her standing by a gated garden. Hanging on the gate was a triangle with a yellow background and black skull and crossbones: the standard hazard symbol for poison. 'Danger, Do Not Touch The Plants' was written in large letters below the warning sign and the article was entitled 'These Plants May Kill'.

'Look at this, it's a very recent article. Joan kept encouraging me to read it but stupidly I put it off, too distracted until now. It's Gloria Lynne at a recent flower show – the poison garden was her exhibit and won a gold ribbon, the title speaks for itself. She also runs a research charity for medicines that can be obtained from poisonous and other plants,' Anna said.

'Holy shit!' he exclaimed and scanned through the article, which had pictures and names of the plants in English and Latin. deadly nightshade (*Atropa belladonna*), ragwort (*senecio jacobaea*), wolfsbane (*Aconitum*) and henbane (*Hyoscyamus niger*) were just a few amongst a long list.

Anna was impatient for him to finish reading, pacing up and down, completely unable to keep still. He turned over a page to reveal a picture of Gloria standing next to a plant that was the shape of an upturned bell and at least three meters high. Its colours were resplendent, the stalk green speckled with cream on the outside, supporting a single bell-shaped leaf with ribbed sides and a frilled edge, which was a rich crimson.

'Look at the size of that,' he breathed, as Anna looked over his shoulder, eager to see what he was talking about.

'Are you referring to the plant or Gloria?' she asked acerbically and they both laughed. She was aware of how tense she had become and how much of their time had been dominated by the discussion of her case.

Blane closed the magazine and was about to place it back on the table when he suddenly flicked it open again. 'Eh! Eh! I should have spotted the connection right away: deadly nightshade, known as *Atropa BellaDONNA*.' He emphasized the final two syllables of its Latin name.

Anna got his gist and put her hands on his shoulders, squeezing them in excitement as she remembered her visit to Lynne House.

'Gloria has a big Doberman. Vicious thing, nearly went for Dewar and me. I distinctly remember Gloria shouted, "Atropa, heel!"'

'It gets better,' Blane said and flicked over the page. Anna sat down beside him and gripped his arm, listening intently as he continued. 'This huge plant Gloria's standing next to is Amorphophallus titanum. It says here that it's an endangered species that's very complex to grow.'

'Gloria has a massive greenhouse – well, more like a botanical garden really – seems she likes to grow plants that can kill. Is the Amorpho-thingy poisonous?'

'No, but its nickname, because it has a putrid smell, is the corpse tree, and the translation of its name from Latin is "Titan" and, you won't believe, "ARUM".'

'Bloody hell, the first name of her and Samuel's son!'

'I would say that Gloria knows exactly how to use atropine for medicinal purposes and as a poison,' Blane said and deliberately paused for Anna to make the connection.

Anna's cheeks were red as she gripped her fists. 'Poison. Gloria Lynne knows exactly what can cure and what can kill!'

'Hang on, sweetheart, because we need to be able to prove that,' Blane said quietly, trying to calm her down.

'We can,' Anna replied, and then held her hands up in a submissive gesture as if to apologize for becoming so loud. She wasn't arguing with him, she just needed his support and wanted him to see that there was more deceit and lies behind Gloria Lynne than anyone had realized.

Blane no longer felt tired and stood up, this new information making him feel almost as excited as Anna.

'Tell me everything you can about Gloria,' he demanded, pacing the room.

Anna sat with her legs curled up beneath her.

'Well, I only met her once so I don't know much beyond what I've already told you, and of course what Bill Roberts sent us.'

He gestured in a circle with his hand. 'Tell me about the day you and Dewar went to her house, what she was like, what she did and said.'

'She's got a really overbearing presence about her, as if she looks down her nose at anyone she perceives to be below her status. She said she's strict with her daughters, but personally I'd say overprotective and she spoils them to get her own way. Oh, and vain – by the look of her she's had some nip and tuck along the way,' Anna added.

'Everything you've mentioned so far is not unusual with many of the rich and powerful,' Blane remarked, eager for more details. 'What did she have to say about Josh?'

'Not much really, said she only met him once and wished she'd had the opportunity to get to know him better.'

'Okay, take this on board. What if she didn't know Josh was her long-lost son Arum? What do you think? Did she know?' Blane asked.

Anna racked her brain, weighing up if it could be true, but shrugged her shoulders. 'All right, let me think it through. Let's say that Samuel had never made contact with Gloria for something like thirty years, but the fact is he must have always known that Josh Reynolds was his son Arum, as would his sisters Esme and Marisha.'

'Would Esme and Marisha have known about Gloria's new life in the UK with Lord Lynne?' Blane asked.

'Gloria is so often in the papers, on TV and in glossy magazines that I'd say that they must have, but I don't think Esme would ever have told Josh the truth about his real parents, or her illegal adoption of him. I think she went to her grave never knowing who Donna really was or she'd have done something to try and part them,' Anna said.

'What about the other sister, Marisha – could she have said something?' Blane asked.

Anna told him that Marisha didn't even know Josh was dead until she and Barolli broke it to her. He gave her a puzzled look, and Anna explained that Marisha had confessed she had not had contact with Esme or Josh for years, after a family disagreement.

'Then it's also possible that even now Gloria doesn't know that Josh was really Arum,' Blane pointed out.

'She knows. I'm certain of that,' Anna said with conviction as she got to her feet.

Blane began flicking through his notes. 'The money from the safe, you said it was found hidden at Esme's and forty thousand was found in Marisha's freezer?'

'That's right,' Anna said, pacing round the room.

'And you believe that only Samuel did the decorating at both Josh and Esme's?'

'Yes, which means Marisha lied to me about him going back to Jamaica,' Anna remarked.

'It also means that when Samuel was decorating, Josh obviously had no idea he was his real father.'

Anna looked at him and sat beside him with her hands on her knees, waiting to hear what he was going to say next. She felt almost childlike compared to him as he had such authority and intuition and she knew he was slowly piecing together the most complicated jigsaw puzzle she had ever worked on.

'Okay, Anna, here we go. I would say that Samuel is the common denominator. Because of the decorating he would have had keys for both Josh and Esme's flats. Also, he stayed at his sister Marisha's, who just happened to lie to you about his movements and hid money in the freezer.'

'Oh, my God, do you think Samuel killed his own son?' she gasped.

'If he did, it could only be for the money, but even then he'd have to know the safe code, or somehow force Josh to open it so he could get the gun.'

She sighed, shaking her head. 'But it doesn't make sense, does it? I can't see Marisha being involved in murder either, not knowingly.' Once again it seemed to be one step forward, two steps back.

'Wait a minute, think about all the birth and marriage certificates Samuel Peters ordered.'

'What about them?

'There all connected to Gloria, her bigamous marriages and Arum the son she abandoned. The certificates expose her as a liar and a fraud. There can be only one reason Samuel wanted them,' Blane said.

Anna hesitated as she looked at him and in unison they both exclaimed, 'BLACKMAIL!' followed by a high five.

They were on a real high, as they realized that if Samuel, and possibly Marisha, were blackmailing Gloria they needed to dig deeper and find further evidence to prove it. It was clear from the request for a copy of Donna's Jamaican birth certificate that Samuel had discovered that she was Gloria's daughter.

Blane lay down on the floor, his elbows behind his head, and began to do some slow sit-ups, explaining that due to an old back injury, sitting in one position for too long caused the muscle to tighten up so he needed to stretch. But it didn't prevent him from speculating that if Samuel was blackmailing Gloria he must have made contact with her either physically or by phone. Anna suggested that whilst decorating Josh's flat Samuel could have seen something that linked Gloria to Donna, maybe even a photograph. Blane arched his back up from the floor to stretch it further, wondering if Samuel could maybe have got Gloria's details from an address book at the flat.

At this idea, Anna immediately sent Joan an e-mail asking her to get a record of calls made from Marisha's house and mobile phones from August 2012 through to the end of the year, and to see if Gloria's house phone was called from Marisha's.

Then the reaction set in; after the buoyant elation they now became subdued, having hit a wall with the lack of evidence to show blackmail had actually taken place. Anna reckoned that if they were right, Gloria would not have reported any threats to the police as she had too much to lose by way of her standing in the world of high society. They both agreed that she might have paid Samuel and hence the forty thousand in the freezer. However, that didn't explain why the money from the safe ended up at Esme's flat.

Anna downloaded the Word file of Barolli and Dewar's interview with Marisha. Blane came over to sit beside her and she snuggled up to him as they read through the interview notes. Anna told him that at the time of the interview Barolli suspected Marisha had been drinking or taking drugs, and once Anna had finished the document she commented it was obvious Marisha was a liar and drunk, and was therefore not reliable.

'Maybe, but Marisha must be involved in some way as she's lied to you about Samuel. She knows something,' Blane said, checking the wine bottle, which was empty.

'Probably where Samuel is, as she hasn't reported him missing. And the money in her freezer explains all the new electrical equipment she had at her flat,' Anna added, while opening the file containing the Charity Ball photographs in order to see if Gloria was missing from the pictures taken between ten p.m. and midnight.

Blane picked up their glasses and headed towards the kitchen area, pausing to wonder if there was something more than just alcohol that had caused Marisha's behaviour during the interview. As he reached for a bottle of Pinot Noir from the wine rack, Anna asked him what he meant. As he found two clean glasses and filled them with red wine he reminded her of the case of the care worker in the old people's home who was poisoning the residents with atropine.

'The agent who compiled the report used a mnemonic to describe the symptoms of an atropine overdose: hot as a hare, blind as a bat, dry as a bone, red as a beet, and mad as a hatter,' he said as he handed Anna her glass.

Sipping the new wine, Anna asked him what the connection was.

'Everything Barolli has written about Marisha's behaviour fits with atropine poisoning – dilated pupils, Marisha complained of being hot, but shivering and not sweating, difficulty focusing and thirsty. It can cause a red skin rash, difficult to see on a black person, but Barolli said she scratched her arm so much she drew blood. Also makes you dizzy and hallucinate, thus the reference to mad as a hatter.'

Anna took in what he had just said, gasped and jumped up.

'It's just an observation, I might be wrong,' Blane said, taking a sip of wine.

'Oh, my God, Barolli thought it was the chicken!' Anna exclaimed.

'Barolli thought what was a chicken?' Blane asked, confused.

'No, he was really ill after we'd been to see Marisha. He thought it was the chicken from a takeaway,' Anna said. She paused and tapped the table, trying to remember how Barolli had described his symptoms, then looked up.

'Barolli said his heart was palpitating, the room was spinning and everything was a psychedelic blur. Also, his temperature hit the roof but he wasn't sweating.'

She took a long sip of her wine, and had to sit down as the realization of what had actually happened dawned on her.

'My God, we were at Marisha's flat. She made us a coffee and asked if we wanted some spiced rum in it. Barolli said yes and Marisha went to pour some in his cup. I made a comment about not drinking on duty, but as Marisha pulled the bottle away some rum went into Barolli's coffee.'

Blane was surprised. 'She was going to poison you both?'

'I remember she said she didn't drink and it was Samuel's rum. I don't think she realized there was poison in the bottle – she'd have to be totally mad to try and kill two police officers in her own home, let alone knowingly drink some herself the day she came into the police station.'

'Can you remember if it was a full bottle?' Blane asked.

'Just over half full, I think – does it matter?'

'The thing is, if the whole bottle was originally laced with atropine, then who drank the other half?' Blane queried, swirling his wine round in the glass.

'Samuel? But surely he would have dropped down dead at the flat,' Anna remarked.

He explained to Anna that atropine could be a bit like alcohol in how quickly it could affect you, depending on age, body weight, whether you'd eaten and so on. Therefore, it was possible that Samuel, like Marisha, had drunk some, left the house and it had gradually worked into his system and he could have dropped down dead in the street somewhere.

Anna was straight on the phone to Joan, asking her to inform the hospital that Marisha might be suffering from atropine poisoning. Joan said she'd get right on to it and Anna told her to call back when she'd spoken with the medical staff.

'If Samuel dropped dead in the street, and it could have been a heart attack brought on by consuming atropine,' Anna said, 'then his death would be treated as non-suspicious and there wouldn't have been a full forensic post mortem.'

'No suspicion of poisoning, therefore no toxicology tests for it, and if he has no form of identity on him he would be listed as a John Doe.'

Anna's mobile rang, it was Joan but before the constable could say a word, Anna launched into yet another list of requests.

'Joan, thanks for calling back. I need you to check all the

mortuaries in London and see if they have any unidentified bodies of black men matching Samuel Peters' description.'

They could hear Joan's sharp intake of breath. 'Oh, my God, this is getting crazy. Do you think he's been murdered as well?'

'It's possible.'

'I really think you need to tell Mike Lewis, Anna. The hospital was asking questions and—'

Detecting the worry in Joan's voice, Anna interjected: 'I will contact him tomorrow morning.'

'It's just that I feel I'm being a bit underhand and subversive.'

Blane went over to his computer and began checking on the Internet.

'You are doing a fantastic job and you know you are my most valued confidante,' Anna assured Joan, trying to calm her. 'If there's anything you think I'm missing or need to know then call me.'

'You leave it with me, Anna. I'll find Samuel Peters for you, dead or alive.'

By now, Anna was starting to flag and asked Blane if she could have some coffee.

'Good idea, we could both do with some,' he agreed, leaving his computer. While he prepared the beans, Anna made another quick call to Pete Jenkins, who was enjoying his Sunday evening dinner at home.

'What now?' he asked, swallowing a piece of his Yorkshire pudding by the sound of it.

Anna could hear his wife in the background asking if it was 'her again'. Anna apologized and said she'd be quick and Pete told her she'd better be.

'There's one other thing, and don't worry, it's not unethical or breaching human rights or anything like that.'

'I'm listening,' Pete said, and gave a big sigh.

'Josh Reynolds' blood sample – am I right in saying it was only ever tested for alcohol and common drugs of abuse?'

'Yes, that's the standard testing. Why?'

'So any poisons or medicines would be missed?'

'We only look for poisons if the evidence in the case suggests it. They're expensive tests to run and—'

Anna interrupted him: 'I think you may find atropine.'

She went on to hastily explain her reasoning and her theory that Marisha and Samuel might also have been poisoned with the same drug.

'My team are still working at Marisha's flat and I noticed a rum bottle on her coffee table in the living room. I'll have it brought to the lab first thing tomorrow morning and do a test,' Pete promised. 'Far be it from me to flatter you but good job, Anna – that bottle might very well have been discarded if you hadn't said anything.'

Blane handed Anna a cup of coffee.

'Thanks, I need this. I was starting to get a bit slurred talking to Joan, I'm sure she was suspicious. I hope I didn't sound two-faced flattering her but she does need coddling now and then, and it helps get results.'

He carried his own mug to the table, reminding her that she had wanted to look at the pictures of Gloria at the Charity Ball. She sipped her coffee, baffled at how the poisoned rum came to be at Marisha's. True, Gloria could have given Samuel the bottle, but they both agreed that if he was blackmailing her he wouldn't be stupid enough to accept it. The other possibility was that Gloria visited Marisha's and secretly laced the bottle of rum with atropine.

Blane looked again at the notes Barolli made of Marisha's interview. 'Let's just backtrack for a minute. We suspect that Samuel was blackmailing Gloria, and we suspect the money in the freezer was a pay-off. In the interview, Marisha said, "Samuel didn't steal the money" and "the rich bitch" gave it to him. Gloria could have gone to Marisha's flat to pay Samuel off; if she already had the poison with her she could have seen the rum and taken the opportunity . . .'

Anna picked up on his reasoning. 'She could have poured it into the bottle. Brilliant, and if we're right, that's why Marisha had no idea when she offered Barolli some and also drank it herself later on.' She was elated; it was yet another major step in completing the jigsaw, and she was beyond impressed by Blane's ability and observations.

He wandered back to stand in front of his computer, describing how while she was on the phone to Joan he had been mulling over her and Dewar's visit to Gloria's house and had done some research on the Internet, particularly about the Salviati and Mazzoni paintings, which Gloria had said were of the three Moirai.

'Come and have a look at this.' He brought the two pictures up side by side on the screen.

'Gloria made reference to Greek mythology, saying they were the daughters of Zeus.'

'Yes,' a confused-looking Anna replied.

'Bear with me on this, but psychologically it's interesting that Gloria didn't paint the whole picture.'

Anna nudged him with her elbow. 'Come on then, Picasso, don't keep me in suspense.'

'I remembered something from my college days.'

'Really, that far back?' she grinned.

'The Moirai are goddesses, also known as the three Fates, and they determine the destiny of man, controlling the thread of life from birth to death.'

He knew he had Anna's full attention as he brought up another web page about the Moirai and read from it.

'Clotho, whose name means Spinner, spun the thread of life, Lachesis, the apportioner, measured the thread of life, and Atropos, also known as AISA, cut the thread of life.'

Anna was intrigued as he returned to the Salviati painting that depicted the three women as ugly and old. 'There's Clotho at the back holding the spindle of thread, in front of her Lachesis stretching the thread between the fingers of each hand and beside her Aisa holding the shears to cut the thread. The ancient Greeks believed that no one, not even a god, could sway the Fates as they controlled the metaphorical thread of life of every mortal from birth to death, and it was impossible for anyone to control their own destiny.'

'Don't go so fast,' protested Anna. 'The other painting, by Mazzoni, where they are almost angelic, does it have the same meaning?'

'Yes, it's just the way the artist chose to depict them. So now we can see that both atropine and the genus name for deadly nightshade, *Atropa bellaDONNA*, are derived from Atropos.'

Anna gazed at him, extremely impressed, and completely enthralled by his intellect and quiet authority.

'Are there any flaws in your makeup or are you always so bloody brilliant?'

'Funny you should mention makeup because Roman women would use atropine as eye drops to dilate their pupils in order to make them appear more sexually aroused. The word belladonna, as I'm sure you know, means beautiful woman.'

Anna couldn't help but giggle, because she hadn't known what belladonna meant. He flushed, embarrassed, thinking she was laughing at him.

Anna put her arms around him and squeezed him with great affection. 'I wasn't laughing at you, Don – more at myself because you blow me away with all this amazing information.'

'I thank you very much, and I think this whole thing with plants and poison may be beyond an obsession with Gloria: it's more like a psychotic fixation.'

'Like that woman in the old people's home you spoke about. She thinks she's a god who can control people's destiny?' Anna asked.

Blane nodded, and picking up his pen he began to write in his notebook. 'I believe Gloria has many of the characteristics of a sociopath, plus a deep hatred of men, including her own father.'

Anna was not sure he was correct. 'Then why did she get married three times and name a charity after her father?'

'It isn't about his legacy, it's about making her look good. Xavier and Henry she married for the money and Samuel got her pregnant.'

Anna sucked in her breath since she thought he had made a valid point.

Blane continued: 'Even her son Arum Joshua meant that little to her she gave him away.'

'In fairness it could also be that Gloria wanted Arum to have a better life.'

'Possibly, but the Arum plant is also known as the corpse tree. Is Gloria implying that as far as she was concerned he was dead to her from the moment he was born?'

'That's disgusting, but if you're right then Gloria really is sick in the head.' Anna sighed. 'Could you fill me in some more about a sociopath's behaviour?'

Blane was on familiar territory as he described how sociopaths could appear to be absolutely charming, form relationships and even marry, but they lacked any depth or meaning as they cared only about themselves. Incapable of any true emotions, from love to shame to guilt, they could be easily angered but were just as quick to forgive. They thrived on reward and gratification and didn't worry about the consequences of their actions because they had no conscience or moral code.

'Are you saying that on face value, you can't find anything not to like about them?' Anna asked.

'No, what I am saying is that they are extremely competent at manipulating people through their lies and deceit.'

'Do you think she may have been treated for it – you know, by a psychologist or doctor?' Anna asked.

'There's no form of psychotherapy or medication that works with an adult sociopath. You can't change someone who has no desire to change.'

Anna's laptop pinged with the arrival of an e-mail, and Blane took the opportunity to put some fresh logs on the fire while she read it. He had felt unbelievably aroused when Anna hugged him earlier, so much so that he just wanted to take her hand and lead her straight into the bedroom.

'I've got a bit of a headache – could we take some time out from the case?' he suggested. 'Maybe sit on the sofa and chat about something else?' But Anna was already distracted so missed what he'd said; instead, she turned and wafted her hand towards her laptop screen. He realized they had one thing in common, which could destroy any serious relationship between them: they both allowed their work to dominate their private lives.

'Wait until you read what Joan's sent about Lord Henry Lynne. He had one son, Robert, who was married to a Maria, and they both died in a helicopter crash in Surrey,' Anna said and made a hissing sound between her teeth

'I doubt if you can put that down to Lady Lynne.'

Anna clicked on a web link Joan had sent from a newspaper article with the heading ROBERT AND MARIA LYNNE IN HELICOPTER TRAGEDY. What she read next made her jaw drop. Lady Gloria Lynne spoke of her sadness at the loss of her stepson and daughter-in-law, and of her and Lord Henry's love for them, and how in some ways she felt responsible for their tragic accident, as she had invited Robert and Maria to Lynne House for lunch. Anna felt her heart pounding; she couldn't believe what she was reading. 'If what I'm thinking is right, Don, then Gloria is more evil than either of us imagined. They had lunch at her home, where she could have poisoned them, then they left to get into the helicopter—'

'Anna, you really need to think twice about where you're going with this as you've no evidence to support—'

'There's a member of the public who said that the helicopter was swerving from side to side but no smoke or unusual sounds were coming from it.'

'The important factor is what an Air Accident Investigation concluded,' Blane said sharply. He leaned over Anna's shoulder to search the Internet for details. 'Here it is, conclusion was pilot error and he'd been drinking.' Irritably, he went to get the wine bottle to pour himself another glass and offered some to Anna, but she declined as she read on.

'It says here, Gloria Lynne told Air Accident he'd only had two gin and tonics all afternoon.' She jumped up, clapping her hands. 'Gloria poisoned Robert Lynne with atropine before he got in that helicopter; she knew it would gradually subdue him, he'd crash and everyone would think it was an accident.

Everything in Lord Henry's will passed to Gloria. Then three months later he pops his clogs as well.'

Blane now read the article in more detail. As much as he didn't like to admit it, he was beginning to think Anna was possibly right.

'Lord Henry was so ill Gloria dealt with all the funeral arrangements and Maria and Robert were, guess what ...?' Anna asked excitedly.

'Both cremated,' Blane replied and rested his arms around her shoulders, thinking about kissing her, but she broke away from him.

'She also organized everything for Donna after Josh's death, including his funeral, and he was cremated as well. Lucky Pete Jenkins still has his blood sample.'

'Just calm down, think it through, because if you do find atropine in it we know it was Gloria, but not how and when she administered it.'

Anna nodded and then told him about Curtis Bowman's evidence that a man, believed to be Samuel, went to the Trojan on the afternoon of the fifth and spoke with Josh.

'So let's just imagine that Samuel told Josh the truth about his real birth parents. He'd feel very depressed, you agree?' Anna asked him.

'And the only other person who could confirm or deny it was Gloria.'

'Yes – my God, I know I am right, because that would explain the route he took in the Ferrari out of London on the A40 and the A3 coming back in. I am certain that Josh drove out to Weybridge to confront Gloria,' Anna said.

Blane nodded and observed that if Gloria knew that Josh was now aware of her past it would be a reason to want him dead and kill Samuel as well. What he couldn't get his head round was if Gloria had already given Josh poison, how had he ended up shot in his flat?

'Unless Gloria knew the atropine didn't work and had to finish the job off so drove Donna's car to his flat,' Anna suggested.

'I think that could be it, but it's all speculation, Anna, you need some hard evidence,' Blane said, trying to be realistic, and by now feeling exhausted by all the speculation they had been tossing around. Anna, however, appeared to be on a roll yet again as she started looking through the Charity Ball photographs to see if Gloria was absent from the shots taken between the times she knew Donna's Mini was missing from the hotel car park. A wave of despair came over her as Gloria's smiling face beamed out from a number of pictures, and she slapped the images with the flat of her hand.

'Gloria didn't leave the ball. Shit. Shit. I feel totally confused with this whole bloody case,' Anna said.

'Let's give it a rest for tonight, clear our heads and look at it all again tomorrow,' Blane said, reaching for her hand with every intention of guiding her into his bedroom.

Anna withdrew her hand and rubbed her head; although she was frustrated – not as frustrated as Blane now was – she wouldn't give up.

'Okay, we know that someone went off in Donna's car, we know from the photographs it wasn't Donna or Gloria and Samuel has no driving licence, so logically that leaves only one other person,' Anna said, almost as if talking to herself.

There was a brief pause before her eyes lit up and she looked at Blane. 'Aisa, my God, Josh Reynolds was having an affair with his other half-sister and using Esme's flat as a love nest!'

'It's a possibility . . .'

'I'm right, I know I'm right, it has to be Aisa. She also had access to the Lynne Foundation charity accounts that money was stolen from.'

'Wait, wait, don't jump the gun, is there any evidence to support an affair?' he asked.

'Fuck it, I don't think so because Donna looked at Josh's e-mails and texts but never found anything and neither did our Technical Support Unit.'

From being almost jubilant, Anna rapidly deflated, shaking her head.

'There is a way – he could have been using Skype or Cate,' Blane suggested.

'We considered Skype and he didn't use it, but what's Cate?' Anna asked.

'Call and Text Eraser, it's a phone app that lets someone who's cheating keep messages from lovers invisible to their partner. It works through a PIN number and there's no icon on the phone's screen – only the love cheat can read the messages.'

'How do you know about that then?' Anna demanded.

'The office Lothario was boasting about it, wife caught him in a hotel with another woman in the end.'

'Good, serves him right.'

She rested her head on her hands and sighed. 'We are still left with so many unanswered questions. If Samuel was blackmailing Gloria first, why didn't she report it to the police?'

'As you said, she's high-profile and wouldn't want it made public. Maybe you're looking at this case in the wrong way.'

Anna glanced up at him. 'The wrong way! After what we've been coming up with all evening, how do you mean the wrong way, for goodness' sake?'

'It's hard to explain without going into great detail.'

Irritably, he wished that their discussion would finish. It wasn't that he didn't care but he was simply finding it harder and harder to concentrate. The more interested Anna was in the case the less he felt she was interested in him.

'You feeling okay?' Anna asked, inwardly worried that he was becoming bored.

'I'm fine,' he groaned, 'just a slight headache trying to get my head around your case. It's like a kaleidoscope of information and trying to separate all the colours is not easy.'

'I'd really like to know what you're thinking,' Anna told him.

He gave a long sigh, and drained his wine before deciding to share his theory. 'I am getting tired out, but consider this proposition: Samuel told Josh to spite Gloria. Josh then went to Gloria's but she would of course deny it and probably say

Samuel was lying and trying to blackmail her. She slips Josh some atropine and he makes it home but is unwell. The atropine makes him more and more emotional; he's confused, trying to make sense of it all – with me so far?'

'Yes, yes, go on.'

'Okay, Josh calls Aisa, he loves her and needs to see her. He gradually gets more and more depressed, having discovered he was committing incest, with not one, but two women. He considers ending it all and gets the gun out the safe. Aisa leaves the Savoy Hotel and arrives at his flat in Bayswater and he tells her everything . . .' He paused to let Anna take in what he was saying, but she was perfectly up to speed with him, nodding her head.

'Yes, go on.'

'This is just a maybe but what if Josh puts the gun to his head, Aisa tries to grab it, and bang it goes off, which would account for why his gun hand was in an unusual position. She panics and runs.'

Anna frowned and chewed at her lips before adding to his theory. 'If Samuel wrote the suicide note and stole the money, he had to have gone to the flat. So maybe he saw Aisa there, and could have seen her run off before he let himself in with his set of keys.'

'Possible, and gives him another thing to blackmail Gloria with,' Blane commented.

'The suicide note would also help to lead the police in the wrong direction and suit Samuel's purpose,' Anna said.

Turning to the Charity Ball photographs again, she concentrated on the pictures taken during and after the fireworks display.

'Aisa's nowhere amongst the crowd on the balcony, then twelve thirty-five, there she is back in the ballroom with Gloria.' Anna paused, looking closely at the photos before continuing.

'Aisa is wearing a different evening dress. If she went to Josh's in the one she first had on she could have got blood on it when he shot himself.'

She turned to look at Blane for confirmation, but he was now sitting on the sofa with his eyes closed. Slowly she went over to sit beside him, and laid her legs across his.

'Gloria confirmed Aisa's alibi about being sick, which means she's bloody well lying again. She knows exactly what happened to Josh, either from Samuel or Aisa herself,' Anna said, nudging him.

Blane yawned and opened his eyes. 'Gloria is an adept liar who can think and react to any given situation very quickly. She would have primed Aisa on exactly what to say.'

'And there was me thinking you'd stopped listening . . .'

She leaned towards him as if to kiss him, but stopped before their lips met. 'Wait a minute. Why hasn't Gloria done more to protect Donna, fight her corner? She's been arrested for murder.'

'In Gloria's world, sacrifices have to be made to save her own skin. She can't say anything and risk being found out herself. As for Aisa spilling the beans, I doubt that will happen either – she won't cross her mother and risk being cut off from her world of luxury and wealth.'

Anna nodded. 'It all sounds so simple, yet underneath the surface is a tangled web of deceit and lies spanning thirty-odd years. What was it Sherlock Holmes said about eliminating the impossible and whatever you're left with—'

'However improbable, must be the truth,' Blane said, yawning even harder.

Anna's head was spinning with a whirlwind of information. 'That's the problem here, Don. My team is making a big mistake and will end up suffering the consequences. How on earth do I explain in a phone call to Mike Lewis everything we have discussed – he'll think I'm totally delusional. Even then, because of Gloria's standing, Mike will have to at the least go and speak with Deputy Commissioner Walters.'

'You don't make a phone call,' Blane said matter-of-factly.

'What? I don't tell Mike anything?' Anna asked, surprised.

'You have to tell them face to face. You're the only person

who's got a handle on this whole sordid mess. Gloria has to be arrested immediately and only you have the full knowledge of what has been uncovered, so only you can interview her and Aisa.'

'You sound like you want to get rid of me.'

'That's the last thing I want to do, and more than anything I want to be with you.' He felt somewhat relieved at finally getting his feelings out.

'I feel the same way, Don. I want and need to be with you,' Anna confessed. Then she grinned wryly. 'Plus, if I walk off the FBI course and go back now, it would be the end of my career. My superiors would never forgive me for blowing a chance someone else could have had.'

'We run three courses a year, and you just solved a major missing-persons case over here, so you leave it to me to speak with the FBI Director and get you on the next one.'

He cupped her face between his hands. He had been impatient to tell her how he felt and to make love with her; now he was arranging for her to leave not just his log cabin but return to England.

'There's a late flight tonight to Heathrow and you'd be back in London by about mid morning. I can call our guys at the airport and see if I can get you on it and they will rush you through Customs.'

'I could always get a flight tomorrow morning,' Anna said, nervous of stating the obvious.

'Only daytime flight is the ten a.m., and that would mean you'd get home nearer midnight on Monday. This way you can sleep on the plane and be fresher for the morning when you see your bosses.'

'Okay.' She stood up and was about to collect her things when he stopped her.

'Listen, I've been wanting to make love with you all day. Maybe fate is playing a big part in this, because I wanted it all to be special and romantic. I envisaged us having the next ten weeks together, really getting to know each other.'

Anna smiled, and kissed him, whispering, 'I want that too.' She kissed him again. 'We do still have time, you know.'

He hesitated for only a moment before he scooped her up in his arms in case she changed her mind and carried her into the bedroom.

Chapter Thirty-One

Blane's colleagues at Dulles Airport were able to secure a seat on the Heathrow flight for Anna so he rushed her back to the FBI Academy where she literally flung her clothes into her case and they raced to the airport. They hardly spoke to each other on the journey, speeding along the highway, blue lights flashing; somehow it just didn't seem the right time or place for either of them to discuss a future together. Anna felt in many ways that Blane was a reflection of her, both in thought and working practices. She feared they were too much alike, and wondered if he might be thinking the same. Anna knew that whatever happened they would have to make sure they found a world together outside of crime investigation if there was to be anything lasting between them.

When they arrived at the check-in, an FBI agent was waiting for them with a flight ticket. He shook hands with Blane who introduced Anna.

'Agent Nathan will get you fast-tracked through to departures. He'll need your passport, Anna,' Blane said.

She rummaged in her handbag and passed the passport over to Agent Nathan who promptly carried her bag to the check-in desk. Blane stood patiently as she answered all the usual questions about packing her own case and carrying no weapons, and then her flight number and gate flashed on the departure screen, alerting them that the passengers were boarding.

'My God, we only just made it,' she said.

Blane took Anna to one side; she nervously wondered what

he was going to say about his feelings for her and what she'd say
in return.

'I just wanted to tell you that Gloria Lynne will be deceitful,
she'll show no remorse or ever admit guilt, and will really know
how to play the "pity card". She will be a consummate actress
and twist accusations round so she looks like the victim. Gloria
will be a very, very clever woman.'

Anna didn't quite know what to say, as she wasn't expecting
this subject, but she realized he was concerned for her.

'Agent Nathan will take you to the plane now. You have a
safe journey, Anna, and I hope it all pans out for you.'

'What?' She had assumed he would be able to accompany
her. He gave a small shrug of his shoulders, and was unpre-
pared for the way she flung her arms around him, hugging him
tightly.

'Thank you, thank you for everything,' she said.

'Well, after tonight, the bedroom scene rather than anything
else, I want us to see each other again and the sooner the better,'
Blane replied, even as he recognized it sounded false, yet not
knowing what else to say because she looked as if she was about
to burst into tears. Agent Nathan pointed to his watch, indicating that time was pressing.

'I'll call to tell you how everything goes,' she said.

He bent forward and kissed her on the cheek, feeling like he
was terminating their relationship. Truthfully, he had wanted so
much more from her, but he knew that circumstances had now
made that impossible.

'Have a safe trip, and e-mail me when you have the time. I
have to get back to the car as it's in a no-waiting zone,' Blane
said, not wanting to prolong the moment. He didn't look back
as Anna hurriedly followed FBI Agent Nathan to the front of
the security queues.

As she sat in first class awaiting take-off, Anna couldn't believe
that so little time had passed since she was last at the airport – it
seemed so much longer with all that had happened. She smiled,

recalling Langton's upgrade at Heathrow, and it dawned on her that she still hadn't spoken to him since he left to hunt for Fitzpatrick. Even though she figured that he would have made contact with her if anything had happened, she realized she was just trying to find reasons not to phone and tell him that she was flying home. Knowing that he would undoubtedly shout at her when he found out, she picked up her mobile and dialled his number.

Langton answered straight away. 'What are you doing up so late, you've got the Yellow Brick Road tomorrow morning?' he asked and laughed.

'Any luck with Fitzpatrick?' she asked awkwardly.

'Well let's put it this way, the FBI SWAT team have saved the British and American taxpayers a lot of money.'

Anna was finding it hard to concentrate and didn't really take in what Langton was implying. 'Sorry, what do you mean?'

'He resisted arrest, pulled a gun and the FBI pumped him full of bullets. So, no lengthy trial at the taxpayers' expense.'

'Are you okay?' she asked, somewhat alarmed.

'Yeah fine, bit of a tense moment in more ways than one. All a bit sad though – his young son was there and witnessed it all. He'll have to go into care as there's no other family and what the trauma will do to him God only knows.'

'Poor kid,' Anna said. 'Still, you got Fitzpatrick.'

'Yeah, but in some ways it still feels like he's the one that got away. I'd love to have slapped the handcuffs on him and told him he's nicked.'

Anna was racking her brains how to tell Langton that she was about to return to London, but he sensed something was wrong.

'You sound a bit down. Is everything all right?' he asked.

'Not really, I need to tell you what's happened.'

'Is it that bloody Don Blane? Did he try something?'

'No, it's nothing like that,' Anna said.

Langton could tell she was still hiding something. 'Fucking FBI are so up themselves. Don't let him get you down, I've got all the red tape Internal Affairs going on here, what with Fitzpatrick being killed, but I should be back at Quantico late tomorrow—'

'I won't be there, I'm actually leaving,' Anna cut accross him, realizing it was now or never.

'What the fuck has he done to upset you?' Langton shouted.

'Nothing, Don helped me unravel the evidence in the Josh Reynolds case and Donna did not murder him. Gloria Lynne has fooled us all, she will stop at nothing to get her way and may have murdered at least five people.'

'Jesus Christ, Anna, Blane knows nothing about the fucking Josh Reynolds investigation. You're being taken in by a load of profiling psychobabble.'

'He knows more than you realize and he's made me see things clearly,' she insisted. 'You've always gone on and on at me about being a team player, well I'm not going to sit back and watch my team be duped by a lying sociopath like Gloria Lynne.'

Langton could tell that he had struck a nerve where Don Blane was concerned but he also knew that Anna was being deeply serious and must have found evidence to support her beliefs. 'Are you one hundred per cent sure about Gloria?' he asked.

'Yes, but as yet I don't have all the evidence to prove it. There's a lot of costly forensic work that needs doing and I'm certain it will prove my theories. Gloria started her murdering spree in Jamaica over twenty years ago, using a poison called atropine. I think she used the same substance on Lord Lynne when they were on holiday in Egypt, then—'

'Just hold on, you're talking about crimes that didn't even happen in the UK – they don't come under our jurisdiction,' Langton said, feeling he had to interrupt.

'It would take too long to explain right now but it's all related to why Josh Reynolds may have killed himself.'

'I don't bloody believe this. You're now back to square one that Josh did commit suicide!' Langton exclaimed.

'Possibly, but I think Aisa was in the flat when the gun went off. She was having an affair with Josh. It's possible Samuel saw her leave the flat and used that knowledge, along with other historical facts, to blackmail Gloria.'

'Holy shit, this is making my head spin – what facts?'

'Samuel Peters was Gloria's first husband, Josh was their son and Donna and Aisa are blood sisters through her marriage to Xavier Alleyne,' Anna informed Langton.

'So Josh was married to one half-sister, and sleeping with the other? I don't bloody believe it, this case gives me a damn headache.'

'You have no idea how long it took to put all the pieces together but I've copies of all the birth and marriage certificates to prove it, and I am certain none of them knew they were in incestuous relationships.'

'My God, this'll be major fodder for the press, considering who Lady Lynne is and all her big-time contacts,' Langton groaned.

'Gloria Lynne has to be arrested immediately. I wouldn't put it past her to kill her daughters to save her own skin.'

'No, no, just wait a second. You cannot arrest Gloria without higher authority. You need to talk to Walters first, you know that.'

'And you know full well he will want a complete report and all the evidence before making a decision,' Anna retorted.

'That's just the way it goes when it comes to the rich and powerful . . .'

'Well, the way I see it, the law is the same for everyone, and if I have reasonable suspicion that Gloria has committed a crime then it's my duty to arrest her.'

Langton knew from the tone of her voice that Anna was determined to have her way, and he was growing increasingly worried that she hadn't grasped the political situation she was walking into and that her stubbornness would be the downfall of her career.

'Anna, just hold off. We can fly out together and be back in

London by Tuesday. You can give me a full run-down and I will go with you to see Walters and plead your case.'

'I'm already on the plane – it's going to be taking off any minute'

'What?'

'I've got to go,' she said and he snapped back angrily.

'Anna, it's just one more day, that's all I'm asking, please wait for me to get back and we can sit down and discuss it all.'

'I don't know if I can do that, I can't risk Walters saying no when other people's lives may be in danger. There's enough to justify Gloria's arrest and interview.'

'I don't doubt that, but just hear me out . . .' Langton paused before continuing. 'Here's the deal, you wait for my return, we don't go to Walters as I've decided from the evidence you presented to me that Gloria should be arrested. I will make the arrest myself and interview her with you.'

'No, I can't let you do that; now you've got Fitzpatrick you could make Commander. I won't let you throw that chance away for me,' Anna said, upset at Langton's suggestion.

'It's too late. Walters decided my promotion fate ages ago and even with Fitzpatrick dead he's not going to give me anything. Walters has always been out to get me. He'll use any excuse, no point in pretending otherwise. If Gloria's arrest goes pear-shaped on my watch, who cares? Walters can shout at me but he'll have no grounds to sack me. I've got nothing to lose and I relish the chance to stick two fingers up at him.'

Anna realized that Langton was prepared to take the fall to protect her career, and no matter how noble, she thought it was wrong. There had to be a better alternative but she needed time to think of something that he would agree to.

'I'll wait until Tuesday,' Anna said reluctantly.

'Good, I'm glad you're seeing sense. Don't tell anyone else about what we've said, not even Mike Lewis. You can tell him you've had a brief conversation with me and I told you to get back to London and I'm on my way back to discuss your findings.

Tell the team about Aisa, but don't say anything yet about Gloria being a murder suspect.'

Anna sighed. 'That won't be easy, as her being blackmailed by Samuel led to her poisoning Josh.'

'Well it's up you, but remember walls have ears in the Met and that's how Walters likes to keep up with what's going on.'

'Don't worry, I'll be discreet.'

Anna thought he was about to hang up but he continued. 'Oh, and forensic-wise, tell Pete Jenkins to do whatever you need.'

'It could be very expensive.'

'Who cares, if it helps prove your case then blow the bloody budget,' he said and hung up just as the seat-belt warnings came on and the engines started throbbing. The flight attendant cleared the half-finished champagne and untouched nuts, and Anna turned off her mobile and clicked her belt closed.

She recalled Langton's words on the plane out when they were flying to Dulles, but now it seemed that his final success in tracking down Fitzpatrick was not the redemption he had thought it would be. She wondered if Langton had already made his mind up to call it a day and retire. It was humbling to acknowledge that he was prepared to tarnish what might be the last days of his career to save hers.

After take-off, Anna was so tired that she just wanted to recline her seat and fall into a deep sleep but she knew that she'd have to compile a full report of everything she had discovered, and as time was of the essence, she got out her laptop and started to work. Exhausted, she fell asleep whilst still typing her report, and woke when a flight attendant gently shook her to ask if she would like some breakfast. Looking at her watch she realized that she had only slept for an hour but it seemed much longer. It suddenly dawned on her that with all her rushing around she had forgotten to arrange for someone to pick her up at Heathrow.

She asked the flight attendant if they were back on UK time and on being informed it was seven thirty a.m. she used the on-board phone to call Paul Barolli's mobile. To Anna's surprise, he was already up and getting ready for work, and sounded extremely pleased at hearing her voice and interested in how she was doing. Anna told him that she didn't have time to go into details but she needed him to meet her at Heathrow terminal five arrivals in two hours. Barolli immediately asked her what had happened but she swore she would explain all when she saw him, asking him meanwhile not to tell anyone about her return. He promised he wouldn't and Anna knew that she could count on his trust and loyalty.

She nipped to the toilet and had a quick freshen-up then enjoyed a bacon roll and some coffee before landing. Although she was still tired she was now running on adrenalin and looking forward to being back in London and eventually arresting Gloria Lynne.

'Seems like only two seconds ago I was saying bon voyage to you,' Barolli remarked, greeting her with a big smile and taking her bag. He was desperate to find out why Anna had suddenly returned to London, but knowing her so well he figured it was best not to ask and that she would explain in her own time.

'I missed you so much I just had to come home,' she teased.

Barolli laughed. 'I called the office and said I was going to the dentist with a sore tooth.'

'Thanks, Paul, I appreciate this,' Anna said, scrolling through the e-mails on her phone as she walked through the crowds. Her eyes flew to one from Joan sent late the previous evening informing her that there was an unidentified body at Fulham mortuary that had been brought in late evening 6 November 2012 and might be Samuel Peters. Anna couldn't believe the date, as it was the same day Josh's body was found. Her gut told her that Gloria Lynne had visited Samuel that day and poisoned him.

'So you want me to drop you off home or are we going to the office?'

'Fulham mortuary, please.'

'To see Doc Harrow?' Barolli asked.

'Not if I can help it. With a bit of luck we are going to see Samuel Peters,' Anna said confidently.

Barolli was now even more curious. 'I don't wish to appear nosey, but is there any chance you can tell me what the hell is going on?'

'I will, Paul, but it's all rather complicated and I want to speak to everyone at the same time in an office meeting. I can tell you that I am almost certain that Samuel Peters' body is in the mortuary and has been since just after Josh Reynolds died.'

'Bloody hell, and we've been farting around searching for him here there and everywhere!'

Once at the mortuary, Anna and Barolli lost no time in finding the head mortician, who showed them the freezer in which the unidentified body was held. Anna told him that the body was believed to be Samuel Peters, a Jamaican citizen visiting the UK at the time of his death, upon which the mortician wrote the information on the wipe board with a question mark beside it.

'Dropped dead in the street from a heart attack. It's nice to finally have a name. He – sorry, Samuel – was due for a pauper's grave this week so you're a bit lucky. He's as stiff as a Christmas turkey at the moment. If I'd known you were coming I'd have got him out of the freezer so he could thaw out.'

Anna asked where the clothing and property that was taken from Samuel was, and the mortician said it was in the storeroom and once he'd got the body out he'd go and get it. Using a hydraulic trolley-lift table he removed the body from the middle shelf of the freezer and pulled back part of the white shroud that covered the face. The black skin had a light covering of ice on it, most notably round the eyebrows. The mortician pulled a handkerchief out of his pocket and gave Samuel's face a quick wipe-down, making the features more visible.

'Best not touch him; those dreadlocks snap off like icicles when they're frozen. Is it the same Samuel you were looking for?' he asked.

Anna looked at the body and said she believed it was, but a further forensic post mortem would need to be done. She suddenly felt the presence of someone stood behind her before hearing them speak.

'Well I can tell yer now, like, I won't be bloody doing it again. Already said cause of death was heart attack so case closed.'

Anna immediately recognized the voice as that of the objectionable Dr Harrow. Turning to face him, she found he had a cup of tea in one hand and the inevitable biscuit in the other.

Anna was not in the mood to put up with the man or his facetious remarks. 'You're quite right, Dr Harrow, you won't be doing another post mortem. I will be calling upon the services of another pathologist.'

'Yer can't do that, I've done me report and Coroner has accepted it.'

'Oh, yes, I can, and I will be informing the Coroner that this man was probably poisoned with atropine.'

The dishevelled doctor glared at Anna. 'Atropine! Well there's no way I could have known that, is there? I sent his blood off for toxicology!'

'I appreciate that, Dr Harrow, but I have read of poisoning cases where the pathologist suspected something was amiss, simply due to skin rash and dilated pupils. I don't suppose you looked for either, did you?' Anna asked, facing him down. She had not liked him previously and now she felt even more distaste, as the biscuit crumbs scattered over his white overall like dandruff.

Harrow's face looked like a mass of blood vessels that were about to burst.

'How dare you insinuate that I have not done my job in a professional manner? I've bloody years of experience.'

'I am very aware that you have, Dr Harrow, but do not go anywhere near Samuel Peters' body, because if you do I may find myself having to arrest you for interfering with an investigation,' Anna said.

Harrow gasped, but said nothing and stormed off.

'Was that true about the skin rash and pupils?' Barolli asked.

'As symptoms of atropine poisoning, yes, but the bit about the pathologist suspecting it, I haven't read it anywhere,' she admitted.

'You sly thing, I bet he's in his office right now searching it on the Internet,' Barolli said.

Anna remembered the mnemonic Blane had used.

'They say atropine makes you hot as a hare, blind as a bat, dry as a bone, red as a beet, and mad as a hatter.'

At first, Barolli didn't make the connection. Anna tilted her head and grinned, then it dawned on him.

'It wasn't the bloody chicken! Holy shit, I could have dropped down dead.'

'I suspect it was the spiced rum. Marisha didn't know it was in there when she poured some into your coffee. Looks like she unwittingly drank some herself – that's why she was odd in the interview with you and Dewar and had a heart attack.'

Barolli closed his eyes and shook his head. 'Oh, no, I knew I shouldn't have done it . . .'

'Don't look so worried – you weren't to know.'

'No, not the poison. I told the council hygiene officers to raid the chicken place and shut it down.'

Anna tried but she couldn't stop herself from laughing out loud.

At that moment the mortician returned with a cardboard box that contained Samuel's belongings and Anna put on some protective gloves so she could look through them. The clothes were folded neatly and on top of them sat a large key ring with six keys attached in sets of two.

'I bet these will be for Marisha's, Esme's and Josh Reynolds' flats,' Anna muttered. She picked up a black donkey jacket and started to check through the pockets, even though the mortician assured her that he'd already searched it. Politely insisting she'd like to check again as sometimes things got missed, she placed the coat down on a nearby table, opened it out and started to pat her hands all over the lining. Suddenly she felt a

small bump and traced the tip of her finger over the shiny mate-
rial to get a better feel.

'Something's in here,' Anna said as she put her hand into the
inside pocket and found that it had a deliberate scissor cut in it.
She could feel some loose paper and, on pulling it out from the
pocket, saw that it was five sheets of A4 paper stapled together.
They were folded so that the fifth page was outermost, which
was covered in something that resembled blood spatter.

'I think this may have been on the sofa beside Josh when he
was shot. It's the right size to fit the void that Pete Jenkins spoke
about.'

She read the top page, and then looked at Barolli.

'It's Aisa Alleyne's birth certificate.'

'What are the other pages?' Barolli asked.

Anna told him that they were birth and marriage certificates
that Samuel had ordered online and probably used to blackmail
Gloria. As she spoke she flicked each page over so Barolli could
see whom they referred to.

'My God, this is dynamite, but how on earth did you know?'
He was so impressed he took a step back, shaking his head.

'A colleague of one of the tutors at Quantico made some discreet enquiries in Jamaica, and sent me copies,' Anna said
diplomatically.

She placed the certificates in a plastic property bag that the
mortician gave her. 'Let's take this up to the lab so Pete Jenkins
can get to work on a DNA profile of the blood.'

As soon as she got to the lab, Anna gave Pete Jenkins a hug
and a kiss to thank him for all his hard work. Pete laughed and
she asked him what was so funny, so he told her that after her
second call the previous evening he had commented to his
wife that Anna was so worked up about the Reynolds case that
it wouldn't surprise him if she jumped on a plane and came
home.

'I found these in the lining of Samuel's coat,' Anna said,
handing him the plastic bag containing the certificates. 'Look at

the direction of the blood – could this be what caused the void on Josh's sofa?'

Pete held the certificates up. 'On a first glance, yes, it could, but obviously I'll need to examine it closer, plus there's DNA and fingerprint work to do.'

'Did you manage to get a set of Samuel Peters' fingerprints from the Border Agency?'

'Yes, and I compared them to the set taken from the unidentified body at Fulham mortuary and they matched.' He handed Anna a copy of Samuel's visa application photograph and she confirmed it was the body they had just seen in the mortuary.

'Okay, you'd better come on through,' Pete said, handing Anna and Barolli lab coats and protective gloves to wear before leading them into the working area. Items of property were laid out on sheets of white lab paper. As they moved along the table Pete pointed to each one and gave them a run-down on the forensic results.

'Money from Esme's flat and Marisha's freezer has Samuel's prints on it, as do the paint tins over there.'

Pete then indicated the bottle of spiced rum and on seeing it Barolli raised his eyebrows and shook his head. Pete grinned. 'I heard you got pretty sick. It was probably from this stuff but I'm awaiting the test results. Samuel's prints are all over it and of course Marisha's.'

'I thought she didn't have a criminal record,' Barolli said, remembering he had already checked this.

'To be safe I got one of my guys to go over to the hospital to take a set off her for comparison and elimination. You were right, Anna, there was atropine in her system and your information saved her life. She's still in a coma but stable and they think she will come round.'

Anna was thrilled that things were falling into place, and even more elated when Pete told her that he had started work on the blood sample from Josh Reynolds and early indications showed traces of atropine. Further tests were needed before he could make a positive confirmation, but it looked promising.

'Thanks, Pete, you're an absolute star,' Anna said.

'I hope Mike Lewis is going to be okay about all this extra work as it's going to cost a bob or two.'

'I've spoken with Langton – he said to go ahead and do whatever needs to be done,' Anna told Pete.

'Bloody hell, is he not feeling well?' he exclaimed.

Anna smiled. 'You can do the DNA familial comparison tests now.'

Pete looked round the room and came closer to Anna and Barolli, 'Well between us three, I lifted some DNA from the paint-tin fingerprint of Samuel Peters. The profile fits to him being Josh Reynolds' father.'

'What about Donna's DNA? Is she Josh's half-sister?' Anna asked.

'That's going to take longer. Josh and Samuel's comparison was easy, as I only had to look at the Y chromosome, which passes down from father to son. To say that Josh and Donna are related I have to create and look at their mitochondrial DNA profile, which is passed down by the mother to her children.'

'That would only allow you to say they have the same mother but not who the mother is?' Anna asked, and as Pete nodded she continued, 'So to be a hundred per cent sure, you would need a DNA sample from Gloria Lynne for comparison as well.'

'Easier said than done, I expect, but I'll leave that for you to get,' Pete told her.

'I can't wait, and I will also be getting one from Aisa as it looks like she's wrapped up in Josh's death and was having an affair with him.'

'Fuck me, this case just gets more and more complicated,' Barolli remarked, having hardly said a word as he attempted to take on board all the new information. Some of it was starting to make sense now, but he was still baffled as to exactly who'd done what, where and when. Plus everyone seemed to be jumping into bed with their brother or sister.

Pete promised he would ring or text Anna as soon as he had

any results to give her. She asked Pete if in addition he would take digital photographs of the certificates she had found in Samuel's coat lining and he assured her he would get it done right away and e-mail them over.

As they got in the car to leave the lab it suddenly dawned on Anna that there might just be an alternative solution to Langton putting his neck on the line for her. She'd use Aisa as a lure to get to Gloria. There was plenty of evidence to justify Aisa's arrest, detention for interviewing and taking her DNA and fingerprints for comparison.

Aisa would be Gloria's Achille's heel and her arrest would also entitle Anna to search the whole of Lynne House. Even if she didn't find anything, Anna knew that Aisa would be the bait that would draw Gloria in and force her to confront Anna. She was certain that Gloria had never had to worry about Donna saying anything, simply because her elder daughter knew nothing. It was hard to believe, but Donna was the sacrificial lamb, and it didn't worry Gloria a jot if she was arrested and charged with murder because she herself was then kept in the clear.

Anna suspected that Josh would have shown Aisa the copy of her birth certificate and therefore hoped her prints would be on it. She was also certain, because of Aisa's alibi, that Gloria now knew of Aisa's affair with Josh and that she had left the Charity Ball to see him. Gloria had always been there to keep an eye on Aisa, to control and manipulate her, but sitting in a cell sweating it out, Aisa would crumble. Gloria would no longer have the physical power over her and the truth might finally come out. Anna mulled it all over, sitting beside Barolli, leaning back with her eyes closed. He had wrongly assumed she was having a little nap.

'You want me to drive you back home to your place for a bit of a rest?' he asked.

At once, she shot bolt upright and clapped her hands.

'Got it, I've got it. No, not home, I want to go to the Lynne

Foundation offices to arrest Aisa Lynne,' she announced assertively.

Barolli hit the brakes. 'Are you serious?'

'Never more so, Paul, never more so!'

Chapter Thirty-Two

'I was hoping you'd come back, lying little cow is in her office,' said Jane, the personal assistant at the Lynne Foundation.

Barolli, who was slightly out of breath from struggling to keep up with Anna as she strode up the stairs two at a time, made the introductions.

'Is there something you'd like to tell us?' Anna said.

Jane threw a glance towards the closed office door and lowered her voice. 'Yes, I've been wondering what I should do because I heard about Donna's arrest and the money she allegedly took from the charity funds. Donna's no thief, but *she* is, Aisa is.'

'Do you have any evidence to prove that?' Barolli asked.

Jane unlocked her top drawer with a key. 'I spent all day Friday and this morning going through Donna's accounts and checking the movement of the monies against the days she wasn't here or I had her booked in for a meeting with someone.'

She opened the drawer and removed a blue folder. 'I've highlighted the specific thefts and they were all made at times Donna was out of the office. I always wondered why Aisa sometimes used Donna's computer, but I never thought she was stealing thousands of pounds.'

Anna glanced at the documents, impressed by how competently prepared they were, giving every detail as Jane had described. Anna thanked her, assuring her that she didn't need to worry that Aisa would find out who had drawn up the documents.

'I'm perfectly willing to make a statement and give evidence in court. She's treated me like a skivvy ever since she started working here, so it's about time she had her comeuppance.'

'Are Aisa's mobile phone bills paid by the company?' Anna asked.

'Yes, and if you'd like a copy I can put them in the folder with the other documents.'

'A copy with the dialled numbers for all of 2012 will be fine, thanks.'

'No problem, happy to help you, detective.'

'It's much appreciated, Jane, but for now I'd be grateful if you didn't say anything to Lady Lynne about Aisa's arrest or the paperwork.'

'You can trust me implicitly,' Jane, replied loving every minute of what was happening.

Anne looked to Barolli and gave a small nod of her head.

'Let's do it,' she said and asked him for his handcuffs, which he removed from the pouch attached to his trouser belt. Barolli was surprised by Anna's request, and even more so when she just threw open Aisa's office door without knocking.

'Who the fuck are you?' Aisa exclaimed as she jumped out of her seat.

'Detective Chief Inspector Anna Travis, murder squad,' Anna told her and in one move grabbed Aisa, spun her round, and before she knew it her hands were pulled behind her back and cuffed. 'I am arresting you on suspicion of the murder of Joshua Reynolds, theft from the Lynne charities, perverting the course of justice, obstructing police and serious offences under the Coroners Act,' Anna said forcefully and then read Aisa her rights.

Aisa let out a loud screech as the handcuffs bit into her wrist. 'Ow, you're hurting me, you bitch! My mother will be livid when she finds out I'm being arrested for something I didn't do. I've never stolen any money, Donna took it for Joshua and she bought him the car.'

'What car?' Anna asked innocently.

'The blue Ferrari, you idiot! What other fucking car do you think I'm talking about?'

Anna lightly squeezed the handcuff ratchet, causing Aisa to wince and squeal as the metal pinched her skin.

'Come on, Aisa, behave yourself or they can go even tighter,' Anna warned.

Barolli was shocked, as he had never seen Anna behave as aggressively as this when making an arrest. He thought it was over-the-top as the handcuffs were not necessary for someone as diminutive as Aisa. Anna caught the look of surprise on his face and winked, at which point Barolli understood everything was deliberate and intended to put the frighteners on Aisa.

'Is there a problem, Inspector Barolli?' Anna demanded loudly.

Barolli instantly was onto the fact she wanted him to play the good cop to her bad – an old trick, yes, but one that Aisa would not realize was being pulled on her.

'No, ma'am,' Barolli said nervously for Aisa's benefit.

'Have you spoken to Donna or her barrister Mr Holme about the Ferrari?' Anna asked Aisa.

'No, she's been in prison. My mother spoke with Mr Holme but not me as yet. You've got this all wrong and you'll pay for treating me like this.'

'Tell me, Inspector Barolli, what colour would you naturally associate with a Ferrari?'

'Red, ma'am, or maybe yellow, but a blue one, that must be a very rare sight indeed.'

'So how do you know it's a blue Ferrari?' Anna asked, making direct eye contact with Aisa.

The wide-eyed gawping look on her face clearly showed that the young woman knew she'd just put her foot in it as she visibly struggled to think of an explanation.

'I overheard my mother speaking to Mr Holme about it on the phone. We were in the kitchen at the time, you can ask her, she'll tell you it's true,' Aisa said nervously.

'Well, if Lady Lynne says it's true then it must be. I mean, Lady Lynne wouldn't lie to protect you, would she, Aisa?'

Anna asked with deliberate scepticism.

'No, my mother would never lie for me, or anyone, for that matter.'

'I would hope not, Aisa, a lady of her standing lie, now that would be unthinkable,' Anna said sarcastically.

Barolli was finding it all very entertaining and thought his colleague was giving a star performance.

'I agree with you, ma'am, Lady Lynne wouldn't lie,' he added for good measure.

Anna continued with the strategy. 'On the night of the Charity Ball, when you became so ill and had to go and lie down, Lady Lynne told me personally how concerned she was for your well-being – she said she even left the ball to see how you were.'

Aisa nodded.

'That was so caring of her, wasn't it?' Anna asked with mock concern.

'Yes, she checked on me a few times. It made me feel better so I went back downstairs to the ball,' Aisa said, but she was not quite so confident.

'Now that's the thing, Aisa, the times your mother came to check on you, were they while you were out in Donna's Mini, or maybe visiting Mr Reynolds at his flat when he was shot through the head, or do you have an identical twin your mother comforted in the hotel room?'

Aisa grimaced despairingly as she realized that she had allowed herself to be trapped.

Anna stared her straight in the eye. 'I don't think Mummy's going to be too pleased, Aisa, do you?'

Aisa's face twisted with anxiety. 'I want to speak to her and Mr Holme.'

'Of course you can, with pleasure, as soon as we have finished searching Lynne House. From top to bottom this time!' Anna said firmly.

'Please will you take the handcuffs off, they hurt and I don't want everyone in the building or street to see me like this,' Aisa pleaded.

'You should have thought of the consequences of lying about Josh's death and framing your sister for theft. You've only yourself to blame now,' Anna said.

She picked up Aisa's mobile and handbag from her desk, handed them to Barolli and told him to take her out to the car.

Once they were out of sight, Anna returned to Jane to pick up the folder with all the documents and told her a tow truck would be collecting Aisa's Lotus later to take it to the lab.

'I was just wondering,' Jane began. 'Obviously, I won't say anything if Lady Lynne phones, well I will, but I'll say Aisa's gone out shopping again. It's just that I wondered what should I do if the press phone or come here?'

'Good thought, Jane. Obviously, don't say anything about what you've given us regarding the theft, but did you overhear what I arrested Aisa for?'

'Yes, that will be imprinted in my brain for many years to come,' Jane said with a big smile.

'Well you can tell the press that's what you heard the lady detective say,' Anna said and smiled back, longing for the moment when the news of Aisa's arrest went public and aspersions were cast on Gloria Lynne. She could see the headline now, in fact she wished she could write it herself: 'Lady Gloria Lynne, Founder and Director of the Lynne Foundation, defends her daughter Aisa arrested on suspicion of murder, fraud and other related offences.'

Arriving at the car, Anna found Barolli sitting with Aisa, who was in floods of tears.

'Right, let's make our way to Lynne House. I want Aisa to be present while we search it.'

Barolli was confused; although this was fine legally, it was general practice for other officers to do the search while the prisoner was booked in at the station.

'The game commences,' Anna said quietly and once again winked at him.

He realized that it was also part of Anna's 'aggressive' tactic, and he was able to witness even more of her full-throttle energy as she phoned Central Command at Scotland Yard.

'DCI Travis, murder squad. I want two POLSA search units to meet me asap at Weybridge railway station car park.'

There was a brief pause before Anna gave a terse reply: 'Don't ask, just do as I say or you'll have DCS Langton on your back!'

Anna then phoned the office and spoke to Joan, who was totally flummoxed when she heard the DCI was back in London. From the serious tone in Anna's voice Joan didn't dare ask why but was soon informed what was happening.

'I've arrested Aisa Lynne. Muster together as many of the team as you can to meet me and Barolli at Weybridge railway station, and tell Barbara to get a warrant to search Lynne House on the way. Also I want SOCOs, a dog van and some locals to help us.'

'Yes, ma'am. Are you sure about Barbara with the warrant – she did cock it up last time?'

'That's why I can count on her to get it right this time, Joan, and by the way you were spot-on about the body at Fulham. It's Samuel Peters.'

'I thought it might be. Does Mike Lewis know you're back?' Joan asked.

'Not yet, everything is moving so quickly I haven't had a chance to call him yet but I will do shortly,' Anna said and hung up.

Barolli was aware that Anna had hardly had time to draw breath since her flight landed. 'Jet lag not kicking in then?' he asked, smiling, as he turned the steering wheel.

'No way, you have no idea how much I have been waiting to do this, my adrenalin is pumping, it feels like all I have been doing since I left London for Quantico was work this damned case out.'

'Well you have my admiration, though I'm still at a loss as to what exactly you've worked out,' he admitted.

*

Anna and Barolli were the first to arrive at Weybridge railway station followed by two POLSA teams, two local uniform units, a dog support unit van and scene of crime vans, and ten detectives from the office in four cars. Anna noticed Barbara driving one of them and sitting in the front passenger seat was Jessie Dewar. When Anna approached, Barbara handed her the warrant with a big smile, saying it was nice to have her back. Dewar frowned and nodded a curt hello.

'You sure it's a good idea to take Aisa along?' she asked. 'You're just encouraging her mother to start getting all protective and kicking off at us again. Why's she been arrested anyway?'

'How nice to see you too, Agent Dewar. As it happens I'm very interested in seeing exactly how Lady Lynne reacts when she sees her daughter. The reason for her arrest is because she has lied through her teeth and was screwing Josh Reynolds. I can also prove the missing charity money is down to her,' Anna said curtly.

Dewar was embarrassed and, realizing how little she knew of what had been uncovered, decided it was best to just listen to what she had to say.

Anna asked everyone to gather round, apologizing for not having time to go into every detail as to why Lynne House was being searched again, but this time it would be the whole premises, inside, outside, top to bottom. As expected, people asked if there was anything they were specifically looking for. Anna showed them a picture of Aisa at the Charity Ball in the dress she was wearing in the early part of the evening.

'If it has not been destroyed then it could be on the premises and possibly bloodstained. Also of importance are any birth or marriage certificates, documents linking Aisa Lynne and Josh Reynolds or referring to the purchase of a blue Ferrari. Look for letters or notes that appear threatening or coded in any way, and old invoices for the purchase of spiced rum. Myself, Barolli, Barbara and Dan Ross will search Aisa and Lady Lynne's bedrooms and the greenhouse. Any questions?' Anna asked, before instructing everyone to follow her in a convoy.

Dewar huffed and didn't look at all happy. 'What am I supposed to be doing during all this searching?'

'I'd like you to sit with Aisa,' Anna said, loving it, but at the
same time appearing very controlled and diplomatic.

'Why can't I take part in the search?' Dewar demanded.

'If you find anything that could be used as evidence it may be
ruled inadmissible seizure,' Anna said, pointing to the warrant
where it specified the Magistrate was giving an officer from the
Metropolitan Police power to enter and search the premises.

Dewar, far from pleased, knew she had no choice but to do
as she was asked, but was determined to get the last word in.

'Bit overkill, isn't it, just over forty people and two police
dogs for one middle-aged woman and her daughter?' Dewar
said, not realizing that it was an intentional move to push Gloria
further towards boiling point.

Anna smiled. 'Yes, it is, but look on the bright side – we'll get
the job done in no time and the police dogs will keep Gloria's
Doberman bitch away from you. Oh, and another thing, I don't
want Aisa interviewed or spoken to in the car.'

Dewar stomped off towards Barolli's vehicle with a face like
thunder.

When Katrina, the Polish housekeeper, answered the intercom, Anna told her to open the gates as she was here on official
police business, having arrested Aisa Lynne. Anna could hear
Katrina frantically shouting for Lady Lynne to come quickly.

Anna and Barolli led the convoy up the long driveway to
the front of Lynne House where, as expected, Lady Lynne was
standing waiting. She was speaking on a mobile phone, teeth
gritted and face contorted with anger, yet she was still able to
maintain a calm composure. Anna got out of the car, waited for
Barbara and together they approached Gloria.

'Just one second, Ian, I think DCI Travis has something to
tell me,' Gloria said.

Anna let the sergeant step forward and hand Gloria her copy
of the search warrant. 'I think you'll find this one crosses the Ts

and dots the Is for the whole house and outbuildings,' Barbara said confidently, knowing that this time she had got it right.

'Ian, darling, they have a warrant for the whole house and grounds. This is just scandalous. You need to come over here and sort it out right away.'

Anna thought it interesting that Gloria didn't firstly ask about Aisa.

'My barrister, Mr Holme, would like to speak to you, DCI Travis,' Gloria said haughtily.

'Tell him I'm busy at the moment and I will see him at the Belgravia station when I interview Aisa,' Anna said, realizing that Gloria had not even noticed her daughter sitting in the car sobbing her eyes out.

'I insist you speak to him now,' Gloria said, raising her voice slightly and holding the phone out to Anna, who took it from her and pressed the stop button ending the call.

'As I just told you, I'm busy at the moment,' Anna said with a disparaging smile.

'Where is my daughter?' Gloria asked sharply.

Anna said nothing but merely pointed to the car where Aisa was sitting in the back seat with Dewar. Anna watched Gloria's reaction carefully: the woman said nothing but the look of anger directed at her daughter said it all. Aisa could only glance at her mother briefly before turning away and lowering her head.

'How dare you arrest my daughter? This is nothing more than harassment and victimization of my family.'

Anna moved closer to her. 'I do not have to justify my actions to you, Lady Lynne, but let me assure you I would not have arrested Aisa if I didn't have reason to suspect that she was involved in the death of Arum Joshua Reynolds,' she said deliberately but quietly, staring Gloria straight in the eye.

Again the woman said nothing, but from the expression on her face, Anna knew she had touched a nerve by mentioning the name Arum.

'I want to talk to my daughter in private,' Gloria said as she gently pushed Anna to one side and started to walk towards the car.

Anna raised her voice: 'And should anyone other than a legal representative advise Aisa Lynne on what she should or should not say to police I will treat that as an attempt to pervert the course of justice.'

Gloria stopped in her tracks, turned abruptly, and walked back to stand with her face inches from Anna's.

'You do not want to play games with me, DCI Travis. I can assure you that you will not win,' Gloria whispered so that only Anna heard.

'We'll see about that,' Anna whispered back, then lightly brushed Gloria aside before instructing one of the POLSA units to search the outside grounds around the house. She then asked Barolli, Barbara and a Scene of Crime Officer to assist her in the greenhouse, where she wanted to photograph every plant and take a cutting from each one.

'What on earth have the plants in my greenhouse got to do with this invasion of my property?' Gloria snapped angrily.

'I have reason to believe that Mr Reynolds may have been poisoned by a substance that was extracted from a plant, specifically deadly nightshade.'

'From my greenhouse? That's ridiculous, poisonous plants like nightshade grow in the wild as well,' Gloria said and gave a mocking laugh.

'Is it?' Anna remarked, knowing that the fact Gloria grew poisonous plants was not in itself conclusive evidence that she was in any way guilty of murder. 'You learned from your father, so who's to say Aisa didn't in turn learn from you?'

It was fascinating to watch the masks flit across Gloria's face, as instantly she was able to swing from outrage to courteous icy coldness.

'There is no need to damage them by taking cuttings. Every plant has a name and species card next to it, and I keep an inventory. Although poisonous to the unknowing, they are all used for medicinal purposes ... TO SAVE LIFE,' Gloria said, looking around her as if hoping for audience approval. Anna smiled, virtually copying the same tone of voice.

'How very informative, Lady Lynne, thank you. If you have an inventory of all the plants you grow, along with some photographs, that will be very helpful.'

Gloria dialled a number on her phone and from what she said Anna quickly realized the woman was once again ringing Holme. Gloria told him what was happening and that DCI Travis was being very unreasonable and overbearing and wouldn't even let her speak to her daughter. Mr Holme apparently told Gloria that as Aisa was under arrest and the warrant was issued correctly, then Anna was perfectly entitled to carry out her search.

'Ian, darling, I pay you huge sums of money to look after my interests and right now I feel like you don't even care what DCI Travis is trying to do to me,' Gloria said in a 'poor little me' voice. She listened briefly to the lawyer before again holding the phone towards Anna.

'We will be making an official complaint to the Commissioner about your behaviour. You are attempting to tarnish my good family name and there will be severe repercussions.'

Anna took the phone from Gloria and held it down by her side so that Holme could not hear her reply.

'Which family name would that be, Gloria ... Rediker, Alleyne, Lynne or maybe even Peters?' Anna said before lifting the phone to speak to Mr Holme. On hearing the name Peters, the look of anger on Gloria's face intensified. Anna's line of attack, by dropping subtle hints, was having the desired effect. She could see that Gloria wanted to scream at her and demand answers, but any reaction might backfire on her. Anna knew that she was holding the loaded dice, as Gloria didn't have a clue how much she knew, or what she would reveal to Aisa and, more importantly, what Aisa might reveal to Anna.

Anna revelled in the moment, watching Gloria's eyes blazing with anger as she pressed her manicured hands together with a slow wringing motion that appeared to calm her. Gradually she turned towards her daughter, who was still sitting in the car, and an utterly scornful expression drew her red lips down in a thin scowl. Aisa turned her head a fraction and shifted her eyes sideways, as if trying to look without being seen, but unable to avoid her mother's contemptuous stare she quickly bowed her head again. It was more than obvious to Anna that Aisa was not just afraid of her mother, but terrified.

Gloria stormed off into the house, pushing her way past Barbara and Dan Ross. Noticing that Barbara was about to pass comment on Gloria's behaviour, Anna held her finger up and touched her lips to indicate to her sergeant to say nothing. The more buttons Anna alone could press to up the ante on Gloria the better.

Ian Holme had been waiting on the line throughout this altercation and Anna now told him that Aisa was at Lynne House with them and she would be taken to Belgravia Police Station when the search of the premises had been completed. She decided to reveal to Mr Holme some snippets of information she suspected Aisa had already told Gloria, or Gloria already knew of long before Aisa's arrest. Anna informed him that she had uncovered evidence that suggested Josh had had an affair with Aisa, who had left the Charity Ball to visit him at his flat the night he died, and had also stolen money from the Lynne Foundation.

Holme was surprisingly calm in his reply: 'So you now think Aisa and Donna were both involved in Joshua's death?'

'For what it's worth, Mr Holme, I have always been an advocate of Donna's innocence, but as you know, I don't make the decision as to whether or not someone should be charged.'

'Agreed, but I hope you will speak up if you have evidence that suggests Donna is innocent.'

'You have my word on that, Mr Holme,' Anna said.

She was surprised he didn't ask her more questions about the evidence against Aisa, and suspected that the lawyer was becoming slightly annoyed with Gloria's attitude and derogatory remarks.

'When do you anticipate being ready for interview, DCI Travis?' Holme asked.

'As I'm sure you appreciate, Mr Holme, it will take me some time to complete my search of Lynne House and no doubt you will want some disclosure of the evidence against Aisa.'

Mr Holme asked if she would be conducting an interview later that day but Anna was keen to hold Aisa overnight without interview, the main reason being she wanted her to realize the seriousness of her situation and to make Gloria sweat longer and push her even closer to boiling point. Anna told Mr Holme that, apart from the search and preparing disclosure, she also needed to take Aisa's fingerprints and DNA for examination at the forensic lab.

'Fine, DCI Travis, I will speak with Aisa on the phone and explain why she is being held overnight. Then if I attend Belgravia tomorrow at, say, ten a.m. for disclosure first, followed by a discussion with my client then interview . . .'

'That will be fine, Mr Holme,' Anna said, totally surprised by his compliant attitude and suddenly wondering if he was up to something and his calmness was a lull before the storm.

While the second POLSA team dealt with the search in the sweltering greenhouse Anna decided to check out Aisa's bedroom. She went over to the unmarked car and from her laptop bag retrieved two printouts of Aisa at the ball, one taken early evening and one after midnight.

Anna opened the rear passenger door and told Dewar to stretch her legs whilst she took Aisa upstairs with Barolli, Barbara and Dan Ross to search her bedroom. Dewar's nose was really out of joint; she was furious at the way Anna had dominated the investigation without having the manners to even brief her on her return to London.

As Anna got Aisa out of the car she could see that the young woman was in a very tense nervous state and physically shaking. In some ways, Anna felt bad about the way she was treating her, but it was a case of needs must if her plan was going to work.

Aisa led them upstairs, through the house to where large wooden double doors opened into a huge bedroom. Barbara stood wide-eyed and remarked that it was bigger than the whole of her upstairs. It was different from the period style of the rest of the house, where there were dark oak panelled walls, wooden floors and oriental rugs. This was a very modern room that had been specifically designed for Aisa, with a marble en-suite bath-room-come-wet room and walk-in wardrobes. The walls and ceilings were white, with fresh Egyptian bed linen on a king-size bed that was adorned with small pink cushions.

Anna showed Aisa the two pictures taken at the Charity Ball. 'You wore two different dresses the night of the ball. This yellow one you were wearing earlier in the evening, I've just looked through your wardrobe and it does not appear to be there. Can you tell me where it is now?'

'I got sick over it when I was feeling ill. I'd taken about three dresses with me to the hotel so I changed before going back downstairs,' Aisa said.

'You haven't answered my question. Where is the dress now?'

'I don't know – I threw it away, I think.'

'Did your mother know you were sick on the dress?' Anna asked.

'No, I never told her,' Aisa said.

'That's strange, your mother checked on you a few times yet you didn't you tell her about being sick on the dress?'

'No, I don't think I did. I mean, what is all this about a fuck-ing evening dress? I put it in the bath to soak,' Aisa said, becoming more and more distressed.

'You never tried to have it dry-cleaned, you just threw it away?' Anna persisted and Aisa nodded. 'Tell me what it cost,' Anna asked, interested to see Aisa's reaction.

The young woman paused, swallowed and shrugged her shoulders.

'We can easily check the cost, so why don't you just tell me now?'

'Nearly three thousand pounds, it was a—'

Anna interrupted, looking Aisa in the eye. 'Three thousand and you just slung it out because of vomiting on it?'

Aisa pursed her lips, turning away, and said nothing but Anna continued. 'So, you went back downstairs to the ball in a different gown. Correct?'

Aisa nodded.

'And you spoke with your mother?' Again the young woman nodded. 'Who never even asked you why you were in a different dress?' Aisa made no reply, clenching her hands into fists, her body rigid as she stared at the floor. Plainly, any mention of her mother and the dress in the same sentence was having a nerve-racking effect on her. Anna knew she was lying and it could only be because the dress was bloodstained and Gloria saw it that night.

Anna caught a movement out of the corner of her eye by the bedroom door; she turned and saw Lady Lynne standing on the landing. She was completely still, her face ashen, but her blazing eyes and red-slashed lips made her appear like the wicked Queen from *Snow White*. Anna gave her a friendly smile. 'Ah, Lady Lynne, I wonder if you could help me with a small dilemma? It's about Aisa's evening dress, the one she wore the night of the ball. It seems to have gone missing—'

Gloria interrupted, giving Anna a long icy stare: 'Listen to me, Detective Travis, I am under no obligation to answer any of your questions and neither is my daughter. Do you understand, Aisa? You do not say a word until you have legal advice and representation from Ian Holme.'

'Sorry, I just thought it was a simple question that would have a simple explanation,' Anna said, keeping her smile in place.

Gloria made a dismissive gesture with her hand. 'You may continue the search of these premises without me. If you take anything, please give Katrina a full list. Aisa, do you understand, darling? Ian Holme told me to advise you to say nothing. I'm going to see him now and he will visit you at the station later.'

Aisa nodded like a naughty child, her fists still clenched, her arms stiff at her sides. Gloria walked out, and they could hear her aloof sarcastic tone as she addressed someone on the stairs. 'Please walk back down. It is very unlucky to cross someone on the stairs. Thank you.'

Anna watched from the window as Gloria stormed out of the house, got into her Bentley and sped off down the driveway, churning up the gravel as she accelerated away.

'Not very caring about you, is she? Your mother seems to be more concerned about how all this affects her rather than you,' Anna said, wanting Aisa to turn against her mother and tell the truth.

Aisa's bottom lip trembled and her fear was obvious. Gloria's total lack of any genuine signs of attachment or care for her daughter was chilling. As if in confirmation of what Anna was thinking, Aisa gave her a strange glance, hands uncurling from the tight fists, and then she smiled, showing her neat even white teeth.

'I've remembered it was a Stella McCartney evening dress. I like her designs but it was nothing special.'

Chapter Thirty-Three

It was after three p.m. by the time Anna and Barolli arrived at the Belgravia station with Aisa. Dewar had also accompanied them, having complained that she felt frustrated at having nothing worthwhile to do at Lynne House. Anna had left Barbara in charge of the remainder of the search of Gloria's property but had never really expected to find anything of evidential value. She suspected that Gloria would never be so naïve as to keep anything that would incriminate her, and even if she did, it would be very well hidden and could take an eternity to find on such vast premises.

Barolli, assisted by Dewar, booked Aisa in at the custody desk then took a saliva sample from her for DNA and a set of fingerprints on the live scan machine. Anna told the custody officer that other than a phone conversation with Mr Holme, Aisa was not to be allowed to talk to anyone else. She then asked Barolli and Dewar to take the set of keys that were recovered from Samuel Peters' property at the mortuary and see if they fitted Josh's old Bayswater flat and the locks taken from Esme's flat.

Anna went upstairs and handed Joan Aisa's mobile phone.

'It's nice to see you again so quickly, ma'am, but such a shame that you've had to miss out on the FBI course, or are you just back with us for a few days . . .?'

'It's nice to see you too, Joan, but I haven't got time to discuss the FBI course right now.'

Joan looked flustered. 'Oh, right, sorry. What can I do for you?'

'I need you to get someone from Tech Support to look at Aisa's mobile for an application called Cate and also to do the same on the copy they kept of Josh Reynolds' SIM and micro-card.'

'Who's Cate?'

'Not a she, it's a phone application. Acronym for Call and Text Eraser and commonly used by unfaithful partners,' Anna explained.

'Whatever will they think of next?' Joan remarked, shaking her head, as her desk phone rang. It was Pete Jenkins wanting to speak to Anna.

'Hi, Pete. I arrested Aisa Lynne and her prints are now on the database and her DNA is on its way to you.'

'Do you ever stop for breath?' he asked. 'Okay, I'm bringing up Aisa's prints on the computer right now.'

'Only to speak with you, Pete. Any more good news for me?'

'Yeah, we still had a blood sample in the lab for Samuel Peters from when he was an unidentified body. I've run an initial test and there's a trace of atropine, but I've more tests to do yet.'

Anna was pleased that it was more evidence in support of her theory that Gloria Lynne had more than likely extracted poison from her own plants to poison Reynolds and Samuel.

'What sort of dosages of atropine are we looking at?' she asked.

'It's impossible to determine accurately. Josh Reynolds, being much younger and fitter, would react more slowly, but the initial symptoms would be the same as Barolli and Marisha suffered. A sudden lethal dose is not the best way to poison someone as people ask questions if you sip a drink and keel over instantly. It's better to go slowly but surely, leading to a heart attack and no questions asked.'

'So Gloria knew exactly what she was doing,' Anna remarked.

'Looks that way.'

'Thanks, Pete, and keep me updated.'

'If you want to hang on a minute or two I'm checking Aisa's prints against unidentified marks as we speak.'

'Yeah, sure.'

There was a short pause before Pete continued, 'Right, here we go. Majority of the fingerprints on the Ferrari match Aisa and Josh Reynolds and none for Donna.'

'And the money recovered from Esme's?' Anna asked.

'Sorry but no. I'm still working on the certificates recovered from Samuel Peters' jacket, and so far I've only found Josh Reynolds' and Samuel Peters' fingerprints. However, the other good news is that the blood spatter on the certificates did fit with them being on the sofa at the time the bullet exited Josh Reynolds' left temple.'

Anna hung up, slightly disappointed that Aisa's fingerprints hadn't been found on the certificates, particularly the one referring to her as Aisa Alleyne. This would have meant that she had physically held and most probably looked at it, and to then deny any knowledge of the document would be a blatant lie. It puzzled Anna why Aisa claimed she was adopted when the certificate made it clear she was Gloria's natural daughter; it was something she would need to raise at the interview in the morning.

Heading into her office, Anna got out the folder that Jane, the secretary at the Lynne Foundation, had given her containing the records of Aisa's mobile phone. She immediately noticed that there were a number of calls to Josh Reynolds' mobile, which started at the end of August and increased in intensity until his death. Anna suspected these calls added up to a secret affair and was not surprised to see there were a number of calls from Aisa to Josh on the fifth of November.

Aisa had called him for two minutes just before the Charity Ball started and then again at 9 p.m. and 10.15 p.m., which was just after she must have left the Savoy Hotel in Donna's Mini. From that time on she never phoned Josh's mobile again and, for Anna, there could be only one explanation. Aisa knew Josh was dead and might even have been present when he died.

Significantly, Anna also noticed that there were calls to Josh from Aisa on the days of the illegal transfers of money from the

CCS Medical account, and on the same day as the payment for the blue Ferrari was sent. Anna cross-checked Donna's appointment records, and confirmed Donna was out of the office when the online transactions were made. The evidence was accumulating against Aisa in a most satisfying way; Anna could see that if the young woman did choose to lie there was plenty of hard evidence to hit her with and hopefully convince her that she was only digging a deeper hole for herself.

Anna's reflections were interrupted by a text from Barolli who told her that he had tested Esme's Chubb and Yale locks against the keys from Samuel's property and they fitted perfectly, and he was now on his way with Dewar to Bayswater and Reynolds' flat.

Opening her office door, Anna called out to Joan to ask if she had a copy of the text messages recovered from Josh's mobile. Joan brought over a folder.

'I've also got details of all the calls made from Marisha Peters' landline and mobile, including cell site analysis, going back to July last year. I don't know how you do it, but yet again, your hunch was right,' Joan said. 'Calls were made to Gloria Lynne's house and mobile from Marisha's landline and mobile on more than one occasion.'

'How did you get Gloria Lynne's mobile number?' Anna asked, worried that Joan had obtained it by improper means.

'Off Aisa's phone, which you gave me earlier – just looked in contacts and found one for Mum and then checked it off against Marisha's calls.'

'Brilliant, Joan. At last we have a tangible connection between Samuel Peters and Gloria Lynne. Can you get me details of all the calls from both Gloria's house and mobile phone for the same period and do a cross-comparison?' Anna asked.

'As you have arrested Aisa, the authority to check outgoing landline calls from Lynne House goes without saying as she lives there. But Gloria's mobile will need at least a DCS's authority,' Joan reminded her.

Anna never ceased to be amazed by Joan's desire to please and help and decided that she'd recommend her for promotion when the case was over.

'Put Langton's name on the request.'

Joan looked surprised. 'Are you sure? He's not even in the country!'

'He will be by tomorrow morning and he's already sanctioned my actions, but please don't tell anyone, it's strictly between us.'

Joan nodded and Anna continued, 'Now tell me more about your good work with the phone calls.'

'Obviously, there were also calls from Marisha's phones to Josh's landline and mobile so I've highlighted those in red and any calls to Gloria in blue,' Joan informed her.

'Well they had to be from Samuel because according to Marisha she and Josh hadn't spoken for fifteen years.'

Anna looked closely at the Marisha Peters' landline list, noticing that the first call made to Gloria's house phone was one week after all the online requests for certified copies of marriage and birth certificates were made to the Jamaican Registrar General's office.

'Once Samuel got the certificates he could, as I am damned sure he did, start to blackmail Gloria,' Anna observed.

'That bit makes sense, but why does Gloria kill Marisha months after Samuel? Why not silence them at the same time if she was involved?' Joan asked.

Anna explained to Joan that she suspected there were different strands of events, the first being the initial blackmail, which Marisha might or might not have been party to, but even if she had been, Gloria could well have had no knowledge of her involvement as Samuel would have done all the talking. Anna had also considered the possibility that Gloria thought Samuel and Marisha would drink the rum together and, having heard nothing from either of them since, thought her evil deed was done. Joan wondered why Marisha had not contacted Gloria since Samuel disappeared. Anna told her she thought it was probably a mixture of things, but predominantly fear that whatever had happened to Samuel might happen to her, and no doubt Marisha didn't want to lose the forty thousand in the freezer.

Anna studied the numbers dialled from Marisha's mobile phone and pointed out that the next call recorded to Gloria's mobile phone was at 10 a.m. on 5 November 2012.

'A month passes with no calls to Gloria, then out of the blue there's one the day Josh dies and the cell site is by Marisha's flat. I believe this was a further blackmail attempt on Gloria by Samuel, but this time she chose to ignore it.'

'Why do you think she ignored it?' Joan asked.

'Because Samuel went to the Trojan and Josh was very upset after speaking to him. He told Marcus Williams he had business to attend to, and I think he went to see Gloria as he then knew she was his real mother. Samuel told Josh the truth to spite Gloria.'

'So Samuel got paid off first time round in October, but got greedy and wanted more?' Joan asked, to make sure she understood Anna's logic.

'Yes. He pushed his luck and Gloria killed him, made sure he'd never come back,' Anna added.

Joan nodded and pointed to the list of Marisha's mobile calls. 'Calls were made to Josh's mobile at midday, four fifteen p.m., then also between seven p.m., and nine p.m., but all very brief.'

'It has to be Samuel making the calls and not Marisha,' Anna said. 'Here's one to Gloria at eleven forty p.m. for two minutes. We know Josh was probably dead by then . . .'

She hurriedly flicked through the pages to look at the cell site location for the call.

'The mobile phone mast is right next to Josh's flat in Bayswater – this can't be pure coincidence! Samuel must have seen Aisa leave Josh's flat, went in using the keys Josh gave him and found his body, so he's straight on the phone to Gloria and making further blackmail demands,' Anna deduced.

'But why did Gloria answer her mobile if it was Samuel?' Joan asked, putting a slight dampener on Anna's excitement.

Anna thought about Joan's question. 'Because she did go

upstairs to check on Aisa, who she thought was ill, but as Aisa was not there. Gloria must have wondered where on earth she'd gone.'

Joan, puzzled, told Anna that she didn't follow her reasoning. Anna reminded her that CCTV clearly showed Samuel turning up at the Savoy just before ten p.m. and then the Mini leaving just after.

'We suspect Aisa was in the Mini. Samuel doesn't drive so Aisa would have got to Josh's long before Samuel did.'

'Right, I get you, so you are saying that he arrived at Josh's as Aisa was leaving. But why did Samuel go back to the Savoy?' Joan asked.

It was irritating that Joan couldn't grasp what to Anna was the obvious, but then she had to acknowledge that Joan didn't have the same detailed knowledge of the case as her. Anna also realized how much of what Don Blane had deduced looked to be spot-on.

'Samuel went to see Gloria, probably desperate to get more money out of her,' Anna said.

'Gloria must have been terrified of a confrontation in front of hundreds of her high society friends,' Joan remarked.

'Exactly, so if he demanded more money she'd probably offer him some outrageous amount just to get rid of him. Samuel leaves and goes to Josh's. Gloria had to have been really flustered, she goes upstairs to calm herself and checks on Aisa who, surprise, surprise, is not there.'

Joan clapped her hands together, impressed with Anna's logic.

Anna banged her hand on the desk in realization that more pieces of the puzzle were fitting into place about what actually happened on the night of Josh's death.

'That's it! That explains the stupid suicide note; Gloria's control over Samuel is his greed. God, she's a quick thinker, she must have known instantly how to use him to her advantage even under immeasurable pressure. She is the archetypal Ice Queen.'

Joan was again confused but Anna was on a high. 'I am sort of following but—'

'Joan, listen to me: even if Samuel thought it was a suicide, seeing Aisa leave was a powerful blackmail tool to use against Gloria. Finding the money in Josh's already open safe was a bonus.'

Joan was still unsure, but Anna was adamant.

'Within minutes of seeing Aisa then finding the dead Josh, Samuel was on the phone to Gloria. She couldn't speak with Aisa at that time as she was on her way back to the Savoy. Gloria couldn't really tell Samuel to piss off. But what she could do is offer him even more money to make sure it looked like a suicide, thus Samuel stupidly wrote the suicide note.'

'And with Samuel out of the way and Josh's death declared a suicide Gloria thought she was in the clear,' Joan said, understanding.

'Yes, yes, exactly. I suspect Gloria paid Samuel off the next day. She needed to get close to poison him, and she laced the rum that was already in Marisha's flat.'

Anna put her hands behind her head, sat back in her chair, took a deep breath in and let it all out again. 'Samuel started a catastrophic chain of events on the afternoon of the fifth of November by telling Josh that he was his real father and Gloria his mother. It led to Josh's and eventually his own death.'

She took another deep breath, and skimmed through all Marisha's mobile calls again. 'My God, there are also text messages from Marisha's mobile to Gloria's. Can you—'

Joan interrupted: 'Already on it and legally the provider is supposed to keep sent texts for two years.'

'Joan, I wish I had a whole team made up of clones of you, we'd solve everything in no time.'

'Even I wouldn't wish that on me,' Joan said, leaving the room.

Anna knew that the results of calls and texts made from Gloria's phones would be crucial to her argument that the woman should be arrested and interviewed for the murder of Samuel Peters. Josh's death was a different matter. Anna was certain Gloria had somehow poisoned him, probably hoping he would crash his car, but he had survived. It would seem the atropine, and Samuel's revelations, had caused Josh's delusional state of mind, which resulted in him taking his own life. Gloria had loaded the gun but never actually pulled the trigger. Attempted murder by poison wasn't good enough for Anna – she wanted the arrogant socialite Lady Gloria Lynne hanged, drawn and quartered for the misery she had brought to so many people.

So, though elated, Anna still felt uneasy. Gloria held the keys that could unlock the answers to so many unexplained questions, but she would never give them up, not even if her own life depended on it. Gloria was manipulative, controlling and an expert liar who had always got her own way, sometimes through charm, but mostly by deceit. No matter which way Anna looked at the problem, it would always come back to how much Aisa knew and whether she would be willing to incriminate her mother. Anna decided that before she left the station to go home she would visit Aisa in her cell, not to interview her, but rather to impress on her exactly why she had been arrested and the seriousness of her situation.

Just at that moment her mobile rang and she could see from the caller identification that it was Mike Lewis. She'd totally forgotten to call him and could have kicked herself, she knew he'd be upset and quite rightly so.

'Hi, Mike, I'm really sorry, I meant to phone you earlier—' Anna started to explain but Mike was quick to interrupt her.

'Langton called me so I know exactly why you came back, but that's not the issue right now – your arresting Aisa is.'

Anna jumped in: 'I've plenty of evidence to justify her arrest if that's what you're wondering.'

'Would you just shut up and listen?' Mike snapped. Anna realized something else must have upset him. She apologized and said she was listening.

'Walters has just been screaming down the phone at me, wanting to know why the hell you arrested Aisa Lynne. I'm sorry, Anna, but you left me in the dark so I had to tell him I hadn't a clue what he was talking about.'

'I'm sorry, Mike. I should have called you ages ago. Has Gloria been complaining again?' she said, trying to make light of the situation, but Mike was not impressed.

'Ten out of ten for fucking observation, Anna. Where are you right now?' he asked in a raised voice.

'In my office, are you on your way over?' Anna asked.

'No, but I think Walters may be. He's in a foul mood and baying for blood. So I'd hide somewhere, if I were you.'

'Thanks, Mike, I'll get Joan to say I'm out and meet with you and Langton tomorrow to discuss everything,' Anna said as she hurriedly hid her briefcase behind the sofa.

'Look, I'm keeping well out of it and have agreed to hand the reins back to Langton to oversee the Reynolds case.'

'If I were in your shoes, I'd be doing the same,' Anna said, slinging her handbag over her shoulder.

'Langton's on your side and I understand why you suspect Lady Lynne, but for God's sake make sure you have the evidence to back your actions up,' Mike warned.

'Believe me, I'm working on it as fast as I can, and it's the last thing I need Walters to know about at the moment.' But as Anna ended the call she heard a bellow from behind her.

'I fear you're a bit late, DCI Travis!'

Anna recognized the voice of Deputy Commissioner Walters and turned towards the door, to find she had not made her escape in time.

'You'd better have some bloody good answers because right now your career is hanging by a thread!' he said, standing in the doorway in full uniform, with a look of thunder and contempt on his face. Grimly, Anna reflected that she only had herself to blame for her current predicament, and now was the time to try and dig herself out of one of the biggest holes she had ever been in. As she put her handbag down on the desk she thought of Gloria Lynne and her unerring instinct for self-preservation. Unseen by Walters, she placed her hand inside her bag and removed her Dictaphone, surreptitiously turning it on and casually placing it in her inside jacket pocket.

'Would you like a coffee or tea, sir, I'll get Joan to—'

'Shut up and sit down!' Walters said, pointing to the armchair in the corner of the room. Anna knew he was in no mood for pleasantries and was so fidgety he was unlikely to sit down himself.

'Would you not like an armchair too, sir, they're more comfortable than the sofa,' Anna said with a deliberately serene voice.

'Right now I'd prefer to look down on you, Travis, as the insubordinate officer that you clearly are,' Walters said scathingly.

'I'm sorry, sir, but insubordinate, I don't know what you're referring to.'

'Don't play games with me, Travis. I've had the Commissioner breathing down my neck, YET AGAIN, because of your fucking gung ho attitude. I also had to call Lady Lynne and listen to her complain about your aggressive behaviour, for which I had to apologize on your behalf, YET AGAIN.'

Anna would have loved to rebuke Walters for apologizing to Gloria but knew she couldn't. 'I'm sorry, sir, I didn't mean for that to happen.'

'Sorry is not good enough. Who was that you were on the phone to a moment ago?' Walters demanded to know.

'My course instructor at the FBI Academy, sir. I was just telling him how disappointed you would be when you found out I'd come back to London,' Anna said, knowing that it was a rather feeble answer.

'Then tell me, Travis, why have you thrown the opportunity of a lifetime away? An opportunity, I might remind you, that but for me you would never have had,' Walters said condescendingly.

'I was made aware of information while I was in Quantico that Donna Reynolds was not responsible for the murder of her husband.'

'And what information was that, Travis?' Walters asked with a cynical smile.

'That her sister Aisa Lynne was involved, sir,' Anna said, trying to avoid a lengthy answer.

He stamped his foot on the floor. 'You really are trying my patience, and believe me I can have you directing traffic in the blink of an eye. Now answer my bloody question!' he bellowed.

Anna paused while she thought about how much she should give away in an attempt to appease him, but at the same time she also wanted him to keep losing his composure.

Joan, who had been listening outside, had just received an e-mail from Tech Support that they had found the Cate app on Josh's phone and had attached the list of dates, times and contents of all texts he sent and received. Realizing Anna needed something to keep Walters at bay, she knocked on the office door.

'I'm busy with DCI Travis so get out now!' Walters barked at Joan, who nevertheless handed Anna the documents.

'Sorry, sir, urgent documents DCI Travis ordered proving Aisa Lynne's affair,' Joan said and mouthed the word 'Cate' to Anna.

Anna could have hugged her. 'I have uncovered irrefutable evidence, in the way of text messages from Josh Reynolds' mobile, that he was having an affair with Aisa Lynne. On the night of his death, she went to his flat to see him, possibly because he had ended their affair by phone earlier in the evening.' Anna handed the Cate texts to Walters to read. He grabbed them out of her hand and flicked through the pages, skim-reading them, as Anna continued, 'I also have evidence that proves Aisa Lynne stole money from the Lynne Foundation for Josh Reynolds' benefit.' She handed him the documents that Aisa's secretary had given her and for the first time Walters sat down as he read through them.

Anna decided to keep going, waffling on about Aisa making the fraudulent transfers of monies from the CCS Medical Trust to Josh Reynolds and the purchase of a Ferrari.

'You'd better not be bullshitting me, Travis!'

'As you can see, it's all there in the documents, sir.'

Walters paused as he looked at the papers again. 'I suppose this does merit the arrest and questioning of Aisa Lynne.'

'Thank you, sir. I fear Lady Lynne got a little excited and somewhat exaggerated the circumstances of Aisa's arrest.'

'You need to learn, Travis, that when the likes of Lady Lynne start to warble, cages get rattled, in the highest of places. There was no need for you to take her daughter back to Lynne House to search the premises, you—'

'Yes, sir, I accept that now but—'

Walters pointed his finger at her. 'Shut up, Travis. You wanted to get her back for last time and wind her up, didn't you? Admit it.'

Anna knew she couldn't reveal there was method in her madness for fear of Walters wanting chapter and verse on why she suspected Gloria Lynne of murder. 'Sir, Aisa Lynne had lied to my officers, she made herself a suspect in a murder inquiry.'

'Tell me, do you think Joshua Reynolds was murdered by Aisa Lynne?'

Anna sighed as she decided to give Walters a reasonably honest answer. 'On the balance of probabilities, I'd say that Josh Reynolds was depressed, under the influence of drink and drugs, and shot himself with his own gun. I think Aisa Lynne was in the room at the time and lied so the charity fraud and her affair with Josh would not be discovered.' She was reluctant to say the drug was a poison called atropine as she still awaited Pete Jenkins' full results. She was however caught out by Walters' next question.

'Why have you been interested in an unidentified body at Fulham mortuary?' Walters asked.

Anna wondered how he knew about that visit.

'Sorry, sir, what mortuary was that ...?'

Walters continued in a sarcastic vein: 'Within hours of returning to London, not only did you piss off Lady Lynne, the Commissioner and ME, but also Dr Harrow, who complained to the Coroner, who ... guess what?'

'Phoned you, sir?'

'At last you got something right, Travis,' Walters said with a mocking smile. 'The Coroner also mentioned that you were spouting off and accusing Harrow of missing some poison called atropen.'

'Atropine, sir. The unidentified body is that of Samuel Peters, he was related to Josh Reynolds and died of a heart attack. I was winding Dr Harrow up about the atropine. I also believe Samuel Peters stole large sums of money from Josh,' Anna said.

'You're a laugh a minute, aren't you, Travis? My days would be so boring without you having your bit of fun and upsetting everyone along the way. Let me get this right: you started with a suicide, which became a murder, and now you think it's a suicide again.'

'Yes, sir,' Anna replied.

Walters shook his head in bewilderment and glared at her. 'There's something you aren't telling me, Travis. This doesn't all add up and by God you'd better not be fucking with me!'

Anna said nothing at first, fully aware that by lying to Walters she would be digging herself into a bigger hole and possibly ruining her career. She could argue that she had been economical with the truth, but in reality she knew that she had gone beyond the point of no return. She could not at present reveal everything she suspected about Samuel and Gloria to Walters as she still lacked any substantial evidence and feared that he would terminate her involvement in the case for being underhand. More than anything, she knew she needed Langton's help if she wanted to arrest Gloria Lynne and have someone to defend her actions to Walters.

'I don't know what more to say than I'm sorry, sir, and assure you it won't happen again,' Anna said sheepishly, deliberately eating humble pie.

Walters came closer and closer to Anna, until their noses were almost touching. 'It better not, Travis, or let me assure you, I will destroy your bloody career. You have become too much like Langton – disrespectful and belligerent – and that is something I will not tolerate.'

Anna knew he was being deadly serious as he headed towards the door. How she hated this man for duping her and destroying Langton's prospects of promotion. In one impulsive moment she decided to chance her luck.

'Have you heard from DCS Langton, sir? I deliberately avoided him before I left for Quantico – he was being very offhand with me.'

Walters stopped, turned and looked at Anna. 'Personally, I don't care if I never see or hear of Langton again, Travis, and neither should you if you know what's good for you.'

Anna nodded her head as if in agreement with Walters, knowing she had touched a nerve. 'I think he may have found out that I spoke with you about his part in the Fitzpatrick case and because of me he didn't make Commander.' Walters laughed with an air of scorn.

'Well, if it's any consolation, Travis, you didn't exactly grass him up, as they say. I was a tad duplicitous in getting out of you what I already suspected, but let me assure you his destiny was in my hands, not yours, so don't lose any sleep over it.'

'Thank you, sir, I won't, and I shall avoid Langton when he comes back to London,' Anna lied and Walters smirked.

'The Met's having to implement five hundred million pounds of budget cuts as part of the Coalition's austerity measures. One chief superintendent costs the equivalent of three constables, so you do the maths, Travis, and tell me who's going to be culled first,' Walters said as he opened the door.

'A chief superintendent,' Anna said, feigning pleasure in her answer.

'Called Langton,' Walters said and walked off with a strutting conceit.

'Arrogant prick,' Anna muttered to herself as she put her hand in her pocket and switched off her Dictaphone.

Anna took the *Gardeners' World* magazine with her when she went down to the cells to see Aisa, where she impressed upon the custody officer that due to the sensitive nature of the case

Aisa was not to be allowed any visitors. Anna quietly pulled back the sliding viewing hatch to look at the suspect, who was sitting on the plastic mattress of a hardwood bench. She had wrapped the blue cell blanket round her, but was shivering. The custody officer opened the door for Anna, who said she would only be a few minutes. Anna could see that Aisa's new environment was having the desired effect and decided it was time to take a softer approach. She went to sit down beside Aisa, who moved a few inches away as if intimidated by Anna's presence.

'Mr Holme told me not to say anything to you until he is here to represent me,' Aisa said, attempting to appear curt but failing.

'You don't have to take his advice, but you have to make your own choice about whether or not to tell me the truth,' Anna said, leaning forward to make eye contact with the young woman, who turned her head away.

Anna knew that inwardly Aisa was scared. 'Do you want to talk to me, Aisa – is there something you want to tell me?' she asked in a calm voice.

'My mother also told me I was to say nothing to you without Mr Holme being present.'

'I know Mr Holme will be acting in your best interests, Aisa, but as for your mother, well . . .'

Aisa suddenly turned and looked at Anna. 'What do you mean?'

The distress in her voice at the mention of her mother was all too plain. 'What do you think I mean, Aisa?'

'I don't know. Please can I go home and then come back in the morning for the interview?' Aisa pleaded.

'I'm sorry, Aisa, that's not allowed as you are a suspect in a murder inquiry.'

The look on Aisa's face at the mention of the word murder was one of devastation. 'I swear, Detective Travis, I didn't kill Josh. I loved him and he was going to leave Donna so we could be together.'

'I don't doubt that, Aisa, but now you're in the police station I'm not allowed to ask you questions without Mr Holme being present.'

'Then why are you here?'

'Before I go, Aisa, you need to understand that when I interview you I can only help you if you tell me the truth. If you lie for yourself, or anyone else for that matter, you will only make things worse and could find yourself charged with very serious offences.'

Aisa met Anna's gaze and nodded as she spoke. Her eyes were swollen with tears, she chewed her bottom lip and Anna had a feeling that she might at last be getting through to her.

'Has my mother phoned?' Aisa asked.

Anna lifted the blue blanket up around Aisa's shoulders in a comforting manner. 'Not as far as I am aware. Do you want me to call her for you?' she asked kindly.

Aisa hurriedly looked away. 'No, it's okay, I'm sure she will contact Mr Holme.'

Anna saw the opportunity to dig a little: 'I know you're adopted and may think that Gloria doesn't care for you like a real mum would, but I think she does.'

Anna tried to make eye contact to gauge Aisa's reaction but she just stared at the floor. Anna thought it strange that the young woman didn't pass comment and she suspected Aisa must have discovered the truth, but still couldn't understand why Gloria would tell her she was adopted.

She moved on. 'Your mother is upset because she's just a bit confused by all that's happening, just like you must be.'

Aisa began to cry. 'My mother doesn't get confused, she gets angry when she thinks we've let the family name down.'

'What does she do when she gets angry, Aisa?'

Trembling, Aisa looked at the floor. It was as if Gloria was in the cell staring at her, warning her to keep quiet.

'Nothing, she does nothing. Please, I want you to leave me alone now,' Aisa said, and wiped her eyes on the blanket.

'It's up to you, Aisa, but remember, you don't have to be

scared any more. If you tell the truth, I can protect you from anyone,' Anna said, but it seemed that Gloria's hold on Aisa was stronger than she had realized.

'Very well, Aisa, but there is one thing I'd ask you to think about very hard.'

Anna paused and waited until Aisa met her gaze. 'You and I both know your sister Donna is sitting in a prison cell charged with crimes she didn't commit. She didn't kill Josh, she didn't steal the money and whoever knows the truth about the night Josh died can save her. The least you owe Donna is the truth – or are you worried that your mother will be angry with you?' Anna asked. Aisa began crying uncontrollably and Anna knew she had made her point.

She stood up, got the *Gardeners' World* magazine out of her jacket pocket and threw it down nonchalantly next to Aisa. 'You've probably already been forced to read it by your ever-so-proud and distinguished mother, but if you haven't, it's an article about poisons by a very poisonous woman.'

Chapter Thirty-Four

After leaving Aisa, Anna started back to her office, now more than ready to collect her things and get home. She was so tired that as she walked through the corridor she suddenly had to lean against the wall to keep on her feet. It was as if a sledgehammer had hit her, as she acknowledged she had been firing on all cylinders and hadn't slept properly for two days. She called Barolli to ask if he would take her home, and found herself shaking as she told him she'd be waiting in the car park. Her head started to throb and she had what felt like a panic attack as the exhaustion, combined with jet lag, kicked in. She crouched down, resting against the wall by the station's staff entrance, in need of some fresh air, and thought she might faint. Barolli bent down to ask if she was all right.

'Just get me home, Paul, I've caved in.'

By the time Barolli dropped Anna at her flat it was almost seven. She felt so wiped out she couldn't even be bothered to unpack her suitcase, she just wanted to have a hot bath and relax. Her whole body ached and her headache was even worse; it was as if every ounce of energy had evaporated. She was desperate to speak to Don Blane and apologize for not calling earlier and tell him everything that had occurred in an unbelievably hectic day, but mostly to say how deeply she cared for and missed him. She looked at her watch and realized that it would be two p.m., meaning he would be in class teaching. She didn't want to interrupt him, but not being able to speak to him there and then made her feel even more miserable.

She sat wrapped in a towel as her bath filled, and without any warning she started crying. The tears were still falling as she lowered herself slowly into the hot bath, closed her eyes and wondered how on earth she was going to find the energy for the following morning. She knew she still had to prepare for the disclosure and interviews, and, feeling totally incapable of moving, she remained where she was, topping up with hot water for almost an hour until she forced herself to get out.

Wrapping herself in her big towelling dressing gown, Anna at last began to feel human. She made herself some toast and coffee and carried it to her bed where, propped up by pillows, she gradually felt her headache subside as she sipped her drink. But the depression persisted and yet again she started to cry, and it was a while before it dawned on her exactly what had taken place over the past twenty-four hours. The adrenalin rush of piecing together the new evidence against Gloria Lynne, her dressing-down by Walters, her obsession with the case had totally taken hold of her senses. She replayed in her mind her departure from Quantico, or more importantly how she had left Don Blane at the airport. She regretted her behaviour, and felt ashamed that she had hardly given a moment's thought to him and had failed to contact him. She had accepted his kindness, his advice, and he had managed to secure her a ticket and a flight back to London. She recalled how it had felt to be entwined in his arms as they made love. The u. expected had happened – she had believed it would be impossible to ever have such intimate feelings after the murder of Ken, but it had happened and now she felt disgusted that she had allowed her obsession with Gloria Lynne to interfere with their growing relationship.

It was only three p.m. in Quantico, so Anna decided to send Blane a text telling him that she had finished work and would ring him at six p.m. his time. She couldn't resist ending with a suggestive remark. 'Just stripped off for a hot bath, wish you were with me – if you were, what would you do?' Anna laughed like a mischievous teenager as she pressed Send. She suddenly felt much better and resolved that she wouldn't review the case notes again but that what she really needed was to sleep and rejuvenate herself. Her phone beeped and she was certain it was Don replying but disappointingly it was a message from Langton, saying he had secured a flight and would be back in London early Tuesday morning. Anna texted back that she looked forward to seeing him and had a lot to tell him about the case and specifically Walters.

Walters' overbearing conduct had obviously upset her, but she was glad that his sheer arrogance had led to him revealing the truth about his feelings for Langton. Anna believed that most of Walters' hatred was actually jealousy at all that Langton achieved in his long and highly decorated career. Langton was respected by his troops and had worked hard to get to where he was, was not afraid to speak his mind and he always got the job done. Walters on the other hand had never been what Langton would call a real detective. He had never headed up a murder investigation or any serious crime case, for that matter. Walters had driven his career forward through departments where his role was investigating police malpractice, or developing strategy and planning. As a streetwise cop he couldn't hold a candle to Langton. Walters had always been a yes man, who gladly trod on others to get to the top. But Anna now had the means by which Langton could secure his promotion to Commander.

Her phone beeped once more. Yet again it wasn't Don, but it was good news. Pete Jenkins had texted to say, 'Positive results all round – Samuel – Josh – spiced rum bottle all = ATROPINE!'

Anna took half a sleeping tablet and turned off her bedside light. She was feeling better, looking forward to the interview with Aisa, confident she could crack her, especially after their meeting in the cell. Anna knew that because Aisa had stolen money from a charity, which benefited the needy, it would not go down well with a judge and jury. Undoubtedly, if Aisa were to be found guilty it would result in a term of imprisonment and because of her wealthy background she would be constantly used and abused, by both the inmates and prison staff.

Anna felt herself becoming sleepy but still her mind wouldn't stop ticking. She feared that Gloria's hold over Aisa was even more powerful than she had imagined, but even if Ian Holme advised Aisa to make no comment, Anna knew that she still had a wealth of evidence that would allow her to pose some searching questions.

At last she fell into a deep sleep. Some time later she was woken by the sound of her mobile phone ringing. She had left in the kitchen, and by the time she got herself out of bed to answer it the caller had hung up. She recognized Blane's number and pressed recall.

'Hello?' It was a woman's voice and Anna was surprised, thinking she must have pressed the wrong number.

'I'm sorry, who is this?'

'Who's this?'

'I must have dialled a wrong number,' Anna said, about to hang up.

'Oh, is this Anna from England? It's Beth Jackson, from the course. I'll get Don for you.'

'Thanks,' Anna said, wondering what the hell Beth Jackson was doing answering Don's phone. It felt as if the rug had been pulled from beneath her feet as she desperately tried to calculate what time it was in the US. She almost put the phone down when she heard his familiar voice.

'Hey, you get back okay?'

'Yes, did you just ring me?'

'Yes, I wanted a catch-up, maybe talk a few things through with you.'

'Why did Beth Jackson answer your phone?' Anna asked with a sinking sensation in her stomach.

'I was getting an article for her to read for her case study. It's work, Anna.'

'Okay.' Anna wanted to believe him, but couldn't help having doubts. 'Was there any problem with the Academy Director about my leaving the course?' she asked hesitantly.

'You kidding? I told him how you helped solve the Mandy Anderson case, which absolutely blew him away. Then when I explained your reasons for returning to the UK, he was totally understanding and said you were welcome back to complete the course whenever you want.'

'That's very kind of him,' Anna said.

'He's also sending a letter of appreciation to your Commissioner.'

Anna felt both humbled and honoured, but what she really wanted to ask Don was if he and Beth were at the cabin.

'So, whatever happens, the good news is I will get to be with you for ten weeks when you come out on the next course.'

Anna heard that comment with mixed emotions; more than anything she wanted to be with Don Blane but she feared that he had lost no time in finding a replacement. She had instantly taken a dislike to Beth Jackson when they had met at the Academy and she couldn't help but think that Beth wanted more than just help on her case. However, Anna knew she was still very tired and was unsure if she was thinking clearly. She wanted to trust Don, and to believe that what they had started was real.

'It's been a really hectic time since I got back. Virtually everything you said has been right so far, but I wish you were here right now so we could bounce ideas off each other,' Anna said quietly, but couldn't help but feel there was a massive distance between them.

'I'm always here for you, Anna, twenty-four seven, you know that,' Blane said in his natural comforting way.

When Anna didn't reply he continued, 'What did you want to bounce off of me anyway?'

Anna gave a quick synopsis of all the developments since she had returned to London and Blane listened intently.

'You must be exhausted. I should let you get some sleep,'

Blane said, and Anna feared it was a ruse to avoid talking to her any further and get back to Beth Jackson.

'No, I'm fine. Do you need to go for some reason?' she asked, dreading a 'yes' answer.

'No, not at all, I'm really interested in everything.'

Somewhat relieved, Anna continued, 'I can prove an association between Samuel and Gloria by calls made from Marisha's house and mobile phones, the majority made during the day and night of Josh Reynolds' death.'

'Well done, you must be pleased.'

'Yes, but I'm still waiting for the results from Gloria's phones. If she was calling Marisha's numbers then she's slipped up and will have to answer some serious questions.' Anna grew edgy, as she was certain she could hear Beth Jackson in the background asking him something.

'So that's me up to date. How are things with you?' she asked.

Blane told Anna that after he left her at the airport he went back to the Academy to do some in-depth research on socio-paths and it was quite disturbing.

'I don't mean to put a downer on things, Anna, but you need to tread warily with Gloria.'

Anna detected concern in his voice. 'Don't worry, Don, after her performance today I think I've got the measure of her. She was taking the bait and reacting to it.'

'I don't want to sound negative but you need to understand that things may not be quite what they seem.'

'That's an understatement where Gloria's concerned, isn't it?' Anna countered, not quite sure what he was referring to.

'Gloria's reactions could be deliberate and she may actually be getting the measure of YOU,' Blane said seriously.

Anna was taken aback. 'Well thanks for the vote of confidence, Don. I appreciate your concern but you've never met Gloria and I have.'

Now he sounded irritated. 'That's the thing, Anna, I am concerned. You've only met Gloria twice and it's impossible to get the measure of someone like her that quickly.'

'Your words not mine, Don,' Anna retorted on impulse, then wished she hadn't.

He ignored her remark. 'I'm worried that you aren't fully aware of Gloria's capabilities. If she is as evil and cunning as—'

Anna exhaled loudly as she interrupted him again: 'Well there's no need to be, I'm a big girl and I can take care of myself.'

'Gloria Lynne has more than thirty years of sociopathic behaviour behind her, not to mention at least five murders, and she's never been suspected of anything, not even jaywalking,' Blane pointed out.

'Well that's all going to change because, as you would say, I'm about to hit the home run,' Anna said firmly.

He kept his composure as she defended her ground, not letting him get a word in:

'And another thing, Gloria even phoned the top brass to try and get me kicked off the investigation. I took some flak from Deputy Commissioner Walters, but I'm still on the case, so Lady bloody Lynne lost that battle as well,' Anna said angrily. She couldn't understand how Don could have been so supportive twenty-four hours ago and now he was giving her a lecture on how she should proceed with HER case, as if she didn't have a clue what she was dealing with.

Blane knew that Anna was overconfident after uncovering so much about Gloria Lynne in such a short space of time, imagining that she had Gloria exactly where she wanted her and was about to break her down. Blane's view was very different; he knew that Anna was dealing with a woman who was a mistress of deceit; Gloria Lynne possessed an intellectual cunning that was way beyond Anna's comprehension. Don didn't want to argue, he just wanted Anna to understand. He realized he would need to be more forceful.

'For God's sake, just bear with me and listen to what I have to say, and when I've finished, if you doubt or disagree with anything I've said, then fine. I understand and respect that it's your investigation and not mine.'

Anna took a deep breath, no longer in the mood to continue their conversation. 'I've got to go, Don, and maybe it's best we leave this discussion until later anyway.'

Blane was determined to get his point across. 'Fine, that's up to you, but I'm not the enemy here. Sociopaths like Gloria Lynne make up only five per cent of the population; the problem is they have perfected the art of manipulating the other ninety-five per cent and that includes the likes of you and me.'

'Very informative, Don, but—'

'Please have the decency to let me finish,' Don said in a slightly raised voice. 'I doubt Gloria was trying to get you kicked off the case – she wants to know what's going on, she needs to be the one who's in control and by controlling Walters she will ultimately control you.' Anna said nothing, reluctantly recognizing that it was in her best interest to listen.

'Walters is someone to be used for Gloria's own purpose; she will fake sincerity and friendship with him simply to find out what you're up to. Walters is nothing more than a disposable commodity who no doubt has already been invited to her next big Charity Ball.' Blane paused to let Anna take in what he was telling her.

'I'm listening,' she said quietly.

'Did you know that many sociopaths give huge sums of money to charity simply to enrich their power and reputations and to fool us into thinking they actually care?' Don said in a calmer tone of voice.

Anna realized that Blane was being honest and frank with her: there was no malice, he was just trying to be helpful.

She apologized for being edgy and blamed it on being woken up and the jet lag.

'Listen, I'm sorry too. I know I'm being aggressive about all this, but I just want to protect you. That's why I called, I was worried about you.'

'I know ...' Anna said, 'and honestly, I've taken on board everything you've said.'

Blane promised that he would e-mail her some of the articles he had found about sociopaths and said that there was one last suggestion he'd like to make where Gloria was concerned.

'I'm all ears,' Anna said.

'It's regarding Jessie Dewar,' Blane said hesitantly.

'What about her?' Anna asked.

'Look, she's the one studying for a PhD in Forensic Psychology, so sociopaths, control freaks and similar types are her bread and butter.'

'No way, Don, I can't let her near Gloria, not after what happened last time.'

'I appreciate that, but she understands those kinds of people, what they're really saying and the way into them. Sometimes you need to utilize the skills of others to succeed, even if you're not very fond of them.'

'All right, point made. I'll sit down with Dewar and prepare an interview strategy. I can also let her watch from the video viewing room so she can take notes and advise me when we take breaks,' Anna said, hoping she wouldn't regret it.

'Thanks, Anna, I know she can be a pain at times and you almost need to treat her a little like a sociopath herself.'

'What, use her and abuse her?' Anna asked humorously.

'No, tell her what she likes to hear, how wonderful she is, praise her and—'

'Quit while you're ahead, Don, I've already eaten enough humble pie for one day.'

'Well, good luck with it all. And please, like I said, be very wary of Gloria. She will already have many of the answers memorized in her head. Even if you think you've cornered her, she's cunning and she'll find a way out, and don't be fooled by any crocodile tears.'

'Thanks, Don. I'm sorry I snapped at you. I know you are only trying to help,' Anna sighed.

'Well that's what happens when you mix work with pleasure.'

Anna was unsure how to respond to him, knowing that in the past that very mix had been disastrous where Langton was concerned and she had ever since avoided making that mistake again, but she had believed that with Blane it might be different. There was an uneasy pause, before eventually he asked Anna to let him know how it all went, reminding her that even if Aisa remained silent, or refused to implicate her mother, that Marisha could also answer many of Anna's questions and hopefully bring Gloria Lynne down. Anna told him that Marisha was still in a coma and hospital tests had found atropine in her system, which had apparently brought on the heart attack.

'This may sound a bit OTT but if I were you I'd consider putting a police guard on Marisha,' Blane said.

'What, you think Gloria would go as far as to walk into the hospital and finish her off?'

'I wouldn't put anything past Lady Lynne. She may not do it herself but she sure as hell can afford someone who would,' he said seriously.

Anna swallowed. 'You're right, I'll organize for a uniform PC to sit with Marisha.' There was another awkward pause as both waited for the other to say something. Finally, Anna said she had to go, and he repeated that he was always available if she needed to talk.

'Thank you, and give my regards to Beth,' she said sarcastically. He gave a soft laugh.

'Very funny. Call me and let me know what happens. Okay?'

'Okay,' Anna said, but in truth, she was unsure if she really would call back, at least not for a while.

Anna managed to get a few more hours' sleep before she woke and got ready for the day ahead. She imagined life with Don Blane in Virginia, blissfully happy and fending for themselves in the log cabin, just the two of them with no pressure. However, she knew deep down she was not ready to make a serious commitment, especially to someone who lived thousands of miles away. It had been a lovely dream, one that she had briefly felt possible, but in truth she wasn't convinced Blane was ready to make a commitment either.

Dressed now, in black tights, crisp white shirt, black fitted pencil skirt and a single-breasted jacket, Anna's personalized uniform was in place. She used little makeup, and just applied some lip gloss. Lastly she coiled her thick red hair into a pleat, and stood staring at her reflection in her dressing-table mirror. She had no family alive, no ties, nothing that was really holding her back. This could be the most challenging day in her professional life, might even be a big career move, and she would take on board all of Don's advice. She was more determined than ever to bring Gloria Lynne down, and prove she was right. She wouldn't mind giving Beth Jackson a kick up the arse! she thought, and then laughed at her crassness, telling herself it was better to have Don as her friend and mentor than as a lover. But there was plenty of time, and who knew what would happen? Life had a way of surprising you. She slipped on her black high-heeled shoes, and she was ready.

Chapter Thirty-Five

As Anna drove to work it struck her that Donna, and to a lesser extent Aisa, were both blind to how evil their mother really was. She controlled their behaviour by rewarding them, most frequently with money. Donna had briefly turned against Gloria and behaved in a manner that was clearly designed to annoy her, but there was little doubt that she had genuinely loved Josh Reynolds. Aisa on the other hand was totally spoilt and wanted for nothing, other than her sister's husband, whose affection she gained by lavish gifts of cash and a Ferrari, a trait she had clearly inherited from her mother. Anna wondered if Josh had actually loved Aisa and really been about to leave Donna for her, or was it just the access to large sums money that he desired. Sadly he had taken the answers to that and so many other questions to his grave.

At the station, Anna arranged for a uniform constable to go to the hospital to have Marisha Peters moved to a single room, and to stand guard. Following that, she continued work on the disclosure she needed to serve on Ian Holme before the interview with Aisa. Holme was a formidable advocate, and having watched the video of Mike Lewis and Dewar's interview with Donna she was aware of how astute and ruthless he could be. Her fear was that Holme would unwittingly pass on information to Gloria Lynne, which she could then use to twist or lie her way out of the evidence Anna had uncovered. She decided that it would be best to drip-feed the disclosure by interviewing Aisa, taking a break, serving further disclosure to Holme and then a further interview before repeating the process.

Anna had moved on to preparing a list of questions to ask Aisa when Jessie Dewar walked in and mumbled good morning in a disgruntled tone of voice.

'Thanks for sitting with Aisa while we searched Lynne House and also for helping Barolli to book her in at the station,' Anna said.

Dewar sighed. 'Barolli and I have been to Josh's old flat in Bayswater and two of the keys on the set recovered from Samuel Peters' property at the mortuary did fit the locks.'

'Good work. We now have evidence to prove that Samuel had access to both Josh and Esme's flats.

'Is it really all worth it?' Dewar asked.

'Worth what?' Anna enquired, unsure what the woman meant.

Dewar looked at Anna and shook her head. 'Turning your nose up at the FBI course and coming back here just to show me up?'

Anna could understand why Dewar was annoyed with her, but wanted her to know that she couldn't be further from the truth. Don Blane was right. Anna needed Dewar on her side, especially when it came to having a better understanding of Gloria Lynne and her sociopathic behaviour. Anna asked Dewar to sit down, which she did.

'Look, I know we've had one or two disagreements about the Reynolds investigation, but your input with the suicide note and Josh Reynolds' death scene has been invaluable. Your knowledge of cars led directly to recovery of the Ferrari.'

'Well it doesn't feel that way,' Dewar said with a sullen look on her face.

'You have to believe me, Jessie, I'm not back here to belittle you in any way. I totally understand why you are annoyed with me, but right now I very much need your support, professional advice and assistance.'

Dewar leaned back in her chair and folded her arms, her expression unchanged. 'Why now?'

'While in the States, I became privy to information about

Gloria Lynne that nobody here was aware of,' Anna explained. 'That information led to the discovery of Samuel Peters' body and the arrest of Aisa Lynne. I will go into everything in detail in the office meeting, but what I uncovered at the time was not through the proper legal channels. It is highly sensitive and would have been impossible to convey in a phone call to you, Mike Lewis or anyone else on the team.'

'Did you tell Jimmy Langton this sensitive information or is he in the dark as well?' Dewar asked petulantly.

'He knows everything and he approved my return to London. Because of the explosive nature of the evidence he is on his way back from Quantico to take command of the investigation,' Anna said. To prove her point, she showed her the text Langton had sent the previous evening. Dewar unfolded her arms and sat upright and Anna knew that she had her attention.

'If Jimmy's back then it must be serious,' Dewar said.

'It's all very complicated, but Gloria Lynne is more involved in the death of Josh Reynolds than any of us imagined. If it hadn't been for the guidance and input of your colleague Don Blane then I would never have been able to put what is a very complex puzzle together. Blane himself said that your knowledge and skills would be invaluable in cracking the case against Gloria Lynne,' Anna said, deliberately pandering to Dewar's ego.

'Can you at least give me a brief insight before the meeting?' the agent asked inquisitively.

Anna told Dewar that she had uncovered marriage and birth certificates found hidden in Samuel Peters' jacket that showed he and Gloria Lynne were married and Joshua Reynolds was their legally conceived son, but his birth name was Arum and Gloria gave him up to Esme when he was a baby.

Dewar's eyes lit up. 'Holy shit ... INCEST. Josh was screwing his sister.'

'Half-sisters, to be precise, but incest nevertheless, and they didn't know.'

Dewar let out a loud whistle of surprise before she picked up on what Anna had said.

'Wait a second, you just said sisters, plural, as in two?'

'Yes. Aisa isn't adopted, she's Gloria's real blood daughter and Donna's blood sister.'

'Jesus Christ, all we need now are Harry Potter and the Half-blood Prince to make this a really complicated story!' Dewar exclaimed, making Anna laugh.

'I think Samuel was blackmailing Gloria,' Anna said.

'Was Marisha involved?' Dewar asked.

'Not directly, but I'm sure from the phone records she had knowledge of what was going on and benefited from the blackmail.'

'I've been racking my brains about Marisha's behaviour in the interview Barolli and I had with her. The "bitch" she was talking about was obviously Gloria Lynne, not Donna.'

'Yes, and Marisha wasn't drunk, she was suffering from atropine poisoning.'

Dewar raised her hands, needing Anna to slow down as she digested all the new information. 'So let me try and work this out. Do you think Gloria poisoned Marisha?'

'Yes, and forensics also found atropine in Samuel and Josh's bodies as well. I know it was her, but the problem is, I don't as yet have a shred of hard evidence to prove it.'

'I always knew there was something not quite right about that woman,' Dewar said, but Anna suspected she was just trying to jump on the bandwagon.

'Will you help me try to break down Gloria Lynne?'

Dewar rubbed her hands in anticipation. 'Of course I will, but I need to know everything you know about her.'

Anna looked at her watch. It was just after eight and she had further work to do before the interview with Aisa.

'I'm pushed for time right now, so can I give you

the full story along with the rest of the team at the nine a.m. office meeting?'

'Yeah, fine by me. When you arrest Gloria, I'd like to sit in on the interview.'

It was a request Anna had anticipated but hoped Dewar wouldn't make as the answer would probably offend her.

'That will be up to DCS Langton, but with Ian Holme representing Aisa it could be tricky,' she said tactfully.

Dewar sighed. 'Did you see the interview with Donna? Now I know how he got his nickname Andrex.'

'Yeah, but if it's any consolation I thought he was showing off and a bit hard on you. There's a viewing room you can watch from.'

'Actually, that would be better – I'll be able to scrutinize Gloria Lynne without any distractions,' Dewar conceded.

'Thanks, Jessie, I'll show you the room right after the office meeting.'

Dewar seemed deep in thought as she grabbed her wallet from her handbag. 'I'm going to the canteen, you want anything?' she said as she got up, then sat back down again. 'Did Don Blane say anything about Gloria Lynne having sociopathic tendencies?' she asked, much to Anna's surprise.

'Have you spoken with him?' Anna asked.

'No, but that's the niggling feeling I had about her ever since I met her and her daughters.'

'Why didn't you say so?'

'It was just a gut instinct, nothing more. I had no evidence to support it, so who'd have believed me?'

'Blane thinks she's a sociopath, and I agree with him,' Anna admitted.

'Good, now I know what we're up against and once I hear all the evidence you've uncovered I'll prepare an interview strategy.'

Anna realized how astute Dewar really was and that her earlier mistakes in the investigation had probably all been down to a burning desire to impress her colleagues.

The agent stood up again and headed towards the door, stopped and turned to Anna. 'Gloria Lynne will be the greatest adversary you have ever faced in your career, Anna. As psychologists we advise people involved with sociopaths to leave, run don't walk, and never ever go back – it's the only option for survival,' Dewar said, emphasizing her concerns yet relishing the challenge.

As the agent left, Joan entered, and Anna wondered if she'd ever get any peace and quiet to get on with her work. The constable informed Anna that Barolli had just picked Langton up at Heathrow and the officer guarding Marisha had called to say that she had briefly come out of her coma. Before Joan could finish what she was saying, Anna was out of her seat and hurriedly putting on her jacket to go to the hospital.

'If I can turn Marisha then I can really nail Gloria,' Anna said excitedly, grabbing her notebook and handbag.

'The officer said that her condition is still serious and her heartbeat's irregular,' Joan warned, but there was no stopping Anna now.

'Joan, there's a folder on my laptop I've named "Nightshade". Everything I and Don Blane uncovered about Gloria Lynne and Samuel Peters is in it. There's a lot in there, print it off for Langton and Dewar to read while I'm out and give them everything you got for me as well,' Anna said as she headed for the door then turned back and handed Joan a list from her desk.

'Here's the initial disclosure list for Ian Holme. That's all he's to be given for now and he can have a private consultation with Aisa.'

In the main office, Anna noticed Barbara sitting at her desk tucking into her first bite of a bacon and egg sandwich.

'Barbara, grab your coat and come with me.'

'But I just got my—'

'NOW!' Anna shouted, causing Barbara to drop her sandwich and take a quick swig of her coffee to wash the mouthful down.

Anna got one of the uniform cars to rush her and Barbara to the hospital on blue lights and sirens. Arriving at the ward she spoke with the attending doctor who informed her that Marisha Peters' condition was worsening by the minute and she might not have much longer to live. Anna could see Marisha through the internal window, her eyes closed and lying motionless with a myriad of tubes and heart monitor wires connected to her body, and a ventilator tube extruding from her mouth. Anna felt deflated for all the wrong reasons; she sympathized with Marisha's pitiful condition, but so wanted her to be able to speak, to provide her with the evidence she needed against Gloria Lynne.

Anna asked the doctor if she could go into the room and he opened the door for her and Barbara to enter. The serenity of the room was broken by the soft rhythmic pumping of the ventilator and the heart monitor with its erratic beep reminiscent of a reversing sensor in a car.

Anna walked over to Marisha's side and turned to the doctor. 'Will she be able to hear?'

'She's no longer in a coma, but it's impossible for me to say,' the doctor replied politely.

Anna leaned forward so she could speak quietly. 'I'm sorry it came to this, Marisha, but I promise you I will do everything in my power to see Gloria stands trial for what she has done to you and Samuel.'

There was a sudden change in the rhythm of the heart monitor as the beeps slightly upped in tempo and Marisha's eyelids flickered.

'I'm Anna Travis, Marisha, do you remember me?' she asked and again the monitor changed tempo.

'She is incapable of answering you, detective, and the heart arrhythmia is due to her deteriorating condition,' the doctor insisted.

Slowly, Marisha's bloodshot eyes opened, not fully, but enough for Anna to feel that she was awake.

'If I ask her questions will she be able to move her head or squeeze my hand?' Anna hurriedly asked the doctor.

'No, she suffered a serious stroke while in the coma.'

Anna removed her iPhone from her jacket pocket and started to press the screen, causing the doctor to rebuke her as he reminded her that phone calls could interfere with the medical equipment. Anna assured him she was not about to call anyone and took him to one side, out of his patient's earshot, leaving Barbara wondering what on earth Anna was doing and feeling most uncomfortable standing next to a woman who looked as if she was about to die.

Anna held her phone up in her hand, with the back of it pointing towards the doctor. 'In your professional opinion is Marisha Peters' death imminent?'

'Yes, I've already told you that, and why are you pointing your phone at me?'

'Because I'm video-recording our conversation and I need you to tell Marisha that she may be about to die,' Anna said firmly.

The doctor looked stunned. 'Are you out of your mind?'

'As you know, Marisha was poisoned with atropine and I believe she knows who was responsible. I want to take a dying declaration from her, and for that to be valid in a court of law she needs to understand that she may be about to die.'

'Really, officer, this is preposterous and apart from that she can't even speak.'

'She can move her eyes, though, but if you want her death to be in vain then so be it, doctor, it's your conscience not mine,' Anna said tactfully.

The doctor looked at Marisha for some moments and eventually nodded in submission. Anna handed Barbara her phone to record the dying declaration. Barbara held it in both hands to keep it steady as Anna crouched down beside the bed and took hold of Marisha's hand, which felt cold and clammy. 'Marisha, if you can hear me, I want you to blink three times for yes and twice for no,' Anna said and Marisha's eyelids opened and closed slowly three times.

Anna looked at the doctor, who stepped forward and told Marisha that her heart was failing and she might be about to die. The acceleration in her heart rate was mirrored by the increased beeping of the monitor.

'Marisha, do you understand what the doctor just said?'

Marisha moved her eyelids three times, indicating, yes.

'You understand that you may be about to die?' Anna repeated, followed by three slow blinks from Marisha.

'Is your sister Esme alive?' Anna asked, to a response of two blinks. 'Was Josh Reynolds Esme's birth son?' Again Marisha blinked twice. At first, Barbara was confused, but then realized that Anna was testing Esme's ability to respond in the negative – however, there were some single involuntary blinks between questions. Anna signalled for Barbara to move in a bit closer to film everything.

Anna fired a volley of questions, each receiving three blinks: 'Did Samuel marry a woman called Gloria Rediker?' 'Is that woman now Lady Gloria Lynne?' Anna looked at Barbara to make sure she was recording it all before asking her next question. Barbara nodded and Anna continued.

'Was Samuel blackmailing her?' Anna asked, but Marisha didn't move her eyes. The beeps of the heart-rate monitor intensified and the ventilator pump worked harder. The doctor leaned over Anna and pressed the emergency button on the wall and within seconds two nurses entered the room and he raised his hand for them to wait.

'Please, Marisha, I need you to tell me the truth, and it doesn't matter now if you were involved.'

The look in Marisha's eyes was pitiful.

'Did Samuel tell you how Josh Reynolds died?' Marisha blinked twice. 'Did you know about his death before I came to your flat?' Two blinks, but with each progressive question Marisha's ability to respond was becoming slower, while the heart monitor and ventilator were going into overdrive.

'You need to stop now, officer, the nurses and I need to tend to the patient,' the doctor said but Anna ignored him.

'Did Gloria Lynne give Samuel the money in your freezer?'

Marisha blinked three times as the doctor put his hand on Anna's arm to escort her away, but she shrugged him off.

'Did Gloria visit your flat the day Samuel disappeared?'

Marisha's eyes began to flicker uncontrollably as a rasping sound rattled through her chest and lungs. The doctor waved to the nurses, who stepped forward and pulled Barbara out of the way so they could get to the defibrillator. Suddenly, Marisha's eyes opened wide and looked as if they were about to pop out of her head and she rapidly blinked three times. The doctor told Anna to get out of the room and forced himself between her and Marisha, but Anna moved round to the side of him, her gaze transfixed on Marisha's face.

'Did Gloria give Samuel the spiced rum?' Anna asked in a raised voice. Marisha gasped in air, blinked once, then again before her bloodshot eyeballs bulged even further. The gurgling noise from her mouth sounded as if she was trying to force herself to speak; she blinked one more time and Anna felt she was saying yes to her question. Marisha opened her mouth and the rasping sound was a long slow, 'Yes.'

No sooner had she finished than Marisha flatlined. The doctor and nurses attempted resuscitation, but everyone in the room knew they were only going through the motions as the patient was clearly beyond help.

Anna moved over beside Barbara. 'Did you get it all?' she whispered.

Barbara rammed the phone into Anna's hand with a look of disdain. 'Does your obsession to bring Gloria Lynne down have no boundaries? Or is it just your ego?' she asked, clearly distressed.

'I had no choice,' Anna protested.

'Maybe, maybe not, but sometimes you need to respect people before they're dead. I thought I knew you better, DCI Travis.'

It was clear that the doctor was not entirely happy with Anna's conduct either, but he understood that she had a job to do and agreed to make a statement when he was off duty. She knew though that her obsessive behaviour had left a bad taste in everyone's mouth.

*

Anna knew that Langton would be back at the incident room when she got there. She wondered if it would be an appropriate time to tell him about her fractious meeting with Walters and that she had recorded Walters stating coldly and calmly that he had shafted Langton's career and was about to force him into retirement from the Met.

Although she felt Langton had the right to know what Walters had done, and was going to do to him, she was worried that it would anger him so much he would be straight up to the Yard to have an almighty head-to-head with Walters. Anna knew she was being somewhat selfish in her reasoning, but she needed Langton to help her with Aisa and more importantly the arrest and interview of Gloria Lynne. For the time being, she didn't want him distracted and came to the decision that it was best to tell him later and in private.

Still, she felt that Langton would be pleased with the result from the hospital. Although in effect hearsay evidence, as Marisha could now never testify under oath, a 'dying declaration' was an exception to the rules of evidence in murder and manslaughter cases. There was no doubt that Ian Holme would contest the declaration, but Anna felt she had adhered to the rules and made the recording when death was imminent and Marisha was also fully aware of that fact.

Entering her office, Anna saw Langton and Dewar sitting side by side on the sofa, both holding notebooks and pens. The whole of the coffee table and surrounding floor area were covered in documents, files and photographs, as was her desk. She greeted them both with a smile as she joined them and sat down in an armchair.

'Interesting stuff, isn't it? Even if Aisa sits there in stone-faced silence I think, after what Marisha indicated, that there's enough to arrest Gloria for murder and a number of other offences,' Anna said, pleased with herself.

Langton shook his head and despairingly dropped his notebook and pen onto the coffee table and scooped up a handful of papers from the floor. He held them up, waved them at Anna and then spoke calmly but with authority. 'Interesting is about right, Anna, and certainly this mountain of paperwork raises a lot of questions, but for me the most crucial one is . . . where's the bloody evidence to arrest Gloria Lynne on suspicion of murder?'

Anna could see from the look on Langton's face he was being deadly serious. She had anticipated him being really pissed off about having to return to London so quickly, and even expected the usual heavy dressing-down about her 'overzealous' behaviour, but not this reaction. He had after all promised to back her up about Gloria Lynne.

She was just going to tell him about Marisha's dying declaration when he continued in the same vein.

'And before you start, I am not interested in Xavier Alleyne or Lord Henry Lynne's deaths as they didn't even happen in this country.'

'But the circumstances surrounding their deaths can be used as similar fact evidence so I—'

'Don't jump the gun, that's only in a criminal trial and if the judge allows it, so please just stick to Samuel Peters' death for now.'

'Marisha Peters just passed away in hospital, but I managed to get a dying declaration from her and recorded it on my phone. The doctor is willing to make a statement,' Anna said, desperate to defend her actions and get Langton back on her side. She pulled her iPhone out of her pocket and put it on the table.

'This better be good, bearing in mind that she was no angel herself,' Langton said and sat back to watch the recording.

Anna had intended to explain that Marisha didn't actually speak other than saying yes to the final question about the rum. But now she didn't think it necessary as the video clip would show that Marisha understood everything that was going on. Anna watched the expression on Langton's face as she played the recording but it gave nothing away.

As the video ended he looked up at Anna, totally bewildered. 'She doesn't say a bloody word and when you asked the two most vital questions about Gloria visiting the flat and giving Samuel the rum all I could see was the bloody floor.'

Anna quickly grabbed her phone and played back the last bit. She remembered the nurses had moved Barbara out of the way but only now did she realize it had prevented her from record-ing the whole declaration.

'Shit, I don't believe it. The doctor can confirm Marisha knew what I was asking and was able to answer both positively and negatively,' Anna said, trying to be reassuring.

Langton had so far remained calm but he was clearly not impressed by the video.

'This is worthless. You're clutching at straws, Anna.'

'Marisha said – sorry, I mean indicated – that Samuel was blackmailing Gloria and the money in the freezer was the pro-ceeds,' Anna said.

'Okay, so let's say Marisha was being truthful, technically she's just confessed to being involved in blackmail and clearly spent the proceeds on electrical goods. No judge in the world will allow this as evidence because Marisha just confessed to being untrustworthy.'

'But we know that Samuel was blackmailing Gloria so there-fore we can argue she was telling the truth even though she was dishonest.'

Langton, becoming impatient, gave a loud sigh and stood up to stretch his legs.

'Take Marisha out of the equation and tell me how you know that Samuel was blackmailing Gloria,' he said sharply.

Anna scrambled around the papers on the coffee table and floor, finally finding what she was looking for. She held it up. 'These marriage and birth certificates, why else would Samuel order them online, pay with Marisha's credit card and have them delivered to her flat?'

'Maybe he was doing some genealogy, tracing his and Gloria's family history,' Langton snapped.

'You're just being totally negative now.' Anna was annoyed with what she saw as an unnecessary and flippant remark.

'Am I? You did the CID course to become a detective, didn't you?' Langton asked.

'What's that got to do with anything?' Anna demanded, angry at being belittled.

'So you were taught, just like everyone else, that blackmail is an unjustified threat to make a gain or cause loss to another unless a particular demand is met.'

'Samuel told Gloria that he would expose the fact Josh was their son and in an incestuous marriage with Donna – oh, and I nearly forgot about her bigamous marriage to Xavier. It's all here in the bloody certificates,' Anna said and threw the papers down on the coffee table.

Langton was now livid and Dewar, desperately not wanting to be stuck in the middle, stood up and said she just needed to run to the bathroom. But neither Langton nor Anna heard a word she said or even noticed her leave the room.

'You need a bloody victim to report blackmail for a crime to have been committed and you don't fucking have either. As for the bigamy, I don't give a toss about that as it was over thirty years ago in Jamaica!' Langton shouted as he paced around the room.

Anna stood up to confront him further. 'Neither do I, but what I'm saying is that Samuel used the bigamy and incest to blackmail Gloria. He knew she could never report it for fear of losing kudos in her high society world.'

Langton took a deep breath and sat down again. In his heart he knew that Anna was probably right in everything she was saying, but he feared for her career and future if she arrested someone as powerful as Gloria with nothing more than what seemed to be circumstantial evidence.

'There's the phone calls to Gloria from Marisha's landline and mobile, Josh Reynolds driving out to Weybridge and—' Anna insisted, but he jumped in.

'You can't tell who made the calls or what was said, and you've jack shit to show he actually went to Gloria's house, let alone Weybridge.'

'If Gloria's house or mobile phones show calls to Marisha's phones, that makes the connection even stronger – how can Gloria explain that away?'

'She doesn't have to!' he barked.

Anna shook her head in fury. 'What? So you think Gloria just decided to have a cosy little catch-up chat or two with Samuel the lowly fisherman after thirty years. Come to think of it, maybe that's why he turned up at the Charity Ball ... she bloody well invited him!'

Langton sucked in his breath, determined to remain calm.

'Joan got the results on Gloria's phones and it was a big zilch, not one single call to either of Marisha's phones. Yet again, where you thought there'd be evidence there is none!'

'Because Gloria's not that stupid, she will have used an untraceable pay-as-you-go phone to contact them.'

'Jesus Christ, you have a bloody answer for everything, Anna. Your problem is you just can't admit when you're beaten.'

'BEATEN, I am not beaten and you've lost your ability to see sense. Samuel, Marisha and Josh all had atropine in their bodies and one common denominator – Gloria Lynne!'

Langton was at boiling point. 'Your effing report says you think Josh Reynolds committed suicide!'

'Because he was under the influence of the atropine that Gloria gave him, he didn't know what he was doing.'

'How many times do I have to say it: you've no evidence to prove Gloria Lynne did anything!' Langton said, determined to convince her.

'That's why she needs to be arrested and interviewed!'

Langton folded his arms. 'Let's stop shouting at each other, it's pointless and getting us nowhere.'

'You said you'd back me all the way,' Anna pleaded.

'I am, Anna, I am, but I can't see you put your head on the chopping block like this. I've looked through all the paperwork and the evidence just isn't there. I respect your gut feeling and normally I'd agree with you a hundred per cent, but this time you just have to let it go and move on.'

She was close to tears. 'I can't believe you are prepared to give in so easily.'

'It's not just the lack of evidence, Anna, you're talking about taking on one of the richest and most powerful women in the country. She mixes with prime ministers and royalty, so ask yourself, whose side will the top brass and courts be on?'

Mimicking him, she folded her arms. 'What about you? Fitzpatrick was rich and powerful, but that didn't stop you hunting him down.'

'That's totally different and you know it.'

'Is it? I always thought you believed that anyone who committed a serious crime deserved to be punished, no matter who they are.'

'Sweetheart, you are in a no-win situation that isn't worth risking your career for.'

Anna didn't know what to say. She simply couldn't believe she had come this far to be knocked back by Langton, and realized there and then that he had lost the will to do what he did best, to fight to the end for what he believed in, even when others doubted him.

She began to pick up the documents, unable to look at him.

'Well then, walk away now and leave me to get on with my job. I'll deal with Gloria Lynne with or without your help.'

Langton sighed with frustration. She could make him so mad one moment yet so full of passion the next. He knew he was wrong and was letting her down badly when she needed him most. He was more than certain his career was at an end, and this would undoubtedly be his last case. Suddenly it dawned on him he had nothing to lose. He'd promised to help Anna and he knew that to break that promise would destroy everything they ever had together. She was angrily stacking the files, still avoiding looking at him, and he gave a soft laugh. She turned towards him, and he smiled.

'Okay, okay, you win, and you'll have my help, but first we interview Aisa and see if she's willing to play ball. If not, we break her down until she does and then we screw Lady Gloria Lynne.'

Anna instinctively grabbed him, squeezed him tightly then kissed him hard on the cheek before thanking him. Langton told her that Ian Holme had arrived nearly an hour ago and Joan had served him the disclosure papers. Anna offered to go and get Dewar, take her to the viewing room and see if Mr Holme was ready for Aisa to be interviewed.

'Thank you,' she said gratefully.

'Yeah yeah, go on, let's get this show on the road.'

As the door closed behind her, he sat down heavily on the sofa, rubbing at his head. 'That's me fucked,' he said to himself.

As Anna took Dewar down to the viewing room to show her the layout, she explained that the video cameras were permanently on and relayed a picture to the TV monitors. The room was dark with no windows or natural light, but had a large table with two monitors and chairs at which to sit and write notes, or there were two comfortable armchairs. A cold-water dispenser, along with tea- and coffee-making facilities, stood in one corner of the room. Anna leaned over and switched on the monitors and turned to Dewar as the picture of the interview room came up onto the screens.

'That's about it – you can help yourself to drinks and it's okay to bring in biscuits and sandwiches, as long as you clean up when you've finished.'

'Is it wise to let Gloria speak with her daughter before the interview?' Dewar asked.

Anna thought that Dewar was suggesting it would be a productive move. 'No way, I don't want them anywhere near each other, that's why I stipulated Aisa was to have no visitors.'

Dewar leaned across to get a better look and pointed at the TV monitor. 'Then why are they in the interview room together?'

Anna turned sharply. Gloria Lynne was sitting next to Aisa, her back to the camera, her arm wrapped round her daughter's shoulder and holding her close whilst whispering in her ear. Aisa was trembling and in floods of tears.

'Shit, SHIT! Who the fuck's let that happen?' Anna exclaimed as she ran from the viewing room towards the custody area, leaving Dewar gazing at the monitor. Gloria slowly, almost eerily, turned to face the camera, her impassive face and piercing eyes appearing to stare straight towards Dewar.

Chapter Thirty-Six

Anna was absolutely livid as the custody sergeant explained that he had received a phone call from Deputy Commissioner Walters instructing him that Lady Gloria Lynne was to be allowed to see her daughter. The sergeant said he had informed Walters that DCI Travis had left orders that Aisa was not to have any visitors, but Walters pulled rank and the sergeant was left with no choice but to comply. Anna asked if Walters had given a reason for his actions and the sergeant told her that his exact words were, 'It would be beneficial to the investigation and may lead to a full confession.'

Anna had a quick look at the custody record and saw that Ian Holme had been served disclosure and then had a twenty-minute consultation with Aisa. Gloria had been with Aisa for nearly an hour. Anna stormed off to the interview room and on opening the door she found Gloria standing next to Aisa, who was looking in an even worse state than before. On seeing Anna, Gloria leaned forward, put her arm round her daughter and started her act. 'Don't worry, my darling, Mummy is always here for you, but you must tell DCI Travis the truth about you and Josh.'

Anna felt sick to the stomach knowing that Gloria had what she craved for, total domination and control over her daughter. She had an overwhelming urge to put Gloria up against the wall and tell her exactly what she thought of her sick, warped existence, but she knew that would be futile and playing into Gloria's hands. So Anna fought back her anger, told herself to remain calm and forced a smile.

'Sorry, I thought Mr Holme was with Aisa having a consultation. I was wondering if she was ready to be interviewed,' she
said as if nothing was wrong.

'She will be shortly, won't you, darling? I just need to speak
with Ian to assure him that there will be no more lies from her,
and then she's all yours,' Gloria said, as if Aisa were some form
of commodity to be handed around. Anna held the door open
as Gloria walked out of the room and followed her up the corridor.

'May I ask what you said to your daughter, Lady Lynne, as
she seems really upset?' Anna forced herself to ask politely.

Gloria stopped and deliberately kept her back to Anna for a
few seconds before turning to face her. 'You should be thanking me, Detective Travis. The great Ian Holme could not get
my daughter to tell him anything – but for me, you'd get nothing out of her. I have done what any caring mother would do,
persuaded her to tell you the truth.'

'And that would be in whose best interest?' Anna asked.

But Gloria's only response was to sneer and look her up and
down as if she were a piece of dirt before walking away.

Anna stormed back into her office to tell Langton what had
happened, to find Jessie Dewar was already there and had
informed Langton that something had gone terribly wrong.

'Bloody Walters, she's using him; if he walked in here now,
I'd kill him!' Anna said, gritting her teeth in anger.

Langton told her to take a deep breath, calm down and
explain what had happened. Anna told them about Walters' call
to the custody sergeant, her brief chat with Gloria Lynne, the
state of hopelessness that Aisa was in, and how Gloria was revelling in it all.

'God knows what Walters told her, and if Ian Holme revealed
the disclosure Gloria had everything she needed to prime Aisa,'
Anna said despairingly and banged her hand on the desk.

'Why would Walters tell Gloria anything?' Langton asked.

Anna remembered that she had not as yet told Langton

anything about her confrontational meeting with the Deputy
Commissioner, and now explained how he flew off the
handle after Gloria Lynne complained about Aisa's arrest.
Walters had demanded to know why she was back in London
and she had, at first, only told him about evidence that impli-
cated Aisa. Langton pressed Anna as to what she meant by 'at
first', so she told him that the Coroner had spoken with
Walters as Dr Harrow had made a complaint. She had to tell
Walters that Samuel Peters was related to Josh and stole
money from him, and as far as Walters was concerned Samuel
died of a heart attack.

'Anything else?' Langton glanced towards Dewar.

'No,' Anna said. She knew it was not a good time to mention
everything else that had been said in that extraordinary meeting.

'Basically, you lied to him,' Langton told her.

'I was economical with the truth,' she said, trying to justify
her position.

'This case goes from bad to worse.' Langton sighed.

'If I were in Anna's shoes I'd have done the same,' Dewar said,
coming to her defence.

'Well, I'm no angel when it comes to feeding Walters with
a load of crap. We have to assume that Gloria sweet-talked
Walters into telling her everything he knew. The agenda now is
damage limitation,' Langton said, looking at Dewar again.

Dewar realized that he wanted her input about what Gloria
might have said to Aisa, and how best to deal with the situation,
and so she commented that it was interesting that the woman
had never come to the station to play the loving and caring
mother when Donna was arrested. Dewar believed the reason
for this was that Gloria had nothing to fear simply because
Donna had nothing to tell as she was the only innocent party in
the whole sordid affair.

'That poor girl has been put through hell,' Anna said.

Langton found it hard to comprehend that Gloria Lynne was
prepared to let Donna take the fall.

'A sociopath like Gloria Lynne has no feelings of love for

either of her daughters in the way that a mother should,' Dewar informed them. 'Donna and Aisa are her pawns, little trophies that she likes to pander to so she appears to be the perfect, caring mother.'

'The woman's something else. How has she deceived every-one for so long?' Langton asked.

Dewar explained that Lady Lynne had spent her life impress-ing people of high standing and integrity through lies and deceit. 'The reality is, Gloria doesn't want friends, she craves loyal followers, people who believe in her and thereby unwit-tingly do everything they can to help her achieve her own conceited goals.'

'She's more dangerous than I realized,' Langton said.

'Well I think we know it now, but Gloria Lynne is dangerous because of ignorance ... not her own, but everyone else's understanding of who or what she really is. It's rare that anyone is able to see through the mask of a cold-hearted sociopath,' Dewar said calmly, adding that Aisa and Donna's reputations didn't matter a jot to Gloria, as ultimately she had to be the one in total control.

Langton remained silent for a moment but then said that Donna seemed to be different as she had, prior to meeting Josh Reynolds, rebelled against her mother by leaving the family home to become a stripper.

Dewar smiled. 'Ah, yes, but the grief of others is sheer pleasure to a sociopath – any weakness, especially in a time of sorrow, and they'll move in and take control. No sooner was Josh Reynolds dead than Gloria used the situation to once again take over Donna's life by playing on her grief, organizing Josh's funeral, the sale of the Bayswater flat and the Trojan.' Dewar looked to Anna.

Anna hesitated and then said quietly, 'I think Gloria saw Aisa in her bloodstained dress when she got back to the Savoy from Josh's. Then under immense pressure Aisa confessed to her mother about the affair and being present when Josh shot him-self.'

'Yet again that is just bloody supposition – you don't know what happened,' Langton said, unable to contain his frustration.

Dewar again sided with Anna. 'What we do know about for certain is Aisa's fear of her mother's wrath. She clearly didn't tell her about the theft of the money from CCS Medical, or the love nest at Esme's, as that would have led to the discovery of her buying Josh the Ferrari.'

Langton looked slightly perplexed. 'Okay, I understand Aisa being terrified of Gloria and thus the partial confession, but why didn't she just up and leave like Donna did?'

It was Anna's turn to look to Dewar for an explanation.

'You have to understand that deep down both girls may know Gloria doesn't love them, but that won't necessarily stop them loving her. The difference with Aisa is she's spoilt, likes life in the fast lane, the swanky parties, mixing with celebs, but most of all she likes the money.'

'Is she like her mother – you know, like a mini-sociopath?' Langton asked, still trying to digest the information.

Dewar grinned at his terminology. 'She's inherited her mother's love of money and taste for the good life, but, no, I don't think she's a sociopath in the real sense of the word.'

'If Aisa's terrified of Gloria, and she's primed her about what to say in interview, then basically we're screwed,' Anna predicted.

'You don't know until you interview her and if anyone can break Gloria's hold on her, you can,' insisted Dewar, keen that they remained optimistic.

Langton was still unsure, but like Dewar he felt he should encourage Anna, and so he gave her a rueful smile.

'Let's get on with it, and see what the outcome is.'

Ian Holme was waiting in the corridor as they approached and, recognizing Langton, shook his hand, asking him how he was. From his facial expression and manner, Anna could see that Holme was not being ingratiating, but obviously had a genuine respect for Langton. He asked to speak to them both in private, and so Anna led them into an empty interview room, while Dewar made her way to the viewing suite.

'Aisa Lynne has made full and frank admissions to me about her affair with Josh Reynolds and the use of the charity fund monies,' Holme said. 'On my advice, she has made a prepared statement, which I will read out to you in the interview.'

'Well, dependent on those admissions we may still need to put further questions to her concerning Mr Reynolds' death,' Anna said, making her point clear.

'I have no problem with that, Detective Travis, and I will advise my client accordingly. What I will object to is any line of questioning concerning the fact that Josh Reynolds was Aisa Lynne's half-brother.'

Anna knew that he could only have got the information from Gloria Lynne. The problem was, she didn't know how much the woman had told him.

'Can I ask why, Mr Holme?' Anna asked.

'Neither Aisa nor Donna Lynne are aware that Joshua was really Arum Peters. Lady Lynne herself did not know Josh Reynolds' true identity until recently. She is concerned that any revelation to her daughters, of their incestuous relationship, could have devastating psychological effects.'

Anna knew there and then that Gloria had Ian Holme exactly where she wanted him: he had become one of her followers, a duped disciple who could see no wrong in her.

'Why has Lady Lynne not brought this information to our attention before?' Langton asked.

Holme said that as Lady Lynne's representative he would be breaching her trust if he said anything more, but she had indicated that she would like to talk to DCI Travis after the interview with Aisa. Langton told Mr Holme that he and DCI Travis would join him shortly in the interview room.

As soon as they were alone, Langton turned to Anna.

'You do not raise the birth certificates or anything to do with them.'

'But Samuel gave the documents to Josh who then showed

them to Aisa, so they are relevant evidence about which I am
perfectly entitled to question her.'

'You have no proof of that, and Aisa's prints aren't on the certificates. Don't you get it? Gloria Lynne is trying to rile you.
Even if Aisa already knows about her relationship to Josh, she'll
make out she didn't, act all hysterical and Holme will accuse
you of deliberate oppressive tactics and end the interview.'

Anna knew that he was right, but it galled her that Ian
Holme was so blissfully unaware that Gloria was using him.

'Okay,' she said begrudgingly.

On entering the main interview room, Anna could see that Aisa
looked much calmer than she had when her mother was with
her, and suspected that she was not as nervous because she had
given Ian Holme the story that her mother had concocted. As
she turned on the DVD recording equipment, Anna tried to
make eye contact with Aisa, while Langton made the formal
introductions and reminded the young woman she was still
under caution. She looked down at the floor and simply
nodded. Ian Holme stated that his client fully understood why
she had been arrested and that anything she said could be used
in evidence against her.

'Aisa Lynne has made a prepared statement, which I will read
out on her behalf. She has signed it as being a true version of
events concerning her relationship with Joshua Reynolds,' Holme
said as he placed the statement down on the table in front of
him. He was about to start when Anna interjected.

'Have you made the statement of your own free will, Aisa?'
she asked, still desperately trying to make eye contact.

Aisa kept her head down and spoke quietly. 'Yes, my mother
told me I must tell you the truth.'

Anna sighed. 'I'm sure she did, Aisa. Mummy always knows
what is best for her little girls, doesn't she?'

'We should be grateful that Lady Lynne is such an honourable
woman; many mothers would advise their offspring to say nothing,' Holmes replied, refusing to react to Anna's sarcasm.

Anna would have loved to press Aisa further on exactly what her mother had said but Langton frowned at her and she knew it was best to listen to the statement before proceeding with any further questions. Holme started to read:

Around mid-summer of 2012 I started an affair with my brother-in-law Joshua Reynolds and our love for each other grew quickly over the weeks that followed. We used his deceased mother's flat as a place to meet and carry out our affair.

At the beginning of September, Josh asked me if I could loan him some money as his club, the Trojan, was in financial difficulties and he needed funds to develop the premises. Josh had spoken with my sister Donna about asking my mother Lady Gloria Lynne for a loan, but Donna refused to ask her for any financial help. I did have funds of my own but I didn't want my mother or Donna to know that I would lend Josh the money, as I feared them finding out about our affair and ending it.

I told Josh that I would loan him the money through the Lynne Foundation, and it was agreed that he would repay the loan once the Trojan was back on its feet and in profit. He opened a bank account using his mother's maiden name and address so that all correspondence would go there and Donna wouldn't find out. I made two online transfers to this account from the CCS Medical Trust charity. Each one was for fifty thousand pounds. I also borrowed ninety-eight thousand pounds from CCS Medical to buy Josh a Ferrari as an early Christmas present.

I know CCS Medical is an account that Donna looked after, but it is our biggest charity and I thought that none of the money would be missed in between lending it to Josh, buying the Ferrari, and then repaying it all. I did not mean for Donna to get into trouble but when Josh committed suicide, I didn't know what to do. I couldn't say anything about our affair, I didn't have enough of my own money to repay everything, and I couldn't get the Ferrari from the garage to sell it. I decided to say nothing, and as time passed no one noticed, so I just left it as it was, sort of put it out of my mind. I am truly sorry for what I did but it was my intention that all the money would be repaid.

As Holmes turned a page of the statement, Anna glanced to see if there was any reaction from Aisa, but she remained with her head bowed. Holmes cleared his throat and continued reading:

On the night of 5 November 2012, I did leave the Savoy Hotel in my sister's car to go and see Joshua Reynolds at his flat in Bayswater. In the afternoon I was busy organizing the Charity Ball and had switched my mobile to silent. I remember someone from reception coming to find me saying I had a call from a Mr Peters. I knew it was Josh but I told them to tell the caller that I was busy and I would ring him back. About fifteen minutes later Josh rang the reception again and I went and spoke with him. He sounded really upset about something and said he wanted to come and see me. I told him he couldn't come to the Savoy as it was too risky but I would ring him later while I was getting ready for the ball. He called the hotel again about two hours later and this time he got put through to the room I was sharing with Donna, who was in the shower at the time. He still sounded upset and demanded to see me. I asked him why it was so urgent, but all he said was that it had to do with my mother, Donna and me. The way he sounded really freaked me out. I said I would say I felt ill and come to him later in the evening.

I didn't have my car with me so I used Donna's Mini. When I got to his block of flats I rang the buzzer, but got no answer so I tried ringing his mobile, but again there was no answer. A man came out of the flats through the residents' security door and I took the opportunity to go in and knocked on Josh's flat door but again I got no answer. I should say that the caller ID is blocked on my outgoing calls, and Josh was using a special application thing to hide my calls and texts on his mobile from Donna.

Anna sighed with impatience – it was infuriating to listen to Holme's upper-class voice, and hear just how much detail Aisa had made in her statement. Holme glanced towards her and turned a page, and again cleared his throat. Langton opened a bottle of water and placed it in front of him. Holme sipped a few mouthfuls, and then he continued reading:

At the time, I was really annoyed with Josh as his earlier call had me frightened that we had been found out. My nerves really got to me and on my way back to the Charity Ball, I suddenly felt ill, stopped the car, got out and was sick on the side of the road and down my dress. I put the dress in a bath of cold water when I got back to the hotel. My mother came into the room while I was doing this and asked how I was feeling. I told her much better and she said to put on another dress and come back down to the ball so I did. I didn't try to ring Josh again at the time, I was upset that I had gone to all the trouble of going to the flat to see him and he wasn't even there. It was not until the next day when I heard about his death that I realized this was why he never answered the door or my calls.

I know that I should have told the police at the time but I couldn't, Donna was already devastated and knowing of my and Josh's affair would have totally destroyed her. When I heard that Josh's death was a suicide I was surprised and I wondered if he had killed himself because of our affair. It even crossed my mind that he may not have been able to repay the money and he was worried about that. I also knew that he was very depressed about his business, and upset that his partner and best friend Marcus Williams had been making money by selling the girls to clients for sex.

This statement is true and what I have said is to the best of my memory accurate about what happened between Josh Reynolds and myself. I would like to apologize to my mother, my sister and the police for all the trouble I have caused.

Throughout the reading of the statement, Aisa continued to look at the floor and only during the last few sentences did she begin to cry. Anna had not realized the full extent of Gloria's cunning until now. She had weaselled out of Walters and Ian Holme exactly what she needed to know, then conned her way into a 'visit' with Aisa. Anna knew that Gloria would have manipulated her daughter, terrifying her into submission to do exactly as she was told. The affair with Josh was a betrayal of Donna, but not a criminal act, and in fact Aisa's only admission to a crime was taking money from the CCS Medical charity.

Holme now took longer sips from his water. Langton said nothing, picking at his thumbnail. Anna knew something didn't seem right, and she asked Ian Holme if she could look at the prepared statement.

The room was silent as she read through the document. It took her a few moments to find it but then it hit her: not once had Aisa actually said she stole the money, but always referred to it as a loan. She was about to question Aisa about the inconsistency when Ian Holme pre-empted her.

'In respect of the money given to Josh Reynolds, for the club and to purchase the Ferrari, my client had always considered this a loan that was to be repaid; there was no intention on her behalf to permanently deprive CCS Medical of the funds. Lady Lynne has also informed me that she does not wish to press charges against her daughter and this morning she repaid every penny out of her personal funds.'

Anna looked at Langton, who shrugged his shoulders. They both realized that to prove theft they had to show that Aisa's intention was to appropriate the money with the intention to permanently deprive. Anna knew that Gloria must have discussed the charity money with Ian Holme, who would have advised her, and Aisa, that if it was a loan and repaid there was no case to answer. Holme now followed up his bombshell by stating that as there was no evidence to substantiate any charges against Aisa she should be released forthwith.

Anna was not prepared to give in so easily. 'There is the question of Aisa perverting the course of justice.'

He smiled, as if he was about to address the court.

'Perverting the course of justice is a very serious offence, DCI Travis, and as I'm sure you are aware it carries a maximum sentence of life imprisonment.'

'I am aware of that, Mr Holme, but I don't think Aisa is,' Anna replied flippantly.

Holme placed his pen on the table. 'The original investigation was treated as a suicide and the Coroner's verdict was suicide. There was no suspicion of a criminal offence; if there had been I'm sure your murder squad would have been called in immediately. Aisa Lynne was never asked to provide a witness statement by DI Simms, or to give testimony during the Coroner's inquest. Ergo, officer, my client Aisa Lynne did nothing to intentionally pervert the course of justice.'

Anna was not to be outdone. 'Who said I was talking about the original investigation, Mr Holme? When DI Barolli and Special Agent Dewar went to see Aisa, at the Lynne Foundation, Josh's death was being treated as a murder investigation.' Anna flicked through the printed documents in front of her, found Barolli's report of the meeting with Aisa, and slid it across the table for Ian Holme to read.

'She said she left the party because the lobster and prawn tian made her feel ill and came back down later for the fireworks. There is nothing in her prepared statement about leaving the ball for nearly two hours, ergo she lied to and misled my officers in a criminal investigation.'

Holme was still reading the document as Anna pressed on: 'So tell me, Aisa, why did you lie to my officers?'

Aisa said nothing and could not look up at Anna, but Holme

was again quick to interject. 'For the same reasons as she said in her statement – she did not want her mother Lady Lynne or Donna to find out about her affair with Josh Reynolds.'

'It is also a criminal offence to conspire with another person to pervert the course of justice. Did you discuss what to say today with anyone else, Aisa?' Anna asked briskly and watched as she began to shake.

Langton nudged Anna's leg under the table and the look on his face made it clear that he did not, at this point, want Anna to accuse Lady Lynne of a conspiracy with her daughter. The look on the face of Ian Holme was even more incredulous, but neither of them knew exactly what Anna was up to.

'Are you seriously suggesting that Lady Lynne would tell her daughter to lie?' Holme asked, exasperated.

Anna ignored him and put the CCTV picture of Samuel Peters down on the table in front of her. 'This picture was taken outside the Savoy on the night of the Charity Ball. Do you recognize or know this man?'

Holme was quick to say that the picture had not been disclosed to him before the interview and he would like to know more before Aisa answered.

'Do you know that man? He came to the Savoy minutes before you left to go to Josh's flat,' Anna asked in a raised voice. She knew that she was taking a risk, but considered that if Aisa had been shown the marriage and birth certificates by Josh then she knew the truth about him being her half-brother. If that was the case then she was reasonably certain that Gloria would have discussed Samuel Peters' existence with Aisa. She also wondered if Gloria had said anything about Samuel to Ian Holme. His next outburst confirmed that she had.

'Detective Travis, I warned you before this interview about non-disclosure and oppressive tactics and you are now—'

Anna again ignored him. 'Look at the picture, Aisa, a simple yes or no will suffice.' Aisa slowly raised her head to look at the image.

'I am advising you to make no further comment, Aisa, and I

want this interview terminated NOW,' Holme said, and pushed the picture back towards Anna.

'Yes, I have seen him before,' Aisa said softly and there was an immediate silence in the room. Holme was about to say something but Anna jumped in and asked Aisa where she had seen him. She looked up at Anna, and whispered, 'When I was at Josh's flat, I saw that man there.'

Holme told Aisa that she was not obliged to answer DCI Travis's questions, but Anna could see that she wanted to say more and she gave Aisa a comforting nod to continue.

'He was the man who came out when I was pressing the buzzer. He opened the door and I slipped in past him. I'd never seen him before or since, but I remember him because of the dreadlocks and his age.'

Feeling like the ground was about to open up and swallow her, Anna realized that she had just fallen into a trap. She had shot herself in the foot. She urgently looked at Langton to take over the interview so she had time to think about what to do next, but he shook his head in disbelief as he realized that Gloria had won. Aisa's primed, yet seemingly innocuous reply, had just shifted the whole balance of suspicion onto Samuel Peters as being with Josh Reynolds at the time of his death.

Aisa's statement had clearly described how she had been unable to get a reply from Josh at the flat by phone or knocking. Anna knew that Samuel had keys in his possession for both Josh and Esme's flat. She closed her eyes and gritted her teeth.

Langton knew the case against Aisa being present at Josh's death had just been dealt a knockout blow.

'Thank you for your cooperation and prepared statement, Miss Lynne. This interview is terminated,' he said as he switched off the recording equipment. Holme sat back in his chair with a smug look on his face and asked about Aisa's release. Langton told him that they would like to hear what Lady Lynne had to say first. Holme raised the fact that Donna Lynne was in prison for offences she clearly didn't commit and he wanted her released forthwith. Langton agreed with him and

458   Lynda La Plante

said that he would arrange her immediate release with the CPS and for transport to take her home to Lynne House.

A demoralized Langton, Anna and Dewar regrouped upstairs, gathering once more in Anna's office. Anna apologized to both of them, adding that for Aisa to say what she did about Samuel Peters, Gloria must have anticipated that Anna knew about him and would show Aisa a picture.

'No shit, Sherlock!' Langton snapped back at her.

'In fairness, Jimmy, none of us could have anticipated that happening, and it shows how intelligent and cunning Gloria is,' Dewar said.

'Travis should have known it was coming,' Langton said angrily.

'How could I have?' Anna said, horribly aware that her game of words with Gloria when searching Lynne House had back-fired.

'Because you told that prick Walters that Samuel Peters was related to Josh, and had stolen money from him. You knew he had spoken with Gloria before the interview.'

'Yes, but I didn't know exactly what he'd told her. Aisa is totally under Gloria's spell so I took a gamble but it didn't pay off. We can always do another interview with Aisa after we have spoken with Gloria.'

'What about? The time of bloody day? You have nothing against her and Ian Holme knows that; even perverting the course of justice is on a fine thread,' Langton said. He leaned back in his chair, trying to control his temper.

It suddenly crossed Anna's mind that Aisa's identification of Samuel Peters could be turned to their advantage. 'Ian Holme will tell Gloria about the identification Aisa made from the CCTV picture.'

'Of course he bloody will! Did you not see the smug look on his face? Dead men can't talk, so the blame for everything will be shifted onto Samuel Peters,' Langton replied in anger.

'Samuel Peters can't drive so timing-wise, he couldn't have got to Bayswater before Aisa,' Dewar remarked.

'Don't talk shite! Holme will simply argue he could have got a taxi and been there five or ten minutes before her.'

Anna was determined to make her point. 'That picture was taken at the Savoy. Aisa said she didn't know the man's name and had only ever seen him at Josh's flat. We know that Samuel is Gloria's first husband so I'd like to hear her explanation as to why he was at the Charity Ball,' she said, relieved that she might yet be able to salvage something from her faux pas in the interview.

Langton paused as he thought about this and then told her that she had made a valid suggestion.

'Don't be surprised if Gloria has a convincing explanation,' Dewar said.

'Thanks for the vote of confidence, Jessie,' Anna said, even though she knew Dewar was right.

'Gloria's highly intelligent and will have planned and rehearsed her story over and over again in her mind, right down to the finest details. She will have memorized an answer for every possible twist and turn,' Dewar informed them.

'What about her bloody micro-expressions?' Langton asked.

'Almost impossible to detect,' Dewar said in a matter-of-fact way.

'I thought it was one of your specialities!'

'Yes, but Gloria's had years of practice at refining her body language and facial expressions. She's a master of deceit,' Dewar replied.

Langton felt they were just going over the same old ground. 'You're supposed to be the psychological expert, Jessie, so please tell me something we don't know or haven't already considered about Gloria bloody Lynne.'

'A play has a start, middle and end . . .'

Langton was losing his patience. 'For God's sake get to the point, Dewar.'

'Gloria will have had to memorize the script thoroughly before she can perform it, and her emotions need to match the moment. The story needs to unfold in the order she memorized it – you change the order and she may just fluff or forget her lines and when that happens it can have a knock-on effect,' Dewar said with a wry smile.

Langton took on board what Dewar was saying and conceded it was worth a try, but he knew that Gloria was not just an ordinary actor.

'Psychologically, I can understand Aisa lying because she's terrified of her mother, but even so a second interview with her could be worthwhile,' Dewar added.

'We will listen to what Gloria has to tell us first and I will take the lead in any questions that need to be asked. You do not interrupt and you will not arrest her. Do I make myself clear, Anna?'

'Not really because I—'

'She's expecting you to take her on and I don't want to play into her hands again,' Langton emphasized.

'I'm perfectly capable of handling Gloria Lynne,' Anna told him.

'Don't flatter yourself. The way I see it so far, none of us are. She is winning hands down. If she was able to prime her daughter, Christ only knows what other cards she's ready to play.'

Langton stood up, almost pushing his chair over, and then gave a cool nod and pointed at her. 'Behave yourself. Right?' he warned.

Anna nodded.

Chapter Thirty-Seven

Taking up her position in the darkened viewing room, Dewar found herself looking forward to the psychological assessment of Gloria Lynne. Here was her chance at once to prove herself and to reveal the cunning sociopath as a pathological liar.

Meanwhile, Langton and Anna made for the witness interview room where Lady Lynne and Ian Holme were waiting. Langton introduced himself to Lady Lynne, who proffered her hand like royalty for him to shake.

'A detective chief superintendent, that's a much higher rank than chief inspector, isn't it?' Gloria asked nonchalantly as she smiled and looked at Anna.

'Tell me, Chief Superintendent, do you know the Chief Constable of Surrey, Mr O'Dwyer? He's a very good friend of mine.'

Langton said that he didn't know him personally but they had met at a couple of police seminars. Playing Gloria at her own game, he added that Deputy Commissioner Walters was more acquainted with the Chief Constable than he was. Gloria replied that Mr Walters had been very considerate in allowing her to speak with Aisa and he would no doubt be pleased that she had managed to get her to tell the truth.

Anna asked Lady Lynne and Mr Holme to accompany her and Langton to the custody suite interview room so that they could record the conversation.

'Is Lady Lynne under arrest?' Holme asked, to which Langton assured him she was not.

'Lady Lynne is not happy to talk to you on tape,' Holme informed them.

This was something that had not been anticipated, and Anna knew that for Dewar's skills to be of any use they needed her to be able to see and hear everything that took place.

She explained that as Lady Lynne was a technical witness to her daughter's confession they would need to get a witness statement from her, and the easiest and quickest way was to record it and then write it up in statement form for her to sign later.

'I'm very sorry, Detective Travis, but for personal reasons, and in my daughter's best interest, I simply cannot do that. This room seems perfectly adequate and Mr Holme has already switched off the power to the camera,' Gloria said, as if butter wouldn't melt in her mouth.

Anna was about to try again when Langton spoke: 'Certainly, Lady Lynne, as you suggest, this room will be fine.'

'Thank you. I wonder, would you mind fetching me some water, Detective Travis?' Gloria asked with a smile.

Anna was left with little choice but to comply, aware that under the circumstances she just had to grin and bear Gloria's objectionable behaviour, but took the opportunity to go and tell Dewar that Lady Lynne had refused to be interviewed on tape. Dewar was extremely annoyed but also realized there was nothing that could be done about it and suggested to Anna that she take her Dictaphone in with her. Anna considered it briefly, sorely tempted, but finally deemed it too risky.

She returned to the interview room with four bottles of water and put them down on the table.

As she had expected, Ian Holme asked for confirmation that what was about to be said was not being recorded and remained within the room between the persons present. Langton pointed out that he could not refuse to ignore or act on anything that related to criminal offences being committed. Ian Holme assured him that what he was about to be told were personal matters, and the only criminal offences that had been committed by the Lynne family were without intent and in ignorance of the truth. Anna and Langton both suspected that Gloria Lynne was about to portray herself as the real victim of everything that occurred, but what they were not prepared for was how well she had prepared her lies.

Settling herself in the upright chair, Gloria took a deep breath and took a tissue from her pocket. 'What I am about to tell you is very painful for me and brings back some of my darkest memories that have haunted me all my life.' Her voice and hands trembled slightly as she wiped a tear from her eye.

Anna looked at Langton and raised her eyebrows as if to say, 'Here we go, she can shed tears at will.' Langton just sat and stared at Gloria, as he wanted to listen carefully to everything she had to say.

'When I was seventeen I conceived a child with a man called Samuel Peters. We named our son Arum Joshua Peters. At the time, my mother was dying of cancer and I was her sole carer after my father's death from drug abuse—'

'Sorry to interrupt you, Lady Lynne, but I read a magazine article in which you said your father died of cancer,' Anna said.

Gloria didn't bat an eyelid. 'Really? Well I don't ever discuss how my poor father died, I simply say he passed away, Detective Travis. The writer must have put words in my mouth. Now do you mind if I continue or are you more interested in misleading press articles?' Gloria said and gave a contemptuous smile.

Langton frowned at Anna, apologized and invited Gloria to continue.

'Samuel was a heavy drinker, and I'm sad to say, quick to use his fists when he didn't get his way. I feared for Arum's safety and Samuel constantly pressured me to give him up for adoption. I refused and was beaten by Samuel for what he called my pig-headedness. Under increasing pressure I found it almost impossible to care for Arum properly and I was afraid that Samuel would hurt him. I knew that my sister-in-law Esme was a good woman and she was emigrating to England with Marisha, her sister, so I asked Esme to take Arum with her for what would undoubtedly be a better life.' Gloria now turned on the waterworks for sympathy. Ian Holme fell for it, resting his hand on top of Gloria's briefly and telling her that as much as it hurt her she had to be strong.

Anna was chomping at the bit to say something and couldn't understand why Langton was allowing Gloria to run the show, as control was what she revelled in. But Langton opened a bottle of water and handed it to Gloria to take some, which she did before continuing.

'Esme and I had false documents made up and Arum became Joshua Peters. For the sake of my own sanity, and Arum's future wellbeing, it was agreed that I would have no further contact with him and I have always honoured that commitment I made to Esme and my son.'

Now the crocodile tears really began to flow, which Anna thought was an act worthy of an Oscar. At last, Langton spoke: 'I realize this must be very distressing for you, Lady Lynne, but if it helps, would I be right in saying that when Esme married John Reynolds, Arum now became Joshua Reynolds?'

Gloria blew her nose politely and nodded her head. 'I had no idea that he was my son when Donna met him – you see, I never had any contact with Esme or Arum after she left Jamaica. Had I known at the time they met then I would have said something, done what I could to stop the relationship, and as for Aisa's affair with him, well I never knew about that until today, so that was a fait accompli,' Gloria said, looking very sub-dued.

Langton cleared his throat. 'You sound overly concerned about Aisa's affair with Josh, Lady Lynne. As you said yourself, you knew nothing about it and anyway these things happen. Thankfully, it wasn't incestuous like Donna's relationship with Josh,' he said very quietly.

Gloria promptly had a minor meltdown, crying, swaying as if she was about to faint and grabbing Ian Holme's arm to steady herself. It was obvious she was about to reveal Aisa's parentage and Anna was worried that Langton was starting to believe her, but before she could say anything he played Gloria at her own game.

Langton slapped his hand to his forehead.

'No, oh, my God, please don't tell me Aisa and Josh were related as well!' he exclaimed as, unseen by Gloria and Holme, he tapped Anna's knee beneath the table.

Gloria played her part to the hilt, sighing and shaking her head, as she explained that Aisa was in fact her and Xavier Alleyne's daughter. Langton raised both arms up and in a very wretched voice remarked how tragic to discover that not one but two daughters were sleeping with her son.

Gloria for a second flicked a glance towards Langton, unsure if he was being sarcastic or genuine.

'I'm slightly confused, Lady Lynne, as Aisa told DI Barolli and Agent Dewar she was adopted,' he said.

Yet again, Gloria had an answer that depicted her as the aggrieved party: 'When I met Lord Henry, he assumed, because of the colour of Aisa's skin, that I had adopted her.'

'Did you not tell him the truth?' Langton asked.

'He never asked me, as I said he assumed as much, and when Aisa was naughty one day he told her how lucky she was to find someone as kind as me to adopt her. Before I knew it he was telling everyone, even Donna, that Aisa was adopted, so what could I do? She was just a small child, and would have been so confused if I'd said anything different.'

'What a terrible predicament to find yourself in, Lady Lynne,' Langton said, looking concerned. Thinking of Dewar's advice he decided to try and throw her off track and without pausing changed direction.

'May I ask why you wanted Esme and not Marisha to care for Arum?'

'I don't mean this in a nasty way,' Gloria confided, 'but Marisha was very similar to her brother Samuel – she liked to put her own needs before others'.'

'What happened between you and Samuel after you gave Arum to Esme?' Langton asked.

'I left him, or should I say I ran away when his drinking and violence became worse. I couldn't get off the island as I had no money, so I went to Montego Bay, where I met and married Xavier.' Gloria paused to blow her nose, and this time Anna tapped Langton's knee beneath the table, wanting him to hold back on the subject of the bigamous marriage. However, Gloria, sharp as ever, went on to say that what she was about to tell them next was shameful but it was the truth. When Xavier proposed to her, she told him about her marriage to Samuel, but not about their son Arum as she had made a promise to Esme. She and Xavier returned to the fishing village where Samuel lived and Gloria asked him for a divorce but he refused. Xavier had said that he loved her and the marriage to Samuel didn't matter, so he arranged for a private ceremony at the plantation and her wedding certificate recorded that she was a widow.

'So you're marriage to Xavier was bigamous,' Langton said with mock surprise, noticing that Gloria shied away from using the word.

'Yes, but we loved each other deeply and saw no wrong in what we had done. When he died it was tragic, a terrible wretched time for me,' Gloria replied, turning up the crocodile tears.

'Well it was many years ago now, but of course you then married Lord Henry ...'

The expression on Gloria's face changed to one of insult but her voice remained calm. 'I filed for divorce from Samuel in Jamaica and it was granted, so my marriage to Henry was lawful, as is my title of Lady Lynne.'

Anna had wrongly assumed that Gloria had never divorced Samuel, but it didn't change her view about him blackmailing her. She knew that in this instance Gloria was telling the truth as her divorce could be easily checked and a lie would not serve her purpose. She had noticed that so far Gloria had not given her the slightest attention, not even a casual glance. Anna would have liked to think that it was because she unnerved her, but she recognized that Gloria was merely trying to belittle her, by treating her as insignificant. Gloria's sob story just got better and better as it went along and Anna wondered, but for her knowledge that the woman was a sociopath, would she also have been taken in by her deceit and lies? The answer, she thought, was probably 'yes'.

Langton spread his hands flat on the table between them.

'Well I don't know what to say, Lady Lynne. I really feel for you – it must have been like a bolt out of the blue discovering that Josh Reynolds was actually Arum, the son that you had no choice but to give up thirty years ago.'

'Thank you, Mr Langton, for being so kind. You cannot believe the pain it caused me when Arum took his own life,' Gloria said and blew her nose. 'I couldn't grieve the way a mother should for fear that Donna would find out who he really was.' She reached into her handbag to get some more tissues but had run out. Langton produced a clean folded handkerchief from his pocket, flicked it open like a waiter with a napkin and handed it to her.

'I've been so moved by your strength and character in times of great hardship that I feel I've missed something,' he said, hoping that Gloria would invite his next question, but she just gave him a doe-eyed look.

'I was wondering when and how you came to know that Joshua Reynolds was your son Arum.'

Anna, thinking that Langton had articulated and timed his question perfectly, fully expected a change in facial expression and a defensive reaction from Gloria, but none came.

'From Samuel, of course – I would have thought that was rather obvious to a man of your intellect, Chief Superintendent,' Gloria said, and deliberately paused, but just as Langton was about to continue, she cut back in.

'I did tell Deputy Commissioner Walters about Samuel when I spoke with him on the phone.'

Langton and Anna were taken aback by this and again

Langton was about to speak but Gloria continued: 'Not in as fine detail as I have just divulged to you.'

Langton asked Gloria when Walters had phoned her and she told him it was the previous evening.

'What did he tell you?'

Gloria explained that Walters had informed her why Aisa had been arrested, at which moment many things about her erratic behaviour when Josh died suddenly fitted into place. Walters had said that although DCI Travis suspected Josh had committed suicide it was believed Aisa was present at the time and this shocked her.

Gloria couldn't remember Walters' exact words but he asked if she knew a Samuel Peters who was related to Joshua. She told him that Samuel was her former husband, and he had been in contact with her since coming to London for his sister Esme's funeral. Gloria went on to say that she was stunned when Walters informed her that Detective Travis had told him Samuel had died of a heart attack. She had asked him when but he didn't know and she felt Travis was mistaken as Samuel had told her he was going back to Jamaica.

'When did Samuel tell you he was going back to Jamaica?' Langton asked.

'Well, it was a little embarrassing really, he turned up at the Charity Ball drunk and looking like a tramp, he'd obviously been hitting the rum again.'

'I'm more interested in what he spoke to you about, Lady Lynne,' Langton said, becoming irritated.

Gloria explained that Samuel asked her if he she had managed to end Josh and Donna's relationship and she told him she was still working on it. He was annoyed and said that he knew he should have told Josh himself, but it was too late as he was returning to Jamaica in the morning.

Langton, aware he was being taken for a fool, was tiring of Gloria's lies and theatrics. Although a dangerous move, which could play to Gloria's advantage, he decided to challenge her story.

'Just like that, unannounced he turns up out of the blue after thirty years?' Langton asked, raising his voice.

'There's no need to be aggressive, Mr Langton, Lady Lynne is trying to be helpful,' Ian Holme said and Langton glared at him.

'It's fine, Ian, I can understand Mr Langton being annoyed that Mr Walters failed to pass on our conversation. Sorry, what was your question again?' Gloria asked, and as Langton was about to repeat it, she continued: 'Oh, yes, about Samuel. Well he actually phoned me a few times, he was doing some decorating at Donna and Josh's flat and he saw a photograph of me with the girls. He recognized me even after all these years. I didn't know at the time, but found out later that he got my number by taking a quick peek in Donna's address book.'

Langton felt himself becoming more and more annoyed as each lie rolled so comfortably off Gloria's lips, and it angered him that someone of Ian Holme's intellect couldn't see her for what she really was. Langton had no hard evidence with which to challenge Gloria, no witnesses, no nothing, and it was clear to him she knew it. She was no longer just the actor in a play; she was now directing the bloody show!

Unabated, Gloria continued, patting and refolding Langton's handkerchief, explaining that on the first occasion Samuel phoned her she wanted nothing to do with him. He claimed he was a changed man and urgently needed to speak to her but wouldn't say what it was about.

'I was obviously stunned to hear he was in London, and I was equally rather scared to even agree to see him. I asked for a contact number and said I would call him back.'

Langton was desperate to try to slow Gloria down, but it was easy for her, as she had memorized a script of lies that made her appear totally innocent of any wrongdoing. Unable to take notes, he was finding it hard to recollect everything that she had said so far.

'Why would you want to call Samuel back when he had treated you so badly in the past?' he asked, trying to break her flow.

'If you hadn't interrupted me so quickly, I was about to tell you that I didn't call him back. The reality was I didn't want anything to do with him. I ignored him, thinking he'd just go away, and I still had no idea who Josh really was at that time. I then received another call from Samuel who told me that Josh was actually Arum. That was enough to persuade me that we needed to sit down and talk so he said he would get back to me with a time and a place, which he did a few days later.'

Anna could see that Langton was becoming exasperated and finding it hard to keep up with Gloria, while it was easier for her to take in everything as she was just listening. She knew that the woman had concocted a story that would cover every angle. Walters had been putty in Gloria's hands, and his blabbing mouth had effectively destroyed any chance they had of proving she was a liar. Although Langton had said he would be the one to lay his neck on the line, that did not seem fair to Anna. Enough is enough, she thought to herself. If she could get Gloria to admit the blackmail she knew she could use it against her.

'Was Samuel Peters trying to blackmail you?' she asked. The room went silent as everyone turned to look at her. She thought that Langton would say something or at the least tell her to go get some more water to stop her going further, but he didn't.

'I beg your pardon, just who do you think you're speaking to, Detective Travis?' Ian Holme asked, looking down his nose at her.

'Gloria, Mr Holme,' Anna replied calmly, ignoring the woman's official title. 'It's a perfectly reasonable question and one to which I'd expect an honest answer.'

'Are you seriously suggesting Lady Lynne would allow herself to be blackmailed and not report it? I think you need to have a word with DCI Travis, Mr Langton, her behaviour is not acceptable.'

Langton looked at Anna and smiled. 'She's being DEADLY serious, Mr Holme. The reason Gloria may not be admitting blackmail is because of the untold damage the truth about her past would do to her seemingly good character.'

'This is outrageous. Lady Lynne has been more than helpful. She has persuaded her daughter to tell you the truth and gone through an emotional rollercoaster herself in telling you about her past. I think, Lady Lynne, that it would be best to terminate this interview now,' Holme advised her.

Anna had to admit Gloria was a consummate actress: she rested her hand on Holme's arm, patting him as if to calm him. 'I'm fine, Ian, dear, the officers are just doing their job, and if you knew Samuel's past like I do then it's understandable that they are suspecting blackmail.'

She withdrew her hand and looked directly at Anna. 'The answer to your question however is, no. One cannot bear grudges forever, but more importantly out of concern for Donna and my son Joshua, as I shall refer to him, I did meet with Samuel. We discussed how best to deal with the situation, he wanted to tell Josh, but I said that would do more harm than good. We agreed that neither of them should ever know the truth and it would be best left to me to split the pair of them up.'

'And exactly how were you going to do that?' Anna asked.

'Well, I couldn't just do it overnight, could I, Detective Travis? They had been in a sexual relationship for quite some time so the sin was already unknowingly committed. I don't expect you to understand how emotional I felt – after all, you're not a mother, are you?' Gloria simpered in an attempt to rile her.

Anna opened her folder and got out a photographed copy of all the marriage and birth certificates. 'Samuel Peters ordered all these documents online. He used them to blackmail you, didn't he?'

Holme was about to speak on Gloria's behalf but again she gently squeezed his arm, indicating she was happy to continue. She spread the photographed documents out on the table and looked over them.

'I know, I know about these because he showed them all to me. You have to understand it was also very emotional for him.

He hadn't seen Josh in thirty years and had lost all contact with Esme. He thought he might have been jumping to conclusions and needed to know if he was right before coming to me, so he obtained all the certificates.'

She frowned and tapped one of them with her red fingernail. 'Can I ask why there is blood on Aisa's birth certificate? It is blood, isn't it?'

'Because they were on the sofa next to Josh when a bullet went straight through his head,' Anna said.

'Must you be so uncaring and graphic about my son's death?' Gloria said, voice trembling, but Anna knew she didn't really care about her son or anyone else for that matter.

Gloria's expression suddenly changed to one of shock as she then started shaking, crying and gripping Ian Holme's arm. 'The certificates were on the sofa? Oh, my God, no, he didn't, please tell me he didn't, why would Samuel tell Josh, why?'

Ian Holme asked to see the picture of the man on the CCTV and Anna handed it to him. 'Is this Samuel, Lady Lynne?'

Gloria nodded and sobbed uncontrollably as Ian Holme glared at Langton and Travis. 'You know full well that Aisa Lynne said this man was leaving Josh's flat when she arrived. I demand to know if any property was missing from Josh Reynolds' flat.'

'We're not sure,' Anna said, realizing that Gloria had yet again turned the tables to her advantage.

'What do you mean, you're not sure? I will walk out of here straight to the Royal Courts of Justice if I have to, and get a sub-poena to see all your evidence!' Holme shouted.

Langton also knew that matters were going from bad to worse, and that they had managed to salvage nothing. Gloria had played her part magnificently from start to finish; she knew they had only circumstantial evidence. She had fooled everyone and she had the best legal mind in the business on her side. Anna leaned over and whispered to Langton that they still needed to ask Gloria about the atropine poisoning, but he shook his head; he knew his hand was forced.

'There was a substantial amount of money found at Esme Peters' flat that had Josh Reynolds' and Samuel's fingerprints on it. Forensic evidence suggests it came from Josh's safe.'

'Did Samuel Peters have access to that flat?' Holmes snapped.

'Yes, and also to Josh Reynolds', we found keys in his possession,' Anna said, feeling it was not fair to let Langton take all the flak for something she had started.

'You told Walters that you thought Josh Reynolds committed suicide; for the life of me I cannot see what made you think Lady Lynne was involved in his death,' Holme protested.

Anna licked her lips and faced him. 'Mr Holme, I believed that Lady Lynne was involved in a cover-up, and I am sure she paid Samuel Peters money to keep quiet about Aisa being there when her son Joshua Reynolds died.' She was trying very hard to maintain a calm positive delivery to keep Holme from overreacting. It didn't work.

Holme was so angry he banged the table. 'I have never seen such shameless breaches of the rules of evidence in my career. You have not heard the end of this, detectives, I will be taking this matter up with the Commissioner himself.'

'No, Ian, you will not,' Gloria said in a motherly fashion.

'Lady Lynne, you and your daughters have been treated dreadfully.'

'I know, and I think Chief Superintendent Langton has been very much influenced by Detective Travis.'

'Nevertheless—'

Gloria again interrupted her lawyer: 'As I said, Ian, I do not bear grudges, and Detective Travis was only doing her job, she was clearly convinced that I was somehow involved in Josh's death and being blackmailed by Samuel. Admittedly, she has not conducted her investigation in an open and forthright manner; however, we achieve nothing if all we seek is retribution. I hope Detective Travis has learned a lesson here today and we can all move on.'

Anna was fuming but Langton was the first to put his hand out and apologize to Gloria. Anna knew he was doing it for her sake but found it hard to accept he was giving in so easily. She so wanted to give Gloria a piece of her mind, but the look on Langton's face said that it was finished.

'I trust that as agreed everything that I have told you will remain strictly confidential?'

Langton and Anna looked at each other. The reality was they'd both have liked to tell Gloria the deal was off, but they knew their hands were tied.

Ian Holme added to Gloria's question: 'I have of course recorded the conversation on my Dictaphone and the micro-card will be given to Lady Lynne for safekeeping. Both she and I will treat any breach of confidence as a slur on her good character, and sue the Met.'

There were other questions Anna badly wanted to put to Gloria, but she knew the woman would have the perfect answer. Anna was forced to admit defeat. Langton asked her to take Ian Holme to the custody area and have Aisa released immediately. He himself remained sitting opposite Gloria, who had taken out her powder compact and was carefully checking her appearance, dabbing beneath her eyes with the handkerchief he had given to her. Her mascara had left dark smudges beneath her eyes, and her cheeks showed a faint tear-stained line in her foundation.

'Dear oh dear, I look dreadful,' she said coyly and then she snapped the gold compact closed.

Chapter Thirty-Eight

As Anna went down the cells to tell Aisa that she was being released without charge, she was deeply depressed. She'd started the day on such a high, convinced that she could get the truth out of Aisa and use her evidence against Gloria Lynne, but everything had backfired on her. Anna had known Gloria would be the greatest challenge she would ever face in an interview situation, but the truth was she had underestimated Gloria's guile and cunning, and now not only did Anna feel she'd let herself down, but worse, Langton, Mike Lewis and everyone else on the team, even Dewar.

She'd had to sit and watch Gloria Lynne's masterful performance of deception and lies as she never once revealed the slightest chink in her armour. Defeat was never an easy pill to swallow in a murder investigation. Over the last few years, under Langton's guidance, Anna had learned to accept that being a detective had its ups and downs and to take comfort from the old adage, 'You win some, you lose some'. This was different: she'd been outwitted and humiliated by a woman she believed to be a serial killer, and Anna hated to feel she had failed.

After Aisa's release, Anna decided to walk round the block, get some fresh air and try and make sense of everything that had occurred. It dawned on her she'd never managed to have the office meeting to tell the team about her suspicions and the facts she had uncovered against Gloria Lynne. Most of them knew bits and pieces, but no one apart from Joan had the full story.

Anna couldn't leave them in the dark, and yet what she would be able to say was now restricted by Gloria's threat to sue if confidentiality was broken. It would be embarrassing for her, but Anna knew that she would just have to swallow her pride and brief the team as best she could.

Entering the incident room, she could see that the team was gathered together and Langton was addressing them. He stood tall and proud as he addressed the officers, and there was a look of admiration and respect on the faces of everyone in the room, even though he must be suffering from jet lag and exhaustion. Although she had come in midway through his debrief she heard enough to realize that he was taking full responsibility for everything, even claiming that he called her back from Quantico. She knew he was doing it to take the burden of pressure off her shoulders and keep the team's faith in her. He had promised to take the flak and he was sticking to his word.

Without revealing anything confidential, Langton acknowledged that they might feel there were many unanswered questions, but sometimes when politics and policing collided, hands were tied and not everyone could be privy to all the information. He reassured the team that they hadn't been on a pointless journey – lessons had been learned, and each and every one of them should feel immensely proud of their contribution throughout the investigation. Langton ended by making it clear that the reinvestigation into Josh Reynolds' death was now closed and the Coroner's verdict of suicide was correct. He emphasized strongly that there was to be no gossip about the case outside the room, and if anyone betrayed his trust there would be severe repercussions. Sternly he asked if anyone had any questions, and although there was a mixture of confused and gloomy faces around the room, not one person said a word.

Langton's expression changed as he smiled and shook his head. 'Cheer up, you miserable lot, you look like you've all been to a funeral.'

'There's always a wake after a funeral, guvnor!' boomed the inimitable voice of Detective Dan Ross and everyone gave a loud cheer.

Langton got his wallet out of his pocket and an even louder cheer went up as he pulled out two fifty-pound notes.

'Go on then, get some nibbles as well. Spiced rum okay for you, DI Barolli?' he asked to more laughter.

Barolli, playing up to his colleagues, took a theatrical bow. 'As long as it's *atropine*-free, sir, or I'll be tripping out and dancing on the ceiling again.'

When everyone else had turned back to their desks Langton took Anna into her office to tell her that he had spoken privately with Joan and instructed her that everything she knew about the case was strictly between her, Anna and himself. He had also told her to close down the investigation on the HOLMES murder inquiry computer and ensure the files were only accessible by a security code that was then to be given solely to him.

'Don't you trust me?' Anna asked.

'I know how much you're hurting right now, I've been there myself, but I don't want you dwelling on the past, going over and over the case files.'

'I just feel that there was more we could have put to her – the atropine, money in the freezer—'

Langton wanted to draw a line under the discussion. 'Listen, she'd secured Aisa's silence and Walters had revealed your hand. I'm sorry to be blunt, but with all your main witnesses dead only Gloria knows the truth. We were just fishing for evidence in a pool of questionable circumstances.'

Anna knew that he was right and arguing with him was pointless.

'I feel like you did about Fitzpatrick.'

'You'll just have to learn to accept that Gloria Lynne is your one that got away. You win—'

'Some, you lose some. I know that, but at least you got closure.'

'It wasn't pretty though, Anna. When I saw the look on his son's face as he clutched his dead father, I asked myself if it was all worthwhile.'

'Was it?'

'The end result was out of my control, but the anger that raged inside me wasn't. Like a fool I let it eat away at me and it nearly cost me my job, certainly my promotion, but worst of all it destroyed my marriage to Laura.'

Anna was shocked. 'Are you separated?'

'Yes, going to the States to get Fitzpatrick was the final straw. I've been a poor husband and father. I put my needs and the Met before my family. I've learned the hard way and I beg you, don't go down the same road as me, because you will regret it in the long run.'

'You will try and save your marriage, won't you?'

'Yes, and there's only one way to do that. I—'

The office door suddenly flew open and Deputy Commissioner Walters walked in, slamming the door behind him, making Anna jump. 'What the fuck do you two think you're playing at?' he bellowed, his face crimson-red and body shaking with anger.

Langton didn't bat an eyelid. 'Now let me think about this. Only one of two people could have called you. I doubt it was Lady Lynne as you served your purpose and would no longer be of any use to her. Ian Holme QC is of course in the same Freemasons Lodge as you so—'

Walters cut Langton off and exploded in fury: 'You've both lied and given me the ammunition to destroy your careers and, believe me, that's just what I'm going to do!'

Anna had never seen a senior officer lose his temper to this extent.

Langton remained calm. 'DCI Travis acted on my orders. I was in charge of this case so if you're pissed off then direct your anger at me.'

Walters ignored Langton and came face to face with Anna, prodding her on the shoulder.

'You, Travis, have done nothing short of instigating a vendetta against Lady Lynne and her daughters!'

Langton took hold of Anna's arm and gently ushered her to one side. She couldn't believe it when Langton suddenly grabbed Walters by the scruff of his jacket and forced him up against the wall with a thud.

'You speak to her like that again, or raise your voice once more, and I won't be responsible for my actions,' Langton said through gritted teeth.

'Take your hands of me, Langton, or you'll regret it.'

Langton squeezed Walters' lapels tighter and lifted him onto his tiptoes. 'You can threaten me all you like, but first YOU WILL apologize to DCI Travis. Do I make myself clear?'

A shaking Walters nodded and complied, though his apology was insincere as he muttered, 'Sorry.'

'Not good enough,' Langton whispered to Walters, 'try again with more feeling.'

'I am very sorry for my overbearing conduct and rudeness.'

Langton loosened his grip, stepped away and a flustered Walters straightened his uniform.

'Assaulting a senior officer is a serious offence and one for which—'

Anna was quick to interrupt. 'What assault, sir?' she said, stone-faced.

Langton smiled at her and glared at the flummoxed Walters.

'You witnessed it, Travis, you saw what Langton did and it's in your best interest to back me,' Walters said, confident Anna would bear witness against Langton for the sake of her own career.

'I saw nothing untoward, sir, and I can't believe you'd expect me to lie,' Anna replied and folded her arms defiantly.

Walters seemed lost for words but Langton wasn't done with him yet:

'Your sycophantic manner with Lady Lynne has ruined the investigation. She used you to find out what was going on and get to her daughter Aisa. You revealed evidence, which let them both walk away scot-free. Jeopardizing a criminal investigation is a serious disciplinary offence.'

'Not to mention misconduct in a public office,' Anna added and smiled at Langton.

'You have no proof and the outcome is still one of suicide. I know your little chat with Lady Lynne was off the record, no tape, no notes, nothing. As for Travis, well she came running to my door over the Fitzpatrick case. She couldn't wait to drop you in the shit to further her own career,' Walters sneered.

'You little prick. I know you fooled her and used it to shaft my promotion to Commander with the Mayor's office.'

'Well you've shafted yourself now. I'm suspending you both from duty whilst you are both investigated for misconduct in a public office. Your warrant cards . . . NOW!'

'I told you I made all the decisions on the Reynolds case, so you only need to suspend me,' Langton said.

Anna decided this was the ideal time to speak up. 'I don't think you want to suspend anyone, sir, it's really not in your best interest.'

'Just shut your mouth, Travis, and hand over that card,' growled Walters.

'Have you forgotten our little conversation yesterday?' Anna asked.

Walters gave a cynical laugh. 'How could I ever forget it, Travis? You shot yourself in the foot by lying to me. Like Josh Reynolds, you put the gun to your own head. Now give me your bloody warrant card.'

Langton looked despairingly at Anna, as if to ask what on earth she was playing at. He was beyond caring what Walters did to him, but Anna, he felt, was playing into the man's hands and throwing away her career unnecessarily.

'It's okay, James, I can handle Deputy Commissioner Walters. Yesterday evening, he admitted how he duped me over the Fitzpatrick case to ruin your promotion. He called you disrespectful and belligerent and said he was going to use the budget cuts to "cull" you.'

'She's lying. I never said anything of the sort,' Walters said adamantly.

'Well let me refresh your memory.' Anna calmly walked over to her handbag, retrieved her Dictaphone and held it up so they could all see.

Anna pressed play and took great delight, as did Langton, in watching Walters squirm as he listened to his voice say everything he had just so steadfastly denied.

Langton and Anna smiled at each other, and in unison turned to Walters to hear what had to say for himself. He just stood there his mouth gawping wide as it sank in that the tables had been turned and his career was in their hands.

'Well that's the most powerful piece of evidence I've heard all day,' Langton said, rubbing it in.

Anna joined in. 'I take it the suspension is rescinded and our sins are forgiven, sir?'

'The case is closed as a suicide; make sure there's a report on my desk by the end of next week please,' Walters muttered and turned to walk out of the door.

'Not so fast, Walters,' Langton said, causing him to stop.

He turned as Langton walked up to him and grabbed hold of his hand. He winced in trepidation as Langton pressed his warrant card into his palm. 'I've had enough of all this crap, so take this as my official retirement.'

Walters was relieved yet surprised. 'Well if you insist that's what you want . . .'

Langton held his hand up, indicating he had more to say.

'I don't ask for anything more than I deserve after a long and distinguished career in the Met. I've solved more bloody crimes, and put criminals behind bars, than you've had hot dinners, so you will recommend me for the Queen's Police Medal.

'You know I can't do that.'

'I don't believe in the word can't and neither should you, unless you want me to go straight down the Mayor's office, followed by a solicitor's, to let them listen to DCI Travis's enlightening recording.'

'There's no need for that – I'll see what I can do.'

'You just make sure it happens, and while you're at it, I want you to recommend DCI Travis's promotion to Detective Superintendent on the next boards.'

Walters knew he had no choice but to comply. He nodded and walked out of the room.

Langton punched the air with joy. 'God, that felt good, that was a bloody masterstroke you pulled. Did you see the look on his face when you played the recording?' He laughed in delight as he slumped down into an armchair.

'If you'd asked to be made Commander, he'd have had no choice – you didn't need to give him your resignation,' Anna said, hoping that he would reconsider his position.

'I was just about to tell you I was retiring when Walters walked in. I'll miss the job, the thrill of the chase and the wonderful and dedicated people I've worked with, none more so than you, Anna. For once my decision isn't about me though, it's for Laura and the children. I want to save my marriage and see my kids grow up.'

Anna was immensely sad. They'd been through so much together, even right up to the end with Gloria Lynne, and the prospect of losing her mentor scared her more than she wanted to imagine. No matter how much they had argued he had always been there for her, making sense out of confusion and supporting her through the turmoils of being a murder squad detective. She knew that but for Langton she would never have achieved so much and become a DCI in such a short space of time. He'd now even secured her promotion to Superintendent, albeit through a bit of skulduggery. She wanted to beg him to stay but knew that would be selfish and it was clear his mind was made up.

'You will keep in touch, won't you?' she asked quietly.

Langton could see the sadness in her eyes; he got up, stood in front of her and gently placed his hands on her shoulders.

'Of course I bloody will, but I won't be talking shop any more and I'm expecting to be guest of honour at the team's

Christmas lunch,' Langton said, trying to make light of what for him was also a very emotional moment.

He drew her close, put his arms around her, gave her a long loving hug, and whispered softly in her ear, 'I'm the one who owes you a big thank-you for putting up with me for so long. Working with you has been a pleasure and a privilege that I will always cherish.' He kissed her lightly on the cheek and stepped back. 'Right, let's have a drink with the rest of the motley crew.'

'I don't really feel up to it right now, not after Gloria Lynne,' she said, trying to conceal the fact that Langton walking away hurt her more than losing to Gloria.

'It sometimes does you good to drown your sorrows,' he said with a smile of encouragement, 'but more importantly you owe it to your team. They stuck by you because they admire and respect you for who you are and your leadership. For them to be strong, you have to be strong. If you just walk out the door you'll damage that respect.'

As Anna and Langton joined the rest of the team in the main office, Barolli was recounting the effects of atropine and Dan Ross was having fun barracking him. As the merriment continued and Anna chatted to Joan, Langton looked over at her, smiled and raised his glass. As she raised her glass in return she knew it was a private moment between two people, a toast to both their futures.

Langton stayed on for about an hour and, not long after, most of the team drifted over to the pub. Anna was in her office tidying up her desk and getting her things together to go home when Jessie Dewar walked in. She asked Anna if she was okay.

'I'm fine, Jessie.' Anna sighed. 'Other than being completely exhausted, that is.'

Dewar apologized for not being able to provide her and Langton with a detailed psychological profile of Gloria Lynne, but Anna reassured her she wasn't to know that Gloria wouldn't allow the interview to be recorded.

'Well, I don't expect it's of any use to you now but it may be of interest anyway,' Dewar said, and she handed Anna a document she had drafted while Langton and Anna were interviewing Gloria. Dewar explained that she had thought Gloria might be arrested, so she had prepared a strategy for a further interview with her.

'It's just some advice and tactics on how to deal with and counter someone who's a sociopath,' Dewar said.

Anna thanked her and promised she would read it.

Dewar stepped forward and put her hand out to Anna.

'Although we've had our disagreements, I'd just like to say I've enjoyed working with you and learned a lot.'

Anna shook her hand. 'I hope the next case we both work on will be more straightforward.'

'Sadly my time with the Met is over. The FBI Academy Director called me to say he wanted me back in the States to help on a serial-killer case. Flight's booked for Saturday morning, so I best get off and start getting my bits and pieces together.' Dewar turned to leave when Anna said she wanted to ask her something.

'From a psychological aspect, where did I go wrong with Gloria?'

'You didn't, we all did. I think all your suspicions are right but we all underestimated her. With hindsight, as you'll see in my report, we should have played her at her own game.'

Anna asked Dewar what she meant and the agent explained that a sociopath's ability to act normally is determined by the information they have available to them.

'Gloria, thanks mostly to Walters and Ian Holme, knew what you knew, so she twisted and used it to her advantage,' Dewar said.

'How could I have countered that?' Anna asked.

'By trying to confuse her, and the best way to do that is to feed her false information: if she's confused and you are not, then you are the one in control.'

'And then?' Anna wondered.

'You hoist her by her own petard, point out her failures, and tell her she's a phoney and a shyster.'

'Bit late now, I guess.'

'Sadly, yes, you need to strike while the iron is hot,' Dewar said. 'Well, guess I'll see you in the morning.'

As she left the room, Anna sat down once more and began to read her report. As she finished it she stood up, slammed both hands on the desk, and let out a yell of pent-up emotion. That iron was still very hot!

As she drove out to Weybridge, Anna did her best to calm her nerves, knowing it was a dangerous thing to walk into the witch's lair alone. Needing a viable reason to go to Lynne House she had gathered together the flat keys, and other documents, that could be legitimately restored to Donna Lynne. It didn't matter to her whether Donna or Aisa were in, the purpose of her visit was much deeper than a polite house call.

Although Dewar's advice was thought-provoking, her suggestion to feed Gloria false information and berate her was of no value to the criminal investigation. Lying about the evidence to a suspect or being oppressive in an interview was not allowed and any resulting confession would be rendered worthless.

Anna realized that Gloria had deliberately used the confines of the police station, and the legal representation of Ian Holme, to suit her purpose. She still had no evidence against Gloria and was only too aware that arresting her was not an option. For Anna this was personal, a need to show Gloria up for the evil bitch that she was. Anna knew that Gloria was not as smart as she thought she was; it was now time for her to be the one in control, and play Gloria at her own game, on her own ground!

Arriving at Lynne House, Anna wondered if she would even get past the front gates. But as she got out of the car and before she could press the intercom, she was aware of the movement of the security camera, and then the gates slowly opened. Anna had the strangest feeling that it was Gloria who was watching and luring her in. She drove up to the house, her heart beating ten to the dozen, forcing herself to breathe in and exhale slowly to keep calm. As she pulled up at the front door, Gloria appeared, dressed in a white, full-length, toga-style dress and gold sandals. The lights from the interior of the house spilled out into the dark night, illuminating Gloria from behind as if she were an angelic apparition.

'Good evening, Detective Travis, I was expecting you,' she said with a tight unfriendly smile. Security lights came on, and from the direction of the greenhouse came the frantic sound of Atropa, the Doberman guard dog, barking and pulling at her chain attached to the kennel.

Anna, thankful that Gloria wasn't allowing the dog to roam the grounds freely, gathered the box of property from the passenger seat and followed the woman into the house, closing the door behind her. Gloria said nothing as Anna followed her across the large hallway. Gloria suddenly stopped.

'Get to your rooms now!' she shouted.

Anna looked up and had a brief glimpse of Donna and Aisa standing at the top of the stairs. As they hurriedly moved out of sight, like two frightened children, Anna noticed they were both wearing the same white togas and gold sandals as their mother. She wondered if they might be about to go to a fancy dress party.

Entering the library, Gloria closed the door. Anna immediately caught sight of the paintings of the 'Three Fates' and recalled Gloria saying she preferred the angelic Mazzoni depiction as it was 'appealing to the eye and their soft white robes are exquisite'. Numbly, she realized that Gloria and her daughters were dressed exactly like the Fates in the painting. She noticed a small pair of flower shears on the coffee table and remembered Don Blane telling her about shears being used to cut the thread of life. Anna was beginning to think that Gloria's mental state might finally have spiralled out of control, and wondered if she had made a terrible mistake coming to Lynne House. Gloria went over to the coffee table and picked up the shears, which made Anna's heart pound with fear as she frantically looked round the room for something to protect herself with.

Gloria turned, holding the shears towards Anna. 'I told

Katrina to put these back in the greenhouse before she went out for the evening. Are you all right, Detective Travis, you seem nervous?'

Anna realized Gloria was playing games with her, but now she was angry and there was no way she would be scared off.

'No, not at all, Lady Lynne.' Anna pointed to the Mazzoni. 'For a moment there, you reminded me of Atropa, or was it Clotho or Lachesis who cut the thread?'

Gloria smiled as she complimented Anna on doing her homework and told her that it was indeed Atropa, or Aisa as she liked to call her, who determined when a person's life ended.

'Tell me, detective, do you believe in fate?'

'We all have a destiny, Lady Lynne, and to an extent we can control what happens to us along the way, but no one has the God-given right to determine when and how we die ... Not even you.'

'You think so?' Gloria smirked, then walked over to the drinks cabinet.

'Would you care to join me in a gin and tonic, detective?'

'No, thank you, I'm driving and wouldn't want to have an accident,' Anna remarked, knowing it was obvious to Gloria why she had declined the offer.

'Did you know that tonic water contains quinine, which comes from the bark of the cinchona tree and is used to treat malaria?'

'Is it similar to atropine?' Anna asked, determined to stand her ground against Gloria's mind games.

Gloria wagged her finger at Anna. 'Too much of either will bring on heart failure and kill you.' Having poured herself a drink Gloria came across to Anna and started to pat-down her jacket pockets and shirt. Anna obligingly raised her arms and told Gloria that she was not wearing a wire and her phone was in the car. Gloria leaned forward and ran her hands up and down the outside of Anna's skirt, then moved her hand underneath, and slowly ran it up and down the inside of her thighs in a suggestive manner.

Although it disgusted Anna she knew that Gloria was trying to intimidate her. 'Satisfied?' she asked, allowing the double meaning to hang in the air.

Gloria sat down in an armchair, casually crossed her legs, and took a sip of her drink.

'Let's not beat about the bush,' she began. 'You despise me because you lost and I won, but what really eats away at your pitiful existence is a desire to know whether you were right or wrong about me.'

Gloria was partially right, but Anna was not going to satisfy her gloating. 'You may believe your lies, Lady Lynne, but what angers you is that I don't, and never will. I seek the truth as evidence. You seek it so that you can manipulate it for your own gain.'

'Then in some ways we are similar, Detective Travis.'

'No, we are not. Unlike you, I don't have a heart that is incapable of feeling the pain of others. I will be given another case, you will be forgotten and I will move on,' Anna said firmly.

Gloria gave a condescending laugh and said it was a valiant but pointless effort to try and defend her own shattered dignity. She paused, sipped her drink again and stared Anna menacingly in the eye.

'Only I can tell you if you were right, Travis, but for that to happen I would need to know exactly what you *think* I did.'

Anna knew Gloria was playing with her and there was always the risk that the woman might admit to nothing if she revealed what she suspected was the truth behind a catalogue of murders. Still, it was now or never, so Anna decided to give Gloria a synopsis of what she believed happened, but not the evidence that had led to her conclusions.

'Samuel Peters discovered that Donna was your daughter. He ordered copies of the birth and marriage certificates to blackmail you about your bigamous past, and your daughter Donna's incestuous relationship with Arum. You paid him fifty thousand, thinking that would be the end of it, but Samuel wanted more and you refused, probably because you had already decided to kill him.' Anna paused to see if Gloria had anything to say but she just waved her hand for Anna to continue.

'To spite you, Samuel told Josh, who now knowing you were his real mother drove out here and confronted you. You wanted your past buried, but Josh, like his father Samuel, was now a threat. You gave him a drink laced with atropine, hoping he would have a fatal car crash on his way home, a method you had used previously to ensure Lord Henry's son and wife died in a helicopter crash.' Anna again paused to watch Gloria's reaction to what she had said so far.

'Are you sure you wouldn't like a gin and tonic?' Gloria scoffed, as she finished hers and poured another. 'Please do continue, I am so enjoying this, it's like listening to a detective story on the radio.' She settled herself back down in the armchair.

'You messed up, the dosage was wrong and Josh made it home, but the atropine meant his brain was not functioning properly and he became suicidal. Josh called Aisa and she went to the flat, tried to stop Josh shooting himself but failed. Wearing a blood-stained dress she ran from the flat and was seen by Samuel—'

Gloria interrupted, standing up and giving a slow handclap. Anna insisted she hadn't finished.

'You don't need to, Travis. I think I know the rest of the story,' Gloria said arrogantly.

'Then I must assume I was right,' Anna said.

Gloria shook her head and sighed. 'Very well, if you really feel the need to unburden yourself.' She wafted her hand dismissively.

'Samuel discovered Josh's body and tried to blackmail you again, this time about Aisa being there. You told Aisa to say nothing; you met with Samuel to pay him off but poisoned him with atropine.'

'And the rest, as they say, is history,' Gloria said patronizingly. She then came closer to Anna, smiling all while as she unpinned a piece of jewellery from her white gown.

'This is a very special brooch, very old, very precious and it's gold and pale blue enamel.' She looked directly into Anna's eyes.

'It's the deadly nightshade flower, and it's a gift from me to you.'

Anna gritted her teeth as Gloria pinned the brooch to her jacket, patting it with her hand, inclining her head to one side.

'So pretty yet so deadly, it suits you.'

Anna responded by saying that she also suspected Xavier and Lord Lynne might have been poisoned with atropine. Gloria, unconcerned, asked why she had not said so earlier.

Anna smiled and deliberately made light of their deaths. 'Didn't happen over here so not my problem.'

'But it angers you to think I killed them,' Gloria scoffed.

'That depends on how close I was to the truth,' Anna replied casually.

'If it's any consolation you didn't miss anyone out and the ingredients were pretty much all there.'

Anna had deliberately said nothing about Marisha and suddenly realized that Gloria had never asked about her at the station. She thought it strange that Gloria had not taken the chance to gloat, and wondered why that might be, even as she allowed the woman to carry on with her melodramatic performance. Her raised voice took on an increasingly theatrical tone, her words enunciated carefully, as she enjoyed showing off to an imaginary audience.

'If I were on a jury I'd believe you and want to convict the defendant for such heinous crimes. The only problem is, you've not one shred of evidence.' She giggled.

'You think not?' Anna replied, stone-faced.

'I don't think, I *know*. You have failed in your efforts to implicate me or my beloved daughters in any wrongdoing and I will continue to be respected as a good mother and a pillar of society, whereas your superiors and colleagues will long remember you as a worthless failure,' Gloria mocked, raising her glass in a victory salute before taking a long drink, then licking her lips.

'Don't flatter yourself, Lady Lynne, you're not that special from where I'm standing. A good liar, yes, but as a mother, you've failed miserably,' Anna said, emphasizing the last three words.

Gloria's facial expression gave nothing away, but Anna knew she had touched a nerve. It was time to try and confuse her.

'It's true, isn't it? Your girls let you down terribly and disgraced your good name. You've given them everything they ever wanted, but what happened?' Anna paused. Gloria opened her mouth to speak but Anna held up her hand, indicating she hadn't finished.

'Aisa steals money from right under your nose, and you didn't even know it was happening – how you could let her make such a fool of you is beyond belief!' Anna noticed Gloria now seemed to need the drink whereas so far it had been a theatrical prop.

'As for Donna, well she betrays you by cavorting naked in front of leering, salivating men with hard-ons. Then she marries Joshua, the very man who hired her and let her display her naked body for his own gain.'

Gloria gulped down her gin and tonic in one, stood up and marched over to the cabinet to pour a third. Her expression had changed, it was as if she was in another world, confused and angry, trying to make sense of it all. Picking up the ice with her hand she dropped it into her glass as she poured a substantial amount of gin, topping it up with just a fraction of tonic. This time she didn't bother with a slice of lemon but took a long swig and then rattled the ice cubes round the glass.

'How very intuitive of you, and, yes, that silly bitch Donna started all this, she's to blame. If she hadn't walked into that filthy, stinking club she'd never have met Joshua. Because of her Samuel came back into my life. If she'd gone to prison it would have been no more than she deserved for what she's done to me.'

Anna was amazed at the sudden change in Gloria's attitude; it was as if her need to blame revealed her true feelings. She also wondered how many gins Gloria had been through before her arrival as her speech was now beginning to slur.

'How right you are, Lady Lynne – Donna meeting Joshua was a disaster, but at least when Samuel came back into your life it was amicable,' Anna suggested.

A look of disgust appeared on Gloria's face. 'Amicable? He's an absolute pig of man; you think I'd willingly let him anywhere near me?'

'So I guess Samuel and Marisha's, sorry I mean Samuel and Arum's deaths are really a blessing in disguise?' Anna asked, hoping a confused Gloria would react to the mention of Marisha's name.

Gloria said nothing at first, but Anna could see she was questioning herself about what she thought she had just heard.

'Why did you say Marisha?'

Anna deliberately looked nervous. 'Just a slip of the tongue, that's all.'

'You're lying, I can tell. What has Marisha got to do with any of this?'

It was now clear that Gloria had never suspected Marisha might be involved, let alone that she was dead. Gloria was evidently worried as Marisha had never been part of her script of lies and now posed a threat. She needed answers to be able to manipulate the information, but Anna was not going to provide them and decided to turn the heat up slowly.

'Deputy Commissioner Walters told you Samuel Peters died of a heart attack, but you said that can't be right because he'd gone back to Jamaica. So thinking about it . . .'

'I demand to know where Marisha is, she's my sister-in-law and I will offer to pay for Samuel's funeral and look after her.'

Gloria was becoming noticeably more agitated, and still Anna avoided answering her.

'Why didn't you ask us at the station if it was true?'

'Ask what, what should I have asked? Has Marisha said anything?'

Anna suspected Gloria wasn't fully aware of what she was saying, or asking, as her brain was working at such a pace to process the new situation.

Anna remained calm, determined to confuse Gloria further. 'I think I've made a terrible mistake. I just assumed . . .'

'What, what mistake have you made, what did you assume?' Gloria asked angrily.

'That it was Samuel's body in the mortuary, but it can't be as he's back in Jamaica, just like you told Walters and like Marisha said. I'm sorry that I wrongly accused you, Lady Lynne, and I realize now that you have just been playing silly games to teach me a lesson.'

Anna was enjoying watching her lies bewilder and anger Gloria, who then raised her voice.

'I don't play games! I controlled when, where and how Samuel would die. I alone determined his and everyone else's fate.'

'It's okay, you don't have to try and fool me any longer,' Anna said, smiling, which infuriated Gloria even more.

'I decided how and when Joshua would die . . .'

'That is ridiculous, everyone knows Josh shot himself,' Anna said, dismissing Gloria's admission as a joke.

'I poisoned him, just like Samuel, and there's nothing you can do about it! Now where is Marisha!' The pupils of her eyes dilated from her anger and increased blood pressure.

'Well if you insist that you really are a murderer then I can't possibly tell you where she is,' Anna said and folded her arms.

'She'll lie like her brother, she doesn't know anything and wasn't even there when I went to see Samuel,' Gloria said, inadvertently revealing Anna had been right about that as well.

'She's dead, Gloria, she never posed a threat to you, but I just made you believe she did. By your own admission, you've proved that I was right all along. I will leave now and you can fester in the knowledge that I beat you at your own game. You will spend the rest of your life thinking about me, constantly looking over your shoulder, scared that I will come for you,' Anna said, coming closer, so close she could smell the gin mixed with the woman's heavy perfume. 'I will never let this go, you can count on that.'

As Anna turned to leave, Gloria gave a howling scream and flung her glass across the room, where it hit the Mazzoni painting and splintered into hundreds of pieces. She was rigid with a crazed fury and totally out of control. As Anna opened the library door she came face to face with Donna and Aisa standing together, holding hands and both crying. She hurriedly closed the door behind her, as Gloria's drunken ranting continued unabated.

'Did you just hear everything your mother said?' Anna asked and both girls nodded.

Aisa looked forlornly at Anna. 'I've told Donna everything about mine and Josh's affair and what my mother made me do. She knows we are real sisters.'

It was clear to Anna that Donna had forgiven Aisa and the two of them needed each other more than anything in the world right now.

'You need to get away from here while your mother's in such a disturbed and unstable state.

'She will destroy you – listen to her, she's deranged and very dangerous and has no love for either of you. Think of your husband, Donna, your lover, Aisa, her son, her own son Joshua blew his brains out, his mind distorted by the poison she'd fed him. You heard her gloating how she had manipulated both of you, and would have let Donna go to prison for *her* crimes. For your own self-preservation get out tonight and never look back.'

The security lights blazed on once more, illuminating Anna's car as she sat inside, shaking, waiting for the automatic gates to open so she could leave Lynne House. As she glanced in the rear-view mirror, the dog began its frantic barking. The big iron gates slowly opened and she reached for her ignition key, just as a movement caught her eye. She turned and looked over her shoulder to see Donna running from the house.

Anna parked just outside the gates and got out of her car to peer through the railings to where Donna was opening the boot of her Mini. Aisa sped out of the house carrying a suitcase, her arms full of clothes which she stuffed into the boot. The girls had obviously taken her advice, but no sooner had Donna got into the driving seat and started up the engine than Gloria flew out from the house, her white robe billowing as she waved her arms and screamed at full volume. The girls shouted in panic and the sound of their voices made the dog even more frenzied and drag at her chains. Anna wished she had waited or taken the daughters in her car as she saw Gloria throw herself at Aisa in an attempt to stop her getting into the Mini, grabbing a handful of the young woman's hair, shouting and clawing as she tried to pull Aisa away, but Donna got out from the car and roughly pushed her mother. Gloria fell backwards onto the gravel then drunkenly tried to get to her feet as both girls jumped into the car. Donna started the engine and the gravel churned up as she reversed at speed, and then made a sliding turn and headed down the driveway.

Gloria, crawling on all fours like the still-frenzied dog, was screaming, 'How dare you leave me! YOU CAN'T LEAVE ME!'

Anna didn't even make it back to her car as the Mini drove past her, very fast, heading down the lane. Whether they saw Anna or not, they made no attempt to stop as she stared at the disappearing rear lights. She could not resist returning to look through the railings, to where the front door remained open wide, but there was no sign of Gloria. The security lights went out, leaving only the lamps from inside to give the house a yellowish glow, foreboding and medieval. The dog had finally fallen silent.

Anna drove back to London still very shaken by the whole encounter. Although she had the satisfaction of knowing she was right, and had managed to warn Aisa and Donna to get away, she was still left frustrated that Lady Lynne was free from any punishment. For now, though, she just had to be content with the fact she had confronted Gloria and that her instincts were correct.

*

The following day, Anna was back at her desk, eager to get on and put the Reynolds case behind her, despite the fact that a few of the team had severe hangovers. Late in the afternoon, she got a call from Langton asking if she'd seen the *Evening Standard* front page about Lady Lynne being found dead at her mansion house.

'What? You are joking?'

'I'm not, darlin'. I phoned the local DCI in Surrey and he gave me the details.'

With a sinking feeling in the pit of her stomach, Anna asked herself: did anyone know she had been to Lynne House? Was he calling to warn her?

Langton continued: 'She was found in her greenhouse by the housekeeper. Apparently, went in there drunk, fell and knocked over a large canister of pesticide. The contents spilled out and gassed her, she didn't even have a face mask on and her dog was found dead beside her.'

'Bloody hell,' Anna said.

'Well, she paid the ultimate price in the end, and her daughters were not even at home. I guess it'll be accidental death.'

Anna agreed and vividly recalled her first ever meeting with Lady Lynne where she explained how dangerous the pesticides were and that she always had to wear protective clothing and a face mask.

'They think she tried to reach for a mask, but the dog was in there with her, so who knows.'

'Yes, who knows? Pity about the dog!' Anna said as she replaced the receiver and sat back in her chair.

The papers were full of the tragic death of Lady Lynne. Donna and Aisa spoke movingly at the funeral and promised the Lynne Foundation would continue the charitable work of Lord Henry and their mother. They never contacted Anna. The toxicology report had stated that Gloria had a very high level of alcohol in her blood, which would have accelerated the effect of the pesticide, and so her death was reported by the Coroner as non-suspicious and accidental.

The files and reports were completed as the team led by Anna prepared for the next case. It had been a huge learning curve and one Anna hoped she would never have to be subjected to again. In her drawer, placed in a small box, as she would never wear it, was the one reminder of Gloria Lynne. It was the gold-and-enamel brooch in the shape of the deadly nightshade flower, so pretty, yet so dangerous, and as toxic as the woman who had given it.

A note to the readers

I am very appreciative to my loyal fans, both for buying my novels and watching the television series derived from the books. Due to necessity, I have sometimes had to alter sections of the plot, to enable the series to translate to television. I have done my upmost to keep them both exciting and not lose the characters' backgrounds.

In the new novel *Wrongful Death*, I refer back to a previous Anna Travis novel that brought in the character of a notorious and dangerous drug dealer, Anthony Fitzpatrick. He became the nemesis for Detective Chief Superintendent James Langton as he was the 'one that got away'. At his first appearance, he is described as fathering two very young daughters. For the *Above Suspicion* series it was decided that to use very young children and to have them escape in a boat was possibly too much of a risk. I therefore changed the daughters to Fitzpatrick escaping with a teenage son. As this was a very big on-screen stunt, I also made the decision that Anna Travis would show her inexperience by not reporting the moment she saw a photograph of the plane used by Fitzpatrick to escape arrest.

I sincerely hope that my readers will appreciate how very difficult it is sometimes to incorporate every detail from the novels. There are very few crime writers who also adapt their own crime novels into television series; it is quite an arduous task to decide what is imperative to be kept in focus for the plot to run smoothly. I hope that *Wrongful Death* will prove to be as successful using the television adaptation references from *Deadly Intent,* and bring to a conclusion the capture of the dangerous drug dealer Anthony Fitzpatrick, who had become one of the FBI's most-wanted criminals.

ABOUT THE AUTHOR

Lynda La Plante's novels, including the Prime Suspect series, have all been international bestsellers. She is an honorary fellow of the British Film Institute and a recipient of the British Academy of Film and Television Arts (BAFTA) Dennis Potter Writers Award. Awarded a CBE, she is a member of the UK Crime Writers Awards Hall of Fame. She lives in London.

www.facebook.com/LyndaLaPlanteCBE

BOOKS BY LYNDA LA PLANTE

BLOOD LINE
An Anna Travis Novel

Available in Paperback and e-Book

Still reeling from the death of her fiancé, Detective Anna
Travis has thrown herself into her new role as the chief
inspector for London's murder squad. When Scotland
Yard's Missing Persons Bureau is unable to locate the son
of a court employee, the superintendent—James Langton,
Anna's former lover—urges her to take on the suspicious
assignment.

PRIME SUSPECT
Available in Paperback and e-Book

Detective Chief Inspector Jane Tennison is determined to catch the madman stalking women in the shadows of London, and after identifying a prime suspect, she'll do anything to make the charges against him stick. But perhaps most terrifying is her obsession with cracking the case, which threatens to destroy her life.

PRIME SUSPECT 2
A Face in the Crowd
Available in Paperback and e-Book

In one of London's poorest communities, filled with racial strife, the murder of a young black woman threatens to tear apart the already divided city. But Jane Tennison won't let anything get in the way of her passion for justice. As long as a killer is at large, stalking her prime suspect is Tennison's prime fixation.

PRIME SUSPECT 3
Silent Victims
Available in Paperback and e-Book

A sex-for-hire street kid is found dead in the apartment of a drag queen. But even more intriguing is the prime suspect—an influential do-gooder who is tied in to the secret lives of politicians, judges, and cops. Detective Jane Tennison has been told whom to arrest—and whom to back off of—but she can't follow orders knowing a destroyer of children is out there.